DEATH ON STONERIDGE

SYRACUSE MYSTERY SERIES BOOK ONE

BRIAN ABBOTT

To Laurie,

From one fellow author to another... enjoy!

Brian Abbott

SOUL MATE PUBLISHING

New York

11-4-15

DEATH ON STONERIDGE

Cover Design by Leah Suttle

This book is a work of fiction. The names, characters, places, and incidents are the products of the author's imagination or are used fictitiously. Any resemblance to actual events, business establishments, locales, or persons, living or dead, is entirely coincidental.

Published in the United States of America by

Soul Mate Publishing

P.O. Box 24

Macedon, New York, 14502

ISBN: 978-1-61935-928-4

ebook ISBN: 978-1-61935-624-5

www.SoulMatePublishing.com

For Teachers who inspire . . .

Acknowledgements

I'd like to thank the following individuals who read or critiqued this book on its journey to publication. Janice Lisbon, Linda Lowen, Deb Mainville, Barbara McClure, Katherine Meluni, Christine Wenger —your notes and encouragements helped greatly in setting this novel on its proper path. Thanks also go to Leah Kaye Suttle for the perfect cover design, and finally, to my editor, Debby Gilbert, for accepting the manuscript and her painstaking care in helping fine-tune the finished novel.

March 1987

PROLOGUE

Her life ebbed, but her death was the beginning.

Who was she? This young wife, with dreams of motherhood, of growing old with her husband, lay against the cold porcelain of the bathtub in her home. She had graduated college and had enrolled in nursing school. Now her vision began to fail her as the crimson flow slowed to a trickle. Perhaps, in her last moments, she thought of what could have been.

Danielle Deveraux died in March. Her death had not been her doing. There had been a confrontation. Heated words exchanged. A brief struggle, and a sharp pain had ripped the flesh of her wrist. She'd cried out. A sudden throbbing pain at the back of her head, and then nothing.

Would the police think anything of the bruise on the back of her head, or would it be assumed she'd slipped in an attempt to get help because she'd changed her mind? Of course, they'd think it was suicide. Why shouldn't they? Slashed wrists, razor, bathtub, and a young woman. Was there any reason to think otherwise? Perhaps a note had been forged for convenience's sake. Her death was meant to be thought a suicide. Yet it was murder that had come to Stoneridge Drive.

Now, it is an invariable fact that a murder must be in want of a detective. But though the "little grey cells" may not be lacking, there is not yet one on this quiet street with the reason and mettle to investigate. And so this murder must wait, as any murder does, for that gifted or lucky individual who stumbles upon the vital thread of clues that leads to inevitable solution.

April 1987

TUESDAY

Claudia Icarios surveyed her dining room. The oval table had been freshly polished and its clutter had been banished to the stately hutch, where it would be more innocuous. With a steady hand, Claudia placed the deck of cards on the table and cut it. Everything was ready for her guests. Once, a crowd of neighbors had competed in the Tuesday Night Bridge Games, treating them like some sort of block party. Sadly, these gatherings had dwindled in the past few years to the "old guard," the small group of original residents, and a few die-hards.

Claudia sighed. In her nearly thirty years living on Stoneridge Drive, she'd seen so many neighbors move on or pass away. She fondly remembered that first group of residents, and the camaraderie they'd shared. She recalled the changing faces of the neighbors as the years rolled too swiftly by. Silently, she lamented the indifference of today's neighbors, especially the younger set, who seldom crossed the boundaries of their yards to chat. Yet she had weathered all the changes. Her short stature and mousy appearance belied her fifty-two years. Few wrinkles lined her face, and her dark brown hair was free of any gray. She had a comfortable life, but lately, she felt something was wrong. She couldn't quite grasp what it was, though. She worried that perhaps she'd seen too much. She thought about Danielle, that young woman down the street, who had committed suicide a month ago. It had been so sudden, so inexplicable. Then a rash of burglaries had plagued the residents of Stoneridge Drive.

This used to be such a quiet neighborhood, Claudia sighed.

The grandfather clock at the end of the hallway began to chime. It was eight o'clock, but when a ninth bell sounded, Claudia thought she'd misheard. Then she realized it was the doorbell. One of her guests, one of her dear neighbors, had arrived.

At first glance, Edith Baxter seemed a tiny, fragile septuagenarian with slightly stooped shoulders. Wrinkles lined her pink complexion, and wisps of white dominated the auburn strands of her hair like clouds on a sunny day. However, these signs of age could not mask the vitality that could be seen in her sky-blue eyes.

"Claudia, have you heard the news?" Edith asked excitedly, as she scurried inside.

"Oh, no, what's happened now?"

"Another robbery."

"Whose house?"

"That Yates couple."

"I trust they weren't home?"

Edith shook her head.

"Is your air-conditioner on? It seems cooler in here," Edith said, folding her arms and rubbing her elbows to warm them.

Claudia noticed her friend wasn't wearing the familiar lavender sweater she was so proud of having knitted herself. *She always feels cold indoors*, Claudia thought, surprised that Edith would have left her sweater behind.

"No, we haven't had our central air looked at yet. Not that I mind the heat, but my husband likes it frigid. He called that company . . . I forget their name. But they can't send anyone until Friday. I did open a few windows so at least we'll have some fresh air. It's not too muggy outside, so it shouldn't be too bad."

The doorbell interrupted further conversation. Claudia barely had time to open the door before Mildred Hawthorne burst in. The stout sixty-seven-year-old strode into the living room like Queen Victoria arriving to speak at Parliament, while Claudia and another arrival, Angela Sparrow, followed behind her as if they were her ladies-in-waiting.

"Where is everyone tonight?" Mildred asked sharply. She expected others to follow her example of punctuality. As she awaited a response, she vainly patted her thick, wavy mane of silver-gray hair. Then, from the sleeve of her light blue sweater, she pulled out a tissue and began cleaning the lenses of her blue-tinted glasses, which she wore on a silver chain about her neck.

Claudia perceived that Mildred must be in one of her moods. She knew Mildred tended to act imperial whenever something happened that didn't go her way. Claudia wondered what it was this time, but she knew better than to ask.

"Brenda Lysik stopped by this morning," Claudia said. "She's working late at Dewitt Enterprises. She mentioned something about an important stockholders meeting next week—"

"Oh, the Board of Directors meeting," Mildred interrupted, grumbling. "I can't tell you how I dread that!" The look on Mildred's face showed utter contempt for something or someone connected to said Board meeting. Quick to change this particular topic, Mildred asked, "What about Evelyn? Hasn't she come back from Italy yet? Has anyone heard from her?"

"Oh, yes," Angela Sparrow answered. "She called me last night. She's been having a wonderful time. She said she can't wait to tell us all about her trip. She's flying back Thursday."

"Just what we need," Mildred said dryly, "another discourse on Italy and its picturesque beauty. Doesn't Evelyn ever go anyplace other than Italy?"

Mildred's latest question was ignored.

"My husband is working late tonight, and I assume Mildred's husband is at his golf club?"

"Claudia, you know very well how difficult it is for me to drag my husband to these bridge games. He'd much rather waste his time drinking with his cronies at his country club. What about Kitty?"

Claudia answered, "She's in Florida with her husband."

"Hrmph," Mildred muttered.

"Oh, yes," Angela said. "Kitty went on that cruise to the Bahamas."

"Is that all the Martinos do?" Mildred rolled her eyes. "Evelyn is always off to Italy or New York City or wherever, and her brother Dean is always dragging Kitty with him here and there. Why can't they just stay home?"

"Mildred, just because your husband never takes you anywhere," Angela said crossly.

Mildred cut her off with another brusque "Hrmph." Irritated by the others' waste of precious time, she urged, "Are we ready for a rubber of bridge, ladies?"

She sat down at the head of the dining room table and waited for Claudia—who as usual sat opposite her—to deal. Mildred snatched up her cards, eager to sort what she hoped would be a good hand. Unfortunately, it wasn't, and Angela opened the bidding.

"One Club."

"One Spade."

Edith debated a moment. "Two Spades."

Claudia passed.

"Three Clubs."

"Pass," Mildred grumbled.

The bidding ended with both Edith and Claudia passing, and Angela opened with the Jack of Clubs. As Dummy, Edith laid down her hand, which Mildred perused carefully before playing a losing card.

"You know," Edith said, "I just received a postcard from Paris with a beautiful view of the Eiffel Tower."

"That's right. How could I forget?" Angela said. In sharp contrast to the other three women, Angela was tall. Though she had just turned sixty in February, Angela remained remarkably youthful in appearance with strawberry-blond hair and periwinkle blue eyes. "I meant to ask you about Tim and Marie. How are they? Are they back from their honeymoon yet?

"No. They come home tomorrow," Edith said.

"Marie is such a lovely match for Timothy. I'm so happy for them," Angela said.

"As am I," said Edith, who then startled her friends with the revelation that she had given the deed of her house to Timothy and Marie as a wedding gift. "It's so hard for newlywed couples to save enough money for a house of their own these days," Edith explained, "and Timothy's apartment is too small for the two of them. I've been happy living here on this street for oh . . . nearly twenty-five years. I just feel it's time to move on, so I've decided to move into Dewitt Manor to be closer to my daughter Sarah and my other grandchildren."

"Oh, but surely you'll come to visit and maybe play a rubber of bridge or two?"

"Yes, Mildred," Edith replied. "Of course, I'll come to visit. After all, I want to keep an eye on my grandson and his new wife."

"I suppose you'll also want to keep an eye on your flower garden?" Claudia hinted.

Edith smiled and said, "Oh, I'm sure they'll be in good hands. Marie finished her studies at Syracuse University with a dual major in biology and education and a minor in botany. All this a semester early! She's such a talented young woman."

"How was the wedding?" Claudia asked.

"Oh, wonderful," Edith answered. "Such an elegant ceremony and the flowers were beautifully arranged. I don't remember the florist's name, though. I'll have to ask my daughter. Oh, and the wedding gown! Marie's mother designed it. It wasn't traditional by any means, but it was stunning."

"Where did they go for their honeymoon?" Mildred asked half-heartedly.

Edith said, "Paris, France. Timothy and Marie were so ecstatic when Sarah gave them the plane tickets. I'll never know how Sarah convinced her husband to go along with it. Jon's not big on spending money, and he's never approved of Timothy's becoming a police officer."

Claudia regarded Edith, who watched the play of cards. She remembered Edith mentioning Jon Dewitt's disapproval before, and her curiosity was piqued.

"Why is that?"

Edith shrugged but didn't lift her eyes from the cards on the table. "I'm not exactly sure, Claudia."

"Now how did Timothy and Marie meet again?"

Edith smiled warmly. "They've known each other for years."

"Yes," Angela said. "I remember having them both in class at Holy Cross." Angela taught the sixth grade class at Holy Cross Elementary and had worked there nearly fifteen years. "I think they started dating in the eighth grade. Even then, at thirteen, you could tell they would be a couple."

"Well, you should have seen the look on Timothy and Marie's face when I handed them the deed to my house," Edith said. "Of course, they were reluctant to accept at first, but I quickly convinced them it was for the best. After all, I came from a large family, and I'm not that comfortable living by myself, especially at my age. They should be moving in Thursday morning."

“Although,” Edith continued, “I fear it won’t be long before Timothy starts worrying. He doesn’t make very much money as a police officer. Although Marie’s been offered a position at the new Syracuse Botanical Gardens.”

“Oh, yes,” Claudia said. “I am looking forward to the Gardens’ grand opening. It’s coming up this May, isn’t it?” When Edith nodded, Claudia continued. “I’ve always felt Syracuse should have one. It will certainly be the perfect place for the Syracuse Gardening Club to meet.”

Edith agreed. Both she and Claudia were members of the Syracuse Gardening Club.

Mildred commented, “I still think they should have put the Gardens in a county park, not a city one.”

She then tried surreptitiously to sneak a peek at the cards in Angela’s hand. Failing to see anything, she reluctantly played her King of Clubs and lost to Edith’s Ace. She was even more vexed when Angela began the next trick with the Ace of Hearts. Gritting her teeth, she played the Two of Hearts, not wanting to give up a decent card.

Claudia, less concerned about the game than her partner, recalled Edith’s news about the most recent burglary.

“Edith told me the Yates house was broken into.”

Mildred gasped. “Another burglary on this street?” Her jowled cheeks grew red with anger. “That’s four in the last month! It’s evil that these robberies keep occurring. And in a respectable neighborhood like this!”

“There have been a number of tragic incidents on this street,” Edith said solemnly.

“You’re referring to poor Danielle Deveraux’s death, aren’t you?” When Edith nodded, Angela continued. “She was such a sweet girl. I think her husband was genuinely devastated by her suicide. When I see him crying as he mows his lawn, I begin to think there’s no happiness in the world.”

The four women paused in reverent silence for a moment. Then Mildred remarked, “It is a shame that Joshua should have such bad luck. He lost out on a wonderful football scholarship when he injured his knee. His father thinks he's a failure, and then this."

"I don't recall you welcoming Danielle with open arms," Angela said.

"That was an entirely different matter," Mildred snapped indignantly. "I didn't think she was suitable for my grandson. I admit I was wrong. I am prone to mistakes." Claudia and Angela rolled their eyes. "I realized that Danielle was the best thing to come along for Joshua. I saw how happy she made him. That's why I was more than happy to help them buy their house here on Stoneridge."

The women's attentions focused more intently on the game after the play of the last trump card. Mildred soon gained the upper hand with the Jack of Spades and continued her winning streak with the Ace. Realizing her team had lost, Angela resumed the conversation.

"How very interesting," Angela said. "Danielle died on March seventeenth, and then one week later the burglaries began. You don't suppose there's a connection?"

Mildred huffed. "What possible connection could there be? I'm sure my grandson has nothing to do with these break-ins."

"I wasn't suggesting that he did, but yours was the first house broken into, Mildred."

"No, Angela, that was the Lysiks' house. And I just don't see what Danielle's suicide could possibly have to do with these burglaries."

"The police didn't think it was suicide initially."

Mildred glared at Claudia.

"My grandson did not kill his wife! Even the police realize that now, I'm sure." Mildred patted her mane of silver hair, and her stony expression defied response. Quietly, Mildred played a useless card. She then professed, "It just goes to show you that it isn't safe on this street anymore. The

Town of DeWitt is supposed to be a respectable suburb. And yet we've had four burglaries in less than a month, as if we lived on the city's South side! I can't believe that so many of our neighbors are planning to go away for next week's school break. This thief, whoever he is, is going to have a field day! The police ought to have caught him by now. For God's sake, Syracuse isn't that big a city!"

"It's not that small either," Angela said.

"I know that. But an awful lot of people know far too much about what other people are doing in this city." Mildred added pointedly, "At least among those who move in the same social classes."

Angela sighed and shook her head in disbelief.

"It's a terrible situation," Claudia commented, as she played her King of Hearts, winning the twelfth trick and assuring the next.

"I'd like to know how this thief always knows when people aren't home."

"That's a good question, Mildred. If only we knew the answer to it," Angela said.

Mildred ignored the sarcasm.

"Well, my grandson came up with the Neighborhood Watch idea after the first burglary," Edith said. "Hopefully that will make this burglar think twice."

Claudia smiled. "I think it's a marvelous idea. There's a Neighborhood Watch Program along Jamesville Road, isn't there?"

"Yes, there is," Edith said. "That's how Timothy came up with the idea. He decided to install the program on our street even before I gave him the deed to my house. He felt it was his responsibility as a police officer. Timothy is very interested in improving the conditions of society wherever he can. I just hope he's never disillusioned. I think it's so important for our young people to have optimism. I've always believed that. There are just too many cynical people in this world."

"You're so right, Edith," Angela said, as she played the final card, ending the game.

As she gathered up the cards and began reshuffling, Edith mused, "Timothy's grown into such a fine young man, but he tends to second-guess himself too much. I wish he had more confidence. You know, he actually thought he was rushing into marriage? He worried he didn't make enough money. I told him he had nothing to worry about. He and Marie will do just fine. She's such a good match for him."

"Yes, but every couple is bound to have their little spats."

"Admittedly yes, Mildred," Edith said sharply. "But I'm sure they'll be just fine once I've vacated the house and they've settled in."

"When are you leaving?"

Despite Mildred's rudeness, Edith answered kindly, "I plan on leaving Friday. That will give me time to help Tim and Marie settle in and move my things into Dewitt Manor. After Easter Sunday, though, I've decided to visit some old friends in Rutland, Vermont."

"How long will you be in Vermont?"

Edith momentarily slipped into her native Quebecois tongue. "*Je ne sais pas,* I don't know, Angela. It's been years since I've been to Rutland, and I am looking forward to seeing all my old friends there. But at my age, I really don't like to travel much. I want to spend enough time in Rutland, but . . . I don't know. I'm really in the mood for gardening. Spring does that to me, you know. I'm sure I could find something to do at the manor that involves gardening. They haven't had a gardener in quite some time, and it certainly would be good for me to get involved with something. I'll have to take my mind off the fact that I'll miss my own garden here."

"Would anyone care for something to drink? Coffee? Tea?" Claudia interjected, thinking to serve the beverages before the next hand. Her guests acquiesced to some iced tea, and Claudia left the room.

"I must say I am rather parched," Mildred said, patting the nape of her neck.

"It's this weather we've been having lately," Edith said. "It's been unusually warm this spring. Not that I mind. I don't like it when the winters linger so long. But we're definitely due for some rain. It's been so muggy this week."

"Yes, but that new weatherman on Channel 3 said we shouldn't expect any significant rain for a few days. In fact, it's supposed to be quite humid tomorrow night," Mildred said.

"This Syracuse weather is so irritating. It's always either too hot or too cold," Edith said, summing up many a Syracusan's thoughts about local weather patterns.

"Isn't it though?" Claudia said, returning with a tray of drinks. "February was so cold, and then March was too rainy. Now April's warmer than usual. And they're saying May will be mild."

"Maybe I should wait to get my central air-conditioner fixed," Angela said. "I do have one of those window air-conditioners, and it should be sufficient."

Feigning sweetness unbecoming of her, Mildred inquired, "Shall we begin the next rubber? I'll deal."

Before anyone could answer, she picked up the deck of cards and expertly shuffled them. She had been thwarted in the last game and was determined to win the next.

WEDNESDAY

"Yes, I called her this morning. I have to do this, Abe. I know she killed my brother."

Sonya Schwartz sat at her immaculately polished dining room table. She idly twirled the phone cord in her fingers as she listened to her husband. "You know I've always suspected. That girl down the street just confirmed some of what I thought . . . Well, I don't know that for sure. But why would she lie? . . . Granted, but I don't think that's the case. My brother's brakes did not fail accidentally . . . Oh, the police botched the investigation!"

The doorbell sounded, and Sonya's brown eyes darted toward her front door. Breathlessly, she blurted, "Look, I've got to go, Abe. She's here. I'll try and get out there later in the week . . . Yes, I know it's Passover. I'm sorry, but this is very important to me. What good is celebrating Passover when my poor brother's ghost isn't at rest?"

Sonya put a hand to her ample bosom and heaved a deep, sorrowful breath. The doorbell rang again insistently.

"I'll talk to you later, Abe . . . Yes, yes. Good-bye."

Sonya dashed to hang up the phone and then ran to her front door. She paused for just a moment to brush her dark, reddish-brown hair with her fingers and smooth out her clothes, an appropriate black ensemble for the occasion. There were times when Sonya was given to dramatics. Her college friends had labeled her a drama queen, and more recently, she had acted in local theatre productions. Now, she opened her front door prepared to give her latest performance.

Her twenty-three-year-old niece stood with her arms folded on the front steps. Rachel Stuart's thin lips and hazel eyes reflected annoyance.

"I don't understand what was so important that I had to race up here."

Putting on a smile, Sonya ushered Rachel inside. "We're family, and I really think we need to talk."

"We haven't spoken in weeks."

"Let's rectify that."

They sat down in the two recliners by the bay window in the living room. Rachel had seldom been to her aunt's house, but she noticed how well kept it was. There was no television, no stereo, no modern technology anywhere in evidence in the room. Rachel did know there was a den where the family watched T.V., but she didn't recall seeing it. The Schwartzs liked to keep their private family life and their public one as separate as possible.

"I'll get right to the point," Sonya said.

"Please do."

"Someone's come forward claiming they have evidence you tampered with your parents' car."

Rachel bristled. "That was an accident!"

Sonya shrugged. "This person seems to think otherwise."

"It's you!" Rachel pointed a finger at her aunt. "You just can't give it up. Why do you persist in persecuting me? I haven't done anything to deserve this."

"My brother gave you every advantage, a loving home, a first-rate education. And what did you do? You disposed of him like yesterday's rubbish when it no longer suited you to have him around!"

"I loved my parents."

"You loved your parents' money."

Rachel stood up and spewed, "You never loved me."

Sonya looked up at her niece and shuddered to see the accusation and menace in those hazel eyes. She gripped the arms of her recliner to keep them from trembling. Not quite meeting her niece's gaze, she stated, "I don't think you know what love is. My brother, God rest his soul, spoiled you. I watched you grow up expecting everyone to cater to your whims. The world doesn't revolve around you, Rachel."

"I don't have to listen to this."

Rachel stalked toward the front door.

"One of these days your husband's going to wake up and see you for what you are." Sonya turned in her chair to see her niece reach for the doorknob. Rachel froze as the words sunk in. "Your college friends already know the truth, don't they? They know how selfish you are. Do you have any friends left, Rachel?"

Rachel glared at Sonya. "Don't underestimate me, Auntie."

With that declaration, Sonya's niece abruptly left and slammed the door behind her. Sonya, having tensed up during the confrontation, let out a deep breath. That certainly didn't go according to plan. Had she really hoped her niece would confess? Sonya looked out the bay window and watched Rachel retreat down Stoneridge Drive. Sonya resolved to find out the truth about her brother's death. Somehow she would bring closure to the loss she felt.

Rachel Stuart glowered as she stalked down Stoneridge Drive. She knew now that it had been a mistake to move here. She never should have stayed in Syracuse! With the money she'd inherited from her parents' death, she could have moved anywhere she wanted. But her husband's family lived here, and she hadn't wanted to push him too far at the time. Maybe it was time to reconsider. Too many things were coming to a head. Her aunt was getting too suspicious. Her husband's sister was moving in just a few houses away. And then there was Lisa.

"That bitch," Rachel spewed. "I'll bet she's the one who blabbed to Sonya."

Rachel looked up and realized she was standing not far from the Yateses' driveway. She considered the brown split-level. Most of the houses on Stoneridge, as part of a development, had bay windows, and Rachel could see a light on inside. She strolled alongside the retaining wall that lined the left side of the driveway. Grinning wickedly, she walked up the slate stairs. A few more steps along the curved walkway and Rachel rang the doorbell. No answer came, so she pushed the doorbell twice in quick succession. At last, the door slowly opened a crack.

Linda Yates, her face ashen, held the doorknob in a vise-like grip. She tried to shut the door, but Rachel pushed passed her.

"Hello, Linda. Remember me?"

Linda was at a loss for words. She absently fussed at her unkempt dark brown hair.

"I'm Rachel Stuart." Rachel looked back at the mousy woman, who cowered by the door avoiding any eye contact. "You remember. I was your sister's roommate. We lived across the street from you on Euclid Avenue near the University."

"I remember," Linda whispered.

A sudden turn of Linda's head struck Rachel as familiar. Funny, she'd never noticed it before. Rachel realized how similar Linda and her sister, Lisa, looked. Clearly there was a strong family resemblance. The only significant difference was their hair. Lisa had blond hair. Although Rachel suspected it wasn't natural.

"I just thought I'd stop by for a visit. It's been so long. And to think how long we've been neighbors here. Are you home alone?"

"W-well," Linda stammered. "The kids are at school, and my husband's at work."

"Oh, I thought Lisa was here."

"What? Why would she be here? She's got classes at S.U."

Rachel had graduated from Syracuse University last May, and she knew full well that Lisa was on campus now.

"Oh, I just thought she might have come to see you." Gesturing vaguely, Rachel added, "Aren't you going to offer me a chair? We can sit and have a nice little chat."

Linda shut her front door and led Rachel up the few steps to the living room.

"Would you like anything to eat or drink?" Linda asked nervously.

"No," Rachel said, sitting on the couch. "That's not why I'm here."

"Yes, why are you here? I would have thought it was apparent that my husband and I want nothing to do with you."

"Yes." Rachel's eyes narrowed. "I have noticed that you and David have given us the cold shoulder. I didn't mind at all. After all, why should I care? But I am here now. And I want some answers."

"From me?"

"Oh, yes. I know you keep tabs on your sister. I want to know what game she thinks she's playing!"

"I don't know what you mean."

"Don't toy with me, Linda! I'm sure we both suspect that Danielle's death was no accident."

Linda flinched. She recalled that day with a shudder.

"Danielle committed suicide," Linda said adamantly.

"Did she really? I heard there was someone seen leaving the Deveraux's house that day."

Linda interrupted, "Surely, that's just a rumor."

"The police took it seriously at the time."

"But they suspected her husband, and he was exonerated. There was no question of anyone else."

Rachel smiled wanly. Tapping her chin, she said, "Now, I don't recall. Where was Lisa the day Danielle died?"

Rachel suddenly laughed. "For that matter, where was your husband?"

Linda pursed her lips and glared at Rachel.

"I think you'd better leave."

Rachel noted the building fury in Linda's brown eyes. Perhaps Lisa's sister wasn't as meek as she thought.

"Calm down. Nobody's accusing anyone . . ."

"Oh, really? Isn't that what you were doing? You like causing trouble for other people. If you have a problem with my sister, then take it up with her and leave me and my husband out of it!"

"Lisa's the one dragging other people into—"

"I don't care! Why even come to me in the first place? I don't control my sister. I don't try to control people like you do."

Rachel clenched her fingers. Composing herself, she replied, "I don't know what you mean. Lisa's the one that likes to interfere. She has something that belongs to me, and I want it back." Rachel stood up to leave. "Just be sure to tell Lisa that I stopped by. And tell her that if she doesn't give me what I want . . . I'll make her life a living hell."

"I don't have to tell my sister anything, Rachel! I'm not responsible for her."

Rachel grew angry. How dare this mousy thing defy her! Her eyes glanced about the room as if trying to search out a reply. They alighted on the baby grand piano in the corner. Rachel looked over her shoulder at Linda and coyly asked, "Oh, by the way, how is your husband?"

"What do you mean?" Linda asked suspiciously.

"Has he overcome that nasty addiction of his? I understand it can be very expensive."

"Just what are you getting at?"

"Well, I'm sure you've noticed that there have been a number of burglaries on our street."

"My husband is not a thief! And he's been sober for some

time. Not that it's any of your business. Besides, our house was broken into Monday night. Or haven't you heard?"

"Oh, but that could have been staged," Rachel scoffed.

Linda stood up and yelled, "Get out of my house!"

Rachel smiled.

"Remember to relay my message to your sister. I expect to hear from her soon. If not, I will be back."

THURSDAY

The driver of the red Jeep Cherokee neared the turn off Jamesville Road. The drive had been a short five minutes from her husband's apartment across from ShoppingTown Mall to their new home on Stoneridge Drive, but she hadn't been this exhilarated to drive a car since she'd first gotten her license. As she slowed down to make her turn, her short brown hair, having been tousled by the wind, fell back in place.

Driving down the slight incline of Stoneridge Drive, she viewed the houses, part of a development of ranch, split-level, and a few two-story homes built at the end of the fifties. She was reminded of TV families with the aproned housewife, the stern and hardworking father, and the towheaded children in white houses with manicured lawns and picket fences. There were no picket fences here and not all the lawns were picture perfect, but the idea could not be shaken from her mind.

Marie Dewitt parked her jeep in the wide driveway of her new home. She swung her long slender legs to the side and slipped out of the jeep with ease. Removing her sunglasses, she revealed doe-brown eyes that soaked in her surroundings. She surveyed the manicured lawn, the trimmed yew bushes in the front yard, and the modest ranch house. Brown with white trim, a bit faded, and gray roof shingles, which appeared newish. It wasn't the mansion she'd grown up in, but this place belonged to her and her husband. Their first home.

Brushing aside stray silky strands of her hair, Marie smiled. How sweet of Tim's grandmother to gift her home to them! Marie had hoped to house hunt for a place of their own, but she had seen how much it meant to Tim and had consented. Looking over the house again, she decided she could make this work. Then she saw Tim's grandmother coming toward her.

"Hello, Marie. Where's Timothy?"

"He should be here soon. He was right behind me." Marie looked up the street for signs of the rental van. In her peripheral vision, she noticed a woman gardening across the street. Then turning back to Edith, she said, "Are you sure about this, Ms. Baxter? I mean giving your house to us?"

"My dear, don't worry about me. It is better to give than to receive."

Marie embraced the dear old lady.

"And remember, call me Grandma," Edith said emphatically. "You're family now."

"Thank you. This really means so much to Tim and me," Marie said. She noticed the woman across the street, having put down her spade and gardening gloves, now approached them.

"Hello, you must be Marie," the woman said, extending her hand. "Edith's told me so much about you. I'm Claudia Icarios. I live in that gray house."

"Nice to meet you."

As Marie continued chatting with the ladies, a rental van drove down the street and pulled into the driveway. Timothy Parker Dewitt hopped down from the vehicle and approached his wife. Dressed in a white sleeveless tee, Tim extended a well-muscled arm and hugged Marie close to him. His soulful brown eyes looked into hers lovingly, and they shared a brief knowing smile.

Edith looked up at her oldest grandson. Somehow he seemed taller than she remembered. Perhaps he had grown an inch? He was only twenty-one years old. He'd also put on some muscle and didn't look as lanky as he had last summer. Still,

Edith could see a marked trace of boyish youth in his features. She also noticed his blond hair was getting a little long.

"Timothy." Edith hugged her grandson. "How are you? How was your trip?"

"Great," said Timothy in a soft tenor voice. "To Claudia, he said, "Hello, Mrs. Icarios."

Having met Tim a few times, Claudia asked, "I heard you went to France."

"Yes, how was your trip?" asked Edith.

"We'll have to show you the photos when they're developed."

Marie chimed in. "Paris was amazing."

She went on to describing some of the sites they'd seen. The Seine. Notre Dame. The Louvre. The Opera House. They might have seen more, too, but they'd spent a good deal of their time in their hotel room with its requisite view of the Eiffel Tower. Of course, Marie glossed over that part in favor of telling the two ladies about evening walks along the Seine and dining outdoors in sidewalk cafés.

"Well, let's get you both settled in," Edith said, ending the discussion of Paris. "There's a Neighborhood Watch Meeting to deal with tonight."

Claudia said her good- byes, and Edith led the newlyweds across the threshold.

Marie had been to Edith's home before, but there was something different this time. Her eyes nearly welled up as she entered. She touched the solid, varnished oak wall divider. Its shelves rose to meet the slightly angled ceiling. The shelves lacked a backing and allowed Marie to see into the living room. They held various family pictures of Edith's daughters and her grandchildren. Marie smiled when she saw Tim's high school senior photo. This divider also contained a built-in planter full of luxuriant ferns. Marie fingered the fronds lightly. So much of this house was Edith's. It reflected her personality.

Opposite the divider, Marie admired a waist-high, black-lacquered cabinet with sliding doors. Atop the cabinet was an electric hurricane lamp next to a vase of flowers.

From this pseudo foyer, Marie could see a hallway leading to the bedrooms on the left, and straight ahead, she saw the octagonal dining table and four chairs. The dining room set looked well-maintained, and the wood freshly varnished. In the corner, a triangular, glass-door cabinet displayed a set of Syracuse China.

No wall separated the dining and living rooms, and Marie thought the wall-to-wall brick red carpet was a little much, but the color was somewhat offset by the white walls and two off-white upholstered couches. The sofa, which could seat six, faced the bay window with its view of the street, while the loveseat, adjacent to the window, backed up against the wall divider.

It was all somewhat bland. True, there were touches of color and life, like the red carpet, the photos, and knickknacks. Edith would need help gathering up all the knickknacks she'd compiled over the years. But it was somehow empty. Like one grandmotherly woman wasn't enough to fill the space. *Perhaps that's why Edith decided to give it up*, thought Marie.

She heard Tim laughing and saw Edith showing him an old family photo.

Marie liked that about Tim. His closeness to his grandmother. She knew he'd mown her lawn and had helped out with odd job repairs. In some ways, it seemed he was closer to his grandmother than his own parents. She hoped he'd be amenable to redecorating.

She glanced at her watch. It was just after eleven o'clock. Not much time until tonight's Neighborhood Watch meeting. Hopefully, they could get the rental van unloaded and have the place looking presentable in time. Marie wished she hadn't agreed to the meeting, at least not so soon after moving in, but she knew it was important to Tim. And there had been all those burglaries . . .

By quarter-past seven, the meeting at the Dewitts' house was well underway. As moderator of the program, Tim explained how it worked to the gaggle of neighbors who had presumably shown up to hear about the program, but most likely were more curious to meet the new neighbors. A few neighbors listened intently. Most of the newer residents feigned patience until the time came for refreshments. They figured the longtime residents would do all the watching anyway. Reluctantly, the group decided on a short follow-up meeting on Saturday to plan a schedule.

" . . . Now, if you see something suspicious, like the example I gave, immediately phone the police. Don't take any rash action on your own. Often times these criminals will commit more than one crime without any qualms. So just remain calm and sensible. And remember, the important thing is not to panic and to report a crime as soon as possible. When your call is answered, the person on the line will ask you a few routine questions. Just be patient and answer the questions as accurately and frankly as you can."

After a pause, Tim asked of the fifteen people gathered before him, "Are there any questions?"

A tall, gaunt man with thin white hair and a gray moustache stood up. Adjusting the monocle over his left eye, Colonel Martin Hawthorne cleared his throat.

"I have one, Mr. Dewitt, or is it Officer Dewitt?" Without giving Tim an opportunity to clarify, the Colonel continued gruffly, "Exactly what are the police doing about these blasted robberies? Are we supposed to catch the man ourselves with this Watch thing? I'll have you know that if I have to make one of those citizen's arrests, I will. And I've got the gun to do it."

"Sit down, Martin!" Mildred Hawthorne commanded. "And stop blustering like a fool!"

Needless to say, the colonel sat down.

Unfortunately for Tim, the colonel's questions instigated an outburst of comments from the occupants of the room. The drone of their voices agreed with the colonel's statements, and Tim tried his best to mollify the crowd and regain control of the situation.

"Everyone, please," Tim said, "we are doing our best to track down this thief. I know we already have officers checking various pawnshops and the like for the items you have reported to us as missing. It's only a matter of time before we nab this guy. All criminals slip up eventually."

"I agree," Edith said, visibly perturbed by the antipathy directed against her grandson. "We just have to be patient, and let the police do their job."

"That's easy for you to say, Ms. Baxter. Your house hasn't been broken into."

"No. I admit it hasn't," Edith said, not sure which of the young men in the room had spoken. "I really haven't anything worth stealing, but patience is prudence, as my mother always said." Claudia Icarios smiled and nodded in agreement, as Edith continued. "Things always turn out right in the end if you're patient."

In order to avoid any further conflicts, Tim hastily remarked, "I think we can conclude this meeting—"

"I think we should all thank Timothy and Marie for the use of their house," Edith added in an encouraging tone, but it only resulted in a few reluctant claps.

To avoid any embarrassing silences, Marie quickly chimed in, "Tim, I think we should serve the refreshments now."

"Let me help you," Edith said, hurrying toward the kitchen.

Tim filled the crystal punch bowl, a wedding gift to the couple, with a concoction of fruit punch, ginger ale, and ice, while Edith brought out chilled trays of deviled eggs, artichoke dip, and other finger foods. Once everything was ready, Marie urged everyone to help him or herself.

While his wife conversed with Mildred Hawthorne, or rather listened to yet another tirade, Dr. Philbin Icarios puttered around the dining room table. The gaunt-faced fifty-two-year-old served as the Onondaga County Medical Examiner, a post he'd held for nearly six years. His gray eyes currently pondered the tray of hors d'oeuvres as if they were specimens on some sterile tray. He absently stroked his peppery gray moustache as he considered which delectable would be least objectionable to his palate.

"Nothing looks quite to my liking either," said a gruff voice behind him.

"Ah, Martin," Philbin said, turning to see the Colonel with a stiff drink in his hands. "Open bar?"

"Some bottles in the kitchen. Southern Comfort. I prefer Kentucky bourbon, but I make do."

"I'm sure you do. How are you faring these days? Have you gotten that security system installed yet?"

"No, Phil. The missus didn't think it was worth the money, and I'm not entirely happy about it. Her only excuse was that she didn't want me coming home at night and setting the thing off because I'd forgotten the code."

"Too troublesome?"

"No, she said it would be too embarrassing."

"I'm surprised she was against the idea. Your house was the first to be burglarized as I seem to recall."

"Actually, Dr. Icarios, it was our house," Shane Lysik said in a soft drawl. A charming thirty-year-old, Shane was an athletic man with dark brown hair and golden tan. He'd been helping himself to some of Edith's hors d'oeuvres and had overheard them even though his sepia brown eyes had been focused on his wife, who was chatting with that couple whose house had been the most recently burglarized.

"Ah, yes, Shane. It was a week before the colonel's, wasn't it? Now I remember."

"Yes, and as I recall, your house hasn't been broken into, Philbin."

With a wily smile, Philbin replied, "No, it hasn't. Though I must confess that should an intruder attempt to do so, he would be staring down the barrel of my Taurus Model 66 Revolver."

"Well, I wouldn't put too much faith in that gun of yours, Phil."

"Why not, Martin?"

"Because I wasn't home to use mine. The blasted punk even stole my Colt Government Model. I only have my Charter Target Bulldog 357 left. Thank God it was hidden well that night!"

"Strange," Shane commented, as he pondered something.

"What's strange?" Philbin asked. "My staying home?"

"No, not that. It's strange that no one's been home when their house was ransacked. We weren't home that night. You weren't either, Colonel, as I remember it. Neither were the Stuarts or the Yateses. It makes a person wonder . . ."

"How does the thief know when people aren't home?" Philbin said, finishing Shane's statement.

Col. Hawthorne, wrongly thinking the doctor's question genuine, answered, "How does any thief know when the house he's burglarizing is vacant? The answer is that no one knows except for the thief himself. And if we knew the answer, then we might be able to catch the blasted culprit!"

While the three men proceeded to speculate, Edith Baxter approached Tim and Marie just after Dr. Craig Logan's departure. "I'm so proud of you, Timothy. And you, too, Marie. I think this meeting was a wonderful success." Edith Baxter smiled. "Now, I'll be moving out tomorrow morning. I don't want to hear any protests. I think you two both need to be alone. Three is a crowd after all. Besides, you're married now, and newlyweds need to make their start without their family interfering in everything. Tim, your mother is picking me up, so there's no need to worry about me."

She looked back at the picked over trays of food on the dining room table. "I should probably start cleaning up." Then she walked away before the newlyweds could say anything.

"I can't believe how good she's been to us," Marie said.

Tim shrugged. "That's the way she's always been. At least with me."

"Yes, but giving us this house. It's such an amazing gesture."

Before Tim could respond, Brenda Lysik approached the newlyweds. A twenty-nine-year-old with silky black hair and gray eyes, Brenda had been working as a secretary at Dewitt Enterprises for nearly five years. Tim had seen her there on a few occasions, but he hadn't realized she lived next door to his grandmother!

"Hello, again. It was so nice of you to host this event. And on your first day moving in!"

Marie answered, "Thank you, Mrs. Lysik."

"Oh, please call me Brenda. Do you know where Edith disappeared to? I just saw her a moment ago."

"Try the kitchen," Tim suggested. "She said she was going to start cleaning up."

"Ah," Brenda said, glancing back and the dining room table, which no longer held quite as many trays of food. "Well, her hors d'oeuvres were wonderful! No wonder they went so quickly. I especially loved the stuffed mushrooms with feta and kasseri cheese. I'd love to get the recipe from her, but some other time perhaps. I should get going, just as soon as I can pull my husband away from that group of sophisticated men over there." Brenda watched her husband chatting with Dr. Icarios and Col. Hawthorne. "They must be practically ready to form a posse and hunt down this burglar by now." Stifling a yawn, she continued. "Well, there's work tomorrow. And I am feeling awfully tired. I just hope nothing happens tonight." After a pause, she asked, "Is Edith staying here long?"

"No, my grandmother's told us she's leaving tomorrow morning."

"I'll be sad to see her go," Brenda said. "She was the first to welcome Shane and me to the neighborhood. I got so used to seeing her out and about in her yard gardening. I'll miss that. It won't be the same at our bridge games either. Oh, but Edith told me that you play bridge?"

"Er, yes," Tim said.

"Maybe you'll join the neighborhood league we've set up. We meet on Tuesday nights when we can."

"I don't know if I can with my schedule," Tim said.

"That is a shame." Brenda continued on a different note, "Well, I'd better drag my husband home. There's a lot of paperwork I have to catch up with tomorrow. I'm working holiday hours on Saturday. Planning for that huge board meeting next Tuesday night requires a lot of attention."

Brenda moved away from the Dewitts and clasped her husband's arm. Her delicate white complexion was a sharp contrast to that of her husband's bronzed look, but they looked well matched together.

While these neighbors had been talking, Mildred and Claudia had settled themselves into the two armchairs in the corner of the living room to chat privately. Having come out the top winner at last night's bridge game, Mildred was in a lighter frame of mind. Still the recent rash of burglaries troubled her.

"Do you really think the burglar lives on our street?" Mildred frowned.

"Or in the neighborhood," Claudia said knowingly.

"I just can't believe—"

"Think about it, Mildred. The Lysiks, then your house, the Stuarts, and most recently the Yates. None of you were home at the time. I don't know about you, but I haven't seen any strange cars casing the neighborhood."

Mildred huffed. "Well, that's just deplorable I tell you. One of our neighbors?"

"I think the police will catch the culprit soon."

"What have the police done?! What leads do they have? Checking pawnshops for stolen items? They won't find anything except a dead end. Although I am glad I was able to use the burglary as an excuse to get rid of my husband's handgun. I only wish I had been able to find the revolver, but he must have misplaced it. I would have found it otherwise. I just can't abide firearms."

Claudia shuddered. "Oh, I know what you mean. I just don't like them. Just the thought of one being in the house . . . and they're too easy to get a hold of these days."

"So true, Claudia. Why look at that man whose body they found in Oakwood Cemetery. They say he was shot in Columbus Circle. Right in front of the county courthouse and the Cathedral! Practically under the nose of the police." Mildred shook her head in disgust. "I won't go downtown anymore. It's not safe," she added.

"You do have to admit that it's not entirely the fault of the police, Mildred. That murder occurred after two in the morning. The police just don't get the funding they need. They can't patrol everywhere all hours of the day. The city politicians are always cutting their budget. I know they're financially strapped, but it doesn't help matters. Of course, no one would have ever imagined a murder would be committed out in the open and in the middle of Columbus Circle!" Claudia paused before continuing. "Oh, no. I'm far more concerned about our judicial system. So many criminals get away with heinous crimes, and those that are put away only serve a couple years before they are out on parole. I'm particularly interested in that Sheldon case."

"Do you mean that young man who killed his girlfriend's father?"

"Yes, the prosecution has a lot of evidence, but much of it is circumstantial. I can't wait to see what happens now that the Grand Jury has issued an indictment."

Mildred shook her head sadly.

"The world is in a terrible mess, Claudia. So much violence and crime. Look at the fighting going on between the Israelis and the Palestinians. I pray a solution will be found for that conflict. Evil seems to be everywhere nowadays even here in this neighborhood. Everybody wants power and money, and no one cares how he gets it as long as he gets it."

Just then Col. Hawthorne and Dr. Icarios walked up to their wives. The colonel said in his gruff, yet booming voice, "Ready to go, ladies?"

Mildred sharply said, "Yes, Martin. I've been waiting for you, you know." Turning to Claudia, Mildred added more sweetly, "I'll see you later, Claudia? We'll have to talk some more. Do you need batteries for tonight?"

"No. I bought some at the mall today. We're all set."

The Icarioses and the Hawthornes were such close friends because they had moved into their houses nearly thirty years ago when the structures were brand new. Presently, the Hawthornes and Icarioses said their good- byes to the Dewitts and left followed by David and Linda Yates.

"They didn't say much," Tim whispered.

"Who?"

"David and Linda Yates. Wasn't their house the most recent to be hit?"

"Well, at least they came," Marie said. "The least the others could have done was call. Obviously, my Aunt Evie couldn't come because she's not back from Italy yet. And Miss Sparrow sprained her ankle. She was told by her doctor to stay off her feet for a few days, but she also called to say she couldn't come tonight."

"What happened to Miss Sparrow?"

"Your grandmother told me she slipped on some loose gravel coming home from their Tuesday Night Bridge Game. At least she and Ms. Llewellyn called to say they couldn't come tonight."

"I just don't get it, Marie. It's like people don't care about their neighbors. Mr. Esterhazy couldn't have cared less about a meeting like this. He brushed aside any involvement because his house hadn't been broken into. His wife came alone! At least she has an interest in neighborhood affairs. Of course, she always has, you know. My grandmother swears she must watch the rest of her neighbors through binoculars."

"Quiet, Tim. She's coming."

"Yoo- hoo." Anne waved to the newlyweds.

Anne Esterhazy was an unnatural blond who liked to be a part of any and every happening in her neighborhood, and if she couldn't be part of it, she wanted to know all about it. She had a slender figure with slightly skinny limbs, but she was pretty in an unconventional sort of way. Her nose was a tad too long and its bridge too narrow, but she had high cheekbones and an oval face. With her quick stride and observant eyes, there was little that she missed. Presently, Anne walked over to the Dewitts with her next-door neighbor Sonya Schwartz in tow.

"Hello, again. It's just so nice to have new neighbors."

"Hello, Mrs. Esterhazy," Marie said. "It's a shame your husband couldn't be here tonight."

"Ha! My lazy husband never wants to do anything but eat and watch television. I practically have to twist his arm just to get him off the couch and do something. Why the house could be falling down and my husband would do absolutely nothing about it. But God forbid that the refrigerator runs out of food or that the television goes haywire. My husband would throw a fit! What about your husband, Sonya? Why isn't he here?"

"He would have been here, but he's out of town. He and our children are visiting his parents in Albany. I hope to join them soon, but I've some unfinished things to take care of."

Unlike her neighbor, Sonya Schwartz wasn't overly talkative about her personal crises, at least in public.

"Oh, that's right. I remember you telling me that. He left the other day, didn't he? But aren't you mad at him? Passover started on Tuesday."

"No, Anne, I'm not mad at him. My husband took the children to visit his parents for Passover."

Perplexed, Anne looked at Sonya, but then shrugged.

"Well, anyway, Sonya and I have to go. It's almost nine o'clock, and I've got to get home so I don't miss *Knots Landing*. I just hope there's no sports program on tonight. My husband thinks he has to watch anything that's labeled a sport without considering anyone else. Well, it's been fun. Bub- bye!"

Tim and Marie sighed with relief to see Anne Esterhazy go, for her words had begun to run together in their heads.

After a brief respite of silence, Marie, an idea having struck her, commented, "Isn't it great?"

"The weather?" Tim teased.

"No, Tim. Don't you realize we don't have to do anything for a whole week? Whatever will we do?"

"Aren't you going to be busy unpacking all the boxes we stashed away in the basement? And didn't you mention some ideas you had for redecorating the house?"

Marie rolled her eyes. "Really, Tim. Couldn't you be a little more romantic?"

"Whatever will you do with me?"

"Don't worry I'll think of something."

"Well," Tim began. "I think we should relax. You know, I never realized how tiring a vacation can be."

Marie smiled. "Well, we were busy."

Tim grinned.

"Hey, Tim," said Todd Stuart, Marie's brother, as he extended a hand to firmly shake Tim's. He and his wife Rachel had come to say their goodbyes. While Rachel attempted small talk with her sister-in-law Marie, Todd took his best friend aside and said, "I have to admit, Tim, this Neighborhood Watch thing wasn't such a bad idea after all."

"I'm glad you think so, Todd."

"Yeah, well, I'm being nice about it. It's hard not to be bitter when your house has been broken into. I certainly hope you and Marie don't have to go through what Rachel and I did. You lose your sense of security, you know? It's—it's had me on edge. I've even purchased a revolver."

Having overheard her brother, Marie asked, "Todd, you don't really think a gun is the answer?"

"I had to do something, Marie," Todd said. "Look. I know how to use it. I took a class. Don't worry about it." Seeing that Marie was still not fully convinced, Todd shifted his gaze toward Tim and quickly changed the topic. "So how's married life been treating you? I hope my big sis hasn't been giving you a hard time."

"Hey, are you kidding? We're still on our honeymoon." Tim grinned.

Todd leaned close and, whispering to his friend, lamented, "It doesn't last forever."

Tim frowned. He wondered what his friend had meant. He would have asked, too, but Rachel insisted they leave, claiming she had a slight headache. So the Dewitts and Stuarts exchanged good-byes and promises to have lunch or dinner together sometime.

After the Stuarts left, Brenda and Shane Lysik, the last of the guests, came to say their good-byes.

"My husband and I have been talking and well—"

Shane interrupted, "We'd like to have a neighborhood party for you. You know just a little welcome. At our house."

"That would be great," Marie said.

Brenda said, "My husband likes parties. He's a bit childish that way, but I like to humor him. It's hard to stay mad at him with his boyish charm."

Shane laughed, embarrassed.

"Let's go, Bren," he said.

"You know it's true," his wife replied, before turning to the Dewitts. "How about next Friday? That will give you enough time to settle in and me enough time to plan for it after Tuesday's board meeting."

"That sounds fine," Marie said.

With the last of the guests gone, Tim and Marie collapsed with fatigue on the couch facing the window. The evening grew increasingly darker. The streetlight at the end of the Lysiks' driveway was on, and the Dewitts watched the shadowy figures of their neighbors returning to their respective homes.

Tim sighed. "Why'd you have to accept? You know I hate parties. Do you know how nervous I was tonight? And I had to give a speech. I mean I know it's part of my job, but—"

Marie shushed her husband with her finger to his lips.

"I'm sure it'll be fun. And you did fine tonight. Besides, I think it's great that the neighbors are friendly. So many neighborhoods aren't you know."

"I guess."

"What time is it?"

"Nine-thirty, why?"

She smiled. "Are you ready for bed?"

Tim smirked. "Yeah, I'm just totally exhausted. Can't wait to hit the pillow."

He leaned over to kiss her.

After a moment, she asked breathlessly, "What about it, Mr. Officer? Coming to bed?"

He feigned hesitance. "I don't know . . ."

"I'll make it worth your while."

"Marie," Tim whispered, shocked. "My grandmother's in the room right across the hall!"

"That'll make it all the more fun."

She led the way down the hallway to the master bedroom, and he didn't hesitate to follow.

Edith Baxter had difficulty focusing on her reading. She sat in bed trying to finish the novel Claudia had lent her, but her mind kept wandering. So many memories replayed themselves in her head. The realization hit her that this was the last night she would spend in the house she had called home since she moved here from Vermont nearly twenty-five years ago.

Once she'd heard her grandson and his wife retire to the master bedroom, Edith slipped out of hers to walk around her house one last time. She ascertained that all the lights were off and remembered how often she had done this before. She made certain the front door was locked and recalled a time when she had not needed to bother with the door's chain. So many memories played out in her mind—some good and some bad—as she had crept about the house.

Returning to her bedroom around 10:30 p.m., Edith paused at the end of the hall and eavesdropped at the closed door of the master bedroom, through which she heard muffled laughter. Happily, she thought of the new beginnings for both herself and her grandson and his wife.

Edith knelt on the bed to open the window ajar. The spring weather was quite humid, and she had wanted to let some cool air circulate in the small bedroom. Then she slipped into bed and resumed her reading.

Again, she attempted to focus on the words, but after a few pages, her eyes were too tired to continue. She rested her eyes. Moments later, she was jolted awake by the sudden slamming of a car door. She heard an anguished cry for help. Then two loud pops sounded. Startled, Edith sat bolt upright in bed.

Somewhere, a car door slammed, and an engine roared to life. As the car sped up the small incline of Stoneridge Drive, the sound of the engine whirred in her ears. Then it died away, followed by silence. Too late, Edith pulled back the curtains and looked out the window. She saw nothing.

As she set her novel on the nightstand, she automatically noted the time. The digital clock displayed the time—11:20—in a deep red color. She scratched her head. What had just happened? What had she heard exactly? She hoped it wasn't another burglary, or worse, something else.

FRIDAY MORNING

Tim Dewitt woke up to the gentle hum of the ceiling fan. Bright sunlight streamed through the windows, but his brown eyes soon adjusted to the bedroom's eastern exposure. For a moment, he felt disoriented before realizing he was waking up in his house. *Our house*, he corrected himself as he turned his head to look at Marie, who still slept soundly nuzzled against his shoulder. He could see her eyes moving beneath her lids and wondered if she was dreaming about their time in Paris. How they had walked along the Seine at dusk or wakened in bed to look out their balconied window with its view of the Eiffel Tower. The trip had been Marie's dream come true. She had taken French classes back in high school, and when they had started to date seriously in their junior year, she would tell him about traveling to France someday. She had loved every minute of being in Paris, and he had loved every minute being there with her.

Tim gently nudged his wife so that she shifted position. She didn't stir from sleep, and he wondered if he had time to bring her breakfast in bed before she woke. He slipped out of bed quietly and padded naked across the carpet to where he had hastily placed his bureau. He pulled out a T-shirt and denim shorts, dressed, and left the bedroom. As his bare feet touched the soft, red carpet, Tim felt an electric rush of reality as the realization sunk in that this house was his, his and Marie's.

Even when he'd arrived yesterday, the house still felt as if it belonged to his grandmother, the place where he had spent happy, childhood days with his brothers and sisters. There was the dining room where his grandmother had taught him how to play various card games. The front room where he had played board games with his siblings. The kitchen where his grandmother would bake various delectables and serve them with iced tea or milk. All of these memories emanated from a house that was now his.

"I can't believe it," he muttered and shook his head incredulously.

He could smell the fresh brew of coffee wafting from the kitchen, and there he found his grandmother sitting, as she always had, at the country-style table sipping her morning cup of coffee with cream and sugar. He suddenly felt as if he were a little boy again and merely visiting his grandmother. But instead of a serene look, he saw his grandmother's knitted brow. Something worried her. He hoped she didn't regret giving up her home of so many years.

"Morning, Grandma. How did you sleep?"

Edith sipped her coffee. She was trying to finish reading the novel she had borrowed from Claudia, but her mind kept returning to the sounds of last night. She had awakened earlier that morning just after dawn and vaguely remembered the events that had captured her attention at 11:20. Someone had called out, "Help me." She remembered that distinctly. She might not have thought anything of it—some of the younger neighbors tended to be rowdy, at times, in the evenings—but those two popping sounds. They really did sound like gunshots. That was before the car engine started. It couldn't have been the car backfiring. The more she thought about, the more she thought she had heard a murder. All morning, she had been thinking through what she heard, trying desperately to rationalize it, but she kept coming back to the same alarming conclusion.

"Are you all right, Grandma?"

Edith looked up at her grandson and smiled wanly. "Oh, I'm sorry, Timothy. I'm fine. Help yourself to coffee, dear, it's a fresh pot." As Tim helped himself to a cup, she wondered how she might ask him if he'd heard anything. "Did you sleep well?"

"Actually, yes." He recalled last night with Marie and contentedly falling asleep shortly after. He stifled what surely would have been a stupid grin and said, "Hosting last night's meeting was a bit draining. I turned on the ceiling fan to keep the room cool. It worked pretty well."

Edith sighed. "I'd forgotten about the fan."

"Are you sure you're all right?"

Edith stood up mechanically and walked over to the window above the kitchen sink. The perplexed look remained on her face, as she stared out the window despondently. After a moment's thought, Edith faced her grandson and asked him a question with the utmost seriousness. "I was wondering if you heard anything last night?"

"What do you mean, Grandma?" Tim asked as he sat at the kitchen table.

Edith sat down opposite him. Her blue eyes looked directly at him. "Last night around eleven-twenty, I heard someone cry out for help twice. Then I heard two gunshots, and a car engine starting and racing up the street."

"Are you sure you weren't dreaming, Grandma?" Tim asked skeptically.

"I'm sure I wasn't. I was reading this novel last night, but I must have drifted off to sleep. Just before eleven-twenty, I was awakened by the sound of a door slamming. I listened at the window, which was open ajar because of the humidity, and I heard . . . I think I may have heard a murder."

"What?"

Edith sighed. "It's so difficult to explain. Let me tell you the whole story once more."

Edith recounted the events she had experienced during the night so vividly that Tim felt he could almost hear those cries and gunshots himself. When she was done, Tim didn't know what to think. In silence, he just sat there looking at the kitchen table.

"Timothy?" Edith recalled her grandson from his thoughts. "I know you must think I imagined the whole thing . . . or that all I heard was a car backfiring or something. But . . ."

She paused for a moment, not certain of just the right words. She picked up her coffee mug and held it in her hands as if she would take a sip, but she hesitated. Several thoughts passed through her mind all at once, and she found it difficult to sort out the details. With some effort, though, she honed in on what had been said at Tuesday night's bridge game. Finally, she looked into Tim's brown eyes.

"Too many things have been happening on this street of late. A suicide, four burglaries. Whatever I heard last night can't be ignored. Of that much I'm certain!"

"But—"

Edith interrupted, "Timothy, please listen. Your mother's picking me up any minute. And I would never forgive myself if I didn't do anything. Now, I can't go snooping around myself. It's not as if I were going to be here anyway. But you could. That's why you set up the Neighborhood Watch, right? For this very sort of thing? And you're a police officer. You know what to do. Just ask around discreetly. Just in case something did happen last night. It could have been another burglary. I pray to God that's all it was, but I fear otherwise."

"Grandma, I'm on vacation. And I can't just go knocking door to door. There's a procedure to follow—"

"I know you, Timothy. You're not the type to sit idly by. I'm just suggesting you get to know your neighbors and ask a few questions. What could be the harm in that?"

For his benefit, Edith gave him that pleading look she so often employed when she desired to be indulged. "Please, Timothy? I need to know you'll do what I asked before I leave."

A sudden honking from a car alerted Edith that her daughter Sarah Dewitt had arrived.

"All right, Grandma," said Tim.

Scurrying about, Edith took her mug to the sink to clean it, suppressed a sly smile, and blurted out a few last words to her grandson.

"Thank you, Timothy. Do take care of yourself and Marie." She hurried to her luggage, which she'd placed by the front door. Waving Timothy aside, Edith snatched up her purse, picked up a suitcase that was far too large for her small stature, and without ceremonially pause, she left.

Tim padded across the beige carpet to the bay window and watched his grandmother sneak one last look at her former home. He wondered—not for the first time—how his grandmother could just up and leave everything behind so decisively, but as he watched his mother putting the suitcase in the trunk of the car, Tim remembered a conversation. This wasn't the first time Edith Baxter had uprooted herself and left behind a home with few possessions to carry with her. She'd been a single mother raising two girls, and she had struggled. Now, happier times prevailed, and both Edith and her daughter waved to Tim before getting in Sarah's car. Tim duly waved back. He was still waving when Marie appeared at the end of the hallway in her peach bathrobe.

Rubbing her eyes, Marie asked, "Was that your mother?"

"Yeah."

"Why didn't she stop in and say hello?"

"I dunno." Tim shrugged.

In fact, he wondered whether his mother was avoiding him. Whatever was bothering her had started just before his wedding. She had seemed preoccupied, and since he'd returned from his honeymoon, they had exchanged little more than pleasantries. Tim wasn't too concerned yet, just curious. He figured she'd tell him what the matter was, when she was ready.

"Tim? Is breakfast ready? I'm famished."

"Oh," he said, breaking away from his thoughts, "Grandma already fixed the coffee, but why don't you get dressed while I cook up something for breakfast."

While Marie showered and dressed, Tim whipped up ham and cheese omelets. He nearly overcooked them. His mind was still reeling from what his grandmother had told him. Something was happening on Stoneridge, but what?

At breakfast, the newlyweds reminisced some more about Paris and plotted their errands for the day. Marie planned to go to the grocery store to stock up. Shortly after they'd finished eating, she left. After a leisurely shower, Tim pulled on a pair of boxers and his denim shorts. He tossed a white T-shirt over his shoulders and towel dried his blond hair, which looked nearly brown when wet. He wondered again if his grandmother might have been mistaken. A car backfiring could easily sound like a gunshot. There was no reason to suspect otherwise. And yet . . .

Tim left the bedroom and sauntered into the living room. He looked out the bay window and absorbed his surroundings. Spring had come early to Syracuse this year, and its stirrings were well under way. The yew bushes were trimmed to perfection, and the lush green lawn looked ready for its first mowing of the year. He regarded the multi-colored tulips and other spring blooming flowers—daffodils, irises, and hyacinths—that his grandmother had planted. The two maple trees' leaves were already blooming, while some of the less fortunate buds, broken off their branches by the wind, lay solemnly on the grass and in the driveway. They lay as bright yellow-green specks of life that would soon shrivel and die. The occasional bug would wander onto the scene, and Tim cringed slightly at the sight of bees and wasps gathering honey and transporting pollen from flower to flower. Caught in this reverie of spring, Tim thought how simple it would be to live by natural laws and not be bound by worries of right and wrong, but then sighed as he considered the chaos that would certainly ensue.

"Why do our lives have to be so complicated?"

He furrowed his brows, thinking again about what his grandmother heard. He looked down the street. That was where the car must have come from. The gunshots had sounded nearby to her, so that meant the site was probably in view. He could just see the large white house belonging to Georgia Llewellyn situated where the street curved. He couldn't recall who lived in the light blue house next door. Todd and his wife lived in the green split-level. Next were Dr. Logan and his two sons in the tan house. Then Tim caught sight of Claudia Icarios in her front yard across the street. She lived in a gray ranch house similar to his own.

His grandmother had told him that Claudia lived for her flowers, and he could see how devoted a gardener she was. Perhaps he could get a sense of the neighborhood from her. She was sensitive to the plight of others, and she was patient enough to listen. Only Tim suspected she'd be too skeptical. Ideally, he could discuss things with Dr. Icarios who served as the county medical examiner. Unfortunately, today, Dr. Icarios would be at work.

Tim paused to scrutinize the white split-level house next to the Icarioses. He didn't recall if anyone was currently living there. In the driveway of the brown split-level next door he could see two young children riding their bicycles under the watchful eye of their father. David Yates looked agitated as he watched his children. He smiled when they looked up at him, but then he'd glance furtively up at the bay window. Presumably his wife was watching from inside.

Tim didn't recall either David or Linda Yates speaking at last night's Neighborhood Watch. They had been content to stay in the background and then quietly leave. Tim guessed that they weren't much older than he was, but he didn't know much else about them.

The next house was another split-level with an unfortunate salmon color. He didn't know the name of the family that lived there, but he had heard they were vacationing somewhere. Tim fancied the idea that they'd left to escape the sickly color of their house.

A Jewish family lived in the next house, a split-level opposite Sonya Schwartz's. They, too, were out of town. Many families had taken off for the Passover and Easter holidays. And next week was the school district's Spring Break. A burglar could have a field day!

Or had the burglar turned murderer?

Tim realized he needed more information about his neighbors or at least some idea of where to start looking. But who could he confide in? Todd would be an obvious choice. Tim had known Todd since they were toddlers, and their high school days at St. John's had only strengthened their friendship, which was further cemented when Tim began dating Marie. Unfortunately, Todd was working today. Tim doubted Marie's brother knew much about his neighbors anyway, since he and Rachel had only moved to Stoneridge a year ago or so.

Tim considered other neighbors. Brenda Lysik? No, she'd be at work, too. Ms. Llewellyn? Of course! Miss Sparrow! His former schoolteacher had helped him on a case once before. She'd be the perfect person to talk to.

"So what is it you wanted to ask me, Tim?" Angela said in that pleasant, caring voice that Tim remembered so well from his school days.

Angela Sparrow had moved to Stoneridge Drive in 1974, two years after she had begun teaching at Holy Cross Elementary School. She served as the sixth grade teacher and had seen several Dewitts and Stuarts pass through her classroom. She also taught English and history to the fifth, seventh, and eighth grades at Holy Cross. In fact, she had encouraged Tim's keen interest in history, especially the history of the Syracuse area, which in turn led to Tim's eagerness to benefit the community around him, and his desire to become a police officer. She had also been very instrumental a year ago when Tim was working on his first case. Angela belonged to the Onondaga Historical Association and had been able to provide Tim with helpful information. Now, Tim once again came to her for advice and information.

"Well, I wanted to ask your opinion of something."

The two neighbors sat on Angela's plush white couch facing her home's bay window with its view of Stoneridge.

"Just tell me what's the matter, dear," Angela said reassuringly, as she adjusted her right ankle on the ottoman set before her.

After leaving Claudia's house Tuesday night, Angela had slipped on some loose gravel. Claudia had driven her to the hospital. Once her sprained ankle had been diagnosed and bandaged, Angela was told to stay off her feet as much as possible for at least a week. Fortunately for her, Holy Cross' Spring Break began yesterday, and with few other necessary appointments, she would easily be able to follow doctor's orders.

"Well," Tim began hesitantly. "My grandmother had her window open last night and—"

Tim stopped abruptly, so Angela filled the awkward silence.

"Oh, that sounds perfectly reasonable. If it hadn't been for my window air-conditioner, I would have had my window open. But pray continue."

"Well, apparently she wasn't able to sleep, ah, that soundly. She was reading and fell asleep, but she woke up when she heard some sounds that disturbed her."

"Take your time, Tim. Don't rush yourself," Angela said encouragingly.

Tim went on to narrate the events that his grandmother had heard last night. Angela sat motionless on the couch as she listened with grave interest. When he'd finished, Tim patiently awaited her opinion.

"I have known Edith for many years now," Angela began, "and I believe her." Tim sighed with relief, and Angela continued, "I do have one question though. Did she happen to tell you from which direction the gunshots came?"

Tim shrugged, saying, "They must have come from down the street. The car drove past our house. I did get the impression that the shots were fired somewhere near the curve in the road, but as I said, that's only an impression based on what my grandmother said."

"That would mean they were nearer to my house than yours?"

"Yes."

"I see," Angela said. "What about the cry for help? Was that a distinctive word or a scream?"

"Again, Grandma gave me the impression that it was a distinctive shout for help."

"And neither you nor Marie heard the shot?"

Tim grinned sheepishly. "I haven't talk to Marie about this yet. But I doubt she heard anything. There's a ceiling fan in our bedroom, and we had it on last night."

Angela reflected a moment, and then asked, "You're probably assuming it might be our burglar?"

Tim nodded. "That's what I was thinking. But I'm not sure how I want to proceed. I'd feel guilty if I didn't check it out. I promised Grandma I would. But on the other hand, what business do I have asking questions about, well, you understand what I mean?"

"Yes, but I think this ought to be pursued. Edith's perceptions shouldn't be ignored. She's too reliable and trustworthy a witness for that." Angela glanced out her window. The ranch house belonging to Lisa Collins caught her attention. As she regarded the college students' home, she began to wonder. "Have you talked to anyone else?"

"No. I really didn't know where to start. Marie and I are new here, and I wasn't sure how to handle our neighbors. I thought you might have an idea of what's been going on lately. Who might be worth talking to? You know . . ."

Angela nodded, but she then asked abruptly, "Do you think it was murder?"

Tim was taken by surprise, but he calmly answered, "That is a possibility. It's also why any investigations *could* be dangerous. Plus I don't want to alarm anyone unnecessarily. After all, everyone's so worked up about the burglaries. And it could have been something quite . . . natural, but it might be embarrassing to someone. You understand what I mean? Besides, there's no evidence or reason to suspect a murder."

"Except for what Edith heard," Angela remarked. "I see how that could be a problem. It would have been so much different if someone had seen what happened."

"Yes, but Grandma only heard what happened. It's not enough." Tim sighed in frustration. "Realistically, I just don't see that there's anything I can do. I'd be overstepping my bounds as an officer. A murder investigation is hands off for a rookie, but if there has been a murder and I could solve it . . ."

Tim considered what it could mean for his career. He weighed the pros and cons of possible actions he could take. What could be the harm in talking to a few of his new neighbors and slipping in a few targeted questions?

"I must say," said Angela, who'd been pondering some questions of her own. "I'm curious as to what Edith heard. There have been an awful lot of unusual occurrences here on Stoneridge. And I, for one, do not think they're coincidences."

"What do you mean exactly?"

"I don't know what Edith has told you, but I find it strange that poor Danielle Deveraux supposedly committed suicide one week before the burglaries began. I cannot help but think that all these events might be linked."

Angela noticed Tim was pondering something, and she asked, "What is it, Tim?"

"It's funny, you know. I remember Todd Stuart dated a Danielle McGinty in high school, but they split up soon after starting college. I'm not sure what went wrong. Todd never really talked about it. And then he started dating Rachel. Of course, I was too busy learning the ropes of the Dewitt Police Department to pay attention."

Tim laughed at the sudden memory, but his laughter soon turned to grim wonder.

"Miss Sparrow, was Joshua Deveraux's wife, was her maiden name McGinty?"

"I'm not sure. I don't think I ever learned her maiden name, but maybe if you tell me what she looked like?"

Tim's brown eyes glazed over as he recalled the Danielle he knew.

"She was the loveliest girl that any of us guys at St. John's Academy had ever seen. When we all saw her at that first dance junior year, we all fell in love with her. I was just getting serious with Marie, so I tried not to pay too much attention. Besides, she had obviously picked Todd. And why not? All the girls agreed he was the handsomest guy at St. John's. Danielle and he were the perfect couple. She had the most wonderful reddish hair and the softest blue eyes. She had that pale Irish complexion and a few freckles on her cheeks. She was tall and kinda statuesque, but she had a kinda grace about her."

"It's such a shame that she should have died so young," Angela said, shaking her head solemnly.

"Then it was Danielle that died?"

"Oh, yes. You described Joshua's wife to a tee. A very sweet girl. A bit fragile. You couldn't help but want to protect her from the harshness of life. I felt as if I had practically lost a daughter, though I never really knew much about her personally. I fear she may have discovered just how painful the real world can be and how unfair it all is."

"Why do you say that?"

"Her husband was having an affair. Didn't you know? Edith didn't tell you?"

"No," Tim said, shaking his head.

"Well, there was a rumor. The suggestion was that he was sleeping with someone in the neighborhood," Angela said, nodding knowingly. "No one's really paid much attention to Joshua Deveraux since the death of his wife. Danielle was the more sociable of the two. We've all sort of kept our distance from him, so that he could have ample time to grieve. Although, I try to speak with him from time to time to see how he's doing, but he's very aloof."

"Could he have murdered his wife?"

Angela shook her head. "Sadly, it has been suggested, but I just don't see it. He genuinely loved her. He certainly was devastated when she died. The whole event, well, it was like Hamlet arriving home too late to save his Ophelia, now that I come to think of it."

After a solemn pause, Angela continued. "She slashed her wrists in the bathtub. She must have been depressed, I suppose, but there were no outward signs. I know there was that rumor that someone was seen near the house that afternoon. Personally, I think that started with Georgia. Georgia Llewellyn is a dear, but she does have a tendency to misinterpret things. She tends to exaggerate certain details. Mostly they're trivial. But sometimes she hears someone else's account of an event, real or imagined, and later she'll say it actually happened and she saw it!"

Angela laughed. She shook her head as she recalled one of Georgia's muddled stories. Then, remembering Danielle's suicide, her smile vanished.

"I'm afraid much of what I know is secondhand. Georgia told me about it that night after it happened. I assume it was mostly accurate. You see, she was there. After Joshua discovered his wife, he ran across the street to get Georgia. He must have remembered her being a nurse. Of course, it was too late by then. He claimed he'd had a flat tire, which delayed his getting home from work. And forgive me for saying this, but I do think the police are a bit too suspicious sometimes. They verified his flat tire story before they even began their investigation. In the end, they ruled it a suicide."

Tim frowned. He felt bad about Danielle. He'd known her, talked to her. She'd always seemed so vibrant to him. And now . . .

He looked down at the rug that covered most of Angela's living room. He barely registered the floral pattern of its border. Something worried him. At first, he couldn't think what, but then he realized the connection he was trying to make.

"How awful," he muttered. He looked up at Angela and realized he'd spoken aloud. "About Danielle, I mean," he added hastily.

"Very sad," Angela said, nodding solemnly. "She died a week before the first burglary at the Lysiks' house."

Tim didn't really pay attention. He was still thinking about Todd's connection to Danielle. They'd dated in high school, and more recently, they'd been living across the street from each other. Todd had never mentioned Danielle to him recently. Had he known she lived on Stoneridge? And what did he know about her suicide?

"Now that's interesting!"

Tim snapped to attention as Angela continued. "Danielle is killed in what I consider a dramatic performance rather than just a suicide, and now, someone else has possibly been murdered in a dramatic final act."

Tim tried to ponder what she'd said, but his mind was elsewhere. Perhaps if he talked to Georgia Llewellyn . . .

"Would Ms. Llewellyn be home now?"

"I suspect so," said Angela in a tone of uncertainty. "She is most days since her retirement."

"Thanks for all your help, Miss Sparrow. I'm sure I'll stop by again. After all, you did help me with a case once before."

Angela nodded. She remembered her small contribution to that case, but that had been an easy matter.

Georgia Mae Llewellyn lived in a two-story white house situated where the road curved like a backward letter "J." Her home was the largest on the street. Her second husband, Albert Kittridge, had been a contractor, and he had purchased the plot and built a home for his new bride in 1959. Albert designed his house to reflect the architectural styles of the South, including a country-style kitchen, parlor, a music room with an ebony grand piano, and a solarium. These rooms catered to his wife's fondness for tending orchids, playing and listening to music, hosting soirées, and reliving her Southern heritage.

Unfortunately, since her husband's chronic illness and eventual death, Georgia had not held any evening parties at her home. Despite this tragedy and though she lived quite alone, the sixty-year-old southern matron remained cheerful. She often played the grand piano and let her mind be absorbed by the music. It was in this state that she nearly failed to hear her doorbell ring.

Undaunted by interruption, Georgia Llewellyn went to her front door and was delighted to see Tim Dewitt on her doorstep. Georgia had always had a fondness for Tim because she had delivered him single-handedly. She had been called over to Edith Baxter's house where Sarah Dewitt had gone into labor during the infamous Blizzard of '66. Georgia had trampled through more than thirty inches of snow to reach the Baxter home late Sunday evening on the 30th of January in 1966. Now the child she had helped to deliver was standing on her very doorstep with a warm smile on his face.

"Why, hello, Timothy," said Georgia in her lilting Southern accent. "I'm sorry I couldn't come to that meeting of yours last night, but I was busy with my spring cleaning. I tell you it is so hard for a person my age to clean a house this large. And then I had to visit my daughter. The poor dear. I can't even begin to tell you how exhausted I was when I returned home at quarter to ten."

Fully refreshed from her exhaustion, Georgia continued smiling brightly, as she absently patted her cotton-like, ash-blond hair.

"Oh, don't worry yourself about that. There'll be another short meeting in a couple weeks," Tim said.

Though Georgia smiled, her crisp blue eyes did not as she replied, "Lovely."

"May I come in?"

"Oh, why of course. How rude of me. Come in."

Georgia ushered Tim inside and led him through the first floor of her house. The décor was stately and evoked the antebellum South. Everything was neatly arranged and well-kept, though there were traces of a recent spring cleaning. They passed through her solarium to the screened porch with its view of her spacious backyard and, as Tim noted, Lisa Collins' backyard. She invited him to sit in one of two white wicker chairs, which flanked a white wicker table with a glass top. Then after offering her gentleman caller a drink, which he declined, Georgia asked, "So how are you and your new bride faring?"

"Oh, Marie and I are fine."

"Oh, that's wonderful to hear. How are the twins, Brett and Denise?"

Georgia recalled how she had also delivered Tim's twin siblings in Kingston, Jamaica, during a hurricane. Her husband had taken ill after that trip, and she had retired from the hospital not long after, but she would never forget that vacation. How odd it had been . . .

"I haven't really seen them since Marie and I got back from our honeymoon, but as far as I know, they're doing great."

"That's so good to hear," said Georgia, smiling. However, she could not quite shake the memory of Tim's birth nor that of the twins. Both had been during severe weather conditions. How curious it was. Trying to put such thoughts aside, Georgia asked, "How's your family? And what brings you to Stoneridge?"

"My family's well, but I'm surprised you haven't heard. My grandmother Edith gave her house to Marie and me as a wedding gift. We just moved in yesterday before the Neighborhood Watch Meeting."

"Oh, how wonderful. You know you were born in that house? And now to think that you'll be living in it. I just know you and Marie will be happy here. The neighbors really care about each other. At least most of them do."

"What do you mean?"

"Oh, I'm surprised you hadn't heard. I know Edith knew about it."

"What is it?" Tim asked, sensing that she was about to tell him her version of Danielle Deveraux's suicide.

"You mean to say you didn't know about Joshua Deveraux's wife's suicide?"

"No, I had no idea," Tim said, telling a white lie.

"Oh yes. It's so hard when one loses a spouse, especially to suicide. My second husband died ten years ago. I really cared for him over my first spouse, who didn't have the decency to die until three years ago! But Albert, my second husband, he was always so patient and kind. When he died, I told myself, 'I will never marry again.' Mind you, you never know, but I do think I shall remain a widow until the end of my days." Georgia paused, before returning to the subject. "Oh, but I was talking about Joshua Deveraux's wife committing suicide. Let's see, it was about a week before the burglaries started. He found her that day, that is, in March. She was lying in the bathtub with her wrists slashed. Well, knowing that I was a nurse, he came to me directly and asked me to help, but by then, it was too late. She must have been dead for at least forty-five minutes before he got home. The sad thing is that he might have saved her. Normally he gets home from work shortly after five-thirty, but that night he wasn't home until close to half-past six. He was delayed by a flat tire. Although, there's been some suggestion that he killed her."

"Why is that?"

"Well, there's been some who've thought he might have put a hole in his spare tire and claimed that he changed a flat. Some think it's possible he stowed his car somewhere, and that he walked to his house and killed his wife."

"But you don't buy that story?"

"I don't know whether I do or not. The rumor is that someone was seen leaving the Deveraux's house earlier that afternoon. And then there's the rumor going around that Joshua Deveraux had been having an affair with someone on this street!"

"It sounds like something out of a soap opera," Tim joked.

"Yes, I suppose it does sound rather like a soap opera. And it's probably just a rumor, but it could very well be the truth. Yes"—Georgia nodded knowingly—"The truth sometimes seems stranger than fiction. Have you ever read some of those true crime stories? They are much more bizarre than any fictional mystery story I've ever read."

"No, I don't like true crime stories."

Georgia sighed complaisantly, and a short awkward pause in the conversation ensued that was eventually broken by Tim's soft voice.

"You know, this weather has been unbearable lately. It was so uncomfortable last night. I hardly got any sleep. Did you sleep well last night?"

"Oh, not at all! I was mad about it, too. I told you that I arrived back here at quarter to ten, exhausted from the day. All I wanted to do was go to bed and get some rest. But, no! That obnoxious young trollop next door was arguing with some boyfriend five minutes after my head hit the pillow."

"How did you happen to hear them?" Tim asked slyly.

"I like to have my window open on humid nights. Reminds me of my childhood days in the South. But then that horrid girl and her boyfriend going at it like two cats in heat. Really, it just got to be too unbearable so I had to shut my window!"

"People have no respect for their neighbors," Tim sympathized.

"So true. I had a terrible time trying to get to sleep despite the fact that I was exhausted."

"What were they arguing about?"

"Oh, I don't know. They were talking about some arrangement. I didn't catch the entire conversation because my hearing isn't what it used to be. But I heard enough. I heard Lisa say, `How dare you! Why should I have told you? What did you ever do for me?' Then the man replied, 'You've changed.' Lisa responded, 'You've got that right. You . . .' The last word sounded like son of a . . . well, you get the picture. It's just that those last three words seemed like they ran so close together that you would have sworn it was one word. Well, I didn't at all approve of the language so I shut my window at that point. I did hear a scream just as I was closing my window."

Georgia bit her lip as she thought about last night.

"All I can say is that the whole situation was much too unbearable to listen to. And such vulgar language. Besides, I wanted my beauty sleep." Georgia patted her ash-blond hair.

Tim suppressed a smile. "Where is Lisa Collins now?" he asked.

"My illustrious neighbor must have left with one of her boyfriends," Georgia said sarcastically. "I do remember hearing a car driving away down the street last night. I suppose it was her car. It's not out in her driveway now, and I saw it in her driveway when I came home last night. Also I didn't see or hear her boyfriend arrive. I assume he came home with her in her car. They drove off down the street at ten-twenty-five, a few minutes after I closed my window. I remember the time because I looked at my alarm clock."

"Sounds like she's having boyfriend trouble, don't you think?"

Georgia rolled her eyes.

"I wouldn't be surprised. I'll bet it wasn't the first time either. I've seen several men calling on her. The boyfriend last night probably found out she was dating another man. In fact, I've seen her with Dr. Logan a few times. A nice man. I knew his family. Well-to-do Texans. Good stock. I couldn't believe that he had taken up with the likes of her. And she's so much younger. But then times have changed. She just doesn't belong in this respectable neighborhood if you ask me."

"She doesn't appear to be the respectable type from what I've seen of her," Tim agreed blindly, for he doubted he'd ever seen Lisa.

"She isn't. Have you seen all the men who call on her? The way she manipulates them. Ever since she moved here, I've always seen some half-naked man doing yard work for her." Georgia's fingertips idly stroked her long neck. She could easily picture the handsome young men she'd seen shirtless from her window. She liked to watch them while enjoying an iced tea. "They didn't get any money for their work. The noises you could hear coming from that house. They're unmentionable."

Georgia shook with disgust.

"You're kidding?"

"Oh, it's awful," Georgia said shrilly. "And her bedroom has to be practically next to mine. That argument last night was about her, ah, indiscretions. I'm sure of it! I tell you it's a wonder no one's tried to kill her."

After a pause in the conversation, Georgia changed the subject and began asking about the new Syracuse Botanical Gardens. She'd heard all about it from Edith and asked about Marie's new job there. Then the conversation drifted onto other current events in and around the Syracuse area. And quite naturally Georgia began asking about Dewitt's Department Store, the Dewitt family business, which had spawned a financial dynasty. Dewitt Enterprises was very active in supporting and sponsoring local community events, including a substantial donation of money to the Onondaga County Parks and Recreation to be held in trust for the Syracuse Botanical Gardens.

Though Tim enjoyed talking to the widow, he was anxious to leave. So when a break came in the conversation, he said, "Well, I should probably get back home. Marie will want me home for lunch. But I'll stop by again, if that's all right with you."

"Why, of course," Georgia said, smilingly sweetly. "And do bring Marie with you next time. I would love to meet her. And I can use my recipe for mint juleps and homemade strawberry-rhubarb pie."

"Sounds great," said Tim, not sure if he liked the idea of rhubarb. "I'm sure Marie would love it."

Tim stood up to leave, and Georgia followed him to the door. But they had no more reached the middle of Georgia's music room, when she suddenly gasped, “Oh, silly me, how I do forget things! Would you do me a huge favor?” When Tim nodded, Georgia explained, “I would do it myself, but I really don’t like my next door neighbor as you probably gathered from our conversation. Well, to get to the point, I have a letter that was mistakenly delivered to me. It belongs to Lisa Collins. I’m afraid our mailman must be farsighted or nearsighted or whatever, because he mistook 208 for my house, 209. So if you would be a dear . . . ”

“Of course,” Tim said, “I’ll take it.”

“Oh, dear me,” Georgia said, looking around perplexedly. “Now where did I put it?” After a moment’s thought, she exclaimed, “Of course, the kitchen. I always keep my mail in there. I’ll just be a moment.”

Left alone in her music room, Tim took the time to look at the furnishings. Wistfully, he admired the furnishings. He had always dreamed of having a moderately large house with well-tailored furnishings like the ones he now saw. As his gaze moved about the room, it came to a stop on a portrait that hung above a black marble fireplace.

The portrait was of a handsome woman in her late-thirties with a little brunette-haired girl, who could be no more than six, standing beside her. The woman was seated in a Victorian chair, and a table next to the girl held an antique fan and two glasses of pink lemonade. In the background, Tim saw an old plantation peering out from behind large magnolia and oak trees bedecked with Spanish moss. Both the woman and the little girl were dressed in clothes reminiscent of the antebellum South.

Georgia re-entered the room with the letter in her hands and saw Tim regarding the portrait. Proudly, she remarked, “That is a portrait of me with my daughter Madelaine.”

“It’s a beautiful portrait.”

“Thank you. Madelaine was always my favorite. She was the one I was visiting yesterday. The poor dear,” said

Georgia, her voice trailing off. A flash of anger seemed to appear in her eyes for a moment, but the aged Southern belle soon regained her cheerful composure. "Well, before I forget, here's the letter. I must confess that I've had it at least a week, but I haven't opened it."

Tim wasn't so sure of that last fact when he looked at the crinkled envelope, but it appeared to be sealed. So Tim said his good- byes to Georgia Llewellyn and left her white "Southern mansion." It was 11:30, and Tim knew Marie would have lunch ready by noon. He didn't hurry home, however, for he was thinking about his recent conversation. The discrepancy between the times was bewildering to Tim as was the fact that Georgia had said the car had driven down the street.

When he reached the edge of Lisa's driveway, he took one long look at the single-story house; the place didn't appear lived in. He glanced over at the green split-level house next door. He also noticed the narrow strip of grass separating the two houses' driveways. Lisa lived next door to the Stuarts, whose house had been burglarized. *Is Lisa involved with the thief? Could she have told the thief when her neighbors weren't home? Or was she the culprit? But how?*

He didn't think she'd lived in the neighborhood long, and how could she know what her neighbors were up to? She attended college classes, didn't she? She most likely wouldn't be home much. But how does a college student afford a house? Unless . . .

Tim shifted his attention to the split-level house belonging to the Stuarts. He and Todd Stuart had graduated from St. John's Academy nearly four years ago. He'd felt somewhat left behind when Todd and Marie had gone off to college. And he had to admit that he and his best friend had drifted apart. Their lives had just begun pulling them in different directions. Still they managed to hang out when they could. Then Todd had dropped out of Syracuse University last year and started working as some grunt at some boring office Downtown. Tim saw even less of him. He couldn't help wondering why Todd had given up on his dream of becoming an actor.

Perhaps Rachel was the reason, Tim thought as he watched Todd's wife exit the house. She didn't seem to notice him standing in the street. She just walked around to the back of the house. Judging by the way she was dressed, Tim assumed she was going to do some gardening.

"Huh. She doesn't seem the type," he muttered.

Not that he knew her type. He'd only really gotten to know her when Todd married her two years ago, but she'd never said much about herself. Tim thought she was introverted or even shy, but Marie had argued otherwise. She had made it rather clear that she didn't like her new sister-in-law. In Marie's opinion, Rachel was a bossy shrew who browbeat her brother. Beyond that, Tim didn't know because he'd never pursued the topic. But now he wondered. Rachel and Todd had met at Syracuse University. Did either of them know Lisa?

I should talk to Todd, Tim thought. Only Todd, of course, wasn't home, and Tim wasn't prepared to talk to Rachel. He was certain *that* would be awkward.

So, in the meantime, Tim looked at his digital watch: 12:05. His stomach growled, so he hurried up the street to his house. However, when he reached the end of the Icarioses' driveway, Claudia, who had been working in her yard most of that day, happened to look up and waved to him. She set aside her gardening and approached the young man, who waited patiently for her. At six feet, he towered over the five-foot-four woman, but Tim guessed that Claudia had a far stronger personality than her short stature suggested.

"I noticed you went to visit Angela. How is she?"

"Well enough. She can't really get around without her crutches, though. I understand she needs to stay off her ankle at least a week."

"Such a shame. Do you realize that she slipped on loose gravel about where you're standing? And then the next day the Town cleaned the debris in the road. Now we have clean roads free of loose gravel. What good did it do after the fact?"

Each year the Town of DeWitt Department of Transportation cleaned the salt, sand, dirt, and gravel deposited by winter's reign and the snowplows. Tim noticed the familiar dusty tracks on the side of the road, where the debris had been gathered up by the sweepers. He knew how easy it was to slip on the gravel, too.

"I know what you mean. *C'est la vie*."

"What? Oh, oh yes, I agree."

"I see you're planting new flowers?"

Tim had noticed the basket of annuals and gardening tools near the Icarioses' front steps.

"Oh, yes. I love gardening. I'm a member of the Syracuse Garden Club. In fact, I got those from another member of the club. I had given her some primroses last year, so she thought she'd return the favor with these snapdragons. I tell you there is no greater joy than caring for life. I just can't understand how people can destroy nature's gifts."

Claudia's mood darkened as she recalled something.

"You mean the rain forests?" Tim asked.

"Pardon? Oh, uh, yes. You know I just remembered. I need to put a roast in the oven for tonight. Would you excuse me?"

Claudia hurried away, leaving Tim startled. What had she said? Destroying nature's gifts? He wondered if she'd been thinking of the rain forests or something closer to home. Tim shrugged. It was probably nothing. He crossed the street to his house. He only looked back once as he made his way to his front door. When he did, he thought he saw the curtain in the window of the Icarioses' house move back in place.

"As Alice would say, 'curiouser and curiouser.'"

Tim entered his house and found his wife in the living room. She'd gotten back from the grocery store and was leafing through the latest *Better Homes and Gardens*.

"Where'd you go?" Marie asked, perturbed.

"Didn't you get my . . . oh," Tim said, slapping the palm of his hand against his forehead. He'd forgotten to leave Marie a note. "I'm sorry. I meant to leave a note. I just went to visit Miss Sparrow."

"Oh, how's she doing?"

"Good. I think her sprain is more of a nuisance to her."

Marie nodded as she flipped through her magazine. She spotted a photo of a ranch house with a manicured lawn and gorgeous garden. With a smile, she looked up at Tim and said, "You know, we're really lucky. Most newlywed couples have to wait years before they can afford to buy a nice house."

"I know," Tim said. "I still can't believe it."

"Your grandmother is so sweet. I really envy your family's closeness."

"My father isn't exactly tender-hearted, Marie."

Jon Dewitt had railed about his son's decision to become a police officer, and Tim had never understood why nor had his father ever given him a reason.

"I know," she said.

Changing the subject, Tim asked, "So, um, how did you sleep last night?"

He didn't catch the slight hesitation before she answered, "Fine. Why do you ask?"

"Oh, nothing."

"Oh, no. I know when there's something on your mind. What is it?"

Tim decided to confide in her.

"My grandmother heard something last night."

Marie's cheeks colored with embarrassment. "She didn't!"

"No, not that," Tim said. "She had the window open in her room, and she heard something outside."

"What?"

Tim took a deep breath. Then he explained to Marie in minute detail what his grandmother had told him. She listened with a practiced ear until he finished.

"I don't believe it. It's too absurd!"

"I'm just telling you what she told me."

He clenched his jaw and refrained from saying anything more, but he couldn't believe that his wife doubted him. She didn't act like she thought it was a joke, but rather dismissed it out of hand.

"Frankly, I believe her," he said.

Marie set aside her magazine and walked over to the window.

Furrowing his eyebrows, Tim wondered what she was thinking. Clearly something was on her mind. Had she heard something last night?

"Is she sure of what she heard?" Marie asked. "Couldn't it have been someone just shouting and a car backfiring? I mean that sounds perfectly natural, right?"

"She's sure of what she heard, Marie. Did you hear anything?"

"Did you?" Marie retorted defensively.

Tim folded his arms across his chest.

"Come on, Marie. Tell me what's bothering you."

She started to protest, but then shrugged. "I'm just not sure. I think I heard a car gunning up the street last night. But I didn't hear gunshots."

"But there's something else?"

Marie nodded. "I don't know what time it was. Close to midnight probably. I was thirsty. So I went and got something to drink. I saw someone outside in the streetlight."

"Who?"

"I just don't know. It didn't seem important at the time."

"Try not to think about it, and it'll come to you," Tim suggested.

"I know," she said, scrutinizing the streetlight, "but I just can't help thinking about it!"

Tim slipped the envelope Georgia Llewellyn had given him out of his pocket and sat down on the couch. He toyed with the paper addressed to Lisa Collins.

After a moment, an idea came to him, and he asked, "What do you know about Lisa Collins? She would be a senior at Syracuse University."

"At S.U.? Well, I knew a Lisa Collins in the VPA Program. She dated Todd briefly. Surely she's not the Lisa that lives on this street?" Tim nodded. Marie continued. "Wow. I never would have thought. How did she afford a house? I know her dream is to become an actress, and she's not the starving artist type, but still. I thought she was living on campus."

"How did you—?"

"She and I took a couple of classes together."

"When?"

"I told you about Lisa. I can't believe you don't remember. She starred in some of the student dramas at Syracuse Stage. I thought she was a little full of herself. Todd's much more grounded about his acting. At least he was at the time. I can't believe he dated her."

He vaguely recalled a conversation about some wannabe actress who wasn't good enough to be dating Marie's brother.

"Oh, yeah. I remember now. Strange how the two of you became friends?"

"Well, not exactly. She was more of an acquaintance. Lisa was really friends with Janessa. Apparently, they went to elementary school together. Until about the third grade. Then Lisa's family moved or something."

"Really?" Tim said. He had met Marie's college roommate several times. In fact, Janessa had been Marie's maid of honor at their wedding.

"Yeah. I don't remember all the details. But can you imagine? They hadn't seen each other in years, and then they end up in the same college class! When they recognized each other's names, they began quizzing each other about the past. Next thing you know they're catching up and chatting about grade school."

"And you two met when you took a class?"

"Sort of. Janessa introduced us. But we did end up taking a biology class Sophomore year. We were lab partners. That's how I knew about her acting. Stupidly, I introduced her to Todd." She rolled her eyes. "At least it didn't last. Todd ended up dating Rachel, who was Lisa's roommate. In fact, they lived in the house next door to us. You know, that apartment Janessa and I moved into Sophomore year?"

Tim nodded. He remembered the large green Victorian on the corner of Euclid Avenue. He'd helped Marie and her roommate move in. The place was affectionately known as Aunt Phyllis's Boarding House, named for the woman who ran it. A lot of university students rented rooms and apartments in that section of the city. But he was stunned that Rachel and Lisa had lived next door to Marie then.

"How did I not know this?"

With a playful smile, Marie said, "Well you were busy staking out speeders as a rookie cop."

"Very funny."

Marie giggled. "Well, actually that was the following year. You were working at that awful job and taking classes up at O.C.C.. And I spent more time at your place than you did at mine."

Tim grinned. "Oh, yeah."

He'd graduated from Onondaga Community College with a two-year degree before enrolling in the police academy.

"Now, let's see, where was I?" Marie tapped a finger against her lips. "I didn't see much of Lisa after the end of the fall semester. She and Todd had broken up by then. And she and Janessa didn't really hang out much. Janessa was too involved with that guy, Rick Gray. God, they must have broken up and gotten back together like five times in four years of college!"

"How long were Rachel and Lisa roommates?"

"I'm not sure. I'd say two years. Oh, but there was a third girl! I've forgotten about Danielle. You remember Danielle McGinty? I wonder what ever happened to her."

Tim nodded grimly. "I'm afraid she's dead, Marie."

"Dead?"

Tim recounted what Angela Sparrow and Georgia Llewellyn had told him about the unfortunate Danielle Deveraux.

"It must be her," Marie said, astonished. "You mean she lived on Stoneridge, too?"

"Apparently."

"How sad." Marie shuddered.

"Do you think Lisa knew Josh?" Tim asked.

"Oh, I'm sure of it. She was Danielle's maid of honor."

Tim's jaw dropped. He'd experienced it before, but he realized again just how small a world it was. At least in Syracuse. People's paths did tend to cross. Still it never failed to amaze him.

"Do you know where Lisa might be now?"

"No, why?"

Tim regarded the envelope in his hands. It had spurred him to ask Marie about Lisa. Wondering what other information it might lead to, he explained, "Ms. Llewellyn gave me this letter to give her. It was mailed to her house by mistake."

"Ask Rachel Stuart. They were roommates once."

Rachel Stuart, née Weiss, was not pretty. Her features were striking, but her nose was too large for her round face.

Her dark brown eyebrows, either naturally or plucked, were too narrow and sharp, giving her a haughty look. Her ample figure was hidden beneath the gray sweatshirt and blue jeans.

Rachel huffed when she heard the doorbell ring. She hated answering the door, especially when it was someone wanting to persuade her to do something. She was surprised, however, to see her newest neighbor on her doorstep.

Intelligent hazel eyes looked down on Tim, who felt somewhat embarrassed under the cold appraisal. Still he smiled cheerily and said hello.

"Can I help you?" Rachel asked in a harsh voice.

"I hope so. My name's—"

"I know who you are. What do you want? If you're looking for Todd, he's at work."

"Well, actually I was looking for Lisa Collins. She doesn't appear to be home at the moment, so I was wondering if you knew when she might be back?"

"Why should I know? I don't run my neighbors' lives."

"But I thought you might know her."

"I couldn't care less about that bitch next door. Why are you so interested in her?"

"I have this letter addressed to her. It was delivered to our house by mistake."

Rachel's complexion paled when she saw the letter in Tim's hand.

"Oh. Would you like to leave it here?" Rachel tried to maintain her composure. "I can give it to her when I see her."

"That's okay. I'd best hold on to it."

A pause ensued.

"Was there anything else?" Rachel asked impatiently.

"I'm sorry I was just thinking about the weather," Tim said, as he wiped his brow. "It's been so hot lately. The humidity makes it difficult to get any sleep. We had to open our window last night to let in the breeze, but then we had to contend with all the noise coming from outside."

"Then I'm glad the repairman fixed our air conditioner."

"He did? When?" Tim asked, confused.

"Uh, well, it was yesterday morning."

Feeling the need to elaborate, Rachel added, "Mrs. Icarios had dropped by to lend me her shovel, and the repairman just showed up. I assumed Todd had called and forgotten to tell me. He gets so caught up in things, it's no wonder he forgets. But then you're his brother-in-law, aren't you? You know what I mean."

"Er, yeah. I guess." Tim scowled. He didn't care for her sarcasm.

"Look, I'm sorry to have been so short with you. I've just been having one of those days. I've been doing some landscaping in back, and it's very tiring."

"I know what you mean," Tim said with a weak smile. "Well, I better get going. Sorry to have disturbed you."

"Oh, that's all right," Rachel said rather dismissively.

Tim was miffed. He didn't like Rachel, and he couldn't understand why Todd would have or could have married her. He hated when people were condescending to him or dishonest with him. Rachel had done both! He'd seen the look on her face when he'd shown her the letter. She recognized it. Somehow he had to find an excuse to talk to her again.

In the meantime, Tim stopped at the end of the Stuarts' driveway and turned to look back at Lisa's ranch house. He remembered the previous owner had added the light blue siding and had had the roof redone last summer, shortly before putting the house on the market. He'd noticed the 'For Sale' sign often enough when he'd come over to mow his grandmother's lawn. He'd even considered looking into it. It would have been a convenient place for him and Marie to live, but he knew that they didn't make enough money between them to buy a house like the one his grandmother had given them, like the one Lisa apparently owned. How does a college student, with financial obligations to pay for college, manage to buy and pay the mortgage on a house? He didn't recall ever hearing that Lisa came from a wealthy family.

Tim shook his head. What did he know? All he had to go on was neighbors' gossip, his grandmother's testimony, and his own muddled mind. Not a good start to an investigation. Tim glanced around quickly to see that no one was watching and casually walked up to the house. He peered through the glass of the garage door, but couldn't really see anything. He did notice there was no car inside.

Fairly certain Lisa wasn't home, Tim walked up to the front door. He rang the doorbell. He wasn't surprised that no one answered. However, he did take the opportunity to look around. He checked for signs of a break-in, but the screen door and the front door looked intact. Not wanting to linger and be seen snooping around, Tim hurried back home. In his haste, he missed seeing the stain of blood on the corner of the steps.

FRIDAY AFTERNOON

"Why, Mrs. Esterhazy, what are you doing here?" Tim asked. He'd returned home to find Anne Esterhazy parked on the couch. When had she arrived? He didn't think he'd been gone that long, but Marie was perched on the edge of the couch and staring at him wide-eyed as if to say, 'Get me out of here!'

Tim smiled cordially at Anne, who immediately launched into one of her ramblings.

"Oh, hello, Tim. Just call me Anne. Everyone does. I just thought I'd stop by for a chat. I didn't realize that you two had moved here permanently. I knew that you married recently, but I had no idea! Well, Sonya told me all about it last night. I can't believe I didn't realize it. Here, I'd assumed you two had come just to talk about the Neighborhood Watch, since you're a police officer and all. Well, now I know better. So I just had to make my famous casserole. I hope you like it. It's my favorite recipe. I figured you probably haven't had time to go to the supermarket yet. And casserole is really the best house-warming gift. Besides, I know what it's like to have bare cupboards. I practically have to jumpstart my husband to go shopping. Of course, he always manages to pick up beer, soda, and snacks for himself, but he never thinks of the really important stuff like milk, eggs, and vegetables. He claims he's too tired after work. Like I have all this energy. He's a car salesman, you know. A real charmer. That's why I married him. But sometimes I wonder what I was thinking."

Anne shrugged and laughed at her own private joke. Barely taking a breath, she continued. "Well, I'd better get going. I can't leave the kids alone for long. Their father isn't home, and God knows what trouble they'd get into without supervision. I have a suspicion they're hyperactive, but my husband doesn't believe me. I'm only a nurse and wouldn't know anything about that, right? Like he'd know. His idea of exercise is pushing the buttons on the television remote control! Well, bub-bye, Marie. It's been fun. Really, people in this neighborhood hardly ever talk to each other enough.

Anne said her profuse good- byes again as she was ushered out by Tim, who, as politely as he could manage, shut the door behind her.

Marie collapsed on the couch with a huge sigh of relief. Staring out the window, she cringed as she watched Anne perkily jog up the street. She imagined the boisterous unnatural blonde had spied another victim up the street and would imminently swoop down and talk the poor person to death.

"I think she must drink too much caffeine."

"I'm so sorry you had to be cornered by her alone," Tim said sincerely.

"Don't worry," Marie said, "I'll be sure to pay you back."

"Hey, I had no idea she'd come down here for a visit."

"Of course not. Did you deliver the letter?"

Tim tugged the crumpled envelope out from his shorts' pocket.

"Ah, so Lisa is missing."

"We don't know that."

Marie shrugged.

"So what did Rachel have to say?"

"Not much," Tim said. "You know, I don't like her."

"See. Now you know what I've been saying!"

"What does he see in her?"

"I wish I knew." Marie gazed out the window as if she were trying to divine an answer. "Well, never mind that. I have something to tell you."

"Oh? Were you able to pry some information from Mrs. Esterhazy?"

Marie laughed.

"Not likely! She wanted to know all about you and me. More specifically, she wanted to know about me. I don't think I like her."

"You shouldn't have to worry about her too much. I understand that she spends most of her time chatting up Sonya Schwartz. She doesn't usually bother her neighbors down the street. At least, my grandmother never mentioned having too many run-ins with her."

"Sounds like I should compare war stories with Mrs. Schwartz. Maybe she can give me some tips on how to handle The Babbler."

"The what?"

"The Babbler. That's my nickname for Anne Esterhazy."

"I like it." Tim chuckled. "Now, what did you want to tell me?"

"Well, actually it relates to Sonya Schwartz. I remembered that she's Rachel's aunt. You should talk to her. Maybe she might know something about Lisa?"

Tim crossed over to the couch and sat next to Marie.

"I don't know," he told her. "I'm beginning to think there's nothing to all this."

"Why not?"

"Well, what do we really know? Something may have happened last night. My grandmother and Ms. Llewellyn both heard something. Lisa Collins is apparently involved. As far as I know, no one has seen her today. But for all we know, she's on campus up at S.U."

"Do you really think she is, though?"

Tim shook his head. “No, I think she’s missing. But there’s not a lot to go on. Just a lot of talk and rumor. And I don’t think enough time has passed for there to be any official investigation.”

“What are you gonna do then?”

“I don’t know. I promised my grandmother I’d look into it. But I feel kinda foolish going around asking pointless questions. I don’t handle cases like this. I take reports of incidents. I chase speeders. This”—Tim said, waving his hand—“this is a bit beyond me.”

“You know I could help you.”

“What? No.”

“Let me help you find out what happened,” Marie said. “I’m sure it wouldn’t be hard to do.”

“No,” Tim said firmly. “I don’t want you getting involved.”

“Why not? We could be like Myrna Loy and William Powell in *The Thin Man*.”

Tim frowned. “Murder isn’t all fun and games like the movies, Marie.”

“So you do think Lisa was murdered?”

“I didn’t mean . . . I’m just saying that it’s not a good idea. I don’t want you getting hurt.”

“What harm could there be in talking to a few of the neighbors? They might tell me more than they’d tell you.”

Tim shook his head. “Look,” he said. “Let’s just have lunch and forget about all this for a while. I don’t know about you, but I’m famished.”

“All right.” Marie pouted. “But you should talk to Sonya Schwartz after.”

“Yoo- hoo, Sonya.”

To her dismay, Sonya realized that she wouldn’t be able to get in her car and drive off in time to avoid Anne. Her next-door neighbor was nearly to the Schwartz's driveway already, so Sonya waited impatiently. She just hoped whatever Anne had come to say wouldn't take too long.

"I just had to talk to you. I was talking to Mildred earlier. She thinks something happened last night after the Neighborhood Watch meeting. She said that she had heard some car backfiring and some yelling. Or was that the other way around? Oh well, she says that some car went racing up the street Thursday night. Well, Mildred didn't know what to think at the time, mind you, but this morning, she noticed that red car of Lisa Collins's was missing. Well, we all know Lisa never gets up early. Mildred thinks that Lisa has run off with one of her boyfriends. And God only knows which one! She's had a string of men over at that house. Good-looking ones, too. And even two or three at a time! God, I envy her! But Mildred seems to think that Lisa's run off with someone who lives on this street! Imagine!"

Anne barely paused for breath, before continuing. "Well, I thought that was the most ridiculous idea. Lisa's the only one that's gone. And who would she have left with? There're no eligible bachelors on this street. Well, there's Dr. Logan, but he's got two teenage boys. He's not going to leave them behind. So I mentioned Mr. Deveraux. He's a widower now, too. I mentioned that I thought he might have killed his wife to be with Lisa, but Mildred didn't seem to like that idea. She actually got downright rude about it. She insisted that Mr. Deveraux had nothing to do with Lisa and that I ought to be looking at that Mr. Yates or that Stuart guy. Now he's dreamy. Did you see him last night at the Neighborhood Watch meeting? That guy is gorgeous! Course you know all about Todd Stuart."

"Not, really," Sonya sputtered.

"Well," Mrs. Esterhazy continued, unfazed, "I just found out that he's that new neighbor's brother. You know, Marie Dewitt. I just came from there. Now, I could see why Lisa

Collins would have an affair with Todd! But what I don't understand is Mildred's insistence about Mr. Deveraux. Doesn't he work for some kind of repair company? I'll swear I saw him in his repairman's uniform or maybe it's a mechanic's uniform. At any rate, this was Thursday morning. He was going over to, oh, wait. He didn't go to Lisa's house. He went to the Stuarts' house. But why on earth would Rachel Stuart want to cheat on her husband? Course I know I haven't seen Mr. Deveraux up close, but he does look kinda hunky. But Rachel is so plain looking. But then you know all about Rachel Stuart—"

"I'm sorry, Anne. Really. I have to go. I'm late for an appointment." Sonya entered her minivan. "If you'll excuse me." She shut the door and started the engine before her boisterous neighbor could say anything further.

Dumbfounded, Anne Esterhazy simply said good- bye and watched Sonya Schwartz drive away. After the minivan disappeared from sight, Anne turned round and strolled back to her house. That was when she noticed something blue in the corner of her vision.

"Oh, yoo- hoo, Mildred," Anne shouted, as she bore down on the unsuspecting woman dressed in blue.

Mildred Hawthorne, dressed in a blue blouse and navy skirt, had come out to water the flowers surrounding her mailbox. She looked up to see Anne Esterhazy swooping down on her like a vulture and realized she'd made a mistake. Mildred hated being accosted so suddenly like this, but she realized that, on this particular occasion, she was trapped.

"Anne, hello." Mildred smiled wanly. "How are you?"

"Oh, I'm quite well, thank you. I'd be a lot better if I had had a chance to see *Knots Landing* last night, but wouldn't you know there was this college lacrosse game on one of those cable stations. I swear I never should have agreed to get cable! My oaf of a husband watched the game all night! Well, I was fed up with him so I took a late night walk. But how are you, Mildred? You seemed a little depressed when we talked this morning."

"I'm fine. I—"

"Oh, that's so good to hear," Anne interrupted. "I can't stand it when people are sick. I mean, I know I work in a hospital and all, but that's different. It's when the children get sick . . . oh, but my husband is the worst. Really he's a big baby, whining and complaining a lot, all the while saying that he isn't even sick at all. I'm glad that I'm healthy. I hardly ever get sick, but then my family has always had a strong constitution. But I'm rambling on. I wanted to ask you about Lisa Collins. I was just telling Sonya Schwartz about our chat this morning. Well, I told her about the possibility of Lisa having an affair with someone, but she really didn't say anything."

Managing to get a word in edgewise, Mildred said "It's not just a possibility. Lisa *is* having an affair with someone. Claudia told me. I don't know how she came across the information, but I suspect she saw something."

"Really?" Anne said, obviously intrigued.

"Oh, yes."

"Does it have something to do with what you said you heard last night? You thought Lisa had run off with some boyfriend."

"I said she must have had some argument with her boyfriend, Anne."

"Oh, so then she drove off and left him? Or she went with him?"

"I don't know," Mildred said, exasperated.

Anne sighed. "Sometimes I wish I lived further on down the street so I'd know what was happening in this neighborhood. Some people have all the luck. I suppose I ought to speak with Mrs. Icarios, but I don't think she likes me very much."

"Oh, nonsense," Mildred said, as she finished watering her tulips.

"No, it's true," Anne said. "Although I suppose I could ask her if her church is going to have a bake sale for Easter like last year."

"You're not thinking of the Greek Festival in June are you?"

"Oh, no. That's every year. Don't churches have a bake sale on Easter?"

"Some do. But Claudia goes to the Greek church. That's the Eastern Orthodox calendar. Their Easter isn't for a couple weeks."

"Isn't it Easter this Sunday?"

Since Anne was Jewish, Mildred could understand her confusion, but the more immediate concern was getting away from her talkative neighbor.

"Yes, it is. But I really must attend to my houseplants, Anne. If you'll excuse me . . ."

Mildred Hawthorne hurried toward her front door. She called over her shoulder, and said, "We can talk later, dear."

Anne was about to return home, but then she noticed Tim Dewitt approaching. Having finished lunch, Tim had decided to talk to Mrs. Schwartz, not realized she wasn't home just now. Unfortunately, Anne intercepted him before he could find this out.

"Hello, Tim," Anne said cheerfully. "I just wanted to ask your opinion of something."

"Oh, hello, Mrs. Esterhazy. What did you want?"

"Well, I was just telling Sonya Schwartz what Mildred Hawthorne and I know. You see . . ."

Anne Esterhazy repeated the story, and Tim listened with half interest. However, he did catch a little of what she said. In fact, he realized that Mildred Hawthorne had a few interesting things to say, especially regarding last night.

"But you're a twin aren't you, Tim?"

Anne's question caught him of guard.

"Huh?" He tried to process what she'd asked him. "No, I'm not. Are you thinking of my brother and sister?"

"Oh, that's right. They're fraternal twins. That's what your grandmother told me. My two girls are identical. They're so sweet. We also have two boys. Our kids play with Sonya's all the time."

After another fifteen minutes worth of talking, or rather listening, Tim finally escaped from Anne Esterhazy. But instead of proceeding with his original plan to visit Sonya Schwartz, Tim walked down the hill to ring the Hawthornes' doorbell.

Mildred answered her door.

"Why, Tim, what a surprise!"

Mildred smiled and opened her door wider and invited Tim inside.

Unlike most houses on the street, the Hawthorne's living room was at the rear of the house and their kitchen was in front. So the two neighbors passed through the dining room into the living room, where they sat on a comfortable sofa that looked rather Edwardian in design. In fact, except for the kitchen, much of the Hawthorne's house looked like a set for an Edwardian stage drama.

"I wanted to ask you about something I've heard," said Tim once they were settled.

"What is it?"

"Well, Mrs. Esterhazy told me that Lisa Collins is . . ."

Tim recounted what Anne Esterhazy had told him.

"Oh, that stupid woman can never get anything right!"

"What do you mean?"

"What I mean is that Anne Esterhazy is an idiot! I never said that I knew who Lisa was having an affair with or whether or not the man was married! Of course, I'm sure she didn't say that now, did she?" When Tim shook his head, Mildred continued, "I might have known! You can't tell her anything without her getting it wrong. If I had said the man was married, she'd probably come back and say he wasn't. She's so suggestible just like Georgia Llewellyn. I'll bet you anything I could point to a random spot on the grass and say I saw a tiny garden snake, and Anne would turn around to someone and say she saw it, too! Then later she'd say it was ten feet long!"

"Granted, Anne has moments when she is right, but that is a rarity. After all, I know I certainly never said that Joshua Deveraux was having an affair with Lisa Collins. But why are you so interested in that girl's affairs? Edith mentioned you hardly ever pay attention to gossip."

Tim decided to give Mildred a modified version of what he'd learned about last night's events so far. Without identifying his sources, he related the argument Georgia had overheard and the sounds that his grandmother had heard.

"Now it seems Lisa has disappeared," he finished.

"I see," Mildred said thoughtfully. "Claudia must have been right!" Mildred saw Tim looking at her quizzically, and she hurriedly explained, "Claudia thought that Lisa was having trouble with a boyfriend."

"Really? Did she also tell you who Lisa was seeing?"

"If Claudia knows, she didn't tell me. But I know it wasn't Joshua. He was devoted to his wife. Now, I know there've been rumors floating around that he killed her. But that's just rubbish! Danielle Deveraux committed suicide."

"How can you be so sure?"

"I just am," Mildred said indignantly.

"But I heard someone was seen outside the Deveraux's house the day Danielle died."

"Unsubstantiated rumors," hissed Mildred. "The poor girl was depressed."

"About what?"

"Really, Timothy, I think you had better leave," Mildred said stiffly. "This conversation is ended as far as I'm concerned. If you would be so kind as to show yourself out."

Mildred's sudden odd behavior bewildered him, but Tim politely left. He didn't look back, but if he had, he would have seen Mildred narrowing her eyes as she watched him go. Her nostrils flared and she clenched her fingers. She'd talked too much. She would have to be more careful to protect her grandson.

After a tea break, Claudia Icarios was again out in her front yard. Kneeling on a protective pad, she dug in the soil around her mailbox to plant some dahlias and narcissuses. She'd had bought them earlier in the week and had nursed them indoors before deciding where to plant them.

Presently, Claudia noticed Tim strolling down Stoneridge. *What was he up to?* She'd been well aware of his movements throughout the day. It had to be about more than just getting to know his neighbors. Claudia had always viewed the younger neighbors, like the Stuarts, the Yateses, and the Deverauxs, as less amicable than those of her generation. Her younger neighbors just weren't that sociable. Well, except for the Lysiks, they at least had made the effort to get to know their neighbors, but then they were closer to their thirties.

"Hello again, Tim." Claudia stopped hoeing. Perhaps Tim and his wife would follow the Lysiks' example. He was Edith's grandson after all. "What brings you here?"

"I was hoping to clear up a little discrepancy I've encountered."

"Oh? What might that be?" she asked cautiously, as she stood up and brushed particles of debris off.

"You see, I just had a chat with Anne Esterhazy and Mildred Hawthorne. Both of them told me two completely different stories."

Tim briefly explained what the two women had told him.

When he had finished, Claudia said, "I'm afraid both of them are wrong or at least misinformed. It doesn't surprise me that that Esterhazy woman doesn't know what she's talking about, but Mildred should know better."

"So you do know who Lisa is having an affair with?"

"No, I didn't say that," Claudia said. "But . . . is Lisa Collins a friend of yours?"

"Well, no. I—"

"Then why are you asking so many questions lately? I've seen you, you know. I'm often out here in my yard. You've been visiting several of our neighbors. Why?"

"I'd really rather not say."

"Why not? We are neighbors. There are no secrets on this street. Someone always finds out eventually."

"All right," Tim began. "As a policeman, I'm worried about the disappearance of Lisa Collins. That's really all I can say."

"Is that all?"

He ignored her question, and asked, "Is there anything you could tell me about Lisa or her boyfriend? Mrs. Hawthorne said you might know what's going on down the street?"

"Oh, that's true enough. I feel that there's something terribly wrong in this neighborhood. I can't say what it is exactly, but something is not quite . . . right."

"What do you mean?"

"Real life is stranger than fiction, and I don't buy into coincidences. I've read enough true crime stories to know better. Perhaps that makes me too suspicious and cynical at times, but there are too many supposed accidental circumstances in life to pass them off as just mere coincidences. You must agree."

"Yes, but what does that have to do with Lisa Collins?"

"Everything and nothing."

Something in her voice indicated that she was holding back something.

Persistent, Tim asked, "How did you find out about Lisa's affair?"

Claudia sighed.

"It was something Rachel Stuart said to me one day. She's seen me up here in my yard and wondered if she could borrow my shovel. Which reminds me I'll have to get it back from her one of these days. Well, as I was saying, I just put two and two together. That's all."

"Rachel said you were present when an air-conditioning repairman arrived?"

"Yes, I was dropping off my shovel. She'd asked to borrow it earlier this week, but I still needed it. I gave it to her yesterday morning. Why do you ask?"

"What do you know about the repairman?"

"It was Joshua Deveraux from across the street."

"Are you sure?"

"Yes, I've seen him enough times to recognize him."

"Then why didn't Rachel tell me who he was when I asked her?"

Claudia hesitated noticeably before she answered, "You'd have to ask her that."

On a different topic, Tim asked, "Did you hear anything last night?"

"No, why?" Claudia asked nervously.

"Well, earlier when we talked, I got the impression you were about to say something.

"You must be mistaken," Claudia stated firmly. She then excused herself to retrieve some fertilizer she'd forgotten.

Just after 6:30 p.m., Todd Stuart collapsed on the couch in his living room. It had been another soul-sucking day at the office. And just his luck, his department was short-staffed with parents taking vacation time with their kids during the Easter holiday and next week's Spring Break. So he'd been asked to work extra hours and accepted. He figured he and Rachel could use the extra cash.

God his life sucked! He just wanted to be an actor. He'd caught the bug back in high school during his junior year. St. John's had put on a production of *South Pacific*, and he'd landed the role of Lt. Joseph Cable, the doomed lover of an island girl. He'd loved every minute of it, despite the joshing from a few of his friends.

When he'd applied to Syracuse University, Todd had opted to enroll in the Visual and Performing Arts program. His father hit the roof. He refused to pay the tuition and figured that if his son wanted to be a starving actor, then he could do just that. He'd struggled along as a waiter on and off campus.

He met Rachel at a poetry reading. He'd been working at the bar hosting the event. At first, he'd thought her an intellectual snob, but he'd discovered her self-deprecating humor and felt drawn to her. She wasn't like the girls he'd usually date. She wasn't beautiful, but she managed to stand out in a crowd. Perhaps he fell in love with the idea of her.

He'd been on cloud nine all while they were dating and when they'd married in June 1985. But everything came crashing down not long after. He'd discovered Rachel's jealous streak; it nearly tore them apart. He wondered if their marriage would have fallen apart—the victim of marrying too young, too soon—if her parents hadn't died.

They'd grown closer after the tragedy, and after inheriting a sizable income from her parents' estate, Rachel cajoled Todd into moving off campus.

But the money dwindled far too quickly, and the bills mounted. Rachel informed him that they were in dire financial straits. She nagged and pressured him to come up with a solution. So he'd felt obliged to quit college after his Junior year to get a job. He suffered ten long months and counting at a pencil pusher job that bored the hell out of him while

Rachel, who'd graduated from S.U. in May 1986, remained content to idle her days at home. And he felt betrayed.

Presently, Rachel sat in a plush leather armchair reading *Harper's Bazaar*. She was quite content with her life for the most part, but then she knew they weren't flat broke! She'd lied to Todd about how much she'd inherited from her parents. And his lack of financial savvy was convenient for Rachel. She'd convinced him that they were in debt, and in so doing, she'd gotten him away from all the pretty wannabe actresses like Lisa.

Damn, Lisa, Rachel thought. *Why does she hate me so much? What have I ever done to her? She never loved Todd. She just discarded him like a used toy. Is she so jealous that one of her leftovers should fall in love with me?*

Rachel reflected on her ex-roommates Lisa and Danielle. They'd all dated Todd, but he'd married her. But it had always bothered her that Todd would look at Danielle and Lisa with more than just a passing glance. Danielle had been his high school sweetheart. Lisa, his first fling at college. Neither had seemed ready to give him up completely. Rachel recalled how she had plotted. She'd won Todd's heart, and she'd gotten him away from those harpies! But she wondered if he still loved her.

She looked at her husband lying prostrate on the couch. One arm shaded his eyes. Those adorable brown eyes that she could stare at all day. Rachel sighed. All her machinations had been worth it; she was certain of that. One look at Todd right there in their house for her to have and to hold obliterated any and all doubts. He looked rumpled in his dress shirt and tie. He'd loosened the latter and unbuttoned the top two buttons of the former. His clothes fit his athletic build well. She loved his tousled brown hair and tanned skin. True, there were dark lines under his eyes, but that could easily be cured by a few nights of sleep. And though he had taken up smoking, he still had a golden, winsome smile. Unfortunately, Todd seldom smiled nowadays. He'd been moody and anxious lately. Rachel suspected he felt stifled. But she also wondered . . .

"Todd, have you seen Lisa lately?" Rachel tried to sound casual.

"God, Rach," whined Todd, obviously upset. "I just got home from working overtime at a job I hate. Can't I get any peace? I'm tired. Sick and tired of this monotonous life. I want to act." He sat up and looked into Rachel's hazel eyes. "That's what I am, Rachel. An actor."

"Todd, we've gone over that a million times. We can't afford your acting career. You haven't done any professional acting, and you don't have a degree. And you can't get a degree because we don't have the money to afford college tuition and a mortgage. Besides, we have to think about ourselves. There are too many bad memories haunting both of us."

Todd shook his head.

"There's no *us*. It's just you. You just want people to do what you want. God, Danielle was right about you. I should've seen how selfish—" Todd brushed away the strands of hair that had fallen over his eyes. "Why don't you give it a rest, Rachel? Let people live their own lives. God knows, I want to."

Rachel set down her magazine on the table in front of her calmly and carefully. She then addressed Todd in a cold, accusatory voice.

"And when did you talk to Danielle about us? Did you go crawling back to your ex-girlfriend for sympathy? Are you trying to say that you've been sleeping around? It wouldn't be the first time." Todd started to protest, but she cut him off. "Oh, you think I didn't know about your little indiscretions? I know about your fling with Lisa. You're married to *me*,

Todd, and I call the shots. You'd just be staring into the bottom of a bottle if it wasn't for me."

"I'm not a drunk, Rach."

She shrugged. "Maybe not. But you certainly went on a binge after Danielle killed herself. Who helped you get over that?"

"You don't care about me. I'm just a trophy to you."

"Too bad you're stuck with me."

Todd brought his fist down on the table in front of him. Rachel jumped and watched as his tired face contorted into one of pain and grief. He got up, stalked across the room, then grabbed his keys from the table by the stairs.

"Where are you going?"

"Out."

"Out where?" repeated Rachel icily.

"Away from you," he replied just as icily. He stalked down the stairs to the front door, which soon slammed behind him.

"I've warned you," Rachel said, seething.

Evelyn Martino set her percolator to brew a fresh cup of hazelnut coffee. The pleasant aroma began to flitter through the kitchen almost at once, and she breathed in the nutty scent. A divorcee with raven black hair, which she'd dolled up to frame her porcelain doll face, Evelyn glided over to the antique oak table. She served a tray of cheese and crackers and sat down. Her eyes a charming shade of violet, Evelyn looked at the newlyweds sitting across from her.

Evelyn was a close friend to Tim's mother and grandmother. In 1961, she had been the first, along with Claudia Icarios, to befriend Edith and her twin daughters Sarah and Wanda. How long ago that seemed to her now. At that time, she had still been married to her husband and had worked at the medical library in Weiskotten Hall, a part of the Upstate Hospital Complex on the edge of Downtown Syracuse. In the intervening years, she had watched Sarah marry while she herself had endured a miserable divorce. Now she worked for the Dean of the medical college at Weiskotten Hall, while Sarah was an administrator for the Department of Medicine.

So many changes, Evelyn thought, wondering where the time had gone. *Was there ever enough time?* Sadly, she wished there were.

The percolator brought Evelyn back to the present, and as she poured three cups of coffee, she asked, "I heard about Angela's sprain. She called me this morning, and I was so shocked. I guess it's true when they say most accidents occur within a short distance from the home."

Evelyn also knew Angela Sparrow quite well since both women attended Pebble Hill Presbyterian Church.

"But that's in reference to cars, isn't it?"

"It doesn't matter, Tim, I'm sure. I'm just glad the city cleaned the roads when they did. The gravel and debris on the roads after winter is atrocious. I've had my car skid on it more than a few times coming down this street."

"And to think that same gravel is used to protect people from skidding on the road in winter when the snow and ice are on the road. Isn't it ironic?" said Marie.

Evelyn tapped idly on the edge of her saucer with her French-manicured nails. "Yes, I think so." She sipped her coffee and savored the hazelnut flavor. After gently dabbing at her lips so as not to smudge her scarlet lipstick, she asked, "So how are you two? I'm sure the wedding was wonderful. I do wish I'd been able to attend.

"Oh, we understand, Aunt Evie," Marie said. "You had made arrangements with that tour long before we set the date for our wedding."

"How was the honeymoon in Paris?"

"Wonderful," Marie said.

"I'd like to go back and actually see more of it."

Marie blushed. "Tim!"

Evelyn, who merely smiled, changed the subject, "Oh, I bought a new deck of cards in Rome. I'm hosting this Tuesday's bridge game, and I plan on using them. I understand you play bridge, Tim?"

"Yes. Grandma Edith taught a couple of us kids."

"But tell us about your trip to Italy, Aunt Evie," Marie said, excited. "How was it?"

"Oh, beautiful. My tour group spent most of our time in Rome, seeing the sites there and at the Vatican. I tell you, a tour group is the only way to see a country."

Marie thought carefully for a moment before saying, "*Quanto tempo e rimasto a Roma*?"

Tim looked at Marie in bewilderment, as Evelyn smiled and said, "*Oh, Quattro giorni*."

"I didn't know you knew Italian, Marie?" Tim said.

"Well, I don't know it all that well. Aunt Evie taught me some, and I took two semesters of it at Syracuse University. I have a friend who speaks Italian, and I sort of learned it to have private conversations with her."

"I think it's very important for a person to know a few languages. It really does help a person out there in the world," Evelyn explained to Tim.

"Yes, but please continue with your story," Marie urged.

"Well, I should start from the beginning. We flew into Rome. From there we traveled north to stay in Venice, Milan, and Florence with a brief stop in Pisa to see the tower. Then we returned to Rome for the weekend. We toured the city and visited the Vatican. Then we went south to see Naples and Pompeii. We flew back from Naples. It was a two-week trip, but in that time we really saw a good deal of the country. I can't emphasize enough how important it is to take a tour. You see and learn so much more about the country's culture that way. Of course, the main thing is that you are not alone so the culture shock isn't as troubling."

"You arrived back last night, didn't you?" Tim asked. He and Marie exchanged a look.

"Yes, it was about a quarter to eleven when I finally got home. Angela told me there was a Neighborhood Watch meeting earlier that night?"

Tim nodded. "Yeah. With four burglaries in less than a month, I thought it would be a good idea."

"Four?"

"The Yateses' house was broken into Monday night," Marie answered.

Evelyn sipped her coffee delicately.

"I'm just glad I have a security system. And the decal's right on the window to ward off any would-be thief. Otherwise, my house might have been broken into. It's horrid that these burglaries keep happening."

"Oh, I agree with you, Aunt Evie. You know I think there was another burglary last night."

"Thursday night?"

"Yes. I heard a car race up the street as if it were being chased by the police."

"Oh, yes. I heard that. That was quite late. It must have been after eleven."

"Oh, you had your window opened, too? That's how I heard the car," Marie said, as she shifted in her seat.

"When I get back from a trip, I like to have the windows open. It lets the house breathe. Gets the air circulating."

"Did you see the car?"

"No, I was reading. I hadn't quite finished the book I'd been reading on the plane. You know, it was funny, though. I was reading one of those murder mysteries—I love mysteries—and I had gotten to the part in the book where the murderer was about to be caught. Somebody on the tour had suggested the book to me so I was expecting the gunshots that occurred at the climax of the book. Then I'll swear I actually heard gunshots when I was reading about them. I thought it was just my overactive imagination, but it sounded as if the shots had come from outside. Now, you don't have this in your living room, but in my living room the middle pane of that bay window can be opened for circulation. I had opened it because of the humidity that night. So I guess I, well, I'm not really sure what I thought I heard. I suppose it was just a car backfiring. I did see a car race up the hill afterwards."

"You saw the car?" Tim asked.

"Not very well," Evelyn said. "I was distracted by some flashes of light across the street. But it was red. It looked like some sort of sports car. In fact, I'll swear it was Lisa Collins's car. I've often seen her racing up the street like that."

"You didn't hear anything else before that?" Marie asked.

"No, I didn't really hear anything except the car backfiring and driving up the street. You see, I was reading the novel in Italian, and I'm not used to that. I have some difficulty maintaining my concentration so I can translate what I'm reading. I'm much better at interactive conversation in Italian than the mechanics of it."

Their conversation drifted on to other topics of family happenings and recent events in the Syracuse area. Tim pondered this new information as Marie helped her aunt clear up the cups and saucers, and then he and Marie said their goodbyes.

They remained quiet on the short stroll to their driveway. There, under the canopy of the two maple trees flanking the paved asphalt, Tim stopped.

"What are you thinking?" Marie asked.

"Your aunt can corroborate some of what my grandmother heard," he noted, as he looked down Stoneridge. His brown eyes focused on one particular tan house. "It would seem that something has happened to Lisa Collins."

"But what?"

"I wish I knew. I mean what do we really know? There have been several speculations about various people having extramarital affairs, and it would appear a young college student has vanished. That's not a murder mystery. It's a soap opera!"

Marie laid her hands on his shoulders and kneaded them softly. "We've got to be patient. Sooner or later, the murderer is going to make a mistake. We just have to wait and keep asking questions."

Tim turned around and took her hand. Gazing into her brown eyes, he just smiled.

"We?"

"You're not alone in this. I can help."

He took hold of her hand, leaned in, and kissed her. A feeling of warmth flooded his body. "Let's go inside."

As they walked hand-in-hand toward home, Tim wanted to think only of a night alone with Marie, of making passionate love, and waking up in each other's arms.

But there was that nagging wonder. Did the neighbors hold secrets to Lisa's mysterious disappearance, or had some interloper disturbed the quiet suburbia of Stoneridge?

I have to do something, he thought. *But what?*

SATURDAY

The smell of eggs and fresh-squeezed orange juice, sizzled bacon, and toasted bread pervaded Marie's sleep, and when these aromas woke her up, Tim surprised her with breakfast in bed. Marie gave her thoughtful husband a passionate kiss. She then savored his culinary offerings. Though her husband tended toward sloppy in the kitchen, he was a better cook than she. A fact she was reminded of as she ate.

Tim snagged a slice of bacon from Marie's plate. He noshed on it while he explained his intention to visit Angela Sparrow again.

"You think Miss Sparrow will know what Lisa's been up to?" Marie asked.

"I hope so. If not, I'll have to go talk to Lisa's sister, and I'd rather not do that."

"Why not? Surely Linda Yates, of all people, should be interested to know what's happened to her sister."

"If something's happened to her," Tim reminded.

"Oh, come on, Tim. We tried calling Lisa's after visiting my aunt last night, and there was no answer. No one's seen her since when? Something happened."

"Yeah, well, maybe." Tim rose from the bed. "Look, I'd better get going. I called Miss Sparrow and told her I'd drop by around nine."

He leaned over and kissed her on the cheek before leaving. Marie, meanwhile, stared at her near-empty plate. Distractedly, she finished off her juice. Then an idea struck her. She set aside the wooden tray and got out of bed. After a quick shower, she dressed casually in a peach silk blouse, black skirt, sheer stockings, and low-heeled black pumps. She completed her ensemble with a corded gold necklace and pearl earrings. She studied the effect in the full-length mirror mounted on the back of her bedroom door. She looked ready for a day of shopping at an expensive boutique, but her plan was to have a little chat with her sister-in-law.

Nearly a half hour after her husband's departure, Marie headed out her front door. The heat struck her. The temperature had gone up since last night, and the steamy spring morning begged for a breeze. Feels more like summer, thought Marie, as she walked down Stoneridge.

She didn't see her brother's car in his driveway and wondered where he'd go so early on a Saturday. But she did notice Rachel, dressed in frumpy gardening clothes, out in the yard. What did Rachel do all day? Did she ever go anywhere? Did she even have a car, or did she just share Todd's? Marie and Tim were currently sharing the use of her Jeep until they could pick up Tim's jalopy from the repair shop. She'd have to convince him to get a new car. His just wasn't reliable. Course, he so hated to spend money!

Presently, Marie reached the end of the Stuarts' driveway. Rachel was kneeling on the lawn near the front steps. Marie watched her pull weeds from the rock garden that lined the front of the house. The idea of her sister-in-law gardening puzzled Marie. Ever since she was a little girl, Marie had loved flowers, their colors, their endless variety. She found the whole world of botany and biology fascinating. In college, Marie had been able to pursue her passion and discovered a new one: teaching. She would love to teach others about nature. She would have eagerly talked to Rachel about it. But not once had Rachel ever broached the subject.

Now, as Marie stood not more than a few feet away from her, she wondered if Rachel cared about anyone other than herself.

"Hello."

Rachel let out a sharp scream when she turned and saw her sister-in-law standing over her.

"Must you sneak up on a person like that?"

"I'm sorry. I didn't mean to startle you."

Rachel Stuart stood and faced Marie. "What are you doing here? If you're looking for Todd, he's not home. He's at work. At least I assume he is. He didn't come home last night."

"What? Is he all right?"

"Oh, I'm sure he's fine. He likely crashed at one of his friend's," Rachel said, mincing the last word.

"Why?"

"Oh, didn't you know? Doesn't your brother talk to you?" Seeing Marie's bewildered look, Rachel enlightened her. "He doesn't love me anymore. I'm sure you're happy about that. You've never liked me."

"I barely know you."

Rachel shrugged. "That's not my problem."

Rachel removed her canvas gloves and stuck them in her jeans pocket. She looked Marie up and down and suppressed a sneer. Was Marie trying to show her up with a presumed sense of fashion? Rachel waited for her sister-in-law to get to the point of her visit. Only Marie was too flustered to say anything.

"Well," Rachel said, "you must have come over for some reason."

"Um, well, I was wondering. Do you know if Joshua Deveraux might take on odd jobs?"

"Why would I possibly know that?"

"I understand he came to fix your air conditioner this week. Was that through his company or on his own?"

Rachel pursed her already thin lips.

"What are you up to?"

"I—"

"I'm not stupid. You and your husband have been asking a lot of questions all of a sudden." Rachel narrowed her eyes as she regarded Marie. "Why? Why all the interest in Lisa Collins?"

"I knew her."

"From what I've heard, you barely knew her."

"How would you know?" Marie said defensively.

"For your information, I shared a flat with Lisa. With Danielle, too. The three of us were friends." Rachel smiled wanly. "For a time."

"Yes, isn't it strange that Danielle should be dead and Lisa should be missing? That would make you the only one of the three left. Now what do you suppose that means?"

"I don't see that that's any of your concern or your husband's. And I don't like being treated like a common criminal. You should teach your husband some manners. It's not polite to pry."

"And you would know about being polite?"

Rachel looked away from her sister-in-law in disgust. She noticed the mailman's truck drive up to Lisa's mailbox.

"Oh, what does it matter?" Rachel wondered if Tim or Marie had opened the letter she'd sent Lisa. She suspected they hadn't yet. "You think I care what happens to Lisa? I'd sooner see her rot. She's been nothing but trouble since she came to this neighborhood. She's tormented me, Danielle, her sister Linda, and her brother-in-law, David."

The mailman pulled up to the Stuarts' mailbox and stuffed a mix of letters, bills, and magazines inside. Marie watched him drive up to the Logan's house before asking, "Was she seeing someone?"

"You mean a boyfriend?" Rachel laughed. "Lisa's had numerous boyfriends. She's always been a flirt. I even saw her chatting up Dr. Logan next door. I'm sure they went out a few times, too. Lisa likes men. She also likes money. So I'm sure Dr. Logan appealed to her."

"Do you know where she's gone? She seems to have disappeared."

"Oh, she hasn't gone far," Rachel attested.

"You seem quite sure of yourself."

Rachel cracked a wry smile. She didn't say anything, though. Instead, she walked over to her mailbox. Marie followed, asking more questions about Lisa, but Rachel ignored her. She sorted through her mail until she came to a curious envelope with no return address. Thumbing it open, Rachel read the contents. Her cheeks grew red with anger.

"What is it?" Marie asked, trying to see what the note said.

Rachel crumpled the letter and glared at her. "It's none of your business." She waved a hand at Marie. "Why don't you just go? And tell your husband to stop asking so many questions."

Rachel stormed across her yard. She yanked open her front door and slammed it behind her.

Shane Lysik dressed lazily in his old athletic gear sporting the Syracuse University logo. His navy jersey with its faded orange lettering had lost its sleeves long ago, and the orange shorts looked well worn. Since he planned on washing his car, he wore only brown flip-flops on his feet. He'd likely lose the shoes and shirt while he worked outdoors and catch some rays. The good-ole Texas boy had enjoyed the Friday Night Lights of high school football and brought his skills as a running back to S.U., and six years after graduating, he still retained his athletic physique, which he didn't shy at showing off.

Shane found his wife sitting at the dining room table. She was dressed in her pink business suit and matching high-heeled shoes. Her gray eyes scanned the piles of paper neatly spread out on the oak table. From time to time, she'd take a sip of her iced tea and then carefully set the glass back on a patterned porcelain coaster.

Brenda Lysik couldn't be more Shane's opposite. She loved lounging indoors and reading, while he reveled in the outdoors and exercising. Whereas Brenda was like a marble statue formed in antiquity, Shane was gregarious and animated. Her demeanor was often reserved and aloof, his was charismatic and approachable. Though they did not seem the perfect match, they seldom argued.

"You're not working today, are you?"

Brenda looked up at her husband and nodded. "It's this Board meeting Tuesday night. I just have to go into the office for a couple hours this afternoon."

Shane frowned. He knew it would end up being longer than just a couple hours. Brenda had succumbed to her boss's vision of pliable, workaholic employees. True, as a secretary at Dewitt Enterprises, Brenda had to prep documents needed for the infamous Board of Directors meeting Tuesday night, but Shane couldn't imagine why it couldn't wait until Monday. Surely all the important papers had been readied before now anyway!

"Aw, come on, Bren. I was hoping we could sit out on the deck and relax in the sun."

Looking over Tuesday night's agenda, Brenda replied, "Oh, no. You can sit out in the sun if you want. My skin just burns. Besides, it's going to be too hot today. I'd rather be indoors."

Or at work, Shane thought wryly.

"Just don't get too comfortable out there," Brenda continued. "You don't want to fall asleep and get sunburned."

"I doubt it. I slept fine last night."

"Did you? You were tossing and turning last night something awful."

Shane rubbed the back of his neck as he asked guiltily, "I didn't keep you awake, did I?"

"No. But are you sure those pills you're taking are working?"

He shrugged. "I've been feeling better."

Brenda tore her attention away from her paperwork and really looked at her husband. She didn't see any dark circles under his eyes, and he did look more rested. Still, something nagged at her.

"Are you sure everything's okay? I'm worried about this bout of insomnia."

"I'm fine, Bren. Really. Work's just been a little rough lately with the restructuring our department's undergoing. It'll be fine, though. Look, I'm gonna head out and start on my car."

Brenda didn't pursue the topic and returned to her paperwork while her husband headed for the garage.

As he gathered up a bucket, sponges, car wax and the other things he needed, Shane thought about Brenda. He remembered meeting her at college. She'd been studious even then, but she'd let loose and have fun at campus parties and events. On some of their dates, they'd gone dancing or even bowling. On their honeymoon, they vacationed on the beaches of the Caribbean, snorkeled through coral reefs, and got tangled in the sheets and mosquito netting of their bed. So what had happened? It seemed like everything changed last year when they had moved here to Stoneridge. Now, all she ever seemed to do was work or sit at home and read a book or magazine.

Shane opened his garage door. He squinted as the bright, inviting sunshine washed over him. He unwound the hose while he pondered what he could do to entice Brenda into relaxing more. For God's sake, he was a psychiatrist; he ought to know what to do! But when the person in question was close to you, it was difficult to gain the necessary distance to be truly objective. Maybe if he talked to Craig. Shane looked over at his neighbor's house across the street.

Since Craig Logan and his two boys moved to Stoneridge last August, Shane and he had certainly hit it off. Both men had been raised in Texas, and they both worked at Upstate Hospital, though it was the former connection that bonded the two men more.

Shane started washing his Dodge Aries. Though he hadn't spoken to Craig recently, he figured he could pay him a visit after Brenda went to work. As he soaped up the hood of his car, he noticed Marie Dewitt talking to Rachel Stuart in the latter's yard. They seemed to be having an argument.

Now that's odd, he thought.

From her kitchen, Angela could see Tim admire the interior of her home with its Stickley furniture and woodwork. The built-in benches, bookcases, and sideboards had been the work of her home's previous owner.

A master craftsman at the Stickley factory, the former owner had conformed the house's interior to the ideals of the Craftsman style, which strived for practical, uncluttered spaces. Reluctantly, the man had retired to Florida for health reasons, and Angela had purchased the home in 1974.

Presently, Angela rolled a tea caddy into her dining room, where Tim sat in a chair of Stickley design. The oval table, too, was a Stickley piece. The set had belonged to Angela's mother, who had passed away shortly before Angela had moved to Stoneridge.

"Do you need any help with that?" Tim asked.

No doubt he felt guilty for letting her hobble around on her crutches, she thought. But Angela didn't like a fuss, and she would be remiss in not serving as hostess, offering coffee and shortbread cookies.

Angela had listened to Tim's summations of his investigations for nearly an hour before she suggested some nourishment. She'd thought over what he'd said while she had been in the kitchen. Now it was time to review some of the facts. As she parked the caddy alongside the chair she sat upon, she replied, "Nonsense. I can't just sit all the time. I like to be active." As she served coffee, Angela suggested, "Now why don't you tell me about your visit to Georgia again."

When Tim finished recounting what he'd learned from Georgia Llewellyn yesterday morning, he asked, "What do you think?"

Angela held up a hand to indicate that she needed a few moments. Finally, she said, "I can't help but wonder about the time discrepancy that you mentioned. You said that Georgia heard the argument an hour before Edith heard the gunshots?"

"That's what she said, but you said Ms. Llewellyn isn't reliable because she often muddles her times."

"That's what I was thinking about. We don't spring forward for Daylight Savings until tonight. I can't imagine that Georgia would have mistakenly put her clocks forward already. She does tend to get muddled, though. She could easily be wrong about the time. We'll have to say that she was for now."

Tim nodded. "But what exactly do you think is going on here?" he asked. "I mean, I can't help but think . . ."

"That nothing out of the ordinary has happened?" finished Angela. "That there's a perfectly logical explanation."

"Well, yes. The idea of a murder in the Town of DeWitt is kinda unusual. Statistically there's only been like what? Two in the past five years?"

"That sounds about right," Angela said, "but it does happen. Murder isn't just limited to the city."

"I know. But there's no body. All we know for sure is that Lisa Collins is missing. We might as well wait and see if she turns up."

Angela sipped her coffee. "You're thinking of her car?"

"Yes. Marie's aunt saw a red car racing up the street about the time my grandmother heard those shots. It must have been Lisa's. But was Lisa driving it or someone else?"

"But she hasn't come back," Angela said pointedly. "Where would a college student go on Easter weekend? Surely she would spend Easter with her family, and isn't Linda Yates her sister? You haven't talked to her yet have you?"

Tim sighed. "No. I didn't want to alarm her unnecessarily."

After a few moments of silence, Angela said, "It does seem that much of what we've learned is rather insubstantial."

Tim agreed, "I know. Just about any defense lawyer would say it's only circumstantial evidence that proves nothing. It doesn't even prove that there's been a murder, but it doesn't disprove one either."

"Is there any way to trace Lisa's car?"

"Possibly. I have a few friends on the force who could keep an eye out. I doubt I could request an APB. It's not like we know the car was stolen."

"I just wish I could help. I feel so useless with my ankle."

"That's all right," Tim said. "You've been a great help. After all, you've lived on this street longer than I have. You know these people better than I do."

"Don't say that, Tim. I don't know some of them any better than you. Especially the younger neighbors."

Tim interlocked his fingers on top of the dining room table and furrowed his eyebrows.

"I'm thinking I should maybe wait a bit and see what develops."

"Don't give up, Tim," Angela said.

"I'm not. I'm just not sure what to do. You always see on television or read in books how sure the detective appears because there's always some concrete fact to go on. I know it's not like that in real life. I learned that at the police academy. But I just wish there was that one clue to set the whole situation straight.

"But that's fiction. That shouldn't bother you."

"But it does."

"Why, Tim?" Angela asked, bewildered.

"Because I should be able to solve them. Fiction isn't like police routine, and even then, I'm just starting out. I've helped on one case. The one I came to you about before."

"Oh, yes," Angela said. "I'm glad to have helped."

"But this time it's different. There's something off about it. I'll bet something has happened to Lisa Collins." He pounded his fist on the table. "But someone's gone to a lot of trouble to cover up that fact. The question is why?"

Marie craned her head down the street and wondered if she should join her husband at Miss Sparrows', but then she spied Shane Lysik washing his car. Perhaps the Lysiks might know something about last night's events. She started toward their house, and though she didn't particularly feel comfortable talking to Shane, she couldn't help but admire his lean, muscled body and cut abs. His was a more manly physique than her husband's, which still retained a boyish lankness, although she smiled as she relished how nicely her husband was filling out. It didn't hurt that Tim lifted weights and exercised when he had the chance.

Marie came to an abrupt stop when Shane accidentally sprayed her with water. He'd been rinsing his car as she approached and hadn't seen her. He flicked up his sunglasses to rest in his thick dark brown hair and greeted her with a big, charming grin.

"Hello. Sorry about that, Marie."

"It's just a little water," Marie said, suddenly feeling a little like a foolish schoolgirl. She tried to maintain eye contact with Shane, but his sepia brown eyes were as adorable as the rest of him. “I was wondering if Brenda was home?”

“Yeah, she’s inside. But she’s gonna be leaving for work soon,” answered Shane sardonically.

Marie thanked him and proceeded to the front door. She stole a quick glance back to admire Shane’s muscles as they worked to clean his car. Then reminding herself why she’d come, she rang the doorbell.

Brenda Lysik was a stunning beauty with long raven black hair that was in sharp contrast to her snow-white complexion. With her gray eyes, she looked very much like a marble statue of the goddess Athena come to life, and her shrewdness matched this vision. As she answered her door, Brenda looked imperiously down the straight bridge of her nose, as if vexed that she was interrupted from her important work. Then she gave her a wide smile. “Marie, what a surprise!”

Brenda ushered her into the living room, where they sat in the two armchairs by the window. Brenda chose the chair that was shaded from the sunlight streaming in the room and which had a view of her husband washing his car.

“How are things at the office?” Marie asked. She’d seen the papers strewn on the dining room table.

“I’ll be happy when this board meeting is over,” Brenda said. “But Dewitt’s Department Store does rather brisk business during vacations like Spring Break. That’s very good news for the Dewitt family.”

“I’ll bet. I know Tim doesn’t care much for the business or all the money, but it does support his siblings. Good education is expensive these days. I dread the thought of having to owe all those student loans some of my friends have to deal with. Thank God, Daddy paid my way.”

“Yes, but I understand Tim doesn’t get along well with his father.”

Straying from her initial purpose for visiting, Marie asked, "You don't know why, do you?"

"No," Brenda answered hesitantly. "I'm not that close to the family. I know who's who of course and a few details, but really, I'm just a secretary. I work the front desk to the main offices on the sixteenth floor. I'm sure Jon and Sarah Dewitt know me well enough, but I don't think the rest of the family does."

"But Jon Dewitt doesn't run the company."

"No, he's busy working as an assistant district attorney." Brenda explained, "The company is actually run by Quinton Quartier. He took over as company president after the death of Jon's father some years ago. Jon is merely the chairman of the board."

Marie suspected Tim's father was disappointed that his son hadn't followed in his footsteps. She'd long known Tim had no interest in becoming a lawyer. And though she remembered Tim talking about maybe working at *Dewitt's*, his family's department store, he'd never pursued that path.

"Oh, how inconsiderate of me," Brenda said. "Would you like something to drink? I know the weather's been dreadfully humid. I'd say we're due for some rain soon."

"No, thanks, I'm fine," Marie said. "I'm actually fond of this weather. It's the type of weather you find in botanical gardens."

"That's right. You're going to be working at the Syracuse Botanical Gardens. Edith was telling me about it the other night."

Marie nodded. "It's kind of exciting. My first full-time job."

"When do you start?"

"A week from Monday."

"So how are you settling in?"

"Well," Marie began. She figured now would be as good a time as any to broach the subject of Thursday night. "Don't get me wrong. It's been great so far. I still can't get used to it. But there's something . . ."

How should she phrase it? She found Brenda's visage open and friendly enough, but there was something icy about her neighbor. Marie suspected it wouldn't be a good idea to cross Brenda. "Did you hear anything Thursday night? After the Neighborhood Watch meeting?"

"No," Brenda said, her thin dark eyebrows arching ever so slightly.

Marie inhaled and breathlessly explained that Tim's grandmother had heard someone cry out for help, then two gunshots, a car door slamming, and then the car racing up the street late at night. "Of course, the car passed by our house, so it came from down the street. It's just so mysterious."

"Is she sure it wasn't just a car backfiring?" Brenda asked. She knew that Edith Baxter was not prone to misinterpreting events like Georgia Llewellyn, nor would her former neighbor make it up like someone she knew. Still it sounded illogical.

"I don't know. I didn't *hear* anything. But I don't think she would have made that mistake."

"But gunshots?"

"It could be connected to the burglaries," Marie suggested.

"But no one's reported one."

Marie remembered Tim telling her about the argument Georgia Llewellyn had overheard.

"Perhaps things escalated?"

"It's inconceivable to me," Brenda said sharply. "Someone would have called the police. Someone would have heard something."

"Well, Tim's been asking around. Apparently, Lisa Collins got into an argument Thursday night, and no one has seen her since."

Brenda noticeably stiffened, and her eyes grew stormy. She turned her wrist and not so casually looked at her silver-plated watch. "I don't think you should worry about Lisa Collins. *She* can take care of herself," she said, her voice sounding like the quiet before the storm.

Marie felt as if the room temperature had dropped considerably. It made her uneasy. She didn't know what to say. Fortunately, she didn't have to do anything, for Shane, having finished washing his car, walked in.

Shane set his sunglasses on the console table by the door and pulled on his jersey. "So what have you two been discussing?"

"Nothing important," Marie said nervously. Perhaps it was all in her head, but an inexplicable tension filled the room. Though Shane stood just a few feet from where his wife sat, it seemed as if there were miles between then. Edith had described the Lysiks as a loving couple, but Marie sensed something amiss. Brenda's icy behavior suggested something wasn't right. And was Shane walking on eggshells? He seemed hesitant to come to his wife's side just now.

"I really should be going," Marie said as she gained her feet.

"Don't forget about this coming Friday," Shane said.

"Huh?"

"For the party," he said. "Say around seven o'clock?"

"Oh, yes," said Marie. "How could I have forgotten? It's very nice of you to do that for us. Most neighbors nowadays don't bother."

"It's the least we could do," Brenda said neutrally. "Edith was so welcoming when Shane and I moved in. It just wouldn't feel right if we didn't do something."

"Well, thank you, again. Good- bye," Marie said, anxious to leave.

It's shameful that a married woman should carry on as you do. Does your husband know about your indiscretions?

Stay away from Joshua Deveraux or else!

Rachel wanted to tear the anonymous note to shreds. She huffed. Would she never be free of these torments?! She paced her carpeted living room. Who had threatened her this time? Lisa? Her Auntie Sonya? Or Mildred Hawthorne? Or was there someone else?

As Rachel mulled over the possibilities, she was drawn toward the large front window with its view of Stoneridge. The Stuarts did not have a bay window like so many houses on the drive, and though the view was limited, Rachel scanned the houses she could see. She regarded the green ranch house across the street. It belonged to Josh. Why on earth had she ever taken up with him? Had she felt the need to get back at Danielle? Or had she let herself play with yet another handsome man who had found her intriguing? Both Todd and Josh were drawn to her. She'd been content in winning Todd from Danielle and Lisa, but the idea of flirting with Josh had flattered her ego.

There was only one person who would care that she was still playing games with Josh. Rachel pursed her lips as she peered up the street at the white house with the wood-shingled trim. The Hawthornes lived there. And that snooty woman would do anything to protect her precious grandson.

Rachel left her home and stalked up Stoneridge toward the Hawthornes' house. However, when she reached the end of the Yateses' driveway, she paused. Mildred Hawthorne could wait. Right now, Rachel was interested in the light she saw on. She didn't particularly care who was home, whether it be Linda or David Yates. Chances were that if anyone knew where Lisa had gone, they would. Rachel walked confidently up the terraced slate stairway and along the walkway leading to the front door. She rang the doorbell and waited. No answer came, so she pushed the doorbell twice in quick succession.

Bleary-eyed and with staggered steps, David Yates, his dark-brown hair unkempt, finally opened the door a crack. Before he could say anything, he saw her and panic flickered across his face. He held the doorknob in a vise-like grip. Too late, he tried to shut the door, but Rachel pushed passed him as she spoke.

"Hello, David. Remember me?"

She looked back at the twenty-four-year-old. He was barefoot and hadn't fully buttoned his shirt. He looked as if he'd just rolled out of bed. But she admired his good looks. She'd always thought it a shame that David never found her captivating the way Todd and Josh had. Even now, his green eyes avoided looking at her.

"I'm Rachel Stuart. You know me. Your sister-in-law and I were roommates. We lived just down the block from you on Euclid Avenue. Near the University. You remember?"

He remembered all too well.

"Yes," he said hoarsely.

"I just thought I'd stop by for a visit. It's been so long. And to think how long we've been neighbors here. Is Lisa here?"

"What? Why would she be here?"

David turned to shut the door. He could feel her eyes boring into his back.

"Well, she's not at her place. I just thought she might have come to see you and Linda."

"I haven't seen her in ages."

He faced her and felt claustrophobic in the small foyer of his home. There were three exits from here besides the front door behind him. To his left, were the stairs to the living room. The door to the garage was to his right, and behind Rachel was the open archway leading to a small den.

He wished he could make a fast getaway, but all too well, he knew Rachel's penchant for running people to ground.

"Aren't you going to ask me to sit?"

"Ah, all right."

David gestured toward the den, where Rachel settled on a loveseat. He perched in a chair opposite her. He began picking at his fingernails.

"So where is Linda?"

"At her mother's. She took the kids. Why?"

"No reason. I just thought you or Linda could tell me where Lisa was."

"I haven't seen her. Sorry."

"Don't toy with me, David! You must know where she is. I know how you need a little fix. Oh, don't look so shocked. I know all about your habit. Or did you think that nobody noticed? When did you get the urge again? Was it before or after Danielle died?"

He looked up at her sharply.

"You don't know what you're talking about."

Rachel shrugged.

"I just want to know where Lisa is. That's all."

"I told you I don't know."

Rachel narrowed her eyes and pursed her lips. She shifted in her seat so that she faced away from him, but out of the corner of her eye, she watched him as she said, "Drugs are such an *expensive* habit don't you think? I wonder how much money can be gotten for fencing stolen goods? I know that this burglar couldn't have gotten much out of what he stole from us. A week's supply of heroin? Cocaine? Maybe I should go to the police." She turned to face him directly. "What do you think?"

David froze. He looked about as if searching for some response.

"I . . ."

She rose to her feet. “Just tell Lisa I will find her. We’re not finished—the two of us.”

Having had the last word, Rachel Stuart left. Quite conveniently, she spotted Mildred Hawthorne across the street. Joshua Deveraux’s grandmother was watering the daffodils surrounding her mailbox, and she was just the person Rachel wanted to talk to. Reaching in her pocket, Rachel removed the letter she’d received that morning and accosted the interfering old woman.

“Why, hello, Rachel. What are you doing here?” Mildred asked halfheartedly.

“I just thought I’d have a chat with you.”

“Oh? Well, would you like to come in and have a cup of tea?”

“No, thanks. This won’t take long.” Rachel thrust the letter at Mildred, and said, “Here, read this!”

“What is it?” Mildred asked, feigning innocence. She took up her blue-tinted glasses, which hung about her neck on a silver chain, and read the note. “Stay away from Joshua Deveraux or else!” She looked up at Rachel. “Oh, how awful for you. A poison pen letter. Tsk, tsk! But why show it to me?”

“Because Joshua’s your grandson! And you’ve never approved of my relationship with him.”

“Why should I, my dear? You are married, aren’t you?”

“Don’t be smug with me. If I chose to sleep with your grandson, then that’s my business! You just stay out of it, or I’ll push him over the edge. We both know he’s not the most confident person. You do remember what happened last time? I’m sure you don’t want that to happen again?”

Flustered, Mildred sputtered for an answer.

“No, I didn’t think so,” Rachel said as she turned and walked away.

Malicious thoughts passed through Mildred’s head as she watched that woman walk casually down the street as if she owned it. Mildred crumpled the letter she had sent and stormed back into her house, her gardening forgotten.

Georgia Llewellyn drove her Lincoln Cadillac down Stoneridge Drive. A car sped by her. Belatedly, she realized Brenda Lysik had just passed her. Georgia wondered where her neighbor was off to and in such a hurry. Perhaps a luncheon appointment? Stoneridge was otherwise deserted. She didn't see any of her other neighbors about. She rounded the curve in the road and pulled into her driveway. She parked and stepped out of her car.

Dressed in a long white dress and matching high heels, Georgia reached into her car and retrieved her wide-brimmed sun hat. It, too, was white. She pinned the hat on her head and strolled along her driveway taking stock of her flowers, which lined either side of the asphalt. Her tulips were coming along nicely, but they looked a little peaked. The hot and humid weather was dragging to say the least. Perhaps a little watering would do them good.

Georgia started toward the spot where her garden hose lay wound by the side of her house. Then she noticed Tim Dewitt leaving Angela's house across the street. She watched him amble along up the drive with his hands stuffed in his shorts pocket and his head bowed. She waved to him, and the movement caught his eye. As he headed toward her, Georgia recalled their conversation about Lisa Collins yesterday. She had gotten into an argument with her daughter that morning, and had been reminded of the one that she had overheard. Something in the tone of Lisa's argument bothered her.

"Hello, Ms. Llewellyn."

Georgia looked up and greeted her neighbor with a warm smile. She drawled, "I saw you were at Angela's. Were the two of you discussing the other night? Now, I know this sounds a bit far-fetched, but this is what? The third day Lisa

Collins hasn't been seen nor heard from? Shouldn't someone notify the police? I know you are an officer of the law, but surely there are certain procedures?"

"Ms. Llewellyn, for all we know, Lisa might have just gone on vacation for the weekend," Tim reasoned.

"Yes, but what if she's gone on one she can't come back from? Death is rather permanent, don't you think?"

"That's if she's dead."

"I have a strong suspicion she is."

Tim arched his dark-blond eyebrows, his interest piqued. "What makes you say that?"

Georgia looked about furtively. Further up the street, she noticed Shane Lysik setting up a lawn chair and Claudia Icarios gardening in their respective front yards. She didn't see anyone else.

"Well," she began, "I think Lisa was murdered. I think she was shot. I heard a car backfiring Thursday night. At least, that's what I thought it was. Now, I suspect otherwise."

"Then where's the body?" Tim asked, joining in Georgia's conspiratorial manner.

"Yes, that has been bothering me. It's awfully strange that no one's found the body. I mean, with this virtual heat wave we've been having." Georgia fanned herself for effect. "Well, you know what I mean. Surely someone should have discovered it by now? Unless it's in her house!"

Excitedly, Georgia craned her neck to regard Lisa's house. Her light-hearted demeanor vanished instantly when she caught sight of Rachel Stuart lurking by the side of her next-door neighbor's house. How long had she been there? Had she overheard anything? Everything?

"I'm sure you're looking into it. I shouldn't keep you," Georgia whispered.

Tim got the hint. He'd noticed Rachel, too, stalking toward them like a tiger about to pounce on its prey, and he wasn't in any mood to face her. So he said good-bye to Georgia and retreated back to his house. Rachel barely acknowledged him as he passed her.

Georgia mustered up her good old Southern charm to greet her neighbor cordially, but her smile was returned superficially and she felt belittled. It didn't help that the young woman was three inches taller than her. However, curious by nature and vexing herself for wearing heels that wouldn't have let her escape quicker, Georgia ventured to ask, "May I help you?"

"I hope so, Ms. Llewellyn. I was looking for Lisa Collins. I notice she's not home. Someone mentioned that you heard her leave Thursday night. Is that true?"

Rachel appeared sincere enough, but Georgia was suspicious of her motives. Georgia didn't think Rachel had overheard her conversation with Tim, but she wondered what interest the young woman had in Lisa.

"To be honest, I was rather disturbed by what I heard that night," Georgia began.

In matters that didn't relate to her, Georgia Llewellyn reveled in gossip. The tit-for-tat exchange of juicy tidbits was an art form to her. So she didn't think it any harm to relate to Rachel what she'd already told Tim Dewitt. She elaborated on the argument she'd overheard between Lisa and the supposed boyfriend, and she mentioned hearing Lisa's car racing down Stoneridge. Georgia purposely left out a few details. This included hearing the gunshots and her belief that Lisa was dead. When she'd finished her tale, Georgia looked up into Rachel's hazel eyes and could almost see the young woman thinking.

"Are you sure it was around ten- thirty?" Rachel asked pointedly.

"Well, give or take ten minutes," Georgia admitted, eying Rachel's reactions carefully.

"And you didn't hear a car backfiring?"

Georgia answered nervously, “Oh, no. Nothing like that.”

Rachel suspected the lie her elderly neighbor had told, even though Georgia was desperately trying to hide behind a sweet smile.

“You’re sure now?”

“Oh, quite,” Georgia laughed stiltedly. “I would have been certain to have heard something like that what with my central air-conditioning on the blink. Of course, I did fall asleep not long after I heard that awful argument.”

Rachel nodded sympathetically.

“Really? I’m sure that argument would have frazzled me so that I wouldn’t have been able to sleep at all,” Rachel lied with ease.

“Well, sleep is much easier for one my age. I don’t need any sedatives like Shane Lysik over there,” drawled Georgia. She gestured toward the Lysiks’ front yard, where Shane lay in a lawn chair catching some rays.

Rachel turned and regarded him with interest. She’d noticed him in conversation with Lisa more than a few times.

“Why does he need sedatives?”

Not seeing any harm in this bit of gossip, Georgia readily explained, “Well, Brenda told Angela that her husband’s been suffering from insomnia recently. Angela told me about the whole thing. Course, I think Brenda’s overly worried about her husband. And I can’t understand why. She really should just spend more time with him. She’s a bit of a workaholic.”

“It must be awful for him.”

“I beg your pardon?” Georgia asked, confused.

“For Shane Lysik. I can totally sympathize. My husband and I have been very unsettled since our house was broken into. I can see why Shane would be on edge. Burglaries make you feel violated. Don’t you think?”

“Well, I really wouldn’t know. I suppose you’re right. Only Shane Lysik started having problems sleeping just after

Danielle Deveraux died. Or was it before? Well, I know it was around then."

"Around the same time David Yates started taking drugs again," Rachel muttered under her breath.

"What was that?" Georgia asked suspiciously.

"Oh, it's nothing. I was just thinking how tragic it was that Danielle Deveraux committed suicide."

"Oh, well, I don't think it was suicide."

"What else could it have been?" Rachel asked crossly.

"Murder," Georgia said with a knowing nod. "Oh, yes. I'm surprised you hadn't heard. Someone was seen outside the house that day. Someone in some sort of uniform. The police followed up on that lead. They thought it was Mr. Deveraux, but he'd had a flat tire. I remember the investigating officer wasn't satisfied. He felt there was something wrong about the whole thing. Like it had been staged to look like a suicide."

"But who would want to kill her?"

"Well, it must have been someone she knew."

"Why do you say that?"

"Well, she must have let him inside. I doubt she would have let a stranger in. She wasn't that foolish. But it's the ones you know that you can't always trust. So sad really," Georgia mused. "You can't ever really know someone, can you?"

"No, you never really do know," Rachel agreed cryptically.

What's she up to? wondered Marie.

Marie watched her sister-in-law's movements with interest. She'd seen Rachel visit the Yateses and was curious to know why. She'd witnessed the altercation between Rachel and Mildred. *What was that all about?* Marie continued to spy on Rachel. She saw her sneak up to Lisa's house and look in the windows of the garage. Then Rachel started as if she had heard something. She turned and saw Georgia Llewellyn talking to Tim. Quite suddenly she swooped down on them, but it looked as if Tim broke off the conversation and bypassed her.

As her husband returned home, Marie strained to see Rachel's seemingly chummy chat with Georgia. Marie couldn't help but wonder if these sudden "visits" had anything to do with that letter she'd seen Rachel receive.

"You watching her?" Tim asked when he entered. He had seen his wife at the window staring down the street.

"She's hit them in succession. The Yateses. Mildred Hawthorne. She stopped to snoop around Lisa's house. And now Ms. Llewellyn. She's up to something."

He stood behind her and hugged her as he, too, looked out the window. "Yeah, well, I really don't care about Rachel right now."

"I talked to her."

"Hmm?" Tim said as he nuzzled her neck.

"I talked to Rachel this morning."

He jerked back. "Why?"

Marie turned to face him. "I thought maybe I could get her to talk."

"And?"

"She wants us both to stop asking so many questions."

"Maybe we should."

Marie looked at him quizzically. He then filled her in on his chat with Angela Sparrow and his brief conversation with Georgia before Rachel interrupted them.

"I just don't see what more we can do. I'll call someone at work to check on Lisa's car, but then I don't know." He rubbed the back of his neck. "I really don't want to waste my time off chasing red herrings."

He sighed and walked down the hall to the bedroom leaving Marie to brood. She wasn't satisfied. She looked out the window and at the brown split-level house belonging to David and Linda Yates. Which one of them had Rachel spoken with, and why had she gone there? Marie determined to find out.

Seeing that Rachel was still chatting with Georgia Llewellyn, Marie slipped outside and hurried up the street. She stepped up to the green door and knocked. She thought she heard someone inside playing the piano. She could just make out the notes of some classical piece. Her knocks having gone unheard, she rang the doorbell. Fortunately, the yew bushes planted nearby shielded her from view.

The music stopped. A few moments later, David Yates again opened his front door.

"Hello, Mr. Yates," Marie said cheerfully.

Laconically, David leaned his arm against the doorframe. He was six feet tall and broad shouldered. Marie liked the mussed-up look of his dark brown hair and had trouble looking directly into his stunning green eyes. She took in his bare feet, his faded blue jeans, and the rumpled, button-down white shirt he'd left untucked. She found him devastatingly good-looking.

"Hello," he said, in a soft tenor voice.

"I'm Marie Dewitt. We met the other night at the Neighborhood Watch Meeting. Am I disturbing you?"

He shrugged. "No. Did you want to come in?"

"Are you sure?"

"Yeah. I was just idling."

He ushered her inside, shut the door, and led her up the stairs to the living room. Her brown eyes immediately alighted on the black baby grand piano in the corner.

"Oh, you were playing the piano," she said.

He looked longingly at the ivory keys.

"I play piano and the violin," he said. He thought of Danielle and the beautiful sweet voice that inspired songs he wrote for her siren's gift. "It's just not the same anymore."

Marie sat down on a comfy green couch. The plushness of the material surprised her. She much preferred it to the roughness of the couches that she and Tim had inherited. She really had to go shopping for new furnishings soon. Though she thought Edith Baxter a dear, Marie didn't find her taste in décor appealing.

While Marie was distracted by ideas of grand shopping expeditions, David appraised his visitor and not for the first time. He'd snatched glimpses of her at Thursday's Neighborhood Watch Meeting. He thought her strikingly beautiful, and in some ways she reminded him of Danielle, the redheaded girl whose voice he had adored. It hadn't been long before he'd fallen in love with the girl herself. He remembered the passionate kiss they had once shared.

"What did Rachel want?" Marie asked, recalling her purpose for visiting.

"Hmm?"

Startled by the realization that David had been staring at her, Marie repeated her question.

"She was looking for Lisa."

David straddled the piano bench. The long fingers of his left hand brushed along the keys of the baby grand.

"Have you seen her? Lisa, I mean."

He eyed his platinum wedding band, and his hand trembled.

"Not . . . not for a while," he answered.

"What did Rachel want with Lisa? Did she tell you?"

Perplexed, David looked at Marie.

"Aren't you Todd's sister?" She nodded, and he continued, "Then Rachel's your sister-in-law. So why are you asking me what she's up to?"

She inhaled deeply before replying, "We don't get along."

David weighed her words and muttered, "She's not very likable."

Marie stifled a laugh, which caused David to crack a shy smile. He found he liked his new neighbor. She was vibrant and outgoing, and he was reminded again of Danielle's elfish and carefree bearing. He knew that Danielle had once dated Todd and blurted out, "Did you know Danielle McGinty?"

Marie was taken aback.

"Yes. But not that well."

"You remind me of her," he said wistfully.

"How did you know her?"

"I took classes at S.U. in music. We collaborated on some songs."

And he had fallen in love. A relationship, as he had learned later, that had been encouraged by Rachel Stuart in an effort to draw Danielle away from Todd. Though he had never acted on his feelings but for one lone kiss, his wife had been devastated to learn of his attraction. The guilt had driven him to seek solace in the bottom of several bottles. When he'd finally sobered up, he and Linda had moved here. He'd given up his music and devoted himself to family life. Until Danielle moved in down the street . . .

"I was at work the day she . . . died." He didn't know why he felt the need to explain, but he continued, "I just couldn't believe it when I heard. I couldn't imagine that she'd ever . . . She was so full of life. Danielle would never—"

"David!"

They both turned to see who'd spoken.

Marie saw a mousy-looking woman with mousy brown hair and a rather plain, unmade-up appearance. Linda Yates gripped the banister at the top of the stairs so tightly her knuckles turned white. A mix of fear and panic showed in her dark eyes as she looked up at Marie. "L—Linda," stuttered David. "You're home."

The woman shot a deleterious glance at Marie.

"I didn't realize we had company."

Marie shifted uncomfortably. She was prettier than Linda, and she felt that familiar pang of jealousy that such women often leveled at her.

"I think you should go home now, Marie, is it?" Linda said. "David's been under the weather lately, and he needs his rest."

Apologetically, Marie rose, said her good-byes, and left them alone. For the second time that day, she pitied a married couple that had somehow drifted apart from one another, and she prayed that she and Tim wouldn't end up like that.

In her egocentric little world, Rachel Stuart failed to see Marie hurry up to the Yateses' house. She was far too content to bother about such trivial matters as other people. She felt in charge of the world, and no one would stand in her way. In this euphoric state of mind, it was perfectly natural for her to give into the urge for one last chat. She just couldn't resist having a word with Shane Lysik. Boldly, Rachel walked up to the lawn chair, her figure casting a shadow over the man.

"Is there something I can help you with?" Shane asked, as he removed his sunglasses.

"It's such beautiful weather outside," Rachel stated. "I'm just surprised your wife isn't outside with you."

"My wife doesn't like the sun. Her skin is very delicate."

"That's funny. I thought it was no secret that you were having marital difficulty."

Scowling, Shane said, "Whatever gave you that idea? My wife and I have been happy for a long time."

"That's not what I heard from a certain friend of yours."

Shane arched an eyebrow.

"Oh, surely you know who I mean," Rachel said, feigning astonishment. Confidently, she continued. "I know about you and Lisa Collins. Though you aren't exactly her only beau, I'm afraid. In fact, I've seen her with Dr. Logan on several occasions. Strictly platonic at the moment. Of course, you never know with Lisa. But you would know more about that than I would. You taught a psychology class of hers once. I do believe it was the only time she ever got an A in class."

"I don't know who you think you are, but my life is none of your business."

Shane put his sunglasses back on and resumed a comfortable position for sunning himself, but his actions did not move Rachel Stuart to leave.

"Lots of things are not really my business. But I make them my business. I find that, in life, if you want to get ahead, you have to have a little knowledge."

"Then I guess you don't plan on going far," Shane scoffed. "You certainly don't know much about me."

Rachel's face reddened, and she spoke in a rushed voice.

"You think you're so smug. No one makes me look the fool."

"Go away," Shane said nonchalantly.

"Don't say I didn't warn you," said Rachel ominously. "People who cross me don't fare well."

With a smile of satisfaction, she turned and left.

"Yes, but, Anne, you're forgetting that Richard Channing worked for the syndicate . . . yes, he's Angela Channing's son."

Sonya Schwartz twirled the cord of her phone as she thought for the umpteenth time that she really, really, really needed to screen her calls. She and Anne Esterhazy shared a love of primetime's soaps. *Knots Landing, Dallas, Falcon Crest*. They watched them all. And often called each other to chat about this or that plotline. The one thing that Sonya hated, however, was when Anne missed a show and begged for a blow-by-blow of the episode.

"No, that was Lance. You did watch the show, didn't you?"

Of course, Anne would protest that of course she did or she only left the room for a moment. In some ways, Sonya thought she should enjoy this game, but today, she was in no mood. They were currently discussing *Falcon Crest*, but Anne had earlier asked for all the details of Thursday's *Knots Landing*. Obviously, she hadn't watched either show.

Sonya looked up at the clock hanging on the kitchen wall. It was five o'clock. Had she really been on the phone for more than an hour? Getting Anne off the phone would take a miracle. And then her doorbell rang, giving Sonya the perfect excuse.

She interrupted Anne Esterhazy hurriedly, "I'm sorry, Anne, but the doorbell just rang. I have to answer it. I'll talk to you tomorrow. Bye." Sonya hung up the phone before Anne had time to get a word in edgewise. She then went to the front door thinking, *There is such a thing as being saved by the bell!*

Sonya opened the door to find Claudia Icarios on her doorstep. She was startled to see her, but nevertheless, she greeted her warmly and asked her to come in.

"Hello, Sonya."

Claudia had been in her front yard much of that day. Thus, she had watched her neighbors with much interest. She had seen Tim walk down to the Stuarts' house and later to Miss Sparrow's home. She had also witnessed the movements of Rachel Stuart. Then Claudia had been called indoors by her husband, who had been working on the *New York Times* crossword puzzle, to take a phone call.

It had been Mildred Hawthorne calling, for she had been grievously upset by Rachel Stuart's visit. Mildred had confided her fears and worries in Claudia, who then tried to ease her neighbor's mind. Unfortunately, Claudia could not completely succeed in mollifying Mildred, so she told her good friend that she would use her trump card in trying to deal with Rachel Stuart. Mildred asked what that was, but Claudia wouldn't tell her.

"Please, trust me, Mildred," Claudia had said before the two women had hung up.

Presently, Claudia Icarios sat in one of the two recliners by the bay window in the Schwartzs' living room. From her vantage point she could see her house down the street, but she shifted her attention to Sonya.

"What brings you up here, Claudia?"

"I just stopped by because there's something that I thought you ought to know."

"Oh," Sonya said. "What is it?"

"Well, Mildred called me this afternoon. She's worried about her grandson. It seems your niece threatened to push him over the edge if Mildred doesn't stop interfering in their relationship. Well, I think it's a shame the young people of today no longer respect their marriage vows, don't you?"

"I'm sorry I don't see how I can help you. And I really don't see what business it is of yours."

"Yes, well, Mildred feels the same way about your niece's interference in her family."

"My niece and I don't get along. She didn't listen to her parents, and she doesn't listen to me. She's a spoiled brat. Always has been. We've tried to avoid each other ever since her parents' deaths."

"But you told your husband that you suspect your niece is responsible for her parents' death."

"How did you hear that?"

"I happened to overhear you two talking at the library the other day."

She was referring to the DeWitt Community Library, located in ShoppingTown Mall—not an ideal place for a confidential conversation with so many neighbors crossing paths there—and Sonya vexed herself for being so careless.

"Claudia! I don't think library board members are supposed to snoop into the affairs of library patrons. Now, I'm sorry. I can't help you or Mildred."

"Sonya, something has to be done about Rachel."

"Please leave," Sonya said, flustered.

Claudia rose and quietly left, but her words echoed in Sonya's mind. *Something has to be done about Rachel.*

"Thank you so much for doing this," said Angela Sparrow.

It was just after five o'clock, and Angela was propped up on her crutches in her kitchen watching Joshua Deveraux fix her faucet.

"Not a problem, Miss Sparrow," said her neighbor in a deep, baritone voice. "It looks like it's just a loose washer."

"I thought as much, but I just couldn't do it myself."

She'd had no trouble loosening the part just after seeing Josh pull into his driveway.

"It'll just be a minute," he said.

He looked back at her and gave her a winsome smile. Then he turned back to fix the offending part.

Angela patiently waited until she could steer the conversation in a fruitful direction. She watched his sure movements as he deftly repaired the leak she'd created. Even as he hunched over the sink, he towered over her. Angela judged he must be six three. She herself was five eleven, though she tended to stoop her shoulders involuntarily.

She didn't know her twenty-four year-old neighbor well, but he knew her as a friend of his grandmother. Still, he'd always been friendly and engaging with her as good neighbors are. Yet, since his wife's death, she'd notice the sadness that pervaded him. The comely young man with the pranksterish teenager's visage now moped about as if preoccupied by his loss. He would still smile at her when she greeted him, but it wasn't the broad grin she was used to, nor did the smile reach his hazel-green eyes.

"There," Joshua said in a satisfied tone. "All done."

"Thank you again."

He shrugged his broad shoulders.

"Just being neighborly," he said. "Besides, I do this sort of thing for my grandmother all the time. She insists Granddad is useless with his hands."

"Yes, the colonel does tend to be a bit clumsy at times," Angela agreed. "Still it is useful to have a man around the house to do those odd jobs." She indicated the sink with a nod of her head. "Or just to feel safe. I must say I've been a bit unnerved by these burglaries."

Joshua scratched at his right earlobe. He hesitated a moment. "You never married?"

Angela hadn't anticipated that!

"Would you care for something? A soda? Coffee? I should offer you something." She started toward the coffee pot, and he shifted aside to give her move room.

Embarrassed, he stammered, "I'm sorry. I didn't mean to offend—"

"No," Angela said as she set about making up a pot, "you didn't offend. It's just a difficult question to answer." She tried not to think of past loves.

"I understand. You don't have to answer. I just . . ." He looked down at his hands. Absently he rubbed his right palm with his left thumb. The thumb began tracing lines on his palm. The pattern formed the letter M. "I miss Danielle."

He stopped fidgeting with his hands and looked at Angela in earnest. "I feel I can tell you, Miss Sparrow, because you're a friend. You're not like everyone else because you listen to people's problems like . . ."

Joshua failed to finish his statement, but Angela picked up on the fact that he meant to say, 'like his late wife Danielle.'

"I understand," Angela said encouragingly.

"I don't think Danielle committed suicide."

"What? But . . . " Angela was at a loss for words.

Joshua continued, "I was looking at the note again. It's not, it just doesn't look like Danielle's handwriting. It looks similar, though."

He took his wallet out of his pocket, extracted a worn slip of paper, and showed it to her.

"The police told me that her fingerprints were on the note. I didn't question it at the time. I guess it looks like her handwriting, but I . . . there was a lot on my mind then. But the more I look at it, the more I'm convinced it's not Danielle's handwriting."

"I don't know what to say."

"I'd take it to the police, but I don't have any copies of Danielle's handwriting anymore. And they wouldn't believe me anyway. And I'm worried about—"

He turned to look out the kitchen window. He could see the row of rose bushes that delineated the edge of Miss Sparrow's backyard and the start of his. He recalled happier times spent with his wife outdoors.

"About what?"

"I think my house was broken into Thursday night while I was at the movies."

"Have you reported this to the police?"

"No. I'm kind of reluctant to make a big deal about it. It's not like my house was ransacked, and only one thing's missing."

"Then how do you know your house was broken into?" Angela asked, bewildered.

"Well, when I came back home, I found my front door unlocked. I'm pretty sure I locked it before I left, so I searched my house to see if anything valuable was missing. I thought that to be quite reasonable with all the burglaries that have been happening, but I couldn't find anything missing. So I just assumed that I hadn't locked the door after all. There just didn't seem to be any other explanation . . . until this morning that is. I opened the drawer in the nightstand next to my bed and found my handgun missing."

"I see," Angela said. She considered the implication for a moment. "And you think the gun was stolen on Thursday night?"

"Well, yes. But I don't understand why anyone would want to steal a gun and nothing else. It just doesn't make sense. I suppose I could have misplaced it, since I sometimes do things like that. I have a tendency to misplace my painting materials and other things, but I've always kept my gun in that nightstand drawer by the bed. It just doesn't figure."

Joshua seemed to be talking to himself rather than to her. He seemed to be reasoning out his confused thoughts aloud.

"Joshua?" Angela snapped her neighbor out of his trance-like state. "When did you come home from the cinema?"

"I don't know exactly. I left my house around nine. The movie started at nine-thirty. I'd gone to Camillus Mall, to the theaters there, since it was the only place the movie *Criminal Denials* was running. I must have gotten home around midnight."

"Yes. I see . . . it would seem that Thursday night has been more eventful than I thought," Angela mused.

"What?"

"It's nothing. I was just talking to myself. These burglaries are just getting out of hand."

"Oh, yeah. I would have gone to the Neighborhood Watch meeting, but I get too nervous around a lot of people like that."

Angela understood. She remembered Mildred having explained how self-conscious and withdrawn her grandson had become since he'd lost out on a football scholarship in high school. And since his wife's death, he'd seemed more neurotic than usual. She had known Joshua for about a year, and she knew what he was like. She knew that he had become a repairman because he did not like working with a lot of people directly, but he was good with his hands.

Again, he absently wrung his wrists. He felt comfortable talking to Miss Sparrow, but he was still nervous. He wanted to tell her something but feared she would think him mad.

"What is it, Joshua?"

"It's—it's just that," he stuttered. "I think I've heard her."

Perplexed, Angela asked, "Who?"

"Danielle. I'll be in my studio or the living room. I think I hear her in the bathroom. Where she died. She's calling to me. She wants me to help her rest." He paused, his gaze falling to his wrists. "I find myself looking for her in that room. I know she's not there, but her voice . . ."

"It's all right, Joshua," Angela said soothingly. "We all hear our loved ones who have departed. Their memories, their selves, are kept alive inside us. So it's perfectly natural for you to experience—"

"It's not like that," he interrupted. "It . . . it's not in my head. I hear her voice." He paused, before continuing awkwardly. "I should probably get home."

"Yes, of course, Joshua, by all means," Angela said, disconcerted. She hoped she hadn't alienated the young man. She truly felt for his situation, but she didn't know what else she could do. "You'll pardon me if I do not show you to the door."

He noted the bandage on Angela's ankle and nodded, though he didn't say a word as he left.

As he plodded up the street to his house, he remembered how, in high school, he had been the star quarterback on his football team. Life had been golden then. He'd won a college scholarship and a cheerleader girlfriend. But during the final game of the season, he'd injured his knee. The scholarship was withdrawn, and his girlfriend had turned out to be the stereotypical superficial blonde who didn't hesitate in dumping him. His confidence had been shattered.

With a sigh, Joshua reached the end of his driveway and was intercepted by Rachel Stuart.

"Hello, Josh."

He turned around defensively.

"I was wondering if you knew where Lisa is?"

He sputtered, "Why should I know where she is?"

"Oh, I don't know. Just a thought I suppose. It's just that I would have thought you might have gone somewhere. After all, I haven't seen very much of you lately. One would think you were trying to avoid me."

She laughed.

Inwardly, Josh cringed. Something about that laugh unnerved him.

"I can't do this, Rachel. It's a mistake."

"Don't lie to me, Josh. I know everything now," Rachel stated loftily.

"I don't understand?"

"No, I don't suppose you would, but then you've been avoiding me. Why?"

He scratched at his wrist nervously. He'd never felt comfortable around Rachel.

"Maybe it's because I've found out who you really are," Joshua said.

"What has Lisa been telling you?" Rachel asked vehemently.

"What makes you think she's told me anything? And why are you so concerned about her?"

"Watch yourself, Josh. I don't like being toyed with. You of all people should know that. You were lucky to have that alibi, when your wife was found dead. How convenient to have a flat tire. Such a shame that you were out fixing it while poor Danielle perished. But you're always fixing things, aren't you? You're so good with your hands. I just can't believe it would take you so long to fix something as simple as a tire. Unless it was on purpose?"

His body stiffened.

"You don't know what you're talking about," he muttered.

"Of course that alibi could be destroyed if someone could place you at your house earlier that day. Anyone could have seen something and not have understood its significance until later . . . like now."

"I know how dangerous you really are, Rachel," Joshua said, narrowing his eyes at her. "I know that all too well," he said as his looked down at his wrists and remembered how she'd bound him to the bed. At first, he'd like it, but then she had taken things too far.

"Really, Josh," Rachel said, advancing on him, "you treat me so badly. Was I ever so mean to you that you would treat me like this?"

"No."

She laid her hands on his broad shoulders, causing him to flinch. He tried to pull back, but she dug in her fingertips like talons.

"Rachel," he protested.

"Tut, tut," Rachel said, as she reached for the top button on his white shirt.

"Rachel, it's over."

Emotionally he knew theirs was an empty relationship, but physically he was still turned on by her. And when she made a play for him, his resistance fell away faster than their clothes. He didn't stop her as she unbuttoned his shirt and began to kiss him.

"Are you nuts? We can't do this out here on the street."

"Well, then we should go inside."

"What about Todd?"

"He's not home," Rachel said, smiling impishly at Joshua.

Joshua glanced up and down the street to ascertain that they were not seen by anyone. Then he led the way to his front door, which he'd left unlocked. He often did that when his mind was on other things, but his worries and other cares were already forgotten now.

Joshua entered his house, kicked off his loafers, and barely had time to turn around before Rachel doffed his shirt and discarded it on the floor. What would she do to him this time? He hoped not the handcuffs again. Then her hands reached out to the waistband of his jeans, and he didn't want to think anymore.

In their haste, neither he nor Rachel had noticed they had been watched. Returning from her visit to Rachel's aunt, Claudia Icarios had seen both of them in his yard. She had witnessed Rachel's advances with alarm and shock. She did not approve of such goings-on, but there was little to do about it in today's world. However, Claudia knew one thing full well. Something had to be done . . .

EASTER SUNDAY

Holy Cross Church and its rectory were built in 1950, not long after the Mission of Our Lady of Solace became the Parish of Holy Cross. Initially serving just sixty Catholic families in the DeWitt area, the congregation grew and a school was proposed. Eight years after the church's solemn dedication, Holy Cross School opened to first through fourth grades. A grade was added each year until 1963, when Holy Cross' first pastor the Rev. Joseph Ritchie presided over the school's first eighth grade graduation. Sadly, Father Ritchie passed away nine months later.

This Easter Sunday, some forty-seven years later, the parking lot was packed with cars. Both Tim and Marie had looked down the slope of the lot to where the L-shaped school stood. The Sisters of St. Francis had staffed the school since it opened, and today, though not all the teachers were nuns, the sisters still maintained a very active presence.

Tim fondly recalled his years at Holy Cross as he and Marie crossed the parking lot to the church's front entrance. Fortunately, they had arrived early. The church was filling up fast, but they found an empty pew near the middle on the right side. Tim, like many of the men, had dressed in a suit. Marie, like many of the women, had dressed in a fashionable spring dress. They smiled as they watched families arriving with their children dressed up in suits and dresses that mimicked their parents. Then they were joined by Tim's mother and grandmother and those of his siblings that had chosen Catholicism.

Tim didn't consider himself religious. His church attendance was sporadic at best and he'd never felt strongly about his faith. Marie, on the other hand, had been raised Catholic and had easily won the decision of their choice of church. He noticed her parents sitting on the other side of the church near the side chapel, which had been open for today. Church might be just more than half full on regular Sundays, but Easters always packed them in like sardines. Marie's brother Todd, like many a wayward churchgoer, showed up in a brown suit and took a seat next to their parents. He sat glumly waiting for Mass to begin.

Many regular churchgoers bemoaned the influx of twice-a-year-Catholics, but they were nonetheless welcoming. Most viewed the spectacle of dresses and suits admirably and frowned at those who rolled out of bed in jeans and a T-shirt. Casual dress was certainly on the rise in recent years.

A hush fell over the assembly as the lector announced the beginning of Mass. Long-time pastor Monsignor O'Brien presided. Today's homily, though not rousing, was reflective and contained a few bits of Irish humor. So far the day had been a chance for Tim and Marie to forget about the troubles on Stoneridge. That would not be the case after Mass ended.

"Timothy," Edith Baxter said, taking her grandson aside. "I do so hope you and Marie are settling in nicely."

Since leaving her home of so many years, Edith had occupied her time with her younger grandchildren and gardening at DeWitt Manor. Yet her thoughts would often stray to the events she'd overheard on Thursday night. Now, while her daughter Sarah chatted with acquaintances and Marie greeted her family, Edith wasted little time in asking, "What have you found out?"

While Tim related what had transpired to his grandmother, Marie half-listened to her father berating her brother's lack of direction in life. As usual, Todd got defensive, and her mother tried to keep the peace. Marie got tired of it.

Her attention wandered, and she was surprised to see the Hawthornes. The colonel and his wife were in conversation with another couple by the church entrance. Marie had heard that Mildred was an active member of DeWitt Community Church, so why would they attend Easter Mass here at Holy Cross? Then she saw Joshua Deveraux leaning against the railing of the church steps nearby. He seemed to be idly waiting for the Hawthornes. Impulsively, Marie approached him and tapped him on the shoulder, causing him to flinch.

"Oh, I'm sorry," Marie said, "I didn't mean to startle you."

Josh flashed a winning smile. "Nah, it's all right. Though I'm afraid I don't . . ."

"Oh, I'm your new neighbor." Marie looked toward Tim, and said, "My husband and I just moved in."

Josh followed Marie's gaze.

"Oh. Isn't that Ms. Baxter?"

"Yes, she's Tim's grandmother. We moved into her house. It was a rather generous wedding gift."

Josh nodded agreement. "So you're Todd's sister then? He mentioned you were moving to the neighborhood."

"Yes. We hosted the Neighborhood Watch meeting. You didn't come."

He looked past her toward the line of cars departing the church's parking lot. "Sorry," he muttered. "I'm . . . I don't like being in crowds."

"It must be difficult to face your neighbors after your wife's death," Marie said sympathetically.

He bristled and bowed his head.

"I'm sorry. I didn't mean to upset you. I just heard the story from my husband. If you don't want to talk about it."

Josh looked up and smiled weakly. "It's all right. I . . . it's been . . . difficult to deal with."

He raised his right hand to finger his earlobe distractedly, as he often did when he was agitated. The motion caused the cuff of his shirt to fall back, and Marie noticed the bruise marks that ringed his wrist. Josh saw her notice and quickly shoved his hands in the pockets of his jeans. His cheeks reddened ever so slightly. The last thing he wanted was for Todd's sister to wonder about the handcuff marks he'd acquired from his last encounter with Todd's wife!

"Marie, what a pleasant surprise."

Mildred Hawthorne tried hard not to mince words, but she'd been aghast to turn and see Marie talking to her grandson. Immediately, she'd swooped in to put a stop to that.

"Are you ready to go, Joshua?" Mildred turned to Marie. "Martin and I thought we'd take my grandson out to Sunday brunch. He really does need to get out more. If you'll excuse us. Martin, do get the car ready. Come along, Joshua."

Taken aback, Marie watched Mildred lead Josh away.

Meanwhile, Tim had finished telling his grandmother what had transpired since she'd left. She stood in silence a few moments before saying, "I wish someone besides Marie and Evelyn had heard what I did, or preferably, something more substantial. Neither of them heard enough of the event. But quite a few things you mentioned appear suggestive. You will pursue the matter of course?"

"Of course, Grandma. I think you're right, that something did happen. Lisa Collins hasn't been seen since Thursday as far as I know."

"You also might want to check into Danielle's death. I must admit that I was rather suspicious of her death at the time. I couldn't help but think that her husband might have had something to do with it. It so often happens that way, you know."

"Yeah, Miss Sparrow mentioned the police were looking into Joshua Deveraux's alibi."

"Angela is quite sensible. I'm glad you have her to confide in. It makes me feel less guilty about leaving."

"Grandma, I couldn't have you go snooping around in something that could be potentially dangerous."

"I know, Timothy. I just hope you don't let your wife get too involved."

"I'll take care of her, Grandma. I'd never want anything to happen to Marie."

Tim's eyes sought out Marie. She was currently talking to her parents, or more particularly to her father.

Edith smiled. "Yes, dear. I also know that Zachary Stuart would never want anything to happen to his only daughter either."

"Er, yes, well." Tim cleared his throat. "Um, I was wondering whether or not there was anything else you might know about what happened."

"Actually, I have been thinking about it. Did you notice any signs of a struggle?"

Tim shook his head. "I was only able to give a cursory look at Lisa's place. There didn't seem to be anything unusual. Although . . ."

Tim regretted not having taken more time to search Lisa's. He hadn't wanted to ignite neighborhood gossip.

"Perhaps I should stay. I could talk to . . ."

"Grandma, you're not Miss Marple. You just enjoy yourself on your trip." Earlier Edith had told him about her decision to visit some old friends back in Rutland, Vermont. "Marie and I will be fine. If something has happened to Lisa, I will take care of it."

"Well, I know you'll be careful. I'd better go find your mother. I have a lot of packing to do."

Tim would have followed, to say goodbye to his mother, but just then Todd walked over to greet him.

"Hey, Tim."

"Hi, Todd. I heard you didn't come home the other night."

"I crashed at a friend's place," Todd muttered.

"Is everything all right?"

"I just needed some space."

Tim didn't think Todd was telling the whole truth, but he didn't press the matter. Instead, he decided to take the opportunity to ask, "Say, I was wondering if you heard anything unusual Thursday night after the Watch meeting?"

Todd furrowed his brow. He must have thought it an odd question, but he answered frankly, "No, we went to bed early that night. I musta been asleep by ten, at least. Why?"

"Look, you know Lisa Collins, right?"

"What about her?"

"Well, it's just that Lisa has disappeared, and my wife is concerned. She and Lisa had attended a class at Syracuse University."

"You don't have to lie to me, Tim," Todd said.

"Huh?"

"You have a tendency of lowering your eyes when you lie or don't tell the whole truth."

"Gee, I'll have to remember that. Thanks," said Tim, who then explained what his grandmother had heard on Thursday night. When he'd finished, Todd laughed.

"What? What's so funny?"

"That's ridiculous. No idiot in his right mind would commit a murder like that. He'd just be asking for attention. Half the neighborhood would know about it. Some of the nosiest people in New York State live on Stoneridge Drive! Trust me."

"I know, but doesn't it seem strange to you that Lisa Collins has been missing for three days now?"

Todd answered. "No. Lisa's always done what she wants. She comes and goes as she pleases. She'll turn up sooner or later. You just watch. No offense, but all your grandmother probably heard was Lisa tearing up the road in her sports car like usual."

"But how does she afford college and a house and a sports car for God's sake?"

Todd shrugged.

"What can I say, Tim? I don't know. I haven't talked to Lisa much since we broke up."

Marie, having said goodbye to her parents, sidled up to her brother and nudged him.

"Hey, you two, what are you talking about?"

"Nothing," Todd muttered. "I should get going. I've gotta pick up a few groceries and the Sunday paper and hightail it home. Rachel will be wondering what's keeping me."

Tim watched his friend depart and exchanged a look with Marie. He wondered if she were thinking the same thing. Todd acted like a dog that had been kicked hard and felt dejected. What could have happened to him? And was Rachel to blame?

The morning's bright sunny skies were slowly giving way to ominous clouds looming on the western horizon. However, these omens of an impending rainstorm were lost on Tim Dewitt. He was thinking about the argument he'd just had with Marie. It had started on the drive home from church. Marie had wanted to know about his conversation with Todd, but though he'd given her the gist of it, Marie didn't believe he was telling her everything. When they arrived home, Marie lit into him. He wasn't telling her about his investigations. He was being overprotective. He didn't trust her enough.

Perhaps he should have taken it all more seriously, but he had honestly felt Marie needed to vent because she was so concerned about and angry at her brother. He just didn't appreciate being the convenient punching bag. He shouldn't have called her on it, though. She'd started to cry, and he'd reached out to comfort her. Normally, she'd let him hug her and tell her everything would be all right, but this time she insisted she needed time to think. She muttered something about picking up the Sunday newspaper and some groceries and left!

He still couldn't believe it, and he couldn't understand what had riled up Marie. He wondered if it could have had something to do with last night's conversation. Marie had been trying to tell him something about Rachel, something that had happened earlier in the day. He just hadn't been listening. He'd been so preoccupied thinking about Lisa's disappearance. He had tried to wrap his mind around various possibilities of what had happened but hadn't come up with anything insightful. And afterwards, he was just too tired.

"Damn it," he huffed. He couldn't keep chasing after phantom gunshots and cries for help. There had to be something concrete. This uncertainty about what had occurred was getting to both of them. Something had to happen soon.

While he mulled this over, he saw the Lysiks pulling into their driveway. He watched them get out of the car and begin unloading groceries. Tim nearly chuckled. It seemed as if everyone planned to shop for groceries today. Tim glanced at his watch. It was nearly one o'clock. He looked out the bay window again. Perhaps he should talk to Brenda or Shane. If they didn't have anything to add to what he'd already found out, then maybe it was time to move on.

Having jogged the short distance to the Lysiks' driveway, Tim said, "Hey," as he approached Brenda.

She pulled out a bag full of groceries from the backseat of the red sedan. "Oh, Tim. How are you?"

"Fine."

Shane returned to the car and greeted Tim. "How's the new house?" he asked.

"Technically it's not new," Brenda said, handing the groceries to her husband. "I understand most of these houses were built in the late-fifties."

She handed another bag to her husband.

"Is that the last of them?" he asked.

She nodded.

"So how does it feel?" she said, turning to Tim.

"Uh, great," Tim said, though he wasn't precisely certain what Brenda had meant.

Shane went inside with the groceries as Brenda asked, "Where's Marie?"

"Out," said Tim, who couldn't help looking over his shoulder at Lisa Collins's house, which was not so very far away. His gaze shifted to the house that belonged to Dr. Craig Logan. Then he noted the streetlight near the end of the Lysiks' driveway.

"Tim?"

"Oh, I'm sorry, Brenda. It's just so quiet and peaceful, an average street in suburbia. It's hard to believe a murder could have been committed here."

Brenda seemed shocked to hear Tim say 'murder.' She regarded him curiously. Then she, too, turned to look down Stoneridge Drive. She barely glanced at the ranch and split-level homes that lined both sides of the street as it curved toward the north. Trees and other shrubbery adorned the area much like any other street in the Town of Dewitt. Telephone poles, some with streetlights, and wires also lined the street. Indeed, Stoneridge Drive was just like any other suburban street.

Frowning, Brenda asked, "Tim, you're not making any sense. You think a murder happened on Stoneridge?"

As if he had not heard Brenda's question, Tim asked, "Did you happen to hear anything around eleven-twenty Thursday night?"

"No, why?"

"You didn't have your window open?"

"Yes, but I was fast asleep by eleven. I told your wife that when she stopped by yesterday," Brenda said. "What is going on?"

"You don't know?"

"Know about what?" Brenda asked. "Murder?"

"Have you seen Lisa Collins recently?"

"No, I haven't."

Tim detected a hint of animosity in Brenda's voice.

"I take it you don't care for—"

"Miss Collins?" Brenda interrupted. "No, I can't say I do. She's a notorious flirt, and I don't like her falling all over my husband."

An awkward pause ensued. Brenda glanced over Tim's shoulder, and he turned to see what had caught her attention. He saw Claudia Icarios leaving her front yard and walking down the street. Such a simple act as this struck him as odd. Perhaps it was because, since he had moved in, he had rarely seen her anywhere but in that front yard. He wondered where she was going.

Watching Claudia pass the Logans' house across the street, Tim uttered, "I can't help think something's happened to Lisa."

Brenda recalled her brief conversation with Tim's wife yesterday.

"I had hoped Marie was kidding. You're not seriously saying that there's been a murder? A murder on this street would be absolutely ridiculous. If someone was murdered half the neighborhood would have seen it. I've lived on this street long enough to know that nothing of that sort could happen without someone knowing about it."

"What about the burglaries?" Tim asked.

He noticed Claudia approach the Stuarts' front door. Todd hadn't come back from wherever he'd gone after church, so Claudia must be looking for Rachel, but why? He brushed aside his thoughts and turned his attention to Brenda, who answered, "I'll bet someone in this neighborhood knows who's responsible for the thefts. They're probably just too scared or reluctant to come forward for whatever reason. And no murder could occur on this street without someone witnessing it."

"Would it be reported if someone did witness it?" Tim asked in disbelief.

"A murder? Of course."

"Are you so sure? If there's one thing I know, it's that one can never be sure without knowing all the facts."

Brenda Lysik shook her head, dismayed. She was about to respond when a strangled scream pierced the air.

Tim's heart shot into overdrive. The next, his police training kicked in, and he ran. For an instant, it seemed as if time slowed. Tim thought he heard footsteps following him, but he didn't look back. Out of the periphery of his vision, he saw someone dressed in white hurrying up the street toward him. Then he rounded the corner of the Stuarts' house.

The first thing he saw was Rachel Stuart sprawled on the ground by her back door. It appeared as if she'd been gardening—kneeling on a gardening pad and planting annuals, creating life while someone had taken hers. Tim swallowed hard. Rachel's skull had been crushed.

Then Tim looked up and saw Claudia standing a few steps away, holding a shovel with visible traces of blood on it. The everyday gardening tool fell from Claudia's hands as Georgia Llewellyn huffed around the side of the house.

"What is it?" Georgia asked. "What's happened?"

"Oh, my God!" said Brenda, who'd followed Tim.

They heard a car screech to a halt and one of its doors slam seconds before Todd Stuart appeared. He called out, "Rachel?!"

Georgia Llewellyn rushed over to him, saying, "Come with me, Mr. Stuart. You mustn't see."

Pushing past Georgia, Todd came to a dead stop the moment his eyes fell upon the figure of his wife lying motionless on the lawn. "Oh, my God," he cried. "Who did this?"

"I found her," Claudia said blankly, "the shovel, too. She was . . ."

She could say no more. The shock she had experienced overwhelmed her. With an effort, she closed her eyes to blot out the image of Rachel dead and to gather her wits about her.

Todd rushed forward and crumpled to the ground beside his wife. "Get a doctor!"

Shane Lysik arrived at the scene as Todd scooped up his wife and held her limply in his arms.

"What's going on?"

Tim's horror grew as he witnessed his friend call out Rachel's name as if he were merely trying to wake her. Not wanting to hear Todd's pitiful cries, Tim backed away. He turned and heard Brenda calmly explaining to her husband what she'd seen.

"Shane," Tim interrupted. "Do you know if Dr. Logan's home?"

"I think so."

"Could you get him? Hopefully, he has something to calm Todd." Tim noticed Anne Esterhazy running toward them. "I need to make sure the scene isn't disturbed any more than it has already."

Others no doubt watched from their windows. Murder had struck close to home. Shane sprinted next door to the Logans'. He banged on the door and tapped his foot nervously. When D.J. Logan opened the door, Shane nearly shouted at the fourteen-year-old.

"I need your father. There's been a terrible—"

"Who is it, D.J.?" asked a baritone voice from inside.

Dr. Craig Logan appeared in the doorway and stood behind his son. He greeted Shane, but there was no time for pleasantries. Shane blurted out the details. The doctor excused himself for a moment to retrieve a little black bag—inherited from his grandfather—that had not been seen for a generation or more. Then the two men hurried back to the Stuarts' backyard.

"What's happened here?" Dr. Logan asked with the trace of a twang in his voice.

"Rachel Stuart's dead," Tim reported. "I need you to—"

"No, she's not!" Todd snapped.

"Mr. Stuart, please," Georgia said. "You need to let Dr. Logan look at her."

"Please," Dr. Logan said gently, "give me some room."

"I'm certain he'll need to be sedated," Georgia murmured to the doctor, as Todd backed away and sat on the grass clutching his knees to his chest.

Tim looked away from Todd. He didn't want to see his best friend sobbing like a ten-year-old. Instead, he informed Shane, "I asked your wife to call the police."

"Aren't you the police?"

"Yes, but I need a C.O. I mean, I need the crime scene unit."

Tim turned from Shane to see Dr. Logan, having opened his black bag, fumble about. Disconcertment, bewilderment, and apprehension flashed across Dr. Logan's face as if he saw that something wasn't there that should be. However, the doctor was quick to extract a sedative to calm Todd Stuart's nerves. With that done, he then turned his attention to the body of Rachel Stuart.

"She hasn't been dead long."

Forty minutes later, regular police procedure in dealing with a murder had been mostly completed, and the body had been taken away. Tim had been regulated to the sidelines, and Sergeant Jack Griffin of the Town of DeWitt Police had taken charge of the case. His C.O. was about a decade older than him. Still considered young for a sergeant, or so Tim had been told.

He watched Jack cast his blue-green eyes over the gathered gaggle of neighbors. What he saw was a typical suburban mix, not unlike his own neighbors just a few streets away. Tim had heard him mutter to an officer earlier about increasing crime in the township. It was no longer atypical for the city's criminal derelicts to drift into the Town of DeWitt for some action. Most common were the petty larcenies and robberies. This street had already had that. But murder? That was a whole new league. Murder was not commonplace in the Town of DeWitt.

Jack took Tim aside a few paces and conferred with him. He asked for Tim's account, which Tim gave succinctly.

When Tim was finished, Jack asked, "You were across the street where?"

"The second brown house. With the red car in the driveway."

Jack nodded.

"The doctor here seems to think she's been dead about two hours."

"Marie and I were probably at church when it happened then. So was Todd Stuart. We both saw him at church."

"I know he's your brother-in-law," Jack said, "but the time of death won't be fully established until there's been an autopsy. He could have just as easily killed her before—"

Tim interrupted, "He wouldn't have—"

Jack cut him off.

"I'm not saying he did, but you and I both know the statistics. You can't let your personal emotions get in the way of an investigation."

"There's more going on here, Jack." He glanced at his neighbors standing about the Stuarts' front yard and lowered his voice. "A neighbor has been missing since Thursday, and my grandmother heard gunshots that night."

"Why didn't you report it?"

Tim closed his mouth. He wasn't sure how to answer. He'd asked himself that very question.

"We'll talk about that later," Jack said. "Right now, I've got to take statements from the other witnesses."

Sgt. Griffin crossed the lawn and approached Claudia.

"Mrs. Icarios? Why did you come down to see Rachel Stuart?"

"I came to retrieve my shovel. The one that was used to . . . to kill . . ." Claudia gulped nervously, before continuing. "She had borrowed it from me last week, and I wanted it back, as I have some digging to do in order to plant some new rose bushes."

"And you found her dead?"

"Yes, I did, Sergeant. I rang the doorbell but didn't get any answer. I know that Rachel Stuart spends a good deal of time outside gardening, so I thought I'd check the backyard. That's when I found her. I don't know why I picked up the shovel. I just didn't know what I was doing..."

"That's a reasonable reaction, Sergeant," Shane Lysik stated. "In fact, it sounds perfectly plausible, considering the shock she must have experienced. She finds her shovel next to a dead body. She picks up the shovel that she came for, as if she were in a trance. Then reality hits her, and she screams."

"And who are you?" Jack asked, slightly perturbed by the interruption.

"Shane Lysik. I'm a psychiatrist at University Hospital."

Jack made a note of what Shane had said before turning to ask the doctor, "Dr. Logan? Do you agree with that estimation given by Dr. Lysik?"

"Well, I don't know much about psychiatry, but I'd say Shane's evaluation is very probable."

"All right," Jack said. He shifted his weight from one foot to the other. Then he turned to face Georgia Llewellyn, who looked at him like a deer startled by a car's headlights.

"Ms. Llewellyn? You were the second person on the scene?" prompted Jack.

Snapping out of her trance, Georgia replied, "Oh, yes. Yes, I think I was. I had just been having tea with Miss Sparrow across the street. I was on my way home when I heard the scream. I live in the white house just down the street." She pointed to her house. "I saw Tim running toward the backyard and I followed through the gap there." She indicated the six or seven foot opening between the Stuarts house and the one that belonged to Lisa Collins. "I used to be a registered nurse, and I thought I could help."

"Did you see Mrs. Icarios holding the shovel?"

"Did I? I don't know. Was she holding the shovel?"

Tim could see Jack sigh with impatience. He'd clearly picked up on Georgia's reliability—or lack thereof—as a witness. His eyes scanned over the remaining neighbors and settled on Brenda Lysik.

"Did you see the shovel in Mrs. Icarios's hands?" he asked.

"No, Sergeant. If she was holding it, she must have dropped it before I arrived."

"Now you were talking to Tim Dewitt in your driveway just prior?"

"Yes, we were talking about . . ." Brenda abruptly stopped. She quickly recovered herself, though, and said, "I did see Claudia walking to the Stuarts' house. I noticed her go up to the front door. I didn't see her go round the back."

Jack looked over the first responder's notes.

"You did see Mr. Stuart driving down the street?" he asked.

"Yes. I heard a car and looked before I ran across the street. We were in the backyard when we heard his car pulling in the driveway. My husband arrived just after Todd."

"And he went to get Dr. Logan?"

"Yes," Brenda answered, "Mr. Stuart was distraught."

"I suggested a sedative," Georgia added. "He wouldn't let go of his wife. I've seen cases like that before. They always had to give the spouse a sedative."

"Yes," Jack said, gritting his teeth.

Tim suspected what Jack was thinking. His number one suspect was currently and conveniently asleep. Todd Stuart had been helped into his home by Shane Lysik and Dr. Logan, the latter having given him a sedative. There was no way Todd would be answering any questions. Not until nightfall. Jack hated those kind of delays. He'd always maintained that left too much opportunity to concoct a cover story, if needed.

"What about you?"

Jack had addressed Anne Esterhazy, who'd been listening attentively to every word.

"Oh, me?" Anne said. "I was in my front yard when I saw all the commotion down here. Naturally, I was curious, so I decided to see what was happening. I passed Brenda Lysik as she went to call the police and just peeked around the corner." She pouted briefly. "I didn't see much, though. Tim was ushering everyone to the front yard to contain the scene, or so he said."

Jack interrupted, "I remember you."

"Huh?" Anne said, startled.

"You went to Tulane University, didn't you? Yeah, quite a few years ago. You were a friend of Justine's ..."

Realization dawned on Anne. "Oh, my Gawd! I should have remembered. Oh, I'm so sorry. How is . . .? Oh, I'm sorry." Anne blushed. "Well, it's good to see you again. As I was saying . . . where was I?"

"Oh, yes. They were taking Mr. Stuart into his house, and Tim told us all to wait for the police here on the front lawn. And this is where I've stayed."

"Well, thank you all for your time," Jack said. "I'll be talking to you again for further information as evidence develops."

After this dismissal, Dr. Logan and Georgia Llewellyn went in to check on Todd Stuart's condition while the others wandered back to their homes.

"Well?" Jack asked, turning to Tim, expecting an explanation.

Jack Griffin had been Tim's Field Training Officer when he had been hired by the DeWitt Police shortly after graduating from the police academy in 1985. This was before Jack had received his promotion to CIU sergeant when his predecessor had retired. At thirty-three, he was the youngest Criminal Investigation Unit Sergeant in the history of the DeWitt Police, but he handled each criminal case with the authority of someone far older.

Through the office grapevine, Tim had heard that Jack's wife, Justine, and their daughter had been killed in a drunk driving incident ten years before. The loss combined with the dismissal of charges against the other driver played a large part in Jack's becoming a cop and his dedication. After joining the Town of DeWitt police force in 1980, Jack had quickly joined the ranks of the C.I.U. department.

Now those hard blue-green eyes stared down at him. He was only two inches taller than Tim, but his muscular build and bearing often appeared larger and more intimidating.

"What? I don't know anything more about this murder than you do."

"Oh, right," Jack said skeptically. "Tim, I know you're on vacation for the week, but I also know that you've been setting up a Neighborhood Watch Program on this street. Surely you know something about these people? You live on this street, for God's sake."

"How's Justin?" Tim asked with a nervous laugh.

Justin was Jack Griffin's thirteen-year-old son. He had been in the car when the accident happened; he was the only survivor, aside from the driver of the other car.

"He's fine, Tim. Don't change the subject."

"What do you want me to tell you?"

"What's going on in this neighborhood? A suicide, four burglaries, and now a murder occurs on this street in less than a month! And now you're telling me one of the neighbors has gone missing too? I've seen less action in a police procedural!"

"Well, it is a long story. I know you've got to get back to the station to report your findings here, but could you drop by later this afternoon . . . say around four?"

"That sounds fine," Jack said. "By the way, how's married life treating you?"

"Great. Marie should be home when you stop by later. I'm sure she'd be glad to see you again."

"Say hello to her for me," Jack said, as he entered his car.

"I will," Tim said.

He lingered in the Stuarts' front yard and peered up and down the street. Hands on his hips, his arms akimbo, he wondered how the hell someone could have snuck up behind Rachel Stuart and killed her in broad daylight. Hadn't anybody seen anything? But then where was he? At church. Easter Sunday, everyone was thinking about their holiday plans and going to church. Who would have seen anything?

Tim looked up the street. Sonya Schwartz and the Esterhazys were Jewish so they wouldn't have been preoccupied by Easter celebrations. Unfortunately, there were a lot of trees and shrubs that would obstruct their view. The Hawthornes and Marie's Aunt Evelyn weren't home when Rachel had been found, but he didn't know about earlier. The Lysiks had been shopping. His gaze moved on to Joshua Deveraux's not-so-typical ranch home and its privacy fence, which extended along the front steps and patio along the front of the house. He didn't know what to think about Deveraux. Marie had mentioned talking to him at church earlier. He'd been with the Hawthornes, his grandparents. Jack suspected Deveraux of killing Danielle, who had once been a roommate of Rachel and Lisa. Tim shook his head. He looked at the pink house next to Deveraux's. Georgia had been there, having tea with Angela Sparrow, and Angela didn't think Joshua Deveraux killed his wife.

"Where's Bryant?"

Tim turned to his right and saw Dr. Logan talking to his son.

"He went biking."

"Damn it," muttered Dr. Logan.

Tim remembered that he hadn't questioned any of the Logans about Thursday night, so he called after the doctor and D.J.

"Could I ask you a few questions, Dr. Logan?"

"Didn't the sergeant just do that?"

"Just some additional questions." Tim glanced at D.J. "For both of you. Could we go inside?"

As he walked to the Logan's house, Tim recalled snippets of conversation he'd heard at the Neighborhood Watch meeting. Claudia Icarios had mentioned that Dr. Logan was a widower and had been for only a short time. When his wife had died a year ago, Craig had decided to leave his position at a New York City Hospital. Though why he'd chosen to move here to Syracuse was something of a mystery.

"So what is it that you couldn't ask me outside?" Craig asked.

They were all seated in the Logan's living room. The house's structure was virtually a mirror image to that of the Dewitts', only there was no wall divider by the door. Father and son were seated on the only couch in the room, while Tim sat in a comfortable armchair.

"It concerns what's happened recently."

"So what is it?" D.J. asked petulantly.

"Well, D.J., two things," Tim said. "I'd like to know where people were before Rachel Stuart was found. I just thought I'd start with you two."

"Why are you so interested in finding that out?" Craig asked. "I thought Sgt. Griffin was in charge of the case. Aren't you on vacation?"

"Yes, but an officer is always on duty. Besides, it's become personal," Tim said. "Please tell me where you were."

Craig gazed out the window. Brushing aside strands of sandy brown hair that had ventured to cover his eyes, Craig murmured a response, "I was here reading a medical journal."

Tim noticed the journal in question resting on the coffee table.

"So you were home all day?"

"No, we did go to church. It is Easter Sunday!" Craig sounded affronted. "I picked up the journal around noon."

"What about you?" Tim said, turning to look at the doctor's son.

Darius Jeremy Logan, known to his friends and family as D.J., was a handsome fourteen-year-old. The boy resembled his father, only his jaw was squarer and his blue eyes lacked the tinge of gray his father's had. D.J. did have his father's slightly upturned nose; however, the bridge of his nose was a tad crooked, the result of an athletic related injury.

D.J. looked Tim in the eyes as he answered, "A friend of mine came over, and we played some one-on-one."

"Who?"

"Justin Griffin."

Sgt. Griffin and his son Justin lived in a modest ranch house on Alcove Place, three streets away from Stoneridge.

"Did you or he see anything?"

"No. We were shooting hoops."

"Kind of hot out for basketball, don't you think?"

"I dunno." D.J. shrugged. "Kinda. It wasn't an intense one-on-one match. We were just hanging out."

"But you didn't see anything suspicious?"

"I dunno."

Tim sighed. "What about Justin?"

"You'd have to ask him."

"You didn't hear anything? Possibly Rachel Stuart screaming?"

"No. Bry was mowing the backyard at the time. I doubt anyone would have heard anything over that racket."

"Hmm," Tim muttered. He wondered if Bryant Logan, the doctor's youngest son, had seen anything.

"Are you finished interrogating my son?" Craig snapped.

"I also wanted to ask the two of you about Thursday night."

"Thursday night?" Craig asked, bewildered.

Tim considered how to broach the subject. He didn't think Dr. Logan had known his grandmother long and might think her a dotty senior citizen ready for the nursing home if he heard her testimony.

"Yes, Dr. Logan. You see," Tim fibbed, "I had my window open that night. I heard two cries, two gunshots, a car door slam and engine starting, and then the car racing up the street. I think that Lisa Collins was murdered Thursday night, after the Neighborhood Watch meeting."

"What?" exclaimed D.J.

Craig, however, showed only skepticism.

"Then where's the body?"

"I don't know as of yet, but my gut tells me that Lisa Collins is dead."

"How do you know you weren't dreaming?" Craig suggested.

"Other people heard the gunshots, doctor. Besides—"

Before Tim could say any more, Bryant Logan burst through the door. Flushed and out of breath, the boy's blue eyes were wide with excitement.

"A body!" the twelve-year-old exclaimed.

Instinctively, Tim knew what the boy would say.

"Dad, I was biking." Bryant took a deep breath. "Down near the creek. I started on the trail . . . on my dirt bike. That's when I saw her. Lying face down in the creek! I rode back as fast as I could. She wasn't moving, Dad. I called to her, but she didn't move."

Bryant trembled and shook as he remembered what he'd seen. His brother stood up and took hold of his shoulders.

"Hey, it's okay, Bry."

Tim studied the two brothers. They were nearly the same height, though they were two years apart in age. He judged them to be roughly five feet nine. Both were tall for their age, but then Dr. Logan himself was six feet two. Familial resemblance was marked among the Logans. Father and sons all had broad shoulders and lank, athletic physiques. Darius was slightly brawnier and Bryant's pug nose a bit wider, but all three possessed the same square-jawed angularity, the same pink lips, and the same style brown hair.

Tim faced Craig and said, "Now, do you believe me, doctor?"

"Yes, it would seem that you were correct."

"I would suggest then that we get down there so you can examine the body. Don't you agree, doctor?"

Craig Logan did not speak. He merely stood up and proceeded to the door, where he picked up his medical bag. Then he and Tim headed down Stoneridge—on foot—toward Cinderbrook Road and beyond that, the creek.

Tim and Craig stood on a narrow bridge over Butternut Creek under increasingly grayer skies. It would rain soon. There was that certain feel to the air, a moist dampness that signaled a storm. Tim, however, was not daunted by the threat of rain, his mind occupied by the grim task at hand. To their left, the creek flowed toward the city and, far beyond that, Oneida Lake. To their right, they could see the body. Trotting down the last small hill to level ground, they paused by a large mound of dirt. The mound blocked the entrance to a dirt path that led into the wilderness between the highway to the east and the neighborhood west of the creek. Following the track south, the two men came to the spot where the corpse lay against the creek bank on some rocks. Someone had obviously dumped her there.

Her pallor appeared bluish; the body bloated as if she had drowned. But when Dr. Logan pulled her out of the water a little and turned the corpse face-up on the dirt trail, Tim saw it. The small, reddish-brown stain of blood formed around a hole in the damp shirt. Tim cringed at the sight. That face. How unreal! Like an unmotivated puppet. Her mud-tangled hair. Eyes that stared blankly at nothing. Like the face of Medusa that even in death could turn a man into stone. Even now, Tim felt frozen to the spot, unable to stop staring.

"She looks terrible," Tim commented.

"She's dead, Tim. What did you expect?"

Tim glared at Craig.

"How long would you say she's been dead?"

"Purely a guess," Craig said, studying the corpse. "Looks to be about three days. An M.E. will need to verify that though."

"Thursday night," Tim concluded.

"You were right, too. She seems to have been shot right through the heart," Craig said.

He pointed to the small wound of dried, crusted blood. More blood stained the V-neck shirt she wore. After a pause, the doctor added, "This is terrible. Two murders committed in a neighborhood where everyone knows everyone else's business."

"You sound like Brenda Lysik."

"Do I?" said Craig, perturbed.

A sudden swift current caused Lisa's hair to separate from her head.

"What happened to her hair?" Tim said. He picked up a stick to examine the blond hair caught among the rocks. "It's a wig!"

The two looked at Lisa's body more carefully.

Craig pointed out, "Look at her hair. She wasn't a blond. She was a brunette."

Tim was shocked. So that was what Rachel had meant by Lisa's unnatural hair color.

Looking around Tim realized how isolated this spot was. The street dead ended at a farm that, as far as Tim knew, was uninhabited, and with no houses down here, it was quite out of the way.

Breaking the silence of the area, police sirens sounded, as two squad cars drove down Cinderbrook Drive. They stopped just past the bridge spanning the creek. Tim watched as Sgt. Griffin and another officer got out of their cars. Instructing the officer to investigate the area, Jack climbed over the mound at the entrance to the small dirt path. While the other officer began tracking some tire tracks embedded in the loose gravel, Jack addressed the doctor and Tim.

"For God's sake, this neighborhood has gone to hell. I might have known you'd be here, Tim," Jack grumbled.

"I know, but, well, a policeman is always on duty," said Tim.

Ignoring Tim's comment, Sgt. Jack Griffin addressed Craig, "How long has she been dead, doc?"

"I estimate three days."

"Be sure to investigate her house, Jack."

"What do you mean, Tim?"

"I mean that this is, or was, Lisa Collins, and she lived next door to the Stuarts, where you just came from."

"What?"

Before Tim could answer Jack, the other officer called to them. He led them to a red sports car, which had been abandoned further down Cinderbrook Drive in a small parking lot by an inoperative radio station.

"I found this car just sitting here," the officer reported. "The tires matched the tire tracks I was following. There're some keys in the ignition."

Tim whispered to Jack, "Lisa Collins had a red car like that."

Jack Griffin noticed the farmhouse next to a barn further down the road. He asked, "Who lives there?"

Tim answered, "No one. As far as I know."

Jack turned to the other officer.

"I'll get the keys out of the ignition and bag them. You go back to your car and radio for C.I.U. Oh, and call someone to have the car towed for inspection. Make routine investigations of the area, and check the farmhouse. I'm going to investigate the victim's house."

A good fifteen minutes later, Sgt. Griffin, Craig Logan, and Tim Dewitt arrived at the front door of Lisa Collins's house. The sergeant tried the set of keys that had been found in the car. After successfully unlocking the door, they entered to find the place in shambles.

"Damn it," the sergeant swore, reacting to the scene first.

Tim stepped carefully around the living room. Cushions and papers were strewn about. A few lamps and a table were overturned, and various knickknacks were shattered or lying broken on the floor near the shelves they'd once occupied. But something was wrong. Like it was all for show. Then he noticed a small leather handbag behind the couch. The purse's contents had partially spilled out.

"This couldn't have been a burglary," Tim said suddenly.

"And how can you be so sure, Tim?"

"Because this isn't missing." He crouched down by the expensive-looking handbag. He took a pen lying on the floor and used it to shift though the purse's contents. "This is Lisa's purse." Tim examined an envelope that had partially fallen out. Lifting the flap with his pen, he saw several crisp hundred-dollar bills. He counted it and said, "There's over five hundred dollars in here! No burglar in his right mind would leave this much money behind. A purse in plain view! This couldn't have been a real robbery."

"Perhaps the perpetrator was caught red-handed by the victim," Jack suggested. "He kills her and then dumps her body down by the creek."

"But why dump the purse or leave it here? Lisa likely would have had it with her. If she came home and surprised a burglar who then killed her, why not take the purse? And if the purse was here when he broke in, then . . ."

"Naturally, he would look in it first," said Jack, finishing Tim's line of reasoning.

"He seemed to have had plenty of time to ransack the place." Tim looked around at the mess and shook his head. "No, something's not right. The murder doesn't fit the scenario, the way I've heard it."

"All right, Tim. Enough's enough," Jack interrupted, rubbing his temples as if a headache were coming on. "We'll get the crime lab boys in here to check things out."

Tim knew the drill. He also knew that murders in the Town of Dewitt were rare occurrences. Very rare. There had only been two in the last eight years that he knew of, and both of those had been easy to wrap up. And they'd just discovered two bodies in one day!

"Hey! I found some bloodstains!"

Tim and Jack hurried over to the doorway, where Craig crouched by steps.

"I would say she was standing in the doorway when she was shot. The bloodstains here on the steps must be where she fell," Craig stated, pointing to dried blood staining the corner of the upper step. More blood stained the left side of the lower step.

"I'd say the shooter was standing approximately five feet away judging from the wound I examined, but I can't be certain. An autopsy would be more accurate."

Sgt. Griffin cleared his throat and said, "All right. Thank you for your help, doctor. You and Tim can go home. I'll call up extra units and finish up here. It's been a tiring day, I think."

The doctor nodded and left. Tim, however, stayed behind to ask, "You'll let me know if you find anything, right, Jack?"

"Yes, just go home, Tim. There's nothing more you can do here," said the sergeant impatiently. As Tim was about to go, Jack called after him, "I'll stop by tomorrow for that talk."

Tim walked up Stoneridge, feeling depressed. The thought of Lisa's corpse stuck in his mind like a discordant chord. She couldn't have been any older than he. How short life can be. *How short it is!* Tim shivered at the very idea of his own mortality. To live forever. How wonderful it would be, if it were possible. But then Tim recalled all the suffering in the world. He could not bear to see others suffer. Not even a hundred years of life could comfort him if he must witness the sufferings of others.

Finding himself standing at the end of the Stuarts' driveway, Tim decided he would check on Todd. They'd been best friends for so long, but Tim realized that they'd drifted apart the last couple years. Their lives had taken them in different directions. *How could it have happened*? *Busy lives*, he supposed. Though now, in some strange way, Fate had drawn them back together again on this street, and as he knocked on the front door, Tim fleetingly wondered to what end.

"Oh, hello, Tim," Georgia said. "You just missed your wife."

"Ms. Llewellyn?"

"I felt I should look after him. At least until his mother comes. I promised Marie, you know." She explained how she'd arranged things with Marie and how she expected Mrs. Stuart any minute. "But what brings you here? Todd's sleeping soundly now, and I'd hate to wake him."

In the light of all the recent tragedy, Georgia's face was a beacon of light in the gloom. An example of goodness still left in the world.

"Don't wake him. I just wanted to know how he's doing."

"Oh, he's fine. But is something wrong?" Georgia asked. Having delivered Tim as a babe nearly single- handed, she seemed to possess an insight into his thoughts and feelings.

Tim confided in her.

"Lisa Collins has been found dead down by the creek on Cinderbrook."

"Oh, dear. Another murder?" Georgia gasped. A groan from inside distracted her attention for a moment, but she soon addressed Tim, "I should check on him. The sedatives may be wearing off."

"That's okay, Ms. Llewellyn. I should be getting home anyway. I think the shock of two murders has finally gotten to me. Besides, it looks like rain."

Shaking her head, Georgia muttered, "How awful. Another murder," before she disappeared into the house to attend to her patient.

Outside, the wind rustled fallen leaf buds and grass clippings, as Tim made his way home. He looked up at the sky and quickened his pace. The clouds gathered like a potent force casting their presence over all below. They came bringing rain, and they would no longer be ignored. Indeed, the drops began to fall.

MONDAY

The morning after Rachel Stuart's murder and the discovery of Lisa Collins's body, Marie puttered about her kitchen waiting for the coffee maker to come to life. She'd spent a restless night tossing in bed, thinking too much about everything. About Rachel. About Todd. About murder.

She never should have left yesterday. She just needed some time away from, well, it didn't matter now. It had happened. She'd come home later than she'd planned yesterday afternoon only to hear that her sister-in-law was dead and Todd had been sedated. Rushing down the street to see him, she'd been thankful—though initially surprised—that Georgia Llewellyn had been looking after him. At least someone had been there for her brother, she'd thought, vexing herself for not being that person. She had tried talking to him, but he'd been groggy from the sedatives he'd been given and was uncommunicative to boot. She'd done what she could though, all the while feeling guilty that it wasn't enough.

As she poured her coffee, she considered checking on Todd again. Tim had gone out on an errand, so she'd have to leave a note. Searching, she found a working pen right away but no paper. Her frustration grew, but then she spotted some paper on the black lacquered cabinet by the front door. When she picked it up, she realized it was the envelope that had been delivered to Ms. Llewellyn's house by mistake. On closer examination, she noticed that the letter had been sent to Lisa Collins by Rachel Stuart!

Full of curiosity, Marie returned to the kitchen, where she sat down at the oak table. Since both the sender and receiver of the letter were dead, Marie opened the envelope and extracted the letter and read.

Lisa—I won't warn you again! Stay away from my husband. I would hate to have to tell the police what I know. And it's no use trying to blackmail me. What little "dirt"—as you put it—is hardly substantial evidence. My parents died in an automobile accident. *I would suggest you not say otherwise. And as for my so-called affair with Josh, I wouldn't go around spreading rumors if I were you. I have plenty of fascinating facts about some rather sordid business transactions you've been conducting. Concrete evidence. Now what do you think your sister would say if she knew you were supplying her husband with heroin? So I advise you to keep your mouth shut. If you tell my husband about Josh or interfere again, I will make you sorry.*

–Rachel Stuart

Marie gasped. What kind of woman had her brother married? Why on earth had she not seen it before? It was too much. Marie dropped the note on the table. What kind of hellish marriage had Todd been trapped in? Had he tried to . . .? No! She shook her head. Her brother would never harm anyone. She knew that. He didn't like confrontation, and he hated to hurt anyone's feelings. If only she hadn't been so busy with college and her wedding plans, maybe things would have been different.

Marie glared at the note. She wanted to crumple up that note and shred it, but knew she couldn't. Besides, what she really wanted to do was tell Rachel off! Of course, *that* wasn't possibly now. So why should she even care that Rachel was dead? Hadn't she gotten what she deserved?

"Oh, God. Todd, I'm sorry," she whispered.

Donna Marie Stuart couldn't coalesce a thought. She stood in her son's kitchen staring blankly at the pot of coffee she'd put on, struggling not to focus on the dripping brown liquid. Her hands with their perfectly manicured nails rose to rub gently at her temples. Perhaps she was getting a migraine. If only she could stop worrying about her son.

She'd looked in on him ten minutes ago. He had been lying in a tangle of sheets on his bed fast asleep. For a moment, she'd remembered him as a teenager when she would rouse him for school. He'd always been a night owl who loathed getting up early. How boyishly innocent he looked in his sleep. Even now, he reminded her of how few short years separated the grown man from the teenaged son.

She should have spoken up about her dislike of Rachel. That girl had smiled to her face while she lied through her teeth. Her son was too good for that manipulative bitch. If only she had put a stop to it, but she tried not to interfere in the lives of her children. She knew it wasn't her place to say anything. Her husband Zachary did enough of that for both of them.

Suddenly, Donna heard the doorbell. At first, she'd thought it was the coffee pot buzzing, but then noticed the coffee had long finished perking. Absently, she arranged her long brown hair more neatly, and hurried to answer the door.

"Hello, Tim. Is Marie not with you?"

"I let her sleep in. She had a rather restless night." He looked up the street at his house, hoping Marie was getting some much-needed rest. "I had an errand to run, and thought I'd stop by."

Tim noticed how haggard his mother-in-law looked but pretended he didn't. Donna had always been a model of perfection when it came to presenting herself—even now she put on a grand smile to welcome him inside—so it was disconcerting to see her tired amber-brown eyes and disheveled appearance. Tim noted for the umpteenth time how much Marie looked like her mother, whereas he knew Todd resembled his father more. Both mother and daughter were stylish and fashionable women. Even in her anxious state, Donna looked as if she'd merely exerted herself gardening and had hurried in to greet unexpected guests.

"So how are you and Marie?" she asked, gesturing for Tim to have a seat.

"Fine," Tim answered, as they sat on the couch in the living room. "How are you holding up?"

"Well enough. This is an awful nightmare really. I never liked Rachel, but I would never have wished her, well, dead. Zachary is concerned that people will think Todd did this. I just can't bear to think that."

Tim suspected Donna was covering for her husband's noticeable absence. He knew Zachary Stuart hated any semblance of scandal. Of course, he knew that Todd didn't get on well with his father any better than Tim did with his.

"I know Todd didn't do this," Tim said confidentially.

"But who then?"

"I don't know, Donna, but I will find out."

Donna sighed as if relieved of a burden. "Thank you. You two were always so close. I . . ." She paused, as if she didn't quite know how to proceed. "I know you both drifted somewhat apart after high school."

Tim looked away. He didn't want her to see the guilt he felt over that. "How is he?"

Her smile dissolved. She berated herself for getting carried away with false facades. Tim was family after all.

Tim had been her son's best friend in high school. After they graduated, she saw them together less and less as they pursued their goals in life. Still, she suspected Rachel was to blame for part of that. She recalled several occasions when she'd call to speak with her son only to be told by Rachel that he was busy or not home.

"I'm worried about him. He's not himself. You know how easy-going he is. Perhaps too easy-going, but nonetheless, Todd . . ." She paused again. "I think Todd has taken Rachel's death badly. It's as if he feels responsible for what happened. Of course, I told him that was ridiculous, but he wouldn't listen to me. I'm worried because Todd doesn't deal with stressful situations well."

"What do you mean?"

"Well, I don't know if Marie told you or not, but I think you ought to know. When my father died, he was devastated. You know how fond of his grandfather he was."

Tim nodded. He remembered.

Donna continued, "Todd began drinking. He had always been allowed to drink on special occasions, and I suppose that was our mistake for not realizing he had a problem. Apparently, Todd thought the alcohol would take away the pain."

"I never knew."

"No one did, but the family. Zachary didn't want it to become public because he was vying for district attorney at the time. So we kept it quiet. Fortunately, the worst of it happened over that summer."

Tim took in the information and realized why Donna was so upset. "Maybe if I talked to him?"

"I don't know," Donna replied. "He hasn't been very receptive to visitors. Ms. Llewellyn's really the only one who's been able to get through to him. She's been such a dear. He refuses to speak with me. But I would appreciate it if you could help."

"I'll try my best," Tim said gravely.

"I'll tell him you're here," said Donna, who disappeared up the stairs.

Tim waited in the living room, until she returned a few minutes later.

"He wants to talk to you," she said, somewhat surprised by her own news. "He's waiting for you upstairs in the den. It's the small room on the right."

"Right. Don't worry, I'll find it."

Tim walked up the stairs, which led from the living room to the second floor of the split-level house. He reached the den and found Todd sitting behind a desk with a faraway look on his face. Tim sat down opposite his friend and waited. He realized suddenly that this was probably the first time he'd been able to sit down and really talk to Todd since his friend had gotten married two years ago. They had been so close in high school, nearly inseparable. And yet he hadn't known about Todd's drinking problem. It disturbed him to think that he had let their relationship falter, that he might not have truly been the friend Todd had needed.

"Have you found out anything yet?"

"Pardon?"

"Have you figured out who killed Rachel?" Todd asked in desperation.

"No," Tim said sadly.

Todd pleaded, "You've got to find out, Tim. You've just got to."

Tim averted his eyes from the genuine pain he could see in Todd's puppy dog, brown eyes. After a few minutes of silence, Tim said, "Saturday night at the watch meeting, you told me that your marriage was a joke. You said your life was a living hell."

Todd felt these words sting him with guilt.

"I know," he said at last. "I may not have had the perfect marriage with Rachel, but I did love her. Yeah, she dominated me like a puppet. I knew that all too well. But I loved her. Sure, I knew she was having an affair with Josh, but I kept hoping she would change. That I could change her. I loved her, didn't I? Despite everything. That's why I stayed with her. To make our marriage work. I could never have killed her. I couldn't have. I . . . You've got to believe me, Tim. I'm being torn to pieces inside not knowing who killed her. I mean, my God! Danielle, then Rachel, and now I hear Lisa's dead, too?"

"Then why are you pushing your family away? Your mother is here to help you. Marie feels like you don't want to see her."

"Everyone I touch is cursed. Tim, they're all dead! Everyone I've ever loved . . ." He started sobbing.

Tim sucked in a breath. Hearing his best friend cried was gut-wrenching. Todd had always been that cheerful, playful guy. The one that everyone had always wanted to be around. He was the last person Tim would have expected to cry. But then life had changed for them both since graduating high school, hadn't it?

Just then Georgia Llewellyn arrived to check on him. When she saw her patient's distraught state, she immediately went to his side for support. She then said to Tim, "Maybe you had better go. He really ought to rest now. He hasn't slept well since Dr. Logan gave him that sedative after, well, I don't dare give him anything."

Dazed, Tim nodded and returned downstairs to the living room, where Donna sat on the couch. She rose to her feet as he entered.

"Well?" she asked hopefully.

Tim shook his head sorrowfully.

"I think he just needs time to grieve. I'm sure it'll take time, but he'll heal. He is strong, Donna."

"He can't go on like this."

"I know," Tim said. "This murderer has gone too far. He's not only taken the lives of two, possibly three, people, but he's wreaking havoc on the lives of everyone affected by these deaths. I will find out who did this."

David Yates had driven home but had yet to get out of his car. Instead, he sat idly strumming the steering wheel. He knew she must be watching him from behind the living room curtains. He didn't want to face her. He'd had enough confrontations for one day. His mind grew numb. He knew he'd have to face her sooner or later. Slouching in the driver's seat, he let his hand fumble for the door. He climbed out of the sedan and staggered up the front steps. He was on automatic pilot. His vision blurred and refocused and his hand shook as he tried to unlock the front door. It swung open on him unexpectedly.

"Why are you home so early, David?" Linda asked shrilly.

"It's nothing."

Linda scrutinized his blue-gray eyes before he averted his gaze. Her heart sank as she realized the one thing she had feared all along.

"Where did you get the heroin?"

"I didn't . . . I'm not on anything."

"Don't lie to me, David! I can see it in your eyes."

"All right, then. Damn it! I got fired today."

"What?"

"Yeah," David huffed. "Grandaddy hasn't been pleased with my performance. He says my attitude's a problem. I'm not taking enough time to learn the business. It's all my fault and all that crap. He doesn't care about me, and he never did. It's just the same old, same old. He cares more about those damned antiques of his than he does me."

"He gave you a chance when no one else would."

"Oh, so you think I'm worthless, too? Hah! Big surprise. I should have known."

"God, David, you had to start using again, didn't you? You were doing so well in rehab. Why now?"

"Damn it. You know why. I went to college with the hope of becoming a musician. I lost out on that when I went into rehab. Along comes Grandaddy offering to take me into the family business. He'll give me a chance. Sure, no problem. Do you know how much I hate antiques? It's all so pretentious! All I have ever wanted was to be a musician. When that was taken away from me, I went nuts. I couldn't go on living like that! I had to find a way out. Surely you can understand that? You of all people?"

"No, I don't understand! You're just making up excuses for the real reason. You couldn't have Danielle, and you started beating up on yourself. It's her fault."

David slapped her across the face. "Don't ever say that! Danielle was an angel. It was that bitch, Rachel. God, I'm glad she's dead, but Danielle . . . She loved me, Lisa."

"Linda."

David collapsed on the couch and held his head in his heads.

"God, I'm sorry. I just . . . I don't know what's come over me."

"It's the drugs, David. I never should have let you take them up again," Linda sobbed.

David stared at her dumbfounded. She started pleading with him to get help. She wanted him to go away again. Sure, shut him up in rehab where he wouldn't be a bother. That wasn't going to happen.

He left the house, slamming the door. She ran after him, but it was too late. He pulled out of the driveway. Before driving off, he saw her throw up her hands in disgust and stalk back inside.

Later that afternoon, Sgt. Jack Griffin sat in the Dewitts' living room, reading the letter from Rachel Stuart to Lisa

Collins. Tim had explained how Georgia Llewellyn had given him the letter and how his wife had come to open it. Now he waited for Jack's thoughts. Jack, however, was not forthcoming. He stared out the window.

"Well?"

"I'm sorry, Tim. My mind's wandering," Jack mumbled. Speaking more clearly, he continued, "It strikes me as ironic that you should find this. I found some rather incriminating evidence in Lisa's purse that linked Rachel Stuart to some hired thug who may have rigged her parents' car. I'm waiting to hear back from the Utica police on it."

"So what else did you find?"

"The gun that killed her, as the autopsy is sure to prove," he said solemnly. "It was under the couch. A Taurus Model 85 5- shot revolver, .38 Special," answered Jack Griffin, who had an extensive knowledge of firearms, which allowed him to easily identify several types of them. "I also ran a check of who in the neighborhood has a registered gun. We've found records for Col. Hawthorne, Dr. Icarios, Dr. Logan, Todd Stuart, and Mr. Deveraux. The make and model may be Mr. Deveraux's, but we're waiting for the ballistic report first. However, it's a strong likelihood the gun we found is the murder weapon. We even found a slug in the door, which looks like the remnants of a .38 special. But like I said we have to wait for the ballistic reports to be certain. Still, I'll bet it's Deveraux' gun."

Tim cocked a brow at his friend and mentor quizzically. Jack's fervor hinted at an animosity toward Joshua Deveraux that made him wonder.

"Anything else?" he asked.

"As a matter of fact, yes," Jack said. "It's rather curious, too. There was a scalpel with dried blood on it. Now that doesn't strike me as the sort of thing most people have lying about the house. Lisa wasn't a medical student, was she?"

"No."

"I didn't think so. I sent it down for analysis. Dr. Icarios is anxious to work on the case. Of course, I'm a bit reluctant to let him. His wife was holding that shovel when Rachel Stuart's body was discovered. It's not that we suspect either of them, but I don't want to botch this one. Double homicides are not commonplace in the Town of DeWitt, and local residents have already voiced their concern with the Town Board and in the papers."

"So who's handling the case?"

"One of the assistants to the medical examiner."

"Will Dr. Icarios see the results?"

"He'll get to review them, but at that point there's not much he can do."

"You mean he can't tamper with the evidence."

"Hey, personally, I don't think the Icarioses have anything to do with this case. I know his wife was holding the shovel, but that Lysik guy's explanation can't be overlooked. Besides, Dr. Icarios did raise that stink about Danielle Deveraux's death."

"What happened in that?" Tim asked, hoping to learn more about the reason behind Jack's sudden fervor a moment ago.

"Deveraux claimed he found his wife dead in the bathtub when he got home late from work. He claimed he'd gotten a flat tire, and his story, on the surface, checked out. But there were some irregularities. The autopsy discovered that his wife had suffered a blow to the head. That could be explained by her possibly slipping in the tub. The problem really lies in the fact that the bloody razor—one of those old-fashioned men's razors—was found too far away from her. Plus, Dr. Icarios wasn't convinced. He couldn't be certain, but he wondered if the razor had been planted. In fact, when he heard about the scalpel we found yesterday, he became excited. He suggested the scalpel be tested for traces of Mrs. Deveraux's blood. We'll do it to humor him, but I can't imagine it wasn't the razor we found. I doubt the murderer would go to all that trouble," Jack said grimly.

"I guess it does sound fantastic," Tim conceded.

"Yes, well, is there any more information you can give me?"

"Jack, I've barely had a chance to process it all. But you might want to talk to your son."

"Why?" Jack asked, alarmed. "He doesn't have anything to do with this, does he?"

"Apparently he was playing basketball with D.J. Logan around the time Rachel Stuart was murdered."

"All right, Tim. I'll talk to him. Right now, I want to see where those reports stand and see if I can't hurry things up a bit. Sorry I can't stay longer, but I'll stop by tomorrow for that little chat. I want to know what's been going on around here."

"I promise I'll fill you in on all the details."

Jack stood up and strode to the front door. He reached for the doorknob and paused. He turned and faced Tim.

"I know I don't have to say this, but be careful, Tim. I don't want you to go snooping around and becoming victim number three. Follow procedures. That's what they're there for. After all, it took a cunning and bold killer to kill Rachel Stuart in broad daylight like that."

Jack opened the front door and almost collided with Marie Dewitt, who struggled with a couple grocery bags as she searched her purse for her keys. Marie looked up at Jack and exclaimed, "Jack Griffin?! I wondered whose car that was in the driveway. I haven't seen you since the wedding reception. How are you?"

"Great. Here let me help you with that," Jack said, as he took the two grocery bags Marie was carrying.

Tim jumped up to help. "Are there more out in the car?"

Marie shook her head, as she asked Jack, "So what brings you here to visit?"

"Business. I wish I could stay, Marie," he said, "but I can't. I'm sure Tim will fill you in on what happened."

Once Jack had left, Tim came over and helped Marie unpack the groceries.

"Did you check in on Todd?" he asked.

Marie nodded. She blinked her eyes, which threatened to tear up. "I got a few of these things for him," she said, indicating a few frozen dinners, some canned vegetables, and a carton of eggs. "I don't know if I can face him again, though. He seemed angry at me."

Tim came and stood behind her, hugging her.

"I'm sure he's not angry at you. He's just trying to cope."

"I haven't been there for him."

Tim turned her around to face him. "Neither of us have," he said, looking into her brown eyes. He noticed she'd been crying again recently.

"I shouldn't have left so abruptly yesterday. I should have come back sooner."

"You couldn't have known what was going to happen," Tim said, as she rested her head against his shoulder. He hoped he sounded reassuring. He'd been shaken by his own visit to Todd that morning.

"I know we haven't had much time to talk since yesterday."

Tim frowned as he remembered. After their stupid argument yesterday morning, Marie had driven off. He'd later learned she'd gone shopping with her former college roommate, Janessa. She'd been blithely spending money while he discovered two dead bodies in their neighborhood and dealt with the fallout. When he'd finally returned home, he saw the bags of clothes and shoes, and the sight had rankled him. But then he saw her sitting at the dining room table crying. One of the neighbors had called her, and she'd gone to see Todd. Georgia Llewellyn had said he'd just missed her when he'd stopped by. Seeing her crying had rent his heart, and he'd gone to her and forgot everything else.

"Sit down," he said now. "It's time you heard what happened."

They sat down at the kitchen table, and Tim quickly related the events of yesterday. He finished his narrative with a more detailed account of the discovery of the two dead bodies, the search of Lisa's house, and Jack's visit this afternoon.

"It's incredible! It's like some movie or story that isn't real. But why didn't you tell me all this last night?"

"With everything that happened? Besides, you looked kinda depressed after talking to Todd." He thought about what he'd seen yesterday, and shook his head. "No, I wish it were just that, but it isn't," he confessed. "I saw both dead bodies with my own eyes. It's a nerve-wracking sight. I don't know if I'll ever get used to it. At least I didn't throw up like some rookie." He smiled grimly. "But, you know, I've been having second thoughts about being a cop."

Marie's eyes widened, and she nearly gasped.

"I thought you always wanted to be a cop? You were so gun ho about it after high school."

"I was. I guess I feel rattled because these are people I know who are dead. I wasn't prepared for that. They talk about the personal toll of the job, but I don't think it's really hit me before now."

Marie reached across the table and held his hand.

"I should stop being morbid, shouldn't I?"

She nodded. "Is there anything I can do?"

"Why should you snoop about? Leave everything to the police and me."

Marie seemed amused by his questions.

"I've always felt that the police need a little extra cooperation at times. This is one of them. But, more important, I want to know who did it. I can't say I liked Rachel because

I didn't, but I worry about Todd. What this could do to his reputation. What it could do to all our reputations."

"Marie, I don't want to see you hurt. Curiosity killed the cat, you know."

"Then I'll just have to live with the fact that I'll only have eight lives left. Besides, I was involved with this little escapade from its beginning. And remember, I saw some of what your grandmother heard. I've also been able to hunt around and ask inconspicuous questions that the police won't be able to ask now; we've both had that opportunity. People didn't suspect anything . . ." She seemed to be searching for the right word. "Amiss. Now, everyone, the murderer especially, will be careful of what he or she says because, in a murder case like this, everyone comes under suspicion. Gossip on this street is rampant, and lies may come out. You and I heard the truth, so to speak, before it becomes twisted."

"I get that. But—"

"You also understand," Marie continued, undaunted, "that you could fall under suspicion? You were in the neighborhood when Rachel was murdered."

"You can't be serious?" Tim said, flabbergasted.

"But it's true! I may be suspected. Granted, these suspicions may be ridiculous, but unless the truth is known . . . everyone is guilty."

"I don't understand."

"Let me put it to you this way. Remember when our class got in trouble in the eighth grade? One of us had broken a window, and no one owned up to having done it? We all would have gotten a detention if Miss Sparrow, who said she had witnessed the incident, hadn't frightened what's-his- name into telling the truth. The same holds true in this situation. Everyone had an opportunity to commit the deed. But if the guilty person doesn't own up to what he or she's done, then everybody suffers. Innocent people shouldn't have something like this hanging over them like a shadow.

Think of D.J.'s father or Mr. Lysik. What would their patients think? What about Todd? People are always ready to suspect the spouse first of all. No, the reputation of the person is ruined! I don't want that to happen. Not to others, not to you, and not to me. This murderer should not be allowed to get away with that!"

Marie's eyes blazed with an intensity Tim had never seen before. Her manner, however, changed as she continued calmly, "So how can I help you?"

"Well," Tim said, "We can't do much of anything now. Oh, now wait a minute."

"What is it?"

"It was something you said, Marie. I just realized its impact now."

Marie repeated her question, which Tim then finally answered, "The bridge game. Grandma Edith's always told me how the ladies like to gossip about recent events during the game. There's no way they would feel secure discussing the murders if I were present. I suspect there aren't many people who'd be forthcoming with me now. Everyone must know I'm a cop."

"So what do you want me to do?" Marie asked, sensing an ulterior motive in Tim's speech.

"Play bridge."

"Oh, come on, Tim. You've tried to teach me the game before, but I told you I'm no good at cards."

"What time is it now?"

Looking at her watch, Marie answered, "Just a little after four."

"Well, the game isn't until tomorrow night. We'll have plenty of time to cram you with everything you need to know in order to play bridge."

"But what should I say about you? They might ask why you didn't come. After all, you're the bridge player."

"Just say I have a headache or something. You're better at lying than I am."

"Gee, thanks."

"Come on, Marie. It's gonna take you a while to pick this up."

"Oh, all right," Marie said, surrendering. "Get a deck of cards."

TUESDAY

Tuesday morning, Sgt. Jack Griffin knocked on the front door of Sonya Schwartz's house. As he waited on the steps, he admired the brick façade, unusual for the homes in the Cinderbrook development. Looking down the street, he saw that Stoneridge Drive appeared quiet and peaceful now. He wondered how things had gone so wrong?

"Can I help you?"

Jack appraised the woman standing in the white doorframe. Dressed in russet-brown clothes and sensible brown shoes, she regarded him with steady, brown eyes. Intelligent eyes.

"My name is Sergeant Jack Griffin. I'm with the DeWitt Police, and we've been investigating the deaths of Rachel Stuart and Lisa Collins. May I come in?"

Sonya ushered him into her living room where they sat in the armchairs by the bay window.

"I understand you were Rachel Stuart's aunt?"

"Y-yes," Sonya said hesitantly.

"I need to ask you were you were Sunday morning."

"I went to Wegmans."

Everyone knew that Wegmans was the place to get groceries in the Eastern suburbs, and Jack knew it was commonplace to run into friends or neighbors while shopping there. No doubt that meant Sonya had a solid alibi.

"I still have my receipts," volunteered Sonya, who'd seen the sergeant frowning.

"Yes, we may need to see them."

"Are you saying I'm a suspect in my niece's murder, Sergeant?"

"Everyone on this street is considered a suspect, Mrs. Schwartz. But it would appear that you had more motive than most."

"Oh?"

"Some evidence has come to light implicating your niece in planning her parents' fatal accident. Your brother was killed in that car crash because his brakes failed."

Tears came to Sonya's eyes.

"Yes. My poor brother and sister-in-law died so that my niece could get their money. I've known for some time that she had a hand in it. I just couldn't prove it."

The sergeant had detected a trace of a New Yawk accent in her voice. The accent became more prominent now.

"I tried to get the Utica police to look into their deaths, but they didn't find anything conclusive. It's not like I could spend all day in Utica trying to get them to keep looking for the truth. I have kids to look after. But my poor brother didn't deserve . . ." She choked back a cry. She took a moment to calm herself. "I confronted my niece. You should know that. I accused her of her parents' murder."

"When was this?"

"Last week. It was Wednesday."

A moment of silence ensued while Jack consulted his notes and debated how much he was willing to reveal. Sonya, meanwhile, glanced out the window.

"Rachel was a self-absorbed child," Sonya said. "She was selfish and self-centered. If she hadn't been killed, I would have suspected her of killing that Lisa Collins girl. They were roommates at college, but they didn't get along. Rachel didn't get along with a lot of people."

"I'm sorry to tell you that a note has been recovered suggesting your niece's complicity in her parents' murder." Jack referred to his notes about another matter. "We've also been tracking some monetary transactions that your niece made to a mechanic in Utica. Apparently, this man was an ex-boyfriend of Rachel's from high school. The Utica police picked him up last night. This morning he confessed to tampering with your brother's car."

Sonya dropped her head in grief, and her brown eyes welled up with tears. She pulled a tissue from the sleeve of her pullover and dried the corner of her eyes. And then she began to smile.

At last, Sonya, her voice still choked with emotion, said, "I suspected for so long. To know that I was right . . ." She paused, and then added angrily, "But it doesn't bring back my brother, does it?"

Jack didn't know how to answer that question.

"You should know," Sonya said, "it was Lisa Collins who said she knew Rachel had had my brother's car tampered with. She promised me that she had proof, but I never saw it."

"Did you tell Rachel?"

"I said someone had come forward with evidence."

Jack pondered this information. Could Rachel have confronted Lisa? But if Rachel killed Lisa, then who killed her? Their deaths had to be related.

"It doesn't make sense," he muttered.

"Excuse me, sergeant?"

"It's nothing," Jack said. "Did Rachel's husband know anything about your niece's involvement in her parents' death?"

"Oh, I doubt it. I think she kept a lot of things from him. I don't think he would have stayed with her if he'd known."

"There has been some suggestion that Rachel was having an affair," Jack stated.

"I wouldn't be surprised. Rachel was never satisfied with her lot in life."

"Is there anyone you can think of who would want Rachel dead?"

"Besides me?" Sonya asked wryly. "I wouldn't like to say. I really can't imagine anyone on this street going so far as to kill . . ."

"Is there something you remember?" Jack prodded.

"I heard a shovel was used to kill my niece."

Jack nearly cracked a smile. The speed of gossip in this neighborhood still amazed him.

"Yes. Claudia Icarios admitted the shovel was hers. Your niece had borrowed it sometime earlier. We didn't find any prints on the shovel other than those belonging to Claudia and the vic—" Jack quickly corrected himself. "Your niece. We believe her killer used gloves."

"But don't you think it strange?"

"Sorry?" Jack said, bewildered.

"Well, it's just odd. I don't think Claudia liked my niece. Why would Rachel borrow a shovel from her? They're not even next-door neighbors. She could have gotten one from Dr. Logan or . . ."

"Lisa?"

"Well, perhaps not Lisa. But she was on friendly terms with Mr. Deveraux across the street. Why borrow the shovel from Claudia?"

"I can't answer that."

"I wonder if she was up to something." Sonya looked out the bay window and saw Claudia kneeling beside her mailbox and tending to some irises planted there. "Rachel tended to do things for a reason," she muttered.

"Is it possible your niece might have been blackmailing someone?"

Sonja's jaw dropped open. "Was she? I wouldn't be surprised."

"I should probably get going," Jack said as he stood up. "There are a few other people I need to talk to. Thank you for your time."

"Oh," Sonya said. "Of course."

She showed the sergeant to the door.

"I noticed your family is not at home," Jack said, as Sonya opened the door.

"They're in Albany visiting family."

"For Passover, yes?"

Sonya nodded.

"And you didn't go with them?"

Sonya smiled warmly. "I had some unfinished business."

"With your niece?" Jack asked.

The smile crumbled.

When Sonya didn't answer, Jack said, "I trust you won't leave town."

Sonya's brown eyes looked directly into Jack's blue-green eyes.

"No, Sergeant. I don't plan on going anywhere."

Satisfied for now, Jack left. He walked to the end of the Schwartz's driveway and headed down the street. He paused when he reached the Esterhazys' house. It amazed him that someone who knew his wife lived there. He was tempted to stop by and chat about Justine, but Tim had told him about Anne Esterhazy's penchant for rambling on and he didn't have the time right now.

He continued on and walked up to the white house with wood trim that belonged to the Hawthornes. While he waited for someone to answer the door, he noticed that he couldn't see much down the street. Several yew bushes lined the sidewalk. The effect created a semi-secluded area that lent the slate-tiled porch and front steps some privacy from prying eyes.

"Yes, can I help you?" Mildred said, opening the door. "Oh, it's you, Sergeant. What brings you here?"

"Just following up on some leads."

Mildred arched an eyebrow. "Won't you come in?"

She ushered him into the kitchen, which was located at the front of her house. Jack noticed a well-apportioned living room beyond and saw an open archway leading presumably to the dining room.

"I understand that your husband reported a Colt Government Model gun stolen when your house was robbed."

"Did he now?" Mildred appeared less than thrilled. "I don't recall that being on the report I submitted."

"Perhaps he added it?" Jack suggested. "In any event, a gun matching your husband's was discovered at a pawn shop in East Syracuse during our routine investigations."

"How can you be sure it's his?"

"The serial number matches the one your husband provided."

Through clenched teeth, Mildred mumbled, "I can't believe he remembered that."

"The manager at the pawnshop described the woman who dropped off the gun."

Mildred pre-empted the sergeant. "Fine. Yes, it was me. I don't like guns, and I saw the burglary as an opportunity to get rid of it."

"You realize that falsely reporting stolen goods is considered a crime."

"I didn't do anything of the kind."

"But your husband did," Jack said pointedly.

"Well," Mildred said, indignant, "that was clearly a mistake."

Jack was silent. He looked hard at Mildred and tried to read her. She returned his gaze with a mix of disdain and indifference.

"I understand your husband likes to bet on the horses."

Off-track betting was allowed in the county to the east of Onondaga. In fact, both of the Hawthornes enjoyed attending the races at Vernon Downs during the summer months.

"What exactly are you implying, Sergeant?"

Jack kept his tone neutral. "A man in debt often finds means to pay them if he's desperate enough."

Mildred's eyes flashed with anger. "My husband is a respected veteran. I would think you would show more courtesy than to imply he was a common thief. Our house was robbed. I suggest you stop wasting time harassing a decorated colonel's wife and do your job." She showed him the door. "Good day," she added curtly.

Jack left the Hawthornes' house. This wasn't exactly a part of his job he enjoyed. His instincts told him the colonel and his wife hadn't really done anything wrong, but it was his job to be thorough. He looked through his notepad briefly and sighed.

Time to check the status of the pending autopsies.

Dressed in shorts and a sweat-soaked T-shirt, Craig Logan jogged down Stoneridge Drive. As he neared the Icarioses' house, he saw Claudia pulling weeds from amongst the irises surrounding her mailbox. She straightened up as his shadow fell upon her.

"Oh, hello, Dr. Logan. It's turning out to be a beautiful day since the rain cleared. Perfect weather for gardening. Were you out jogging again?"

Claudia proffered a hand and Craig helped her to her feet.

"Hello, Claudia. Is your husband home?"

"Oh, no, Philbin's still at work. I thought you knew he was working late today. I think he's anxious to get the autopsy results on, well, our unfortunate neighbors."

"I thought he had recused himself from the case? Conflict of interest or something," Craig said, wiping sweat from his brow.

"Oh, he has. One of the assistant medical examiners is working on the case. Philbin just expects to see a copy of the final results. He wants this whole thing cleared up so our lives can go back to normal."

Craig nodded in understanding. He, too, would like to see a resolution to these murders.

As adjusted her gardening gloves, Claudia asked, "What was it you wanted to see my husband about? I could relay the message."

Craig lied. "Just some professional questions about Mr. Stuart."

Claudia peered into Craig's blue-gray eyes. Perhaps he was being too quick with his answers. He didn't want to be perceived as mendacious.

"Yes. That is a shame," Claudia said, never taking her eyes from Craig's. "I was there, you know. When he had his breakdown. Is he any better?"

"I think he is very troubled young man," Craig said. Her scrutinizing gaze unnerved him and he averted his eyes.

"Shouldn't you see Mr. Lysik then? He's a psychiatrist or psychologist. I would think depression would be—"

"To be honest," Craig interrupted, "I don't exactly relish the idea of going to Shane for help just now."

Claudia frowned.

"But why? I thought you and Mr. Lysik were on friendly terms."

"Er ..." Craig wavered about telling her, but he'd come to know and trust the Icarioses since his arrival on Stoneridge last summer.

"Well, you know that Shane introduced me to Lisa."

"No. No, I didn't," Claudia said.

He hesitated to continue. He'd piqued her curiosity. Shane had been a good friend to him since he'd moved to Stoneridge. They shared that innate Texas welcoming demeanor, but . . .

"It was at the hospital. Shane had been a teaching assistant at the University in the psychology department, and apparently Lisa had been one of his students. She had stopped by to visit him at work, and he introduced us."

"Was she seeing him professionally?"

For a moment, Craig was startled that Claudia should be so astute.

"Oh, you mean was she a patient of his? No, nothing like that. She was just saying hello to one of her former TAs. The three of us had lunch that day . . . oh, it must have been three, four months ago. Shane was called back to the hospital unexpectedly, and Lisa and I . . ."

"You dated her."

"Yes," Craig admitted. He wasn't particularly proud of it now, but he'd been flattered by the attentions of a very pretty younger woman then. "It was great at first," he said. "Then I realized I wasn't the only guy on her social calendar."

He recalled his last date with Lisa a couple weeks ago. It still angered him to think how callous she had been. He'd confronted her about her other boyfriends, in particular, about her married boyfriend, Shane. He'd seen them share a kiss outside an eatery near the hospital one night. She'd brushed him off, saying she didn't have time for jealous men. He'd been so angry then. Presently, he looked at Claudia and saw her large hazel eyes regarding him quizzically. "Sorry. I didn't mean to burden you."

"Oh, that's all right."

"What is it?" Craig asked, noticing her faraway look.

"It's strange really. You and Mr. Lysik both work at Upstate Hospital. Mrs. Esterhazy is a nurse there, and Evelyn Martino works at the medical college there. Mr. Lysik taught at the University, and Lisa, the Stuarts, the Yateses, that poor Danielle Deveraux, and Marie Dewitt all went there. Then Marie is Todd Stuart's sister, Evelyn is his aunt, and then Mildred . . . well, it all just seems so unbelievable. Don't you think?'

Craig shrugged. "I suppose."

"It's almost as if fate intervened and brought all this about."

Craig snorted. “If you believe in that sort of thing.”

“Well, if you’ll excuse me,” Claudia said. “I should get back to weeding. I finally bought a new shovel. I just couldn’t bear the idea of . . . well, I’m anxious to get my new rose bushes firmly planted before sundown.”

“I’ll see you later, Claudia. And tell your husband hello.”

Craig was about to pass on by, when Claudia remarked, “Oh, didn’t you want to talk to Philbin?”

“Oh, it doesn’t really matter.”

Craig left his neighbor to her gardening and continued on down the street. He caught sight of Georgia Llewellyn disappearing into Todd Stuart’s house and started thinking about what she had said yesterday morning. He’d gone to check on the young Mr. Stuart and had gotten into an unwelcome conversation. But what had she said that had rattled him so?

“I’m so glad you came by, Dr. Logan. I’m just not sure what to do. I didn’t dare give Mr. Stuart any more of the sedative. I don’t think it’s good for him, but he’s been very agitated. And his mother keeps asking me all these questions. I’ve just forgotten so much of my training. I haven’t nursed anyone in so long. It’s all because of that Lisa Collins. She never should have come here in the first place. And see, someone killed her. It could be Mr. Deveraux, but really it’s not him I’m wondering about. It’s you. *You went out with her a few times, didn’t you? And I seem to remember that you own a gun.”*

Georgia Llewellyn’s words keep going around in his head. Then suddenly he remembered something Tim had said. *“Evelyn Martino saw the car that drove up the street that night. She said it was a red car. So I wasn’t dreaming or mistaken. It wasn’t your red sports car that Evelyn saw.”*

What were they trying to imply? Did they know something? And why had Claudia given him such a suspicious look? Yes, he’d lied to her about his motives for wanting to talk with her husband, but still. He recalled seeing Claudia talking with that Tim Dewitt. What ideas was he filling her head with? Was Tim trying to pin the blame on him?

As he reached his front door, Craig was getting increasingly irritated. He was beginning to wish Tim had never moved here. Ha! What was it Brenda Lysik had said at the Neighborhood Watch Meeting? They had started talking about allergies somehow. Didn't she say that Tim was allergic to bee stings? How did she happen to know that? Well, he supposed it didn't matter. Craig Logan entered his home with a wry smile on his face.

Marie's head was spinning with bids of spades, hearts, diamonds, and clubs. She feared she had somehow discovered the rabbit hole that led to Alice's Wonderland, and the army of cards was chasing her. She could hear the shrill voice of the Queen of Hearts shouting out, "One No Trump! Off with her head! She doesn't know how to bid." And then the other queens' high-pitched shrieks and murmurs echoed the Queen of Hearts' sentiments.

What was she doing? Marie woke up and rubbed her eyelids with her fingertips. She'd spent much of the last twenty-four hours learning to play Bridge, and soon it would be time to head next door to her aunt's house for a real game. She had insisted on a two-hour nap so that her mind would be sharp for tonight's anticipated gossip, but now she wished she hadn't. She'd loved *Alice's Adventures in Wonderland* and its sequel, *Through the Looking Glass*. Her eighth grade class had been assigned the book in English class. While most of the boys in the class, including Tim, had joked about the real meaning behind, *Eat me*, *Drink Me*, the Caterpillar's Hookah . . . *wink, wink* . . . she had simply enjoyed the fantasy. She'd never imagined it could be a nightmare. But then, wasn't this whole murder case just that?

"Knock, knock."

Marie looked up and saw Tim standing in the bedroom doorway.

"You don't want to oversleep for the big game," he said with a smirk.

"I'm getting up."

She climbed out of bed and dragged herself over to her vanity. Her hair was a mess and her clothes were too rumpled. She looked for her alarm clock, the one she'd forgotten to set.

"It's six-thirty," Tim said helpfully.

Marie restrained herself from throwing a cosmetic's bottle at him. He got the hint, though, and left her alone to get ready. Thirty minutes later, Marie had tidied her hair and changed into a peach blouse and suede skirt. Tim kissed her and wished her good luck, and she was on her way. She walked up to her Aunt Evelyn's house next door and rang the doorbell.

"Marie, I'm so glad you could come."

Evelyn Martino ushered her niece inside, and Marie saw the freshly polished dining room table, the bright glow of the crystal chandelier above it, and the Chippendale chairs pulled out in readiness. Marie hadn't been to her aunt's house in some time, but it was much the same as she remembered. The powder-blue carpeting, the crisp white walls, the dark, polished-wood furniture. It all reminded Marie of the elegant movie sets of the 1950s, an era she knew her aunt favored.

"Angela was just telling me that she was teaching you how to play Bridge earlier today," Evelyn said as she smoothed down her lavender dress, one Marie fancied Doris Day would have worn.

Marie noted her aunt's careful coiffed jet black hair, which was done up in a stylish chignon, before she turned to say hello to Angela Sparrow, who sat on the sofa in living room.

Angela had helped Tim teach Marie the ins and outs of bidding after a doctor's visit in the morning. She was able to forego crutches in favor of a silver-knobbed cane—made of cherry wood—that had belonged to her late mother.

"You should have called me, dear," Evelyn said. "Although I did have a hair appointment this afternoon, and I must admit that Angela is the better player." Evelyn turned to face Miss Sparrow. "It's just so nice that you're able to get around so well. I thought you would be laid up for some time."

"My ankle's much better, thank you. I am grateful that it is; after all, I wouldn't want to miss this bridge game," Angela said. Her implication was not lost on either Marie or her aunt. Both realized that this bridge game was still being held for the sheer desire to ferret information and opinions out of neighbors.

Evelyn nodded as she turned to her niece. "Where's Tim, Marie? I thought he was coming tonight."

"He's got a headache, so he suggested I come to take his place."

"Oh, that's too bad," Evelyn said. "There'll be just the five of us then, I'm afraid."

Marie detected her aunt's disappointed tone. Evelyn loved hosting lavish parties. She judged the success of her parties by the number of those who came and the number of those who left in chipper spirits than they'd arrived. Five was not a party.

Marie recalled past parties that her aunt had hosted. They'd always been elegant affairs with a sort of Hollywood glamour, which her aunt strived to embody. But now, as she looked around, Marie realized that glamour was dated. Like time had frozen in Evelyn's house and she had stepped into a film or TV set from that era when people had their cocktails in hand after work on a weekday evening.

"I'm surprised that Mildred isn't here. She's always early when it comes to bridge games," Angela noted.

Evelyn answered, "Oh, Mildred called earlier. She and Martin have that board meeting tonight. It seems it's rather important. Or at least I got that impression. I didn't even know the Hawthornes were on the board of DeWitt Enterprises. I thought it was family-owned."

Evelyn arched her brow questioningly in Marie's direction.

"Don't look at me. I just married into the family. I don't know anything about the business."

"Well, Brenda Lysik is the recording secretary at the meeting or something," Evelyn said. "So she won't be here tonight either."

"Who else is coming?" Angela inquired.

"We're just waiting for Claudia and Georgia."

"Ms. Llewellyn? I didn't know she could play bridge," Marie said.

"Yes," Angela said. "Quite well in fact. She plays in a local league, so she hasn't really gotten involved with our neighborhood set. But she called me last night to ask about our game. I guess she's tired of driving so far to her league games. I just told her to call Evelyn."

"Which she did," Evelyn said. "And I said that of course she was welcome to come. We're always in search of new players because not everyone can attend our little tournaments all the time. Like tonight."

The doorbell rang again, and Evelyn excused herself.

Angela whispered to Marie, "Whenever your aunt is hosting our bridge game, she acts like Grace Kelly, but plays like Lady Macbeth."

"My aunt's always been like that when hosting a party," Marie commented. "I guess she takes after my grandmother in that respect. I don't think I've ever seen her play bridge though."

"Mildred and Claudia are both formidable opponents, too. In fact, any combination of the three is nerve-racking to say the least."

Evelyn Martino, unaware of the comments made behind her back, greeted her newly arrived guests.

"Welcome to our game, Georgia," Evelyn said as she led Georgia and Claudia inside. "I'm afraid we are a bit short-handed tonight, so we will have to deal out."

"Oh, that's quite all right, Evelyn. I'm sure the rubbers will prove most entertaining."

Marie noticed Georgia had the glint of a ruthless, expert player in her eyes. Feeling out of her league when it came to bridge, Marie only hoped she could hold her own as she focused on learning what secrets her neighbors might be holding onto.

"Shall we sit down, everyone?" Evelyn asked, as she gestured toward her dining room table.

The dark surface of the colonial table gleamed with polish. Four chairs, high-quality replicas of the Chippendale chairs of the late 1700s, were arranged perpendicular to each other. A fifth, identical chair, in the corner of the dining room, would allow the occupant to watch the game in progress without being in the way.

Evelyn walked over to the table and took the farthest chair, the one with its back to the window overlooking the backyard. As she pulled back her chair, Evelyn addressed Claudia.

"Shall we team up, Claudia?"

"Why, not, Evelyn?"

Claudia took the chair opposite Evelyn, leaving the remaining three guests in an awkward position. Georgia, however, quickly suggested Marie and Angela fill the other two spots, since she wanted to see how the others played. Though no one would have suspected, she was determined to win. Georgia took her seat in the fifth chair while Marie sat on Evelyn's left. Angela was the last to take her chair, opposite her partner Marie and next to Georgia.

"How many rubbers should we play?"

Marie suggested, “I think we should play five, Aunt Evie. That way everyone has one turn out of the game.”

The other women looked at Marie strangely. Seeing Marie return a bewildered look, Angela explained, “That’s not quite how it’s done, dear.” Answering Evelyn’s question, Angela said, “I think it’s best not to set a limit. Let’s see how long the rubbers last first.

“That sounds reasonable,” Evelyn said. “Does everyone agree? Good. Would you like to cut the cards, Angela?”

Miss Sparrow nodded and accepted the expensive set of cards, which Evelyn had acquired in Italy, and cut them. She expertly shuffled the cards and began to deal them.

“So, Evelyn,” Claudia said. “I didn’t realize you were Marie’s aunt.”

“Oh, yes. In fact, I talked to Marie’s mother just this morning,” said Evelyn. She thought of her chat with her baby sister over coffee at her nephew’s house.

“Did you talk to Todd?” Marie asked.

“No, it was early, and he was sleeping in.”

After everyone arranged her cards according to suit, the bidding for the first rubber began with Angela at west.

“One Club.”

“One Spade,” said Evelyn with a smile.

“Two Diamonds,” Marie said tentatively.

“Double.”

Angela passed.

“Two Spades.”

“Huh?” Marie’s mind was muddled. “Ah, pass, I think.”

“Three hearts.”

Everyone followed with a resolute ‘Pass’, closing the bidding. The game was afoot, along with the hunt for information.

“So, Ms. Llewellyn, how’s Todd?” Marie asked, after her aunt had laid out the Dummy’s hand. She then played her three of clubs, allowing Angela to win the first trick with her opening ace.

"Not so good, I'm afraid," Georgia replied without removing her eyes from the play of cards; though she was sitting out this rubber, she was clearly analyzing the others' playing skills. "Dr. Logan suggested I give him some valium to calm him down, so he could sleep. I must say I'm really worried about him. Did you know that he's threatened suicide?"

Marie blanched.

"But he's all right, isn't he?"

"Oh, yes," Georgia said, embarrassed by her little faux pas. "You shouldn't worry yourself, dear. Your mother's there now. She plans on staying at least the rest of the week. A family should hold together in situations like this. But I do so dread the thought of that handgun in the house."

"Mr. Stuart owns a gun?" Claudia asked, horrified.

"Yes," Georgia said. "Can you imagine? I nearly had a heart attack when I came across it in the nightstand. I wonder what his wife thought of it. Not everyone feels at ease with firearms in the vicinity."

Marie eyed the reactions of the other players as Claudia defeated her team's chance for a run in clubs with the two of hearts. Then she said, "You know, it's interesting. Tim told me that Lisa was murdered with some kind of handgun. In fact, Sgt. Griffin found a gun in Lisa's house."

Claudia spoke as she played her only spade to Evelyn's ace.

"Oh, I loathe firearms of any kind. I feel they are too dangerous to keep in a household. I keep urging my husband to get rid of his handgun. I'm so afraid that some accident would result because of it. I mean, what would happen if it were to go off while he was cleaning it? Oh, I dread the thought of it. The mere sight of it makes me shudder."

"I know what you mean," Evelyn said. "My ex-husband owned a gun. It always gave me the willies."

Claudia commented, "The colonel has a revolver, too. I remember Mildred telling me that she doesn't like it either. And when her husband wanted to put in a security system, she put her foot down. Said she didn't want that thing waking her up in the middle of the night because he couldn't remember the code number. She said the burglar wouldn't come back because there was nothing left worth stealing. She did, however, use the burglary as an excuse to get rid of one of her husband's guns, but she couldn't find the other because he had misplaced it!"

"Speaking of burglaries, did you know that my next-door neighbor, Joshua Deveraux, had his house broken into? Apparently, it happened Thursday night."

"No. Really?" said Marie.

"Yes," Angela continued. "He said that he had gone out to the movies at Camillus Mall. When he came back, he found his door unlocked. He suspected something wrong and checked his house. Nothing was missing, but later he found his gun gone."

Still keeping her eyes on the play of cards, Georgia said, "You don't think there's a connection between the burglaries and the murders, do you? I mean, Mr. Deveraux's gun is stolen on the same night the police say Lisa Collins was murdered."

"I don't think it's quite that simple," Angela said.

Marie wondered what Claudia thought and noticed the older woman was frowning. Her attentions, however, seemed more focused on the game. It looked like she was mental counting something. Then she switched to the trump suit.

After two tricks were played, Claudia smiled and blurted out, "I seem to be getting all the right cards tonight."

Disappointed by her play of cards in her first real hand of bridge, Marie re- initiated the conversation, partially to learn more information about the murder and hopefully, to distract Claudia.

"I can't believe Rachel was murdered. And in broad daylight! And why was she murdered? Do you think she might have known something in connection to Lisa Collins's murder?"

"She must have," Georgia said. "Lisa was murdered first, after all."

"Yes, but what bothers me," Angela said, "is the air-conditioner. I find it a coincidence that it was fixed that morning on the day Lisa was apparently murdered. It's convenient to the killer that the Stuarts didn't have their window open that night."

"True," Marie said. "But at least one can say that Todd didn't kill her."

"But how can you be so sure?" Claudia asked. "I've read a number of true crime novels, and I know the statistics. It's generally the spouse or a family member."

"But it doesn't fit in this scenario," Marie said crossly. "It doesn't explain Lisa's death. Lisa was killed first."

"Lisa was killed by a boyfriend," Georgia stated firmly. "I remember telling Tim that I overheard an argument she had with him that night."

Georgia related to everyone the story she had told Tim Dewitt.

"All right, but then what about Danielle Deveraux's suicide?" Marie asked. "I've heard talk that she might have been murdered. And isn't just a bit too coincidental that she died only a week before the burglaries started?"

"Well," Georgia said, "it may all be related. I've seen them all having clandestine meetings with each other. That Lisa dated Dr. Logan a couple months ago, and lately I've seen her chatting up Brenda Lysik's husband. She also pestered Joshua Deveraux, especially after his poor wife died. And I've seen her flirt with Todd."

"What about Rachel Stuart?" Claudia put in. "Wasn't she unfaithful to her husband?"

"Sad to say, neither of the Stuarts seemed very concerned about their marital vows." Georgia leaned toward the others. "I've seen Rachel and Joshua Deveraux together. And Mr. Stuart flirted with both Lisa and Danielle. They were all just a little too friendly down the street. Though, come to think of it, I think that Mr. Yates was pining after Danielle, too. Now I'm sure both the Yateses are nice people and that Mrs. Yates is such a sweet thing but they've both been acting very strange lately."

Angela frowned, cleared her throat, and said, "Maybe if we tried to figure out where people were when Rachel Stuart was killed, then we might discover who killed her. You were out on your front lawn at the time, as I seem to recall, Claudia?"

"Y—Yes, I was. I didn't see anything though. I was busy caring for a new exotic type of flower that a friend at my gardening club had given to me. It's called Evening Stock. It blooms in midsummer and has the most beautiful fragrance. In fact, I have another interesting plant called Queen- of-the- Night."

"Oh, yes," Marie said, "I've heard of it. Isn't it also called Night Jasmine?"

"Yes," Claudia answered cheerfully. "It started blooming last week. I even stayed up to watch it one night."

Georgia frowned.

"I don't believe I've ever heard of either of those two flowers," she said.

Georgia liked to think that she was up-to-date on all the latest gardening tips and what flowers grew best locally. Sadly, she was a well-informed beginner compared to Claudia, Edith Baxter, Angela, and a few others in the neighborhood.

Marie, in order to get back to Miss Sparrow's suggestion, said, "Well, Tim and I must have been at church at the time

Rachel was killed." She looked directly at Claudia and added, "And Todd was there, too."

"Yes, but what time was she killed?" Claudia retorted.

"Sgt. Griffin suggested to Tim that it was around eleven o'clock," said Marie, who cheerfully won two tricks with her ace and king of diamonds.

"I was having tea with you at that time, Georgia," Angela said.

"That's right," Georgia said. "I remember now."

"Did you see anything, Georgia? I wasn't facing the window, but I believe you were."

"Nothing special, I'm afraid. I only saw the meter man."

"The meter man?" Marie questioned. "On Easter Sunday? But, Ms. Llewellyn, the meter man already came round earlier this month. Tim's grandmother made a point of telling us that when we first arrived."

Georgia shrugged, "Well, maybe he was a repairman. It was one of those type uniforms."

"Where did he go, Georgia?"

"Oh, I only saw him pass the window, Angela. I don't know where he went. He just walked down the street, that's all. It must have been about ten minutes after eleven."

"Well, I couldn't have seen him then. I was at church," said Evelyn, who attended Pebble Hill Presbyterian Church. The church was less than a half-mile away on Jamesville Road. Angela was also a member of that congregation, but she had gone to Easter service Saturday evening with some friends.

"Except for Claudia, I don't think I saw anyone outside when I came home," Evelyn continued. "Besides, why would the Meter Man be working on Easter Sunday?"

Marie, too, thought that suspect, but then Georgia added in an uncertain tone, "I suppose it could have been a repairman."

The ladies played the rest of the game in silence. Claudia, who had trumped Marie's queen of spades, won the game for her team with one overtrick. The deal then passed to

Evelyn, who deftly but carefully shuffled her new deck. When everyone was ready, Evelyn began the bidding, "One Club."

The contract was made at five clubs with everyone following Evelyn passing, and the second game began with Claudia as Dummy. As Marie played her first card, the ace of hearts, it was her aunt who initiated further conversation.

"You know, this whole affair is horrid. I suspect Mr. Deveraux did it all. He was probably the thief behind these burglaries. How else did he manage to own a house like he did? Most young people his age live in apartments. And he does drive a rather expensive red car for a repairman's pay."

"Oh, that's right, he's a repairman," Marie said, remembering a fact she had earlier come across. "Wasn't he the one who fixed the Stuarts' air-conditioner? Rachel had told Tim that someone had come to fix her air conditioner. She had claimed neither she nor Todd remembered calling for a repairman."

"Well, I know it Joshua who came that day," Claudia said. "I was there at the time because I was loaning her my . . . shovel. But Rachel knew who it was. She knew it was Joshua, and I'll bet she lied about not calling a repairman."

"Oh," Georgia began, "and a mechanic's uniform can look like a repairman's outfit or a meter man's outfit. I suppose that could have been what I saw. In fact, now that I think about it, it was a repairman's uniform."

Angela said, "Well, I still find it hard to believe that Lisa could have afforded her house. She's only a college student. Where would she get the kind of money needed for mortgage payments?"

"What about Todd Stuart?" Claudia suggested. "I still think he could have done it. In such cases, it's often the husband. And, if he was having an affair with Lisa, he could have killed her so that he wouldn't have to split the money. Also, by killing Lisa first, he causes confusion and makes it look like Lisa was the main target."

"What money, Claudia?" Angela asked, confused.

"Why Rachel's insurance money, Angela. The Stuarts had a joint life insurance policy done up. So many people seem to be getting those types of policies nowadays. Todd Stuart will be a rich man. His wife must be worth at least a half million dead."

"Where did the money come from?!" Georgia asked, astounded.

"Well, I overheard the Schwartzs talking in the library one day, and later I asked Mr. Schwartz about it. He told me Sonya's brother ran a garment business in Utica that they sold upon Mr. Weiss' retirement for a sizable profit. When the Weisses died in an automobile accident, half their fortune went to Sonya and the other half to Sonya's niece, Rachel."

There were some gasps of surprise from the other women, as they realized the implication. After a brief pause, Claudia continued. "At Rachel's insistence, the Stuarts took out a joint life insurance policy soon after her parents' death, but I suspect that Todd might have been the initiator of that."

"Todd doesn't care about money," Marie interjected.

"Maybe," Claudia said. "But I know he had to quit college because of money, and I'm sure the insurance will allow him to return to school. Yes, money can be a powerful motive. I think it's possible he's putting this nervous breakdown on as an act. He was an actor at one time, wasn't he, Marie?"

"Yes," Marie said reluctantly.

"See. He would know how to feign a nervous breakdown. What do you think, Georgia. Is he?"

"Well, I don't know. It's been a long time since I've worked as a nurse." Georgia shook her head. "No, I couldn't be sure."

"So he could have been faking?" Claudia asked.

There was no answer though, and the ladies lapsed into silence. The second game ended soon after with Evelyn and Claudia winning. Just as quickly another began. With a contract of four spades, Claudia's side soon won the rubber.

During this play of cards, the conversation trickled to a few remarks about this and that; none of it was of interest to Marie.

Marie couldn't stop stewing over Claudia's suspicions of her brother. Her brother would never kill anyone. She had to be sure about that, right? If only she hadn't been so caught up with her own life the last couple years. She should have talked to Todd when he dropped out of college. She'd thought it odd at the time. But he'd seemed so positive and upbeat then. Even at her wedding a few weeks ago, he'd seemed so happy. Had that been an act only for show? There'd been those odd moments, when he'd thought no one was looking, that she'd seen him looking tired and sad.

As her Aunt Evie graciously switched places with Georgia Llewellyn for the next rubber, Marie resolved to visit her brother and try to get him to open up to her. In the meantime, she had to focus on the game. Getting the neighborhood gossip could help clear up everything. She counted up her cards.

"One Club," she said, barely concealing her excitement.

"One Heart."

Liking her own hand, but not her abundance of clubs, Angela countered, "One Spade."

"Pass."

"Two Clubs?" Marie said, uncertain.

"Pass."

"Three Diamonds."

After Georgia's "Pass," Marie was confused. Why had Angela switched to diamonds? She, herself only had two diamonds. She was better suited in hearts . . .

"Oh. Three Hearts."

The bidding continued and increased in pace until Angela's triumphant, "Seven No Trump!" That left the opposing team flabbergasted.

"Oh, I've never seen a Grand Slam in No Trump before!" said Evelyn with a clap of her hands in delight. "Would anyone like refreshments? Coffee?"

The players acquiesced to coffee and cake, which Evelyn, as hostess, dutifully served as she commented, "I must say I'm disappointed I'm not in this hand."

Though she had bid enthusiastically, Marie, too, was disappointed to realize her hand would be the Dummy and that Miss Sparrow would be playing. The first five tricks were played in silence and with heavy concentration by all players. Despite the players' scrutiny in search of them, mistakes were nonexistent. After Angela's consecutive win of five tricks, the game calmed down to a slower pace with an emphasis more on points scored. The game already indicated that Angela would win the remaining tricks unchallenged.

Meanwhile, Marie thought, her hunt for information continued.

"So who do you think the burglar is?" Marie asked. "I mean, it must be someone who knows when people aren't home."

"You know I was just thinking about that," Claudia said. "Looking back on the robberies, well, Angela you yourself said it at our last bridge night. It must be someone on this street. One of our neighbors is the burglar. One of them is a killer."

"But are they one and the same?" Angela questioned.

"Well, I hope you don't think my brother's responsible for the burglaries, too," Marie said, catching Claudia's eye.

No one commented on Marie's statement.

"Well, I think the burglar is Mr. Deveraux," Georgia said.

"But Mr. Deveraux's house was broken into Thursday night, Georgia. I already told you that," Angela said.

"But how else could he afford to live in his house?"

"Mildred helped him buy the house." All eyes turned to Claudia. "Well, he is her grandson."

Marie recalled her encounter with Mildred Hawthorne after talking to Josh at church on Sunday. She'd been incredulous to learn that Mildred was Josh's grandmother, but here was confirmation of that!

"He could have made that up about his house being broken into," Georgia said. "He probably used his gun to shoot Lisa."

"I still think the murderer could be Todd," Claudia said firmly.

Angered by Claudia's continual accusation of her brother, Marie commented, "And suspicion moves from person to person like a moving finger. The question is, where does it stop? I wonder if it ever does. Suspicion seems to have a habit of hovering over everyone. We all had an opportunity, didn't we? Don't we all have secrets to hide?"

Shocked by Marie's insight, the others fell silent until the end of play, which did not last long. In Angela's capable hands, the game was an easy win.

"I must say, I don't know how the police will ever catch this murderer. There just doesn't seem to be a lot of clues about. There ought to be. Like in those detective novels," Evelyn said.

"But there are plenty of clues, I'm sure, Aunt Evie," Marie said. "There's the gun the police found in Lisa's house."

"They found the gun that killed Lisa?" Georgia asked.

Marie, realizing she had said too much, reluctantly answered, "Yes."

"Now they'll find out who did it. It's only a matter of time," Georgia said with glee.

"I wonder if it is as simple as that," Angela said. "Finding a gun doesn't really prove much. It could have been stolen."

"It's Mr. Deveraux's. You can bet on that. Women's intuition," Georgia said.

Claudia remarked, "You know that's what Mrs. Esterhazy always says. Now there's someone I can't put up with. I'm glad she doesn't know how to play bridge."

"Oh, I agree," Evelyn said. "She is the most overbearing woman. I try to avoid her as much as possible."

"I feel sorry for Mildred," Claudia said. "She lives right next door! She's always saying how Anne Esterhazy never listens to anyone but herself. That is unless you're telling her some bit of gossip that she didn't know. But then she practically turns around and acts as if she's the one who knew all along."

"That reminds me," Marie said. "Mrs. Esterhazy said Mrs. Yates dropped off her children at her mother's house for the week. Sometimes I wonder how that woman comes up with her information."

"Really?" Claudia said, surprised. "I must say I'm surprised. Linda Yates is devoted to her children. Her whole life revolves around them."

Marie shrugged. "That's the indication Mrs. Esterhazy gave."

"They're a quiet couple, aren't they? That's how neighbors should be. Instead of the way Lisa Collins was. I, for one, am glad she's dead. I wouldn't shed a tear for someone like her," Georgia said.

Silence reigned for a moment before Claudia suggested they talk about something else.

A suburban street of a medium-sized city is never truly dark. City lights cast a far-reaching glow over the night sky—obscuring stars that would otherwise be seen—while streetlamps illuminate more immediate areas and cast conical glows of comforting light at spaced intervals.

Instinctually Marie knew this, but, having wished her aunt good night, she followed the other ladies as they strolled down the damp, darkened street and she felt apprehensive. Perhaps this was because she knew a burglar and a murderer—were they one and the same?—lurked somewhere on Stoneridge.

"My goodness, it's dark! What time is it?" Georgia Llewellyn verbalized Marie's thoughts exactly.

"Ten-thirty," Angela answered, glancing at her digital watch. "We must have had rain, though. The street looks wet."

Looking up at the sky, Georgia huffed, "Cloudy. How typical. We hardly ever see the sun, so why should we see stars?"

"We've had a fair bit of sun recently, and you know we need the rain."

"I suppose," Georgia said weakly.

Glancing about, Claudia said, "Well, it's a good thing we're able to walk home in pairs, considering the circumstances."

They soon reached the end of Marie's driveway where Claudia said her goodnights to the other ladies and hurried across the street to her home.

Walking to her own front door, Marie looked back and saw Angela and Georgia strolling past the lamppost at the end of Lysiks' driveway. The light drew her attention, and she paused, trying to recall a forgotten memory. She'd seen someone that night, but not someone she recognized. Who could it have been? Had it been a stranger she'd seen? Could the killer really have been an outsider?

Marie heard a rustling noise in the bushes off to her left. Hoping it was just an animal, she entered her house and then locked and chained the door as a precaution.

"How did it go?"

Tim's voice startled her. She turned and saw him lounging on the couch in just jeans.

"Is everything okay?" He swung his bare feet off the couch and sat up.

"Y—yes," stammered Marie. "It's just, walking home in the dark . . ."

Furrowing his eyebrows in concern, he asked, "I know it was just next door, but you didn't walk home alone?"

She shook her head. "No. We all left together."

"Good." Folding down the corner of a page, Tim set down the spy novel he'd been reading on the nearby end table. "So how did the bridge game go?"

Beaming, Marie said, "It was awesome. I won fifty dollars because I got a grand slam in the second rubber and won in hearts—"

"Wait a minute. Did you say you won fifty dollars?"

"I take it that's pretty good?" Marie asked doubtfully.

"For a bridge game, yeah. It's great!" He stood up and stretched. "So did you hear any good gossip?"

Marie watched him stretch his arms over his head and admired the movement of his muscles elongating. She crossed the room and hugged him, wanting to feel his solid frame and his steady presence. Holding him, feeling his bare skin under her fingertips made it easy to forget such fears that had flittered through her mind outside in the dark. As his strong arms enveloped her, she felt safe, protected.

"What's wrong?"

"It's nothing," she said, looking up at him. She could see the concern in his brown eyes. "It was just some things said about Todd," she admitted. "I just want this all to be over. I wish . . . I want things to be normal. We shouldn't have to be looking over our shoulders wondering which one of our neighbors is a murderer."

"It won't always be like this." Tim caressed her cheek and smiled. "I promise."

Stroking his chest with her fingertips, feeling the warm, smooth skin, she said, "Could we forget what happened, just for tonight?"

"I think we could manage that," he said in a low, sensual voice. And then he kissed her.

WEDNESDAY

Ten o'clock Wednesday morning, Angela Sparrow ushered Tim into her elegant, yet simple abode. The swelling in her ankle had decreased considerably, but she still needed the use of her mother's silver-knobbed cane. Tim helped his hostess close her front door and then crossed over to the dining room table where she had some coffee ready to pour.

Last night had been wonderful. He and Marie had forgotten about the troubles on Stoneridge and had had a marathon lovemaking session before falling blissfully asleep. Then with morning's arrival, they'd faced the realities of the day, and over breakfast Marie had filled him in on the gossip at the bridge game.

Now he studied a large poster on the table, a map of Stoneridge drawn expertly by Angela. He looked over the names, finely penned in calligraphy, before pouring himself some coffee. Then he noticed there was no cream. Tim, who could not understand how anyone could drink coffee without cream and sugar, asked Angela if she had any milk or half-and-half.

"In the refrigerator," she told him.

He volunteered to get it and poured some into his cup. "That's better," he muttered as he sipped what would be his third cup of the day.

When he returned he found Angela sitting at the Stickley dining room table, smoothing down a hand-woven place mat.

"I was just remembering happier times," she said. "Alas that was another time. I know all too well that we can't recapture the past."

He sat down opposite her. " 'The past is the key to not repeating history's mistakes.' That's what you always taught us."

She smiled wanly. "Yes. But sometimes it's best forgotten."

Tim saw a sadness creep across her face. Changing the subject, he said, "Now, this map?"

"Yes," Angela said, smiling proudly. "I do enjoy painting and sketching on occasion. It's just a hobby, mind, but I think it a talent. I'm not as good as Mr. Deveraux is. You should see his work. Still I feel I can hold my own." Looking over her work, she added, "I thought this would be convenient to refer to, and I could tell you a few things I know about our neighbors."

Tim asked, "What about the people on the next street over?"

"I talked to Georgia's neighbor, Kitty Martino. She and her husband live in that corner house on Rosehill Drive. The white stucco one adjacent to Georgia's. Well, she told me that the house next to her, the one behind Lisa's, and the house behind the Stuarts are both for sale. The family in the house behind the Logans is on vacation. And of course, there is a six-foot fence that runs between the backyards of the houses on this street and that one. No, I don't think anyone on Rosehill Drive is involved in this matter. Besides, I don't think anyone on this street really knows anything about their backyard neighbors, except maybe Claudia, who has chatted with the lady of the house behind hers. Although, I believe they're both in the Syracuse Gardening Club. No, I am utterly convinced that the murderer lives on this street."

"I wonder if anyone can be eliminated as a suspect," Tim muttered. "I know Jack's checking on the whereabouts of neighbors out of town just to be sure, but that only confirms what we already suspect. The killer has to be someone on Stoneridge. It's an outside possibility that some old boyfriend could be involved, but too many things seem to depend on knowing the neighborhood intimately. Don't you agree?"

"Oh, quite."

"And I think it's a safe assumption to eliminate ourselves as suspects. Your ankle would make it physically impossible to kill either Lisa or Rachel. I can vouch for Marie and Grandma Edith, too. None of us left the house Thursday night. And I think it's highly unlikely that D.J. and Bryant Logan are involved."

Angela nodded. "That all seems very reasonable. Also, I believe Georgia Llewellyn was with me around the time Rachel Stuart was murdered. Other than that, I don't think the list could be narrowed any further at this point."

Tim sighed in frustration. "Therein lays the problem."

While Tim visited with Miss Sparrow, Marie sat in their living room drinking coffee and reading the latest copy of *Country Living*. She nearly spilt the coffee on her magazine when the doorbell suddenly rang.

"Who the hell is it this time?"

Marie huffed and got off the couch to answer the door. She realized too late that she should have surreptitiously checked to make sure it wasn't Mrs. Esterhazy again, but she was both thankful and shocked to discover David Yates on her doorstep.

Haggard and drawn, David smiled wanly. His white Oxford shirt was haphazardly buttoned, his blue jeans tattered at the knees, and his Dockers looked well-worn. His breathing seemed a bit ragged, as if he'd been running, and he wiped some sweat off his brow with the back of his hand. His eyes would glance at Marie and look away, but she could see that they were bloodshot.

"Why, Mr. Yates, what brings you here?"

"I—I've got to talk to you," stammered David. His green eyes looked imploringly at her. "Can I talk to you? Can I come in?"

Despite her better judgment, she let him in, stepping aside as he stumbled past her. She saw him come to a sudden halt, swaying as if he were suddenly dizzy. A moment later, he shook his head as if trying to clear his mind. Marie sensed something wrong, but she tried to remain calm.

"Mr. Yates?"

"I know—know what they're all saying about me," David said, pacing the living room with his hand touching his forehead as if he had a headache.

"Please sit down. You're making me nervous." When David sat down on the couch beside her, Marie continued, "What are people saying?"

"They're saying I killed them. That I killed Danielle, and that bitch Rachel Stuart. I've seen them talking. The neighbors. They know I loved Danielle. She was everything to me. I'd never kill her. I couldn't. It was someone else. Not Josh. He loved her, too. But Lisa. They think they know everything."

"Who? Who thinks that?"

"That lady across the street. The one two doors down. They all do. I see the way they gossip and look at me. They suspect me. They're saying I did it."

Marie looked into David's anguished eyes. They welled up, but no tears escaped. She stared at those striking eyes, the color of jade. There was just a hint of blue tint in them, but there was a great deal of hurt as well.

"And did you?"

"I didn't kill anyone! I can't prove it. They know I'm no good. And I'm not. Grandfather always said so. I'm nothing but a bastard. Worthless!" He looked directly at her. "I've done things I'm not proud of. But I've never hurt . . . I never meant to hurt anyone. But what does it matter." He threw his hands up in the air as if all hope were lost. "Nothing matters. You'll put me back in that place."

Marie watched his bloodshot eyes shift nervously.

"What place? What are you talking about?"

"You know, don't you? You know who the murderer is? That's why you were asking those questions. About Lisa and Danielle. You knew then. She couldn't hide the truth from you . . . Oh, no. I—It'll all . . ."

"Are you all right?" Marie asked, as he swooned with dizziness. She also noticed he was sweating more than was normal for a man of twenty-four years. Remembering Rachel's note, she wondered if he was stoned.

Recovering his senses, David stuttered, "I—I'm f—fine. It's all the pressure. Everyone closing in on me."

David tugged at his collar. Then he jerked open the top two buttons of his shirt. Marie could see the sheen of sweat on his chest, the dark lines under his eyes, and his pallid complexion. His symptoms alarmed her, but what ailment could it be? Surely he was too young for a heart attack or stroke. Drugs? When he began gasping for breath, Marie jumped to her feet and grabbed hold of his arms.

"What's the matter?"

All at once, Marie knew she had to get a doctor, and she started toward the phone just as the doorbell rang. She bolted for the front door and swung it open. Linda Yates stood there and quietly asked, "Excuse me, but is my husband here?" She craned her neck to look past Marie.

"Yes!" Marie snapped. "He's ill and needs a doctor. Go across the street! Get Dr. Icarios. I think he's home. Please hurry!"

"Oh, my God! What's the matter?"

"Just go!"

Linda hurried across the street and up to Mrs. Icarios, who was out in her yard gardening as usual. She frantically explained to Claudia what was happening.

Marie, rushed back to David and forced him to lie down on the couch. She removed his shoes and swung his bare feet onto the couch. Then she propped up his head with the couch's pillows. She stood back and tried to think calmly for a moment. What should she to do? Something seemed familiar about all this. She strained to remember an incident that had occurred at S. U. during her Freshmen year. She remembered a student collapsing during a biology lab only to have the professor revive the student with some juice. That student had been diabetic.

Marie ran to the kitchen and looked in the refrigerator. There was a pitcher of pink lemonade left over from the last Neighborhood Watch meeting, and she quickly yanked it out of its place, spilling some on the kitchen floor. She grabbed a straw and a glass from the cupboard, poured the lemonade, and dropped two sugar cubes into the drink. Then as fast as she could go without spilling any more of the lemonade, she raced to David's side and forced him to drink.

His breathing was still labored, but she forced him to sit up and sip the lemonade through the straw. Though he spilled a fair bit of the pink liquid on his shirt, he managed to drink enough to calm himself. His breathing began to stabilize as Claudia Icarios, whose husband was not home, arrived with Dr. Logan and Linda Yates in tow.

"What happened?" Dr. Logan asked as he entered and approached David.

"Is he all right?" Linda asked fretfully.

Her heart still racing from all the excitement, Marie answered, "I think he's suffering insulin shock."

Marie stepped aside for Dr. Logan to examine David Yates. She noticed that the doctor seemed to hesitate before opening his black medical bag as if he did not want the others to see something. Despite his precautions as he quickly opened the bag, extracted his stethoscope, and closed it, Marie saw that one of the doctor's scalpels appeared to be missing. She didn't have much time to think on what she'd seen, for Mrs. Icarios, who had been trying to comfort Linda, remarked, "My husband's working today, but I remembered seeing Dr. Logan earlier today. We were very lucky to get a hold of him because he was about to leave for a jog."

After a brief examination of the young man's vital signs, Dr. Logan asked David, "Are you feeling better, Mr. Yates?"

"Y—Yes. A little better."

"Did you take too much insulin this morning?"

"Huh?"

"Are you diabetic, Mr. Yates?"

"Yes! Yes, he is," Linda said.

"Did you take too much insulin this morning?" the doctor asked.

"N—No. I—I don't know. I don't know what happened."

"It's all my fault," Linda cried.

Marie watched her nearly swoon, but Claudia caught hold of her and led her to the couch. It all seemed a little overdramatic, but then Dr. Logan addressed her, "How did you know what was happening?"

Marie explained about the student in her biology class. After she had finished, Dr. Logan said, "Well, Mr. Yates. You are extremely lucky that Mrs. Dewitt here knew what to do. Though a fruit drink like orange juice or lemonade is a good counteract to insulin shock, I recommend you visit the hospital for a check- up. Just to make sure everything's okay."

Dr. Logan began to pack up the few medical devices he had brought with him in his black bag, as Claudia asked of Marie, "Are you all right, dear? I could stay and help out if you think you need me."

"Thank you, no, Mrs. Icarios. I'll be all right."

After Dr. Logan and Claudia had left, Linda Yates slumped on the couch adjacent to the living room window while Marie told David to rest for a few moments. Marie then sat down next to Linda and held the distraught woman's hands.

Drying her tears with a tissue Claudia had given her, Linda whispered, "I'm just so afraid for David. He came home Monday afternoon and said he'd been fired. I tried to tell him he needed help, but he wouldn't listen. He just left and didn't come back. Then he drove home not more than an hour ago. I waited for him in the house, but he didn't come. So I went looking for him, and Mrs. Icarios said he had come here. I hate when he's like this."

"Is your husband taking drugs?"

Linda, fretting with the tissue in her hands, nodded. "It started about the time Danielle died. I think David was having an affair with her, with Danielle. Then she found out her husband had been cheating on her with Rachel Stuart. Well, Danielle did love her husband, so she and he had a long talk one night. The next day she broke it off with David. He went nuts."

She glanced over at his supine form. "David used to accompany Danielle on the piano whenever she sang. He regarded her as a godsend. 'Her voice is like a nightingale's. Every composer dreams of such a beauty, such an angel of music,' he would say. Danielle was fond of David, too, until she met Joshua. He came to fix something in the apartment Danielle shared with Rachel and Lisa. Danielle fell for Joshua, and David was heartbroken. He began using drugs again. A girlfriend in high school had first turned him onto them. When she died of an overdose he enrolled in rehab. I knew about his past, but I loved him. When he turned to drugs, I didn't know what to do. I talked to Danielle, and she was so sweet. She helped me convince him to get help. When he did sober up, we decided it would be best to move here."

She paused a moment, as if remembering happier times. Then she continued. "We were shocked when Joshua and Danielle moved here. I knew it wouldn't be long before David would obsess over Danielle, but I figured it would keep him sober. Then one night Danielle told him there was no chance for them as a couple, and David went out and got drunk. The next day I caught him using." She chocked back a cry. "Two days later, Danielle was dead, and David withdrew from reality. Ever since, I have tried to keep my eye on him. I don't know where he's been getting the drugs. Honestly, I don't."

Marie suspected that Linda had a hunch as to where David was getting his supply. She also suspected that Linda was leaving out something.

Linda held back her tears and continued, "My husband was out that night. The night my sister was killed."

"I am sorry," Marie said sympathetically.

"Please, don't," Linda said. "Lisa and I never really got along so there's really no love lost."

"But you were sisters."

"It never seemed like it, you know? She had all the looks, and well, I had all the brains."

"But you two look so alike. How can you possibly say that?"

Linda blanched slightly.

"Well, I—I'd rather not talk about it. They asked me to come down and identify her. She looked so lifeless there on that gurney. I don't want to think about it." She rubbed at the corner of her eyes. "I'm more worried about David. He, well, the night Lisa died, David . . . he went for a walk around ten o'clock. He said that he needed some fresh air. He didn't come back until midnight. I know he was sober when he left, but he was strung out when he finally came back. Oh, was he ever in a wretched, vile mood. I couldn't understand why. Then when I heard about Lisa's death. I could only think . . . My husband, you see, well, I would see his eyes wander when he would see a pretty woman. I think to him they must have reminded him of Danielle. It's the drugs that do that to him. He can't help it though. He hallucinates. He sees things that aren't there. Oh, I just don't know what to do."

Linda wrung her hands and sobbed. She regarded David as he lay on the opposite couch, resting peacefully. Drying her eyes, she added, “I suspected what he had done before Rachel was killed, but what could I do. I know everyone’s been saying they’re shocked that I let my children spend the week with my mother, but it’s the safety of the children I’m concerned about. I just can’t trust my husband. Not when he’s stoned. I know he’s a decent man, deep down. He would never kill anyone. But it’s like living with Dr. Jekyll and Mr. Hyde. I never know what mood he’ll be in.”

Unsurreptiously, Georgia watched Sgt. Griffin and a couple officers approach Joshua Deveraux’s house. She continued to gawk as the police conversed with Mr. Deveraux. After what looked like heated words, they took him into custody. The sergeant entered the young man’s home while one of the officers ushered Mr. Deveraux into the back of a police cruiser. After it drove off, Georgia’s mind ran wild with all sorts of ideas. She just had to tell someone. So she hurried across to Angela Sparrow’s house and rang the doorbell.

“Angela . . . Oh, Tim, you’ll never guess,” Georgia began breathlessly.

Tim Dewitt stared as she scurried past him like a scatterbrained squirrel. She approached Angela, who sat calmly awaiting whatever news her neighbor could barely inhale enough air to say.

“That sergeant has just arrested Mr. Deveraux.”

“What?” Tim exclaimed.

“Yes! The police just came and took him away.”

“Where are the police now, Georgia?” Angela asked calmly.

“Oh, they’re still at Mr. Deveraux’s. They must have a search warrant. It’s as if they knew!”

"I've gotta talk to Jack," Tim said.

Tim and Georgia jogged, while Angela hobbled along with her cane, up the street to the green house next door. They saw Brenda Lysik, Donna Stuart, and Claudia Icarios already milling about at the end of Deveraux's driveway. Georgia immediately sidled up to Claudia and asked if she'd missed anything.

"They've taken Mr. Deveraux away," Claudia said. "The sergeant's acting like it's an open-and-shut case. I tell you I'm shocked. They think they've found the gloves he used to hold the shovel."

"Where is the sergeant now?" Tim asked.

"Oh, he's inside with another policeman, searching the premises. That officer is keeping everyone out," Claudia said, pointing to the young, sandy-blond-haired officer standing guard by the front door.

"We'll see about *that*," Tim mumbled, as he approached the house. He was barred from entering by the officer, but Tim recognized him and said, "Hey, Ryan, remember me?"

"Tim?"

"Yeah."

"Hey, it's not like you've been at work lately."

"So you think it's okay to forget about me, huh? For God's sake, you were at the creek the other day when we found Lisa's body!"

Ryan shrugged.

"Jack's expecting you. He's in there somewhere. You can go in. And I know I don't need to tell you not to touch anything."

"You're picking up the tab next time at the Queen of Spades diner."

Ryan laughed. "Sure, man."

Jocular teasing aside, Ryan Tierney and Tim were good friends who'd joined the Town of DeWitt police force as rookies together. The Queen of Spades diner had become their favorite hangout on or off duty. Presently, Ryan knuckled Tim lightly on the shoulder as he passed by and entered Joshua Deveraux' house.

"What lies are you telling her?" David sat up and glared at Linda.

They certainly did not look like the happily married couple to Marie.

"I'm just telling the truth, David."

David gripped the edge of the couch and dug his toes into the carpet.

"You're telling her I did it, aren't you? You'd like to put me away. You—"

"I can't bear to see you like this," Linda interrupted. "It's ruining our lives."

"You're telling her that I killed her, aren't you?"

"No, David, I—"

"Don't lie to me, Lisa," David yelled, who stood up and began pacing the room.

She went to him.

"Please, David. Don't do this to yourself." She turned to Marie and said, "He gets like this when he's agitated. You've probably already guessed that Lisa was his supplier. He was so dependent on her that I don't think he realizes she's dead. It's like he can't believe it, and so he hallucinates. It's the same thing with Danielle. He doesn't accept the fact that she's dead.

"Don't ever say her name again!" David said, as he struck her, knocking her to the floor.

Marie jumped up. "Mr. Yates!"

David buried his head in his hands. As Marie helped Linda to her feet, he advanced on Linda, "I'm sorry. I didn't mean to."

"Don't you dare come near me," Linda hissed, withdrawing from David and leaving Marie like the monkey in the middle.

"Don't do this to me. I need you."

Linda started laughing. "All you've ever needed is the drugs. Drugs of any kind. It didn't matter. No one has ever meant anything to you. Not your wife! Not even your own children. Not even Danielle McGinty!"

"Don't!" David cried, covering his eyes. "You know what she meant to me. I never meant to . . . love her."

"What about your wife?" Linda asked. "What about me?"

David pushed past Marie and again tried to approach Linda, who again retreated from him.

"I love you, too," he said. "I always have."

"I don't believe that," Linda said, averting her eyes.

Marie could see Linda no longer had any strength to help David; the poor woman seemed exhausted from trying to hold her family together.

"L—Linda?"

Linda's eyes had already filled with tears, but she shut her eyelids as if to hold them in.

"I can't help you now. I've tried before and failed. I can't be your crutch anymore. I have too much to think of. Lisa, the children."

Linda turned away from David as Marie advanced on him.

"I know it really isn't my place to interfere, but . . ."

Marie stopped when David faced her with a deep-seated pain visible in his eyes. He stood there like a marionette whose strings had been cut but had not yet fallen to the ground in a heap. To Marie, he looked like a broken man.

Marie opened her mouth to speak, but saw him looking over her shoulder. She turned around.

Linda held herself tightly and refused to return David's pleading gaze.

"I'm sorry," David said. "I'll change. Please? Don't leave me too."

Marie saw Linda bite her lip, wavering.

Meanwhile, Tim entered Mr. Deveraux's unkempt living room. He called out Jack Griffin's name and heard a muffled response. A few minutes later, Jack entered from the basement stairs with sooty cheeks and gray dust in his brown hair. Dust also covered most of his uniform.

"What happened to you?"

"Nothing, Tim. Just a little mess in the basement," Jack said, brushing himself off.

"What's going on? You've arrested Josh Deveraux?"

"What? No congratulations?"

"For what? I'm not satisfied that Deveraux committed these murders."

"Aw, come on, Tim. We've just taken the guy in for questioning. Personally, I think he's as guilty as they come. Said he was at the movies Thursday night. No witnesses, of course. Just like last time. A shaky alibi and a dead body. You know about his wife, right?"

Tim nodded.

"So you think he did it? You think he killed his wife and Lisa and Rachel."

"Hell, yeah," Jack said. "The gun we found is registered to him. Ballistics proves that the slug we found in the door matched Deveraux's gun. Ms. Llewellyn already told us that she saw a man dressed like a meter man the morning Rachel Stuart was killed. I'll bet you anything it was Deveraux in his repairman's uniform she saw."

Tim frowned. Something didn't quite make sense.

"Look, Tim, this guy's killed before. I don't buy for a second that his wife committed suicide. I was there. I was the one who investigated it. It wasn't right. The whole thing reeked of being faked. I called in the Sheriff's Department for backup help in the investigation, for Chris'sake."

"But you didn't turn up anything."

Jack huffed. "No, we didn't. But I wasn't satisfied with the verdict of suicide."

"But why would he kill Rachel Stuart?"

"She was probably blackmailing him. We've discovered large deposits to Rachel Stuart's bank account in the last few months. Besides the ballistics report came in. The gun we found was fired twice. He's had it."

"There's got to be something that's being overlooked."

"Nothing's been overlooked, Tim. We found the gloves he must have used to handle the shovel, and the Kelly Repair, Co. uniform that he must have worn. I was just about to ask Ms. Llewellyn if it's the same uniform she saw."

"Isn't there anything else?"

"No! God, Tim, you're not on duty. You're on vacation! This shouldn't even be your concern."

"Well, it is," Tim said angrily, his nostrils flaring. "This is where I live now. Me and Marie. I care what happens in my neighborhood. And you told me an officer is always on duty, vacation or not. I just . . . something doesn't sit right with me about this."

"Hey, Tim, I understand. I was a rookie once too, but this guy is our killer. All the evidence—"

"Evidence can be manufactured. You said it yourself once."

"Well, maybe you can help me. There's an unfinished portrait," Jack said, knowing nothing he could do or say would change Tim's mind. "It's just down the hall here, to the left."

Tim followed Jack down the hall and into a small studio.

An unfinished portrait of a woman rested on the easel awaiting its next brushstroke. The reddish hair was a hazy halo upon her doll-like head. The woman's blue eyes stared out as if imploring she be completed. Just a few more finishing touches.

Tim was neither art critic nor connoisseur, but even he could see that Joshua Deveraux had captured his subject's likeness well.

"That's her. That's Danielle Deveraux. He must have stopped painting after she died."

Jack whistled and said, "She was a beauty."

Tim wondered if Danielle had been murdered, but if so, would an artist kill the subject of his painting before it was finished? He started to say something when he noticed a note on the floor behind the easel. There was something scrawled on it.

Standing in Joshua Deveraux's driveway, Angela Sparrow could not bring herself to believe that her next-door neighbor, that handsome young man, was guilty of these murders. She didn't want to think of it. She leaned on her cane and closed her eyes. Something wasn't right about it. Something she couldn't quite put her finger on. She tried, but her neighbors were conversing and their chatter rang louder in her ears so she listened to their comments.

Georgia was talking to Donna Stuart. "I hate to say this, but fireworks are going to fly when Todd finds out. I'd hate to have to be the one who tells him. His poor wife. I thought it was Mr. Deveraux. He just didn't seem to fit in here, in this neighborhood. He was always so withdrawn. They say you never suspect such a person until it's too late."

"But why would he kill my daughter-in-law?" Donna asked.

"They were having an affair."

"Georgia," Claudia admonished. "I don't think Mr. Stuart's mother needs to hear all the sordid details."

"Under the circumstances," Donna said, "perhaps I should."

Brenda Lysik thought it advisable to change the conversation's direction. "Mr. Deveraux always kept to himself. My husband says that some murderers can be secretive and withdrawn, and you'd never suspect them. They suddenly snap because they've been repressed by society. Really, I think there's a screw loose in men like him. He was a painter, you know. I used to see him outside in his backyard painting sunrises and sunsets. Why—"

They all heard a loud crack.

"What was that?" Georgia gasped, looking about in alarm.

"I won't be your crutch anymore."

David backed away with a horrified look. Then suddenly, he bolted. He sprinted toward his driveway. Several thoughts crammed through his head all at once. He thought he heard Lisa's voice, then a shot. He just had to get out of this damned neighborhood.

David frantically reached for the keys of his car without realizing that his bare feet had been cut by some small pebbles. As he attempted to open the car door, Linda caught him by the arm.

"No, David. You're too distraught to drive."

"Get away from me! You don't care a damn about me."

David wrenched away from her, and she lost her balance. She fell against the retaining wall; the climbing ivy barely cushioned the blow. She slumped to the ground, clutching her head in her hands.

"Stop him," Linda said to Marie, who'd followed them.

David revved up his car engine. He backed up, just as another car drove hazardously in order to block his escape.

The sudden gunshot startled Angela. Her eyes popped open with alarm. Had someone else been murdered? Didn't the police have the culprit in custody? How could this be happening now? And where had it come from?

Realizing that the sound had come from behind her, she turned around and said to the others, "I think it came from Todd Stuart's house."

"Oh, my God!" Donna Stuart said in a panic. "I should never have left him alone."

Georgia cried out, "It's all my fault!"

She hurried across the street ahead of Todd's mother. At a short distance behind them, Tim, having heard the shot, had exited Joshua Deveraux's house and followed. Georgia, having reached the steps first, banged on the door and called out Todd's name. Then Sgt. Griffin arrived beside her and gently pushed her aside.

"He won't answer," she shrieked.

Donna yelled, "Todd! Todd, it's your mother! Open the door! Please."

The door slowly opened. Todd Stuart stood in the doorway with a handgun, recently fired, in his hand. He was barefoot, dressed in jeans, and a shirt half-buttoned and half-tucked. His hair was unruly and his eyes were red.

"I—I couldn't do it," he stuttered and broke down crying.

The gun fell from his hands as he staggered against the doorframe. He started to crumple to the floor, but the sergeant caught hold of him. Georgia Llewellyn, still distressed, helped Jack Griffin and Donna Stuart bring Todd back into his house. Tim and the rest of the ladies, who arrived presently, followed them inside, as Todd was laid on his couch.

"It's my fault," Georgia lamented. "I could have sworn that I locked the drawer containing the gun. I've kept it locked all this time in case of this. I must have forgotten, but I could have sworn I locked it!"

"There, there," Angela said, trying to comfort her.

"Didn't you hide all the bullets, Georgia?" Donna asked harshly.

"Yes. No. The gun was unloaded, I think. Oh, I can't be sure of anything now. It's all my fault. My fault. I'm a nurse! I should know what to do. I can't trust myself anymore. No one can trust me anymore. I forget things."

"Georgia, really. You're being much too hard on yourself," interrupted Angela.

"No, I'm not. Todd Stuart could have killed himself because of me. I wasn't careful. I didn't make sure. I made a mistake about that meter man, too. The meter man had already come. I should have known that. I should have known about this!"

When Donna started crying, Georgia rushed from the living room and ran out the open door. Tim followed and saw her run out into the road.

Then, like a scene from a movie shown in slow motion, Tim saw it happen. The swerving car, the momentary look of horror on Georgia's face as she turned and saw the oncoming car, the squealing tires, the crunch of bones, and the rending sound of the car as metal struck wood. Stunned silence followed.

He didn't think he'd ever forget that surreal moment. It had stunned him for a fraction of a second before instinct took over. He rushed over to Georgia.

He heard Jack Griffin coming up behind him, shouting to Officer Tierney to call for an ambulance. As he knelt beside the crumpled woman, Jack rushed passed him toward the wrecked car.

Tim reached for Georgia's wrist to feel for a pulse as Claudia Icarios and Brenda Lysik joined him. "Ms. Llewellyn? Ms. Llewellyn, can you hear me?"

Her eyes fluttered open and deliriously she looked up at Tim. In her stupor, she said, "What's ya doin', Tim? Acting like you's so knowledgeable. You don't know everythin' smarty pants. I 'eard ze whole thin', I did. The argument, you know. Twas at ten clock that I look out me window. Carry 'er off, 'e did. Put 'er in 'er car an' drove off down street. But nobody 'ud lissen to a muddled ole woman like me."

"Who, Ms. Llewellyn? Who?"

"Don' know. Some man or it coulda been a woman. Them shots is what come later," Georgia slurred as she closed her eyes and lost consciousness.

Just then, they heard Linda Yates cry out. Supported by Marie, she had come down the street and had seen David's wrecked car. She felt woozy again and Marie tried to hold her upright. Brenda lent a hand as her husband arrived on the scene.

"How awful," Brenda said to her husband. "I think she must be dead! That red car ran right into her! Did you see it happen?"

"No," Shane replied. "I was too busy recovering from the shock of almost being shot!"

Having heard Shane Lysik's remark, Tim looked back toward Todd's house. He could see the bullet hole in the window.

"You say you dodged a bullet, Mr. Lysik?"

Shane nodded as Tim muttered, "He must have fired out the window."

"My husband," Linda said weakly. She clutched her head continuously as if her head pounded, ready to explode. Marie and Brenda struggled to keep her on her feet.

Tim, meanwhile, joined Jack by the wrecked car a few feet away and peered in.

David Yates was slumped over the steering wheel. A cut on his brow oozed blood, and his breathing seemed labored. Jack called out his name, but there was no response. Still, he looked relatively unharmed, though unconscious. The front of his car, however, was a mangled wreck from the crash, and the windshield was cracked and broken from where the driver had hit it.

Tim called out to Claudia, "Where's your husband?"

"At work. I don't know where Dr. Logan is."

Jack looked at Tim, "Is Lysik a psychiatrist or psychologist? Maybe he could—"

Just then, Dr. Logan appeared from around the bend of Stoneridge. He reached the accident site, and upon seeing the broken glass scattered about, he asked, "What on earth happened?

Craig Logan wore comfortable running shoes, jogging pants, and a T-shirt drenched with sweat. As he walked toward the car wreck, he muttered, "My God!" Then he noticed Georgia Llewellyn's body in the middle of the road and stopped dead in his tracks.

"Where did you come from, doctor?" Tim asked full of curiosity.

"I was out jogging. What happened?"

"A terrible tragedy," Claudia said, standing beside Georgia's crumpled form.

Craig turned and scanned the shattered windshield, the broken driver's window, and the blood trickling down the side of David Yates' face.

"We ought to get him out of there," Tim said. "Can you get the door open? It doesn't appear to be too bad."

While the men discussed what to do about the unconscious man in the car, Marie said to Brenda, "Help me bring Linda into the house. I think she's bleeding."

"I'm sure it's nothing," Linda protested. "Just see that my husband's all right. I'm fine."

Blood still trickled down Linda's neck from a cut behind her ear, from when she'd hit the rock wall. Marie thought she saw blonde hairs near the bruised cut as she and Brenda helped the distraught woman into the Todd's house.

Meanwhile, Officer Tierney approached his sergeant and informed him the paramedics were on the way.

Throughout, Claudia Icarios stood beside Georgia Llewellyn like a guardian angel. All the while she pondered. She looked toward the car crash site and regarded Shane Lysik. Then she considered something. She glanced back at her own front yard. Had her eyes deceived her? She could see the bullet hole in the window. Its trajectory faced the Lysiks' house. Had Shane Lysik nearly been shot by accident? Things she'd seen with her own eyes did not follow logically. Had Todd Stuart actually attempted suicide? Unfortunately, her concentration was broken when Evelyn Martino appeared at her side.

"This is terrible. I never meant for this to happen. I saw Mr. Yates knock his wife against that retaining wall by their driveway. Then I heard my niece yell for help." She looked down at Georgia and tears welled up in her eyes. "I got in my car to try and block him. If only I'd been faster . . . I blocked the way up the street. I had no idea that Georgia had wandered into the road."

"Tragedy would seem to be the order of the day on Stoneridge. Todd Stuart nearly killed himself."

"Oh, my God! I thought I heard a gunshot," Evelyn said. "Is he okay?

"Yes." Claudia nodded. "He couldn't do it. Thank God. That young man has a strong will to live. He fired the gun out the window, and narrowly missed Mr. Lysik in the process."

Elated that her nephew was all right, she was nonetheless dismayed that someone else was nearly hurt.

Claudia continued. "We all rushed over to Todd Stuart's house. They yelled until he came out of the house with the gun still in his hand. He dropped it right there on the . . . Well, where is it?"

From where she stood, Claudia could see that there was no gun on the Stuarts' doorstep. She hurried over to the steps and looked around. Alarmed, she shouted, "The gun is missing!"

That drew Jack over to investigate. "He dropped it right here on the steps, didn't he?"

Claudia nodded. "It should be here."

Jack also scanned the immediate area. "It's not here now."

"Well, where could it have gone?" Claudia asked. Her voice was drowned out by an ambulance, its sirens blaring, as it turned down the street.

"Oh, heavens," Evelyn said. "I had better move my car before they ram through it."

She hurried up the street as Tim passed by Jack and Claudia and entered Todd's house. Upon his entrance, Miss Sparrow, who had not moved from her seat, opened her eyes and asked, "Is Georgia . . .?"

Tim answered, "It doesn't look good, but I'm not a doctor."

"What about my husband?" Linda asked, holding an ice pack to the back of her head.

Tim answered grimly, "Unconscious, but they think he'll be okay."

She started sobbing, though Tim thought it the type of crying that could almost be mistaken for laughter. Strangely, it reminded him of something Miss Sparrow had said earlier about fearing for the safety of those on Stoneridge. He understood her meaning all too well now. Presently, Tim crossed the room to where Todd Stuart wallowed in self-pity on the couch.

"Todd, where do you keep your gun?"

Todd mumbled, "In the drawer by the bed upstairs."

While Tim went in search of the gun, Jack Griffin led Dr. Logan into Todd Stuart's living room. Dr. Logan, having gone next door to his house to retrieve his medical bag, began to examine Linda's wounds before administering to Todd.

Some minutes later, Tim returned holding aloft a revolver with a pen through its trigger guard.

"It's not loaded," he said. "This gun was upstairs in the locked drawer where Ms. Llewellyn left it. I found the key hidden under the lamp. That means the gun Todd fired wasn't his."

Jack narrowed his eyes. "That's a Colt Agent Revolver, and I'll swear the gun Mr. Stuart dropped on the doorstep outside was a Colt Detective Special."

"I have a Colt Detective Special," Dr. Logan said abstractly, as he examined Linda's superficial wound.

Jack and Tim looked at him.

"Where is your gun now, doctor?" Jack asked.

"At my house. Why?"

"May I see it, doctor?"

"Let me finish here first."

Once he'd finished tending to Mrs. Yates, Dr. Craig Logan led Sgt. Griffin and Tim Dewitt to his house, where they discovered the doctor's gun missing.

Georgia Llewellyn was rushed to Upstate Hospital where she would be listed in serious condition. A second ambulance brought David and Linda Yates to the same hospital for treatment. He was kept overnight to be monitored for a concussion he'd received while Linda was patched up and released.

Meanwhile, the DeWitt police, under Jack Griffin's guidance, took statements from the residents of Stoneridge who'd witnessed the horrific accident. By then, Anne Esterhazy and Mildred Hawthorne had joined their neighbors to quench their curiosities about the afternoon's events.

While the neighbors milled about sharing gossip, Tim and Jack stepped aside to speak in private. They were interrupted moments later by a furious Mildred Hawthorne.

"What's this I hear about you arresting my grandson?"

"Mrs. Hawthorne, please," Jack said. "We've just taken him in for questioning."

"In handcuffs?"

Jack muttered to himself. Aloud, he said, "He is a suspect."

"Nonsense," Mildred protested. "He was with Martin and me at church when they say Rachel Stuart was killed." She whirled on Tim. "Your wife talked to him after Mass. Or did she forget to mention that?"

"So that's what's become of us?" Tim said, but he wasn't just talking to Mildred now. He couldn't stand it anymore. He was frustrated with neighbors—witnesses to two murders—withholding information, flinging accusations, and no doubt spreading malicious gossip. Raising his voice above the drone of the others, he continued. "You've had a supposed suicide, how many burglaries, two murders, and now this accident that nearly took the lives of two people. And nobody knows what happened, but everyone's guilty, right?" He paused as a few murmurs died down. "See, I know something. I know you're all hiding something. Maybe you don't think it's significant, but collectively everything counts. It's all part of the same picture. And I, for one, don't think that picture points to Joshua Deveraux."

He looked at Mildred, whose fury was replaced with a smug look. He glanced at the others, their various faces betraying shock or dismay, and saw that Jack was ready to shut him down, so he'd better hurry up and say what he felt he needed to say.

"Tell me what you know. I'll be home all day tomorrow. Alone. And if anyone's thinking about staying silent . . . let's just remember what happened to Rachel Stuart. I'm convinced she knew something, and she was killed before she could reveal what she knew. I already have a pretty good idea of that completed picture. I just need that corroboration from you. There's a cat among the pigeons, and I'll catch it by the tail!"

Neighbors eyed their neighbors warily. More than a few were stunned by Tim's revelation. Did he really know? Was he bluffing? Soon after, most of Stoneridge's residents withdrew silently, but Marie, Jack Griffin, and Angela Sparrow lingered behind.

"Tim, you're putting yourself in grave danger," Angela said, face twisted in anger.

"No, I'm not. Jack's going to be listening to everything that happens from the kitchen, while I'll be out in the living room. I've already arranged the whole scheme with Jack. Right, Jack?"

"Right," Jack said, gritting his teeth. His eyes flashed a cross look at Tim, who got the message loud and clear. Tim's superior was not happy about that stunt he'd just pulled.

"Tim, what are you thinking?" Marie clasped his arm. Worry was evident on in eyes.

"Find out the information we need to get this killer."

"And get killed in the process?"

At first, saying nothing, Angela shook her head in disgust and hobbled toward her house. Suddenly, she turned around and added, "Remember what you, yourself, said about a cat among the pigeons. This cat is very cunning and may just claim another pigeon if you're not careful."

"Don't worry. I'll be careful."

Unconvinced, Angela left without another word.

"Don't do this, Tim. I really have a bad feeling about this."

"Don't worry, Marie. I'll be fine. And Jack will be in the next room after all."

Dread filled Marie's heart. Her intuition warned her to be afraid.

Later that afternoon, Sonya Schwartz returned home after running some errands. She had barely stepped out of her car, when Anne Esterhazy swooped down on her from out of nowhere.

"Oh, yoo- hoo, Sonya? Have you heard the news?"

Oh, no! Sonya thought.

"No, Anne. What happened?"

"Why, you missed all the excitement. Mr. Deveraux was arrested for the murders, but that Tim Dewitt doesn't think he did it. And then Mr. Yates got in a horrible car accident and nearly killed Ms. Llewellyn. They were both rushed to the hospital in serious condition. I almost wish I were on duty today. Although I don't work in the ER."

"What?!" Sonya said, astounded by the news. "How did . . .?"

Anne Esterhazy went on to narrate what had occurred based on what she had been told by Mildred Hawthorne, who had in turn been told by Claudia Icarios. For once, Anne had completely captivated Sonya until she finished the story and, of course, began rambling.

"I think it's absolutely dreadful the way this neighborhood's gone to hell, but my oaf of a husband still doesn't care. 'So some people have been murdered. Happens every day,' he says. He'd rather sit and eat in front of the television. Meanwhile, I'm scared to death! Did you know they said Mr. Stuart tried to kill himself with a gun that wasn't his? The mysterious gun disappeared right under everyone's nose. It was Mr. Deveraux's doing. I'm sure of it. Brenda Lysik says he's a painter. If you ask me, painters always have some sort of bad disposition. They're not living in the real world. Brenda even said so. If you ask me, the man is a little batty in his belfry. I'm surprised he's only killed two people. He's that type, you know."

"What type?"

"The 'serial killer' type, of course. He's quiet and withdrawn. Lots of serial killers are like that. At least, that's what I've heard."

"Really, Anne. I think you're exaggerating just a little."

"Not at all, Sonya. I'm convinced beyond a reasonable doubt that Mr. Deveraux is the murderer. Mildred Hawthorne insists he was with her when Rachel Stuart was killed, but he could have done it earlier. The police haven't said what the time of death is. And I'll bet the police will find out that he's our burglar, too. How else is he able to afford that house of his? Houses on this street don't come dirt-cheap. And my husband is always complaining about how high our taxes are. Besides I have proof about Mr. Deveraux, and not just about him. I know about a lot of people."

"Be careful, Anne. It's dangerous to say things like that," said Sonya, who knew full well that Anne Esterhazy was letting on that she knew more than she actually did.

"Nonsense, Sonya. I can easily take care of myself," Anne said, nodding with self-importance. She had fully convinced herself that she knew something, though what that might be was anyone's guess.

Farther down the street, Mildred Hawthorne spoke in hushed tones with her neighbor Evelyn Martino in the latter's yard. "I never liked that young man. He was always pestering Joshua's wife. I knew he was no good."

"Poor Georgia."

"I know, Evelyn," Mildred said, shaking her head. "I still can't believe it. Things like that just don't happen every day. These murders have everyone on edge. If only it were all over. First, poor Danielle. Then the burglaries. The murders—" She stopped abruptly. Further down the street, she noticed Angela Sparrow talking to Brenda Lysik. Mildred remarked thoughtfully, "Claudia and I felt sure it was *her* husband."

"Todd? Mildred, he couldn't have. My nephew would

never hurt anyone. He had a complete breakdown. My God! He tried to kill himself!"

However, Mildred had not been talking about Todd Stuart.

"Really, Evelyn. I know he's your nephew, but he was an actor. Those drama types are always overreacting. He wouldn't have killed himself. He probably just staged the whole thing to get attention. I don't think he really liked her all that much. How could he? She was always telling him what to do."

"You mean Rachel Stuart?"

"Really, Evelyn, don't you know what your nephew's been up to? Of course, I meant Rachel Stuart. You should have heard her yelling at him down the street. You see, I was in my garden at the time, and . . ."

Evelyn listened to Mildred's story with grave interest and regret. She could only be horrified now to hear how Rachel had browbeaten her nephew. She'd never spent much time with her nephew or his wife since they'd moved here. She never took the time to get to know Rachel, but whenever she had tried to be polite, Rachel had brusquely brushed her off. Besides, she had her own life to lead. If only she had known . . .

Dusk brought a warm breeze that refreshed the atmosphere. Brenda Lysik, for once, decided it was the perfect weather to be outdoors in, and so she sat out on her front porch. Her husband would have joined her, but he'd been called away by some patient. Still, she hoped he wouldn't be long. They needed to spend more time together. Her work was getting in the way. She knew Shane didn't like it. He wanted her to spend time with him, not a bunch of papers.

Brenda lounged in a lawn chair and sipped her iced tea. Looking up the street, she noticed some neighbors conversing with each other. No doubt they were discussing the day's sad events. She looked down the street and saw Angela Sparrow hobbling up toward her.

"Hello, Brenda, how are you?" Angela asked. "Is your husband all right?"

"Yes, Miss Sparrow. That bullet gave him quite a scare. Him and me both. He said it missed him by mere inches."

"Really? Oh, how fortunate that it missed."

"I know. I couldn't imagine, well, it's just upsetting. The police still haven't been able to extract the bullet. Look, I'll show you."

Brenda helped Angela over to the garage door. She showed the tall, thin woman where a bullet had lodged itself in the garage door near the edge of the house.

"Oh, my. This is terrible! Your husband could have been killed!"

"Oh, I know. You saw how hard he was breathing after his close call. I'm just glad nothing happened. Of course, my husband tends to exaggerate. I doubt he was mere inches away. Still, I'm glad nothing did happen."

"My goodness. Mr. Stuart is certainly a lucky man. He is most fortunate that he didn't accidentally kill your husband. It would have been a terrible tragedy."

"For whom?"

"For everyone involved."

"Oh, yes. Of course. I see what you mean."

Jack Griffin looked forlorn. He and Tim stood in the Dewitts' driveway discussing the day's events. As it was, Jack didn't like the turn of events. He'd seen too much in his time as a police officer. True, he hadn't seen many murders over the course of his career, but he had experienced enough not to take things as lightly as Tim appeared to. "I really wish you hadn't done that," Jack said.

"What?"

"Tim, come on, you know what I mean. Don't you think you're being a little melodramatic with that speech of yours earlier? Setting yourself up as a sitting duck! Tim, you're a police officer. Start acting like one instead of some amateur armchair detective in a mystery novel!"

"I'm trying to do my job, Jack. Just like you. I'll admit my, well, procedures aren't exactly by-the-book, but I think it's the best way to get the answers we need. And the only way to get answers is to take, well, measures."

"Tim," Jack began gravely, "I think we've got the right man. Josh Deveraux may have gotten away with his wife's murder but he's not going to get away with these two."

"No, Jack. I'm not satisfied with Mr. Deveraux as the murderer. Everything's wrong with that. And you're forgetting Mrs. Hawthorne's testimony. No, there's something that's being overlooked. It just seems too simple. I don't know. I think Mr. Deveraux is innocent."

"Oh, come off it, Tim. You know he's guilty. He's gotta be. He killed his wife. That lady, Ms. Llewellyn, was babbling earlier about him having had an affair with Rachel Stuart. And Lisa probably knew about it. I'll bet that's why she had that five hundred dollars in her purse. He went to pay her off and killed her."

"Then why didn't he take the money back? It's a lot of cash."

"I don't know. Maybe he gave it to her earlier and thought she'd already put in the bank or something. We'll find out, Tim."

Tim shook his head, but didn't say anything. He looked instead at the street, at the houses in the neighborhood where he had come to live.

"It's them, you know," he said finally.

Tim looked up and down the street and saw various neighbors outside talking to each other.

"They're hiding something," he said. "Each one of them knows something. Something that would lead to the truth. The problem is that they refuse to reveal their secrets. They lack trust because they're too busy accusing each other in their minds. They don't think logically. They just go around suspecting one another. Always on their guard. Not knowing who to trust. The innocent become guilty until the guilty one is found. Just like Marie said. I can't give up, Jack. We've gotta catch this killer. We can't have another murder."

"Do you really think someone else may be killed?" Jack asked skeptically.

"Someone's already gotten away with two murders, possibly three. Why not another? If the murderer should suspect someone knows something incriminating . . ." He let the thought sink in. "Rachel Stuart probably knew something."

"But, Tim, you shouldn't put yourself at risk."

"I'm not taking a risk. You're going to be there on guard," Tim said. "Or should I worry?"

Carefully weighing his words, Jack answered, "I won't let anything happen, but that doesn't mean that something couldn't go wrong."

"Don't worry," Tim assured him. "I'll be on my guard, too."

"Yes, but this killer is bold. Killing Rachel in broad daylight was a gutsy thing to do. And if Joshua Deveraux isn't the killer. Look, Tim, I just don't want to have to attend the funeral of a friend."

"I won't let that happen!" Tim said firmly.

THURSDAY

Jack Griffin walked the short distance from his house on Alcove Place to the Dewitts'. The five-minute hike gave him time to think. What if Tim was right and he was targeting the wrong man? Could it be that he was too prejudiced to view this case objectively? He had been so dead certain that Deveraux had killed his wife. It had been all wrong. The way the body lay in the tub. The razor on the tile too far away. The hastily written note. It had all been made to look like a typical suicide, but its staginess had been apparent.

Jack looked up. It was starting off as a dismal and cloudy day, although rain did not seem likely. It seemed as if the gray skies were reflecting the clouded state of his mind. He just wanted this case to be over.

Meanwhile, Marie lay in bed and sighed. She knew Jack Griffin would be on his way, and her husband was already in the shower. It would have been the perfect day to sleep in with Tim. The light streaming in the bedroom lacked the brightness of a bright sunny day and suggested cloudy skies. She sighed again. How nice it would have been to cuddle next to Tim. It seemed they hadn't had a peaceful moment alone since last Thursday. Reluctantly, Marie slipped out of bed and prepared for her day ahead. Janessa Farentino, her close friend and former college roommate, was going to pick her up so the two of them could go shopping. She'd picked up clothes on their Sunday outing, and she thought of getting some home furnishings this time out. Still, Marie hadn't been thrilled about being virtually kicked out of the house, but Tim had insisted. He said it would be safer. Well, if he thought things would be too dangerous, why was he going through with this idiocy? Setting himself up as possible bait for the killer. Sometimes Marie felt Tim hadn't quite grown up yet.

Hearing the shower still going, Marie knocked on the door and shouted, "Are you going to be in there all day?"

About twenty minutes later, Marie sat with her husband in their living room listening to Jack Griffin. He related his conversation with his son Justin, who had been playing basketball with D.J. Logan at the time of Rachel Stuart's murder. Unfortunately, the boy had seen and heard nothing. In fact, he had been angered and upset to think of someone being killed so near to him, and his father had tried ineffectually to comfort him.

"He still thinks about his mother," Jack said.

Marie looked toward her husband, who paced across the black-and-white tiled kitchen floor.

"I'm sorry, Jack," Tim said, trying to hide his disappointment.

"Please stop pacing, Tim," Marie pleaded. Turning to Jack, seated across the table from her, she continued, "He didn't sleep much last night. He keeps trying to crack this thing. I know it's important to get to the bottom of it all, but I wish he wouldn't take this risk."

"I tried to talk him out of it," Jack said, throwing up his hands. Addressing Tim he added, "It's a juvenile idea!"

"I'm sorry, you two. But I don't see how else to get these people to talk. It's been like pulling teeth ever since Rachel's body was discovered."

"But, Tim," began Jack, who was interrupted by the doorbell.

Marie answered it. Her former roommate, Janessa Farentino, was at the door. She went to Tim, hugging him protectively, and whispered to him to be careful. He nodded, and she left with Janessa, who waved hello and goodbye to Tim before being dragged off by Marie.

Meanwhile, Tim and Jack set aside talk of the murders for the moment to discuss sports, but it wasn't long before there came a faint knocking at the door. Tim wasn't even certain he'd actually heard a knock, but he went to see if someone was there just as another tentative knock sounded. Opening the door, he found Bryant Logan standing on his doorstep. One would have thought the twelve-year-old boy was a cat caught in a downpour scratching on the door wanting to come in, only it hadn't rained since Tuesday night.

"Hello, Bryant. What brings you here?"

"I heard about what you said yesterday afternoon, you know, after the ambulance came and took Ms. Llewellyn and those other people away. I thought I should come over and tell you something. Can I come in?"

"Yes. I—I just didn't expect—"

Bryant interrupted, "I know. People consider a kid like me wouldn't know anything. Why should I? It's not like I ever get in trouble. But that doesn't mean I don't know things."

"No, I didn't mean it like that."

He thought back to his own childhood and what it had been like. He remembered being asked to leave the room when the adults wanted to talk about something. Adults talking in whispered murmurings. Adults telling him half-truths. Children saw nothing. Children heard nothing. Children didn't understand. They were too young; their only crime was that they were not adults. Even now, Tim was amazed by how often adults neglect the testimony of children. How often they don't listen. If children did speak up and tell what they saw or heard, they were hushed. Don't be a tattletale. What nonsense! Tim remembered when he'd been seven years old. He'd seen something awful. Something he didn't care to remember just now.

"I'm sorry," he said to the boy. "Come in."

"D.J. might have told you," Bryant said, a bit firmer than his earlier, weak tone, "I was mowing the lawn when she was murdered. You know there's that bunch of trees between the Stuarts' house and ours. They're evergreens, but you can still see a little bit between the branches. Friends and I have watched Lisa sunning herself." The boy's face reddened in embarrassment, but he continued in order to draw attention away from it. "I saw it happen. Through the trees." A frightened look crossed Bryant's face, as he said, "I saw him kill her. He wore some sort of uniform. He had the shovel in his hands. I couldn't see his face. I didn't know he'd killed her, 'til later. But after finding that girl's body and hearing that Rachel was dead, I was too scared to say anything."

"It's okay, Bryant. We're all a little scared. These murders are a little too close to home." After a pause, Tim asked, "Are you sure you didn't see the man's face?"

"No. He was facing the other way. I could only make out the uniform he was wearing. It was a brown outfit like what the meter man wears."

"Or a repairman?"

"Yeah, I suppose." Bryant paused before adding, "I'm just afraid I'll be killed next. When I think of what happened to Lisa and Rachel, I know they took Mr. Yates away, but somehow I don't think he was in this alone."

David Yates? The boy must have heard wrong, thought Tim. "What makes you think he did it?"

"Because he takes drugs. He's gotten them from Lisa. The same place D.J.—"

"What about D.J.?"

Bryant averted his eyes. "He got drugs from Lisa," he said solemnly. "But she got the drugs from someone else. That's why I'm afraid. You said that people can get murdered if they know too much. That's what you said yesterday. I heard you."

"I see," Tim said thoughtfully.

"What do you think I should do?"

The boy's blue-green eyes beseeched him.

"Nothing. Just act normal and—"

"But what about D.J.?" Bryant interrupted. "I'm worried about him."

"I'll see what I can do about it."

"Would you?" he asked, brightening up.

"I'll try."

"But you'll . . . you won't say I told you?"

"No," Tim said. "You'd better get home now before you're missed."

After the boy had left, Tim returned to the kitchen, where Jack had already poured the coffee. Looking into his cup, Tim frowned. It was black, and he needed cream and sugar. Before he could add these, though, the doorbell rang. His smile was a self-congratulatory one, for his plan seemed to be working; however, his smile quickly changed into a frown when he opened the door.

"Oh, God," he muttered.

Anne Esterhazy, a.k.a. The Babbler, bustled passed Tim. She started talking almost immediately and, as usual when she was nervous, she gestured incessantly with her hands while she babbled on.

"Mrs. Esterhazy, slow down." He hadn't understood a word she'd said. It was like it had all been one long word!

"Oh, you were so right," Anne said breathlessly. "When you said we were all holding back something, I mean. I just feel so guilty. I should have come forward sooner. Maybe if I had, maybe Rachel Stuart might still be alive. And maybe, maybe yesterday wouldn't have happened."

Anne rambled on, "I am positive my information could have put that Mr. Yates behind bars where he could have caused no harm. I tell you I know something that would shock the neighborhood. I don't know why I didn't say something sooner. But you never think what you see will be important.

I mean it seemed so innocent at the time. But of course, how could I know someone was being murdered! Well, that's why I had to come now. I just knew I had to tell you."

"What do you know, Mrs. Esterhazy?"

"Well, you see, I was out for a walk that night when Lisa Collins was killed. I had just arrived back home when I heard gunshots from down the street at eleven twenty. I even saw that car which drove up the hill. It drove right past me, and I saw the driver of the car. It was a man in a mechanic's uniform."

"Who was it?"

"I don't know. I couldn't see the man's face. But there was someone else outside that night. I saw Mr. Yates leave his house and walk down the street at ten o'clock, when I left on my walk. And—"

Tim interrupted, "You were out walking for an hour and a half?"

"Well, yes, I needed some fresh air. I was angry at my husband. You see, I had had a little domestic squabble with the oaf. I was trying to get him to be more active than he was. I just couldn't take his yelling so I left and missed *Knots Landing*. I think Sonya Schwartz may have suspected that fact, but I tried to bluff my way through. You see, when I went out for my walk, I spent some time with a friend on Rosehill Drive, the next street over from ours. I spent about forty minutes with her, telling her about my problems. It was on my way to her house that I saw Mr. Yates leaving his house."

For a moment, Tim thought Anne may be lying or at least making up half-truths, but he could see the sincerity in her eyes. Tim was very perceptive when it came to people. He may not always remember what they were wearing, but he could always remember the expression on their face. It was a trait he had learned at a young age.

"You were saying about Mr. Yates?"

"Yes, well, I watched him walk down the street towards Lisa Collins's house. Oh, and I noticed some flashes of light coming from the Icarioses' yard, and I saw Mrs. Hawthorne leaving the Icarioses' house and returning to her own."

"Did you see Mrs. Icarios?"

"Not then. But I did see someone in the Icarioses front yard later when I returned to my house. I assumed it was Mrs. Icarios, but I could be wrong. Although I can't imagine who else it could have been, except Mrs. Icarios. Yes, it must have been her."

Tim suspected Anne hadn't actually seen Claudia.

"Did you see anyone else, Mrs. Esterhazy?" Tim asked, hoping he wasn't leading a highly suggestible witness.

"No. Only the man in the mechanic's uniform crossing the street to Lisa's house around ten o'clock. I think the man came from Mr. Deveraux's house. In fact, I'm sure he came from Mr. Deveraux's house."

"Are you sure the man went to Lisa's house?"

"I'm pretty sure he did. He could have gone to the Stuart's house, I suppose," Anne said. "Although it was a week ago now. It's so hard to remember things that happened last week, isn't it?"

Abruptly, she blurted out, "It had to be Lisa's house. Where else could he have gone? Really, I'm sure that has to be what I saw. Anyway, I really must be going now. I've left my children alone, and there's no telling what they'll get into. They were watching TV when I left, but they always get so antsy. They can never pay attention to anything long enough. Bub- bye!"

Anne scurried out the front door and wandered up the street to her house. She was sure she had done the right thing by telling what she knew. She just hoped she had told it right. Perhaps she should ask someone's opinion, but she didn't see anybody about. Maybe Sonya was home. And so

Anne hurried up to her neighbor's house. She didn't see the colonel step out of his house after she'd passed by.

Meanwhile, Tim, glad to be rid of The Babbler, noticed Col. Hawthorne approaching. The colonel had an odd gait. Some stiffness, perhaps an old war injury, caused his left leg to stop short of its full range of motion. He didn't exactly limp, but his stride was not quite normal. Of course, Tim could not help roll his eyes heavenward and wonder how such a clever idea had gone so horribly wrong. Col. Hawthorne was known for rambling extensively on and on about his war experiences, and Tim had been cornered more than once by the old boy.

Between Anne Esterhazy and the colonel, thought Tim just as the colonel's rapped knock sounded.

"Hello, Colonel. What brings you here?"

The man coughed gruffly.

"Was about in the street. Saw that Esterhazy woman drop by. Thought I might do the same."

"Would you like to sit?"

"Ach, no. I don't intend to stay long."

Tim sighed with relief.

"The missus sent me over. Due to present circumstances." He paused a moment and coughed again. "She, er, she thought I should pop by and speak up as it were."

"Oh, and what do you know, Colonel?"

"Well, it has to do with bird watching."

"Bird watching?"

"Ah, yes. I'm sure you've heard of it. It happens to be a hobby of mine."

And I'll bet you also spy on other people at the same time. Tim smiled wryly. He wondered how the colonel had picked up bird watching as a hobby. Still, the colonel could be frank at times. Just as long as he wasn't relating some war story or some boyhood experience which could drone on for ages. As that wasn't the case presently, he came right to the point.

"I happened to be bird watching the day Rachel Stuart was ruthlessly murdered. Was watching some playful goldfinches in a rather obscure area behind that huge yew bush on our lawn. I happened to notice Rachel Stuart gardening in her front yard. She had a shovel with her. I supposed that that was the one that done her in later. Well, like I said, she was gardening. Then for no reason at all she takes the shovel and places it by the garage door. Her husband came out of the house and left. Rachel then disappeared."

"Around the side of the house?"

"No. She went the other way. She looked around cautiously, then crossed the street, and went to Mr. Deveraux's house. She was there for about an hour before she returned to her house and went around the side to the backyard. Only when she passed the garage door, the shovel was gone!"

"It wasn't there?"

"No. You see this meter man fellow had come out of nowhere and had taken it. He then had gone around the side of the house before Rachel Stuart came back."

"Did you see his face?"

"No. His back was to me most of the time. Not to mention he wore a cap which covered his face. The man came back to the front yard after Rachel had gone to the backyard. He didn't have the shovel then. He just walked away down the street."

"Was the man wearing gloves?"

"I, ah, I don't remember. Well, er, really I don't know. He might have been wearing gloves, but then again he might not have. You know, I didn't really pay particular attention. Of course, gloves come in all colors. I tell you this whole affair reminds me of the time when—"

"Ah, colonel, I have another visitor coming," Tim said. He explained how the colonel could make a swift exit. "You can slip out through the basement."

"Where?"

"I'm sure it's the same as your house. The door in the dining room," Tim prompted.

The colonel nodded and left.

Thankful for having avoided one of the colonel's long-winded war stories, Tim opened the front door, and Marie's aunt brushed passed him, gliding into the living room and perching on the couch. Tim maneuvered in front of her, blocking her view out the window so she wouldn't see the colonel. Then he asked, "Are you okay, Ms. Martino?"

"Call me Aunt Evie."

"Okay," Tim said. "What brings you here?"

"You really alarmed me with that speech yesterday. I simply had to come and tell you what I know."

"And what do you know?"

"Not enough to convict someone if that's what you mean." Evelyn sounded disappointed.

"Well, please, tell me what you do know."

"It was Sunday, the day Rachel Stuart was murdered. I was just about to leave for church when Mildred Hawthorne stopped by. She and her husband were headed out, too. Well, Mildred was looking down the street."

Evelyn's tone indicated that she wished the positions had been reversed.

"I noticed she had a very puzzled look on her face. She seemed distressed by something she saw down the street. Finally, I looked back and saw a repairman hurrying off down the street. He was passing Georgia Llewellyn's house. I really didn't know the significance of what I had seen. I still don't think I see the full significance of it, but the fact remains that Mildred saw more than I did. She must have seen the man."

"About what time was this?"

"Oh, just after ten."

"One more question. Where was the colonel when this happened?"

"I don't know," she said, seemingly startled. "I assume he was still inside. I left for church before they did."

"Are you sure? He wasn't out bird watching?"

"Bird watching? That's an odd hobby for someone with a glass eye."

"So he wasn't there?"

"No, I'm sure I would have seen him," Evelyn said. "Tim, I'm sorry but I have to be going. I have a dinner party to get ready for tonight. My mother likes all her dinner guests to dress formally. She's very much against the lax manners in today's generation."

As they stood, she added, "Do be careful, Tim. Marie would be devastated to lose you. This idea of your playing cat-and-mouse today is not a good idea. I don't think this killer knows any bounds."

"I'll be careful."

"Well, just be sure that you are. By the way, either you or Marie should have a talk with Mildred or Claudia. Those two definitely know more than they've been admitting."

When no one else had made an immediate appearance after Evelyn Martino's departure, Tim decided to take advantage of the golden opportunity to break for lunch. While Tim fixed up some sandwiches, Jack made a few phone calls. When the sergeant was done, Tim asked, "Find out anything?"

"Yes," Jack said. "I had them run a check on Lisa's accounts. They could reflect the account of a drug dealer. So that the Logan kid's testimony could be legit. We also rechecked Rachel Stuart's bank accounts and found that she has a separate account with a large amount of cash in it. The money's apparently been in there since spring of last year. Apparently, Rachel has been dipping into the secret savings account and putting it into another account when she had need of money."

"Ah, I see," Tim said.

"By the way," Jack began, "what that Logan kid said about the mechanics' uniform. Well, I didn't mention it before, but we found such a uniform in the trunk of Lisa's car. There was a tear where the name patch had been removed, but it matched the type of uniform used at Kelly Repair, Co., the business Deveraux works at. That and the gun were what led us to make his arrest."

"Then why did you let him go?"

"His grandmother. Mildred Hawthorne threatened to raise a stink. Apparently, she's chummy with the town supervisor's wife."

"Wow."

"Yeah, well, it's not like that would have made me turn him loose, but we also checked up on Deveraux's story about being at the movies Thursday night. Turns out the concessions clerk remembered him. We're still checking to see if he could have slipped out early and made it back in time to kill Lisa—"

The phone rang, interrupting Jack. Tim answered it, but handed the phone over when the person on the line asked for Jack. Tim stood a couple feet away and strained to listen to both ends of the conversation. He wasn't able to make out the full story, but he waited until Jack was finished before asking any questions.

"The autopsy's in, isn't it?" Tim asked, once Jack had hung up.

Jack nodded grimly.

"And?"

"Lisa was killed by a blow to the back of head. She was shot after she was dead."

"What?"

"They've double checked the results. A colleague of Dr. Icarios confirmed it. They found a fracture to the back of the victim's skull, and they found bits of brick in the wound. They also matched traces of blood on the scalpel we found in Lisa's house to Danielle Deveraux." Jack paused before adding, "I can't understand it, Tim. The gun we found, the one belonging to Deveraux, was used to shoot Lisa, but she was already dead. This whole thing is . . . it's bizarre!"

"You tell me. I'm just as baffled as you are."

"Well, at least one thing checked out."

Tim looked at his friend, as Jack said, "Early this morning, one of my officers, you know Ryan Tierney, found Dr. Logan's missing gun behind some bushes in front of Lisa Collins's house. Likely tossed there by someone. Preliminary tests concluded that the slug we dug out of the Lysiks' garage door came from Dr. Logan's gun, the one Todd Stuart fired."

"Curiouser and curiouser," Tim said.

After lunch, Tim didn't have to wait long before another neighbor decided to drop by. Joshua Deveraux hesitated at the end of the Dewitts' driveway. He looked about uncertainly, but took a deep breath and shuffled toward the house. He knocked twice and waited, ready to bolt should no answer be forthcoming. He shifted his weight from left foot to right foot and back again several times. He turned to go just as Tim, shocked by a visit from the accused, opened the door.

"I talked to Miss Sparrow this morning," Joshua said, shoving his hands in his pocket. "She told me what you had said yesterday and said I should come see you. Can I come in?"

"Ah, sure," Tim said, ushering him inside.

"I had told her something," Joshua continued. "She said I should tell you, but first . . ." He looked Tim in the eyes. "I want to thank you."

"Thank me?"

"Yeah. I want to thank you for believing in my innocence," Joshua said sincerely.

"Well, you're welcome," Tim said, flabbergasted. "What was it Miss Sparrow wanted you to tell me?"

"She said I should tell you about a painting in my studio."

"Oh, yes, the portrait. It's of your wife, right?"

"Yes," Joshua said, looking down at his hands. "I'd started it before . . ." Absently, he scratched at his fingernails. "Before she died. I couldn't bring myself to finish it. Dave Yates saw it one day when he stopped by and begged me for it. I didn't agree then. But after a couple days, I just . . . I couldn't bear to look at it anymore. I called Dave and told him. He was planning to pick it up Thursday night."

"The night Lisa was killed?"

"Yeah. I thought he was going to pick it up earlier, but I guess he went to the Neighborhood Watch meeting?" He looked at Tim as if for verification. When Tim nodded, he continued. "Well, I decided to go out. So I left a message on his answering machine, saying I wasn't gonna be there. He must not have gotten it because he did come to my house that night. He left a note on the easel. It said he'd found my door unlocked, that he came in to look at the portrait, and that he'd be in touch. I told the police about the note, but it's missing. I just can't seem to find it anywhere."

A tinge of guilt swept Tim's body, but he tried not to think about it as he said, "I have a few questions, if you don't mind."

"Sure. I'll tell you what I can," Joshua said sincerely.

"Were you and Rachel Stuart having an affair? My wife saw some bruises on your wrist Sunday."

Joshua lowered his eyes and again focused on his hands.

"Rachel and I dated briefly a couple years ago. That was before she married Todd. Then I fell in love with Danielle."

He scratched at the cuticle of his thumb. "But there was something about Rachel. She knew how to go after what she wanted. When she moved here . . ." Joshua choked up with guilt. He looked up at Tim. "Yes. I let Rachel walk all over me again. It only happened a couple times, and I hated myself for doing that to Danielle. When I first found her I thought she'd found out, but . . ."

"Were you having an affair with Lisa, too? Some neighbors saw the two of you together."

"No," Joshua said, looking Tim in the eye. "Lisa and I were just friends. She tried to warn me about Rachel, but I didn't want to hear it. You don't want to face the guilt sometimes, you know? I should have listened though. Lisa had been a good friend to me ever since we met, and I really think it's awful the way everyone perceived her. She wasn't as bad as everyone says. She listened to you and didn't judge you, and she was a hell of a lot better than Rachel."

"All right, I just have one more question. How did you happen to drop by the Stuarts' house on Thursday to fix their air conditioner?"

"My boss got a call and told me a woman had specifically asked for me. I recognized the address. I told my boss I'd do the job after my lunch break. I drove home, had lunch, and then I walked over to Rachel's house. Mrs. Icarios was there at the time, but she left after dropping off that shovel."

"But Rachel denied calling for a repairman that day. At least, that's what she told me."

"I really don't know what to say," Joshua said with a shrug of bewilderment.

An awkward pause ensued until Tim finally asked, "Is there anything else you can think of that might be important?"

Joshua shook his head. Tim then asked him to wait a moment while he took the opportunity to check up on something. He went to his bedroom where he found the jeans he'd worn yesterday. He extracted the small scrap of paper, which he had picked up in Josh Deveraux's studio, and read it.

Josh,

Your door was unlocked, but you weren't home. I just had to look at the painting again. Hope you don't mind. Sorry I missed you. I'll call soon.

Dave

Returning to the living room, Tim showed the note to Joshua.

"Is this the note?"

Joshua confirmed it was. Tim could see he was both relieved and perplexed, but though he looked up at Tim and appeared about to ask a question, Joshua didn't pursue the topic. Instead, Tim asked him if there was anything else he knew, but he couldn't think of anything.

After Joshua's departure, Tim entered the kitchen and handed the note to Jack.

"Why didn't you show this to me before?" Jack demanded.

"Sorry. I picked it up, and then we heard that gunshot, and I forgot about it."

"Next time, follow procedure, Tim," Jack said sternly.

"I will."

Jack sighed heavily as he looked at the note again. Was it possible he was wrong about Deveraux? Then again, how could he be sure this was David Yates' handwriting? He heard Tim ask a question, but the doorbell rang before he could answer.

Dutifully, Tim went to answer the door yet again. When he'd given his speech yesterday, he hadn't quite expected such a response. It seemed like the whole neighborhood wanted to confess something, and it was starting to tire Tim out.

"Why, Shane, what are you doing here?"

"I have to get something off my chest. Can we sit down and talk?"

"Sure. Please come in."

Tim led Shane Lysik to the couch facing the window as he said, "I must say this is a bit of an awkward situation for me. I hadn't expected you to come to me. I just didn't think you knew anything. Your wife said you were taking sleeping pills at night for insomnia."

"Well that's why I came to talk to you. You see, I didn't take my pill on Thursday night. I only pretended I did for my wife's sake. I just couldn't stand taking those pills. However, I found myself restless like I was before . . . before I started taking the sleeping pills. We had gone to bed shortly after getting back from the meeting that night. My wife soon fell asleep, but I got up and walked out to the living room. It must have been around ten o'clock when I saw him."

"Saw who?"

"Well, I don't think it means anything, but I saw Mr. Yates go to Lisa Collins's door. Only I never saw him come out."

"Did you go back to bed?"

"Yes. I went back to bed and lay awake. Then I heard some shots a little after eleven."

"The ones that were fired at eleven- twenty," Tim said.

"Yes, I suppose that's when it happened. But you don't think David Yates killed her? I mean he didn't know her, did he? What motive could he have had?"

"I don't know if he killed her, but I certainly don't know enough to say that he didn't. The whole mess is confusing."

"Yes," Shane interjected.

"I feel I can confide in you since your wife works at Dewitt's. It's just that we've never really gotten a chance to talk to each other."

"I know, Tim."

"This whole business is unreal. Everybody's so jumpy, so frightened. I just don't know when or where it's all going to end. This murderer seems to be more of a fictional character than a real person. I constantly see this person whom I can't find. He's just there. In fact, he seems to be everywhere at once!"

"I'm sure the police will catch their man. You really have to take your mind off it. Don't think about it so much."

"Yeah, I know you're right. Marie will think I'm crazy. Of course, she already thinks that." Tim's face brightened up. "But I did manage to get her out of the house today. I figured it'd be better to tackle people alone."

Tim didn't hear his neighbor's next statement, for he had jumped out of his seat so fast that he almost knocked Shane over.

"Quick. You'll have to leave by the back way. Your wife is coming up the driveway."

Shane appeared agitated, but he shook his head.

"It's better if I go out the front. Brenda won't care that I dropped by."

Shane strode to the front door and opened it before his wife could reach the steps. He gave her a peck on the cheek, whispering, "I'll tell you later." Then he jogged across the Dewitts' front lawn to his house.

Brenda watched him go, but then she stalked up the steps and entered the Dewitts' house.

"Well, Tim, what exactly do you think you're doing? If your mother knew—"

Tim cut her off, "What are you doing here, Brenda. I'd thought you'd be at work?"

As they sat down on the couch adjacent to the window, Brenda answered, "I left early. I wanted to speak with you. I think this approach of yours is foolish. I know you knew about Lisa's murder before her body was discovered, and I know I didn't believe you. I'm sorry, but what are you trying to do? Get yourself killed?"

"I am trying to solve a murder."

"I thought that was the police sergeant's job. You've only been an officer, what, two years?"

"We all pitch in on a case, Brenda."

"But you're on vacation. You should be enjoying your time with your wife. Not chasing down a killer who would just as soon kill you. You should follow your own advice. If the murderer suspects you, then you're in danger. You practically told the murderer yesterday that you're on to him. What's gotten into you?"

Before Tim could say anything, Brenda continued, "Fine. You don't have to explain anything to me. I just want you to be careful. My husband was almost killed because someone wasn't careful." Brenda shuddered for a moment at her own words. She finally said, "I should be going. I just wanted to stop by and make sure you were all right. You will be careful won't you?"

"Of course."

"Good. Remember, tomorrow is the party at our house for you and Marie. It'll start at six, so don't be late."

"We'll see you tomorrow then," Tim said, bewildered by the whole conversation. Was she scolding him? As he showed Brenda to the door, he wondered if any of his neighbors took him seriously. He may not be in his uniform, but he was an officer of the law.

"My son told me that he visited you early this morning," Craig Logan said crossly. He'd arrived about ten minutes after Brenda Lysik's departure. "I'd prefer you not talking to my sons without my being there."

"I'm just trying to get at the truth, Dr. Logan. Why are you so averse to having this mystery solved?"

"I want this business resolved just as much as you do."

"Then why have you been so antagonistic? What do you

know? Is there something you're afraid to tell me? Are you protecting someone?"

"No. I don't know anything," Craig affirmed. He looked away from Tim and stared out the window.

"The police found your gun, Dr. Logan. It was found in the bushes by Lisa Collins's house. Todd nearly killed himself with it yesterday. Do you have any idea how he got it?"

"No."

"The police also found a scalpel in Lisa's house. There was blood on it."

Craig visibly paled.

"Care to explain, Dr. Logan?"

"I didn't kill anyone!" He stared defiantly at Tim. "That scalpel could have come from anywhere. And my gun could have been stolen. There've been an awful lot of burglaries in this neighborhood lately."

"Perhaps the scalpel was stolen from your medical bag?" suggested Tim, who remembered the doctor's actions when they found Rachel dead. Dr. Logan had tried to prevent anyone from seeing into his medical bag. Perhaps he'd discovered or realized that something was missing.

"That's possible. I don't use that medical bag often."

Craig Logan sat back on the couch with renewed confidence.

"Besides," he said, gesturing with his right hand, "what does a scalpel have to do with these murders? Lisa was shot, and Rachel was hit with a shovel."

"Ah, but Danielle Deveraux's wrists were slashed with a sharp object."

Craig sat up straight and jerked his head to look at Tim. He didn't like the smug look on the younger man's face. "That was a suicide," he stated, but he made it almost sound like a question.

Tim shrugged. "Maybe. I think the sergeant is looking

into it." He didn't mention the blood found on the scalpel or that it belonged to Danielle Deveraux.

"I heard she used a razor," Craig said coldly, almost clinically. "I also heard that the husband had a flat tire that day, but the sergeant was suspicious of that story. Yet the police accepted the verdict of suicide."

Tim wondered where Craig had heard his information, but merely said, "Looks can be deceiving."

"My God! What is this neighborhood coming to? Everyone's gone mad. I look around and see everyone accusing his or her neighbor. It's got to stop! It's got to stop I tell you. It's ruining us!"

"I agree, doctor," Tim said. "Perhaps then you will answer a question that's been on my mind. It's been rumored that you and Lisa Collins dated. Is that true?"

"That's none of your business," Craig snapped. He abruptly got up and left, slamming the door behind him.

The sound brought Jack out of the kitchen. He saw Tim get up and move toward the window.

"I hope you don't mind that I told Craig Logan a few details."

Jack moved to sit on the couch Tim had just vacated. "Sometimes, to get at the truth, we have to— Hey, what's this?" He patted the couch. "Did something spill? It's wet."

"Wet?"

"Yes," Jack said, pointing to the spot. He brushed it again with his forefinger and sniffed it, but couldn't identify the smell.

When Tim performed the same task, he began to sneeze violently. His eyes began to water, and he started to wheeze. As quick as he could, he rushed to the master bedroom and to the bathroom there. After ten minutes behind a closed door, Tim stepped out into the hall. He had washed his hands and taken some Benadryl.

"You all right?" asked Jack, who thought he'd heard Tim vomit.

Tim nodded. "The Benadryl helped. There're some paper towels in the kitchen. Would you mind wetting them, maybe with some vinegar, and rubbing the stain? Then turn the couch pillow over."

"Sure, but why?"

"I only have one allergy, Jack." Pointing to the stain, Tim added, "And somehow that contains it."

Tim watched from the relative safety of the hall and waited until Jack flipped the couch cushion over. Then as he stepped into the living room, he heard something buzzing. An occasional tap called his attention to the window.

"Kill it, Jack!"

On some level, Tim knew the fear was irrational, but he couldn't forget how he'd nearly died as a little boy after a bee stung him. He watched, immobile, as Jack snatched one of Marie's home and garden magazines and—having a little difficulty eradicating the bee from the face of the earth—swatted it dead.

"What's gotten into you, Tim?"

"What was it?"

"A yellow jacket. Why?"

"I'm allergic! If I had been stung, it could have been fatal. Only a few people outside the family know."

"The Benadryl," Jack said, remembering something he'd once read.

"It's got diphenhydramine." Tim briefly explained how it countered the toxin in bee stings. Then he said, "Sorry I yelled."

Jack waved that concern aside. "No, I get it. But I don't understand about the stain on the couch? You sure you're not allergic to something else?"

"Only bees and wasps. Whatever it was, it must be similar

to the toxin bees and wasps carry in their stingers. I don't know how that stain got there."

"It couldn't have been there long," Jack said.

"I'm sure it wasn't there before lunch," Tim said, thinking over the events of the day. "I'd say it got there sometime after Josh Deveraux's visit."

"Goddamnit, Tim, Jack said. "I warned you about this . . . this stupid idea of setting yourself up as bait. You could have been killed!"

"I know—"

Jack cut him off. "This isn't a game! You're not playing some part in a mystery novel. There's a procedure to follow, and it's there for a reason." Jack rubbed his temples as if he were experiencing the onset of a headache. "I shouldn't have let you . . ."

"We had to get the information somehow. And you have to admit, this attempt on my life narrows the suspect list dramatically."

"Well, I'm not risking anyone's life to narrow it further. Damn it, Tim, I can't do this anymore!"

"Wha—?" asked Tim, furrowing his eyebrows.

With a heavy sigh, Jack slumped on the couch. Looking up at Tim, he said, "You don't know what it's like. Your wife and kids driving along in a car ..."

Jack blinked back tears.

"There was nothing I could do. Nothing! I wasn't there. My son witnessed the whole thing. He watched his mother and sister die. I had to do something, Tim. I had to. So I became a police officer. Hoping to right wrongs and make this world better for my son. I thought in some way it would make up for my wife and daughter's death."

He shuddered.

"I've investigated murder cases before. I've investigated hundreds of burglaries and drug racketeers. And I've been shot at! Nearly killed once. Tim, I've got a kid barely in high school. He hasn't got anybody else but me. Maybe I'm just getting burned out."

Tim wanted to ease his friend's mind, but he scarcely knew what to say. Then the doorbell rang, and the moment was gone. Both men looked at each other.

Tim trudged to the door. *Who could be it be now?* The doorbell rang again three times in succession before he could open it.

Marie breezed in with several shopping bags in hand and headed for the dining room table.

"So I forgot my key. It's no big deal. I knew you would be home. You practically let the whole neighborhood know that!" Marie paused as she noticed the grim expressions on Tim and Jack's faces. "What's wrong? What's happened?"

Jack answered, "Someone tried to kill Tim."

"Oh, my God!" Marie sunk into the nearest dining room chair. She fought back tears as she looked up at her husband. "Who's next? What more do we have to go through to catch this . . . murderer? Three deaths and so many tragedies. My brother, Ms. Llewellyn, the Yateses . . ."

"Marie, it's okay," Tim said. He knelt by his wife's side and put his hands on her shoulder to comfort her. "We will get to the bottom of this."

After dinner, Marie watched Tim drive off. He'd filled her in on the details of his conversations with their neighbors and was off to meet Jack Griffin at the police station. They planned to look over the various police reports coming in about this case. She wished Tim could have stayed away from work on their vacation. She herself wasn't due back at the Syracuse Botanical Gardens until next week. While out on their shopping expedition, she and Janessa had talked about the Gardens. They had been talking about one of the unfinished exhibits, and it had reminded Marie of something.

Something that had been said at the Tuesday night's bridge game. She had completely forgotten about it until now.

She remembered Janessa had been talking about night-blooming flowers, and Marie had thought it funny that it was the second time in a week someone had mentioned them. The topic had come up at the Tuesday night bridge game. Something about Evening Stock blooming. Hadn't her Aunt Evie and Mrs. Esterhazy both said something about witnessing flashes the night of the murder? The type of flash from a camera, perhaps?

Marie left her house and hurried across the street. She rang the doorbell until Dr. Icarios answered the door.

"May I help you?"

"Yes, Dr. Icarios. I was wondering where your wife is?"

"She's over at the Hawthornes'."

"Oh," Marie said, taken aback. "Thank you."

Dr. Icarios closed his door, and Marie smiled. She was glad, for now she would be able to deal with two people at once. Cautiously, she made her way up the incline of Stoneridge in the darkening twilight. As she went, Marie was startled by an owl hooting off to her right. She sped up until she had reached the end of the Hawthornes driveway, where she paused to catch her breath and felt slightly foolish for being in the least bit frightened. When the owl hooted again ominously, Marie scurried up to the Hawthornes' doorstep, where she knocked on the door with fervor.

Mildred Hawthorne appeared startled to see Marie, but she soon recovered her manners and graciously invited Marie into the living room, where Claudia was sitting on the sofa.

"Where's your husband?" Marie asked Mildred.

"Out. He's at a club meeting for war veterans. Why did you come?"

Marie explained, "Actually, I came here to see both of you. You were both outside the night Lisa Collins was killed, weren't you? I remembered overhearing you two discussing plans at the Neighborhood Watch meeting that night. Mrs. Icarios later gave me the impression she was outside tending to a flower, and she mentioned night-blooming flowers at Tuesday's bridge game. It finally hit me today what that all meant."

"Evening Stock," Claudia said.

"Yes," Marie, "also called Queen- of- the- Night."

"Was that enough to tip you off?" Mildred said, sitting down beside Claudia.

"Well, not quite, Mrs. Hawthorne. Mrs. Esterhazy told my husband she had seen flashes of light—and both of you—that night. More or less. And," Marie added, stretching the truth, "I myself saw the flashes of light that night."

"We better tell her what happened, Mildred."

Marie sat perched in an armchair, waiting anxiously for what they had to say.

"Mildred and I planned to watch the Evening Stock bloom Thursday night," Claudia began. "Mildred had raised one before, but an unexpected early frost killed it off. When I told her about the one I had grown, she was interested in seeing it. So we made plans. It must have been a quarter to eleven when Mildred and I met outside. Mildred had brought a flashlight, so we could see better. The bloom was beautiful. It was worth all the effort."

"After Mildred went home, I thought about taking a picture. I went inside to retrieve my Polaroid camera. When I came outside again, I heard all the commotion. The screams, the gunshots, the car. It was all so superficial. I just couldn't believe my eyes. I was terrified. I watched the car drive past me. I saw the driver. It was a dark-haired man in a mechanic's uniform. I didn't think anyone had seen me because I was near the corner of my house, and it was much too dark. I confided in Mildred what I had seen and she said she'd seen some of it, too ..."

Mildred picked up Claudia's narrative. "We have been trying to figure out who it was we saw that night. But so far we've drawn a blank. I just wish we could have done something more."

"I think there is something you can do. Mrs. Hawthorne, you sent your husband to tell mine something you saw. Why?"

At first, Mildred bristled, but then relenting, she asked, "How did you know?"

"My Aunt Evie told Tim about the talk the two of you had on the day my sister-in-law was killed."

"Perhaps that was a bit foolish on my part," Mildred said begrudgingly. "I really didn't want to deal with your husband. I'm sure he's a dear, but he is a policeman, and I've been trying so hard to protect my grandson, Joshua."

"But don't you think it would be best to tell what you know so that we can find out what happened?"

Mildred looked uncertain, but Claudia urged her, "Mildred, it really is for the best that everything come out into the open."

"Very well."

Mildred gazed out the window and at the newly sprouted leaves of the birch and maple trees on her lawn slowly blowing in the breeze. Dusk had set in and had cast a bluish pall over everything. This encroaching twilight unsettled her.

"I never dreamt . . ." Mildred said sadly. "You see, Joshua tried too hard to please an obstinate father. It became all about football. Being the star player in high school, getting a scholarship to a rah-rah college, and maybe even, well, it must never have been meant to be. Joshua suffered an unfortunate injury his senior year. It devastated him and made his father bitter toward him. Joshua moped about for a bit, but he'd always been good with his hands, and he'd never liked the idea of college anyway. So he moved into an apartment and put himself through trade school. Two years later, after graduating, he got a job with the repair company he still works for today. On one of his first jobs, he met Lisa Collins, Danielle McGinty, and Rachel Weiss, who later became Rachel Stuart, as we all know."

Mildred cleared her throat then continued. "Joshua was called in to repair a broken refrigerator in the girls' flat. They all flirted with him, but Danielle was the one who stole his heart. He fell in love with her at first sight. We all did when we met her. She was a sweet, lovely girl. But then there was Rachel.

"Rachel was jealous of Danielle and Lisa's beauty. I think she vowed to ruin their lives because of it. She certainly didn't care about anyone's interests but her own. She liked to be in control, and she liked power. Whenever she found a way to hold some damaging information over someone else, she'd use that information to its fullest extent. I'm sorry to say that she flattered Todd's ego. She broke up his relationship with Danielle and later Lisa. When she seemed to be losing control of Todd, her parents were mysteriously killed in an automobile accident. Well, poor grief-stricken Rachel found comfort in Todd's arms and convinced him to marry her. Even after the marriage, when Todd's attentions strayed to his ex- flame Danielle or Lisa, Rachel fumed with hatred. She bought the house here on Stoneridge to keep him away from the other two girls. When that didn't work, she used any and every trick she could to ruin everyone's life.

"Perhaps you know that Lisa's sister and brother-in-law lived in the house next door to the girls? Rachel had seen David Yates' interest in Danielle. She made sport of it. She would commiserate with my grandson about David's obsession with Danielle one day, and the next, she would encourage David's advances. She used my grandson like a toy! Joshua let her interest in him lead to other things . . ."

Her voice trailed off, as if she didn't want to utter such unmentionable indiscretions. When she did continue, there was a tinge of chastisement in her tone. "If I'd only known then! I had no inkling of Joshua's prior involvement with Rachel. I helped him and Danielle buy the house here. It wasn't long before Rachel got her hooks into my grandson again. I suppose she turned to her old tricks because the Yateses and then Lisa moved here, and that irritated her.

"You see, David Yates and his wife moved here after his stint in rehab. He'd started taking drugs, apparently not for the first time, after Danielle got engaged to my grandson. Rachel must have found out that David got his supply of drugs from his sister-in-law, and she used that information to blackmail Lisa. That worked for a time. Lisa disappeared from their lives. Then Lisa moved here. I heard the two had a spat shortly after Lisa arrived, and Rachel stalked off in a fury. I think Lisa had unearthed some information about Rachel's parents' accident."

Mildred nodded her head knowingly.

"Well anyway, Rachel still kept up relations with Joshua in the worst of ways. Poor Danielle. She came to me crying about it. I'm not sure how she found out, but I've always suspected Lisa told her. I tried to help Danielle end Joshua's involvement with Rachel, but that awful woman wouldn't leave him alone. Not even after I wrote a poison pen letter to her just days ago! Still, Danielle had other problems. That David Yates was too much in love with her. He cooked up some idea of them collaborating on some song he'd written. He made passes at her. He wouldn't leave her alone. Finally, Danielle had a long talk with David a few days before she died. Danielle told me that she had let David down gently. She was also planning to have it out with Rachel and Lisa."

"But how do you know all this?" Marie asked.

Mildred responded flippantly, "Isn't it a person's prerogative to know about their neighbors? Besides, as much as I dislike my granddaughter Sharon, she had been most informative." Mildred explained that Joshua's younger sister was also a student at S.U. and had known and heard much about the three girls.

Marie nodded, as she pondered what Mildred Hawthorne and Claudia Icarios had told her. She then asked, "You mentioned that Rachel might have been blackmailing Lisa and vice versa? Are you sure?"

"Oh, yes," Mildred said. "Danielle wondered about that, too. She wasn't certain what each had on the other, but she suspected. After all, she had lived with both of these girls for at least two years."

Claudia Icarios then clasped Marie's hand, as she said, "Would you please bring this torment to an end? I don't think this neighborhood can take much more of this. We've even been in the local newspapers. 'Death on Stoneridge: Two Neighbors Murdered!'"

Mildred Hawthorne showed Marie the evening newspaper. "Claudia is right, my dear. This can't go on. We can't live our lives wondering or looking over our shoulders at the slightest noise."

"Don't worry," Marie said, trying to sound reassuring. She wondered why these two old cats hadn't spoken up sooner, but then she considered that what they'd told her was circumstantial hearsay at best. "It won't go on much longer. Thank you for your help."

Marie was about to get up and leave, but remembering something, she turned back toward Claudia.

"I just have one more question, though. Tim's told me a lot about his investigations. That's what led me to you both tonight, in fact. But I can't help but get the feeling that there's something more."

"Whatever could it be?" Mildred asked in utter bewilderment.

"Mrs. Icarios, you mentioned earlier that the two of you have been trying to figure out who the driver of that car was."

"That's right," Mildred said. "We've simply run out of ideas."

"Is that true, Mrs. Icarios?"

Claudia looked at Marie before turning again to gaze out the window. She answered with a soft-spoken "no."

"You suspect someone then?"

"Claudia, why didn't you tell me?" Mildred asked.

"I didn't want to believe, not at first." She turned to Marie. "You must understand, I've read a number of true crime stories. I like to think they've given me a fair insight into the criminal mind, and I suppose that's why I haven't spoken up before. I've been too afraid to. Because I couldn't be sure. After all, what had I seen? Just a neighbor walking home? But it had been the night of the murder."

"Who did you see?" Marie asked.

Claudia looked at Mildred as she said, "I never told you, but I went back outside after I called you that night. I had dropped one of the photos, and I didn't want it to get wet in the morning dew. I heard someone walking. That's when I saw him."

Late Thursday night, unable to sleep easy, Marie paced along the living room carpet, her bare feet shuffling along its softness. Worries plagued her mind. She and her husband had argued about Tim's near death experience, and it had left Marie feeling chilled. So she had slipped out of bed, had put a bathrobe on over her peach negligee, and had come here to the living room to sort matters out.

The midnight hour chimed as Marie approached the bay window with its view of a street now frighteningly quiet. Inky darkness covered everything like a widow's veil, and only the streetlights and lawn lampposts, on some neighbor's properties, illuminated this scene with their soft white light beams. Death seemed to linger in this shadowy night where no light pierced the darkness as if awaiting to pounce on its next victim. Who on this street was that incarnation of death causing them to look over their shoulders, to jump at any odd stray sound? Like a heavy load that was becoming more than just unbearable, the street's plight was like a nightmare that would not end.

Marie looked up and down the street. No one was out and about at this late hour. Not like that night. The events echoed in her head. What Edith Baxter had heard, what her aunt and she herself had seen. All separate pieces that were part of a larger whole. She began to review certain facts she and her husband had unearthed. She first remembered something her husband had told her. "No idiot in his right mind would commit a murder like that. He'd be just asking for attention." But isn't that what had been done? Marie aimlessly passed on to Ms. Llewellyn's testimony. The poor woman had said a car had driven *down* the street at twenty past ten o'clock, after the argument that Thursday night. The gunshots came at 11:20.

Facts started coming into Marie's head randomly.

Lisa was not shot, but died from a blow to the head . . . Ms. Llewellyn is suggestible like Mrs. Esterhazy . . . The painting of Danielle McGinty . . . Mr. Yates's note to Mr. Deveraux . . . The mechanic's uniform . . . The gun that belonged to Dr. Logan, which was found in the bushes . . . The blackmail letter . . . The meter man . . . The scalpel . . . Rachel's expression . . . Insulin and bee stings . . . Lies . . . Gossip . . . The red car . . . Lisa's blond wig . . .

It was all so complicated. Marie wondered where it all led, and where it all ended.

Again, Marie stared out the window in front of her and looked around. Light streamed through the newly budding leaves of the trees on the Dewitts' lawn and caught her eye. She looked intently at the light of the lamppost at the end of the Lysiks' driveway. *If only that lamppost could speak.*

The things it could tell. But then, wasn't the street made up of the people who lived on it? If so, then everyone did see it all. By combining all the information . . . Marie studied the lamppost's light again. This time she saw the truth. She saw it all, like a movie flashback. She remembered what she had seen that night, and she knew. She knew who the murderer was. It was so simple, but it was unbelievable! Marie couldn't believe it was true, but it had to be!

Marie saw a light go off in her brother's house down the street. *If I'm right, he's the last piece of the puzzle. Then all that's left is to set a trap.*

FRIDAY

"Sorry to drop in on you like this."

Marie noticed her brother's tousled brown hair and bloodshot eyes. He looked rather scruffy this morning, and she couldn't recall him looking so unkempt since high school.

"What are you doing here?" Todd asked, as he pulled his bathrobe on over his bare shoulders.

"Do you mind if I come in?"

"Not at all. Come right on in. Everyone else does."

Marie wondered what that comment meant, but then she just attributed her brother's behavior to stress. True, Georgia Llewellyn and their mother had been in and out of his house, hovering about him like twittering wrens, but Marie thought his attitude a little strange considering the sad circumstances. For a moment, she was unnerved by taped up glass; the memory of the bullet hole lingered. She sat down dazedly. Perhaps for the first time, she realized how close she had come to losing her brother.

"I didn't wake you, did I?" Marie asked, as Todd joined her on the couch.

"Well, yeah, but it's okay. It's kinda late, and you couldn't have known."

"Where's Mom?"

"She went out to do some grocery shopping. She left a note," Todd said with a sardonic smile. "If you'll excuse me while I get a cup of coffee. I can't function in the morning without it," he added gruffly.

Averting her eyes from the window, Marie remained silent as she regarded the magazines on the coffee table in front of her. In the meantime, Todd disappeared into the adjoining kitchen. A couple minutes later, he returned with a cup of black coffee and sat down on the couch adjacent to the chair in which Marie was seated. He then propped his bare feet up on the table in front of him and set his coffee on the stand between the couch and the chair. For a fleeting moment, Marie wondered what Rachel Stuart would have thought. Though she hadn't known her sister-in-law well, Marie suspected Todd's late wife would have disapproved. Rachel seemed to have always had a fastidious manner about her and had expected others to submit to her wishes.

"In a way, I'm glad Mom isn't here. I wanted to talk to you alone. I know I haven't really seen much of you in quite a while. We certainly have to get together more often."

"What do you want?" Todd asked bluntly. "And don't tell me this is just a social visit."

"Information."

"I don't know anything about this mess. I haven't exactly been fully conscious through all of it."

"No. But you're fine now, right? Besides, I'm interested in something else."

Todd took a sip of coffee and winced. He liked it black, but his morning grogginess had affected his measuring, and he'd put in far more grounds than usual. Unfortunately, the sugar he'd put in only made it worse.

"What do you want to know?" he asked.

Marie recounted what Mildred Hawthorne had told her last night. Her brother grew very quiet, and when she finished he didn't respond. He just sat there, glumly looking at the mug of coffee on the table.

"Well?"

"What can I say?" He attempted a smile. "She's right. That's what happened. I didn't see it either. Maybe I didn't want to. I should have known better, but you know how it is when you think you're in love."

He looked away from her. Very quietly, he continued, "I should miss her, but I don't. I feel like a heavy load's been lifted off my back. I have my life back, such as it is."

"Todd, why didn't—"

"What? Come to you or Mom? Whine about my life? What good would that have done? Rachel had me house-trained. When she snapped her fingers, I came like a good little boy. Should I go running to my mommy or big sister because I can't take my wife's browbeating? I already felt like less than a man."

"What about Tim? He was your best friend."

"I just couldn't. You and Tim were so happy planning the wedding and . . ."

"Todd, I'm so sorry."

"Yeah, well, what can you do?" He shrugged. "It's over now. Anything else you want to know?"

"Well, there is one thing. I've been informed that there was a man Lisa was dating at the time. Some professor or something of that sort? Possibly a graduate student?"

"I'm not sure who you mean. Lisa dated a lot of guys, and I know she dated more than one professor."

"Could she have dated someone living here on Stoneridge?"

"I don't think so. Although Lisa was flirting pretty heavy with that doctor next door. Craig something?"

"Logan?"

"Yeah, Craig Logan. I'm sure they went out once or twice. At least that's what Rachel told me. Course, I think Shane Lysik had a fling with Lisa."

"What?" Marie feigned surprise since she had already suspected as much.

"Yeah, he dropped by the other day while mom and Ms. Llewellyn were out. We reminisced about college days and about the Stage. He wondered about who had killed Lisa, and we just talked." Todd shrugged. "He said he was sorry about

Rachel. Wondered how I was doing. It was rather depressing, but then again I was in a depressed mood anyway. He left before I almost blew my brains out."

"Yes. Tell me about that. How did you get your hands on that gun?"

"I don't know. I reached for a magazine on that coffee table, and there it was. It was right there. Like it was waiting for me. The natural thing to do seemed to be to pick it up and use it. It all seemed so easy, but I just couldn't go through with it. And once I fired the gun, I felt like I had come out of a trance . . ." Todd trailed off as he was not sure what happened next.

"Did you have any other visitors that day?"

"Only Josh Deveraux."

"When did he stop by?"

"Josh came in the morning, sometime. I haven't been able to keep track of time this week. Mom was still here then, but she gave the two of us some privacy. Shane came later after Mom had left to see what was going on across the street. Something about the police arresting somebody."

"I see. Yes, now I see."

"Why are you asking so many questions?"

"Curiosity."

"Well, you'd better be careful, Marie, or you may end up like Rachel did. And you're too good for that."

"Thanks, I think," Marie said with a smile. "Did Rachel ask too many questions?"

"Well, she was always prying into other people's business. She liked to know about people. I guess it gave her some sort of thrill to be able to know things about people. She was sort of a control freak."

"Where were you last Thursday night?"

"My, aren't you nosy. I suppose you mean after the Neighborhood Watch meeting? I was here that night. I kind of zonked out. I was tired from working, I guess."

"Did you call a repairman to fix your air-conditioner last Thursday?"

"No, why?"

"Just something your wife told Tim."

Todd looked angry.

"Look. I didn't kill anyone if that's what you're getting at."

"I didn't say that."

"No, maybe not. But I've seen the suspicious look Ms. Llewellyn gives me. I hear what people are whispering about. I know what people think."

"Do you? Do you really?"

Abruptly, Todd got up and brought his empty cup to the kitchen.

Marie followed him. "I don't think you know what I'm thinking, Todd. You shouldn't jump to hasty conclusions. Everyone in this neighborhood seems to suspect Mr. Deveraux."

"Josh?" Todd said, flabbergasted. "Ha! Josh wouldn't hurt anyone. He's too naïve."

"People have been known to lose their naïvety."

"Not Josh," Todd maintained.

Marie shrugged, unconvinced.

"Suit yourself, Marie."

"What about Lisa? What was she like?" Marie asked, curious to hear Todd's thoughts.

"She's was fun, I guess. I mean she was an intelligent girl who knew how to have a good time. She wasn't like these peroxide blondes you sometimes meet. The ones who are so air- headed. Kind of like Mrs. Esterhazy."

"Oh, so you've met her, have you?"

"It's kind of hard not to. She seems to pop up everywhere when you least expect it. But she's about the only one in this neighborhood I sorta know. Besides Aunt Evie, Josh, and Dave Yates."

"And Mrs. Yates," Marie added.

"Nah, I don't really know her. She was always so quiet around the Stage. She often came to see her husband during rehearsals and such, but she always sat in the background. She was always so quiet. Of course, when Rachel and I moved here, we sort of kept to ourselves. Rachel wasn't the type of person who liked to be neighborly."

"I see."

"Yes, well, I'd like to get dressed now if you don't mind, but I'll see you tonight at the Lysiks' party."

Marie nodded. Her brother had confirmed a number of her suspicions. Now she needed to confront one more person.

Joshua Deveraux felt numb. He didn't feel like doing anything or going anywhere. He sat slumped on the loveseat in his living room, idly fingering the invitation dropped off by Brenda Lysik that morning. He had nearly missed seeing it when he retrieved his morning paper on the porch and read one of the headlines: "Murders on Stoneridge Still Under Investigation."

He had skimmed through the article, which said the investigation might be taken over by the county sheriff's department if a solution wasn't found soon. Remembering the run-in he had had with the Town of DeWitt police and the questions he had already been asked by the Sheriff's deputies, Joshua had not felt well. His gut felt like it had been wrung like a wet towel. Even worse, the article hinted that the police had a suspect!

At that point, Joshua had nearly dropped the paper. It was then that he had seen the invitation with his name neatly handwritten on the envelope. When he had opened it, he wished he hadn't.

Now, over two hours later, Joshua still felt his gut churning. How could he possible attend a welcoming party and face everybody? Especially after his arrest? Sure, he had been released with no charges having been formally made against him, but still . . .

"Damn Rachel," Joshua thought, aloud. "I never should have gotten involved with her. Rachel never cared about anybody but herself. Now here I am suspended from work, and I'll probably go to jail for nothing!"

Hearing a noise in the master bathroom, Joshua froze. He peered down the hallway and thought he had heard her voice again.

"Danielle?" he called out.

Naturally, there was no answer. It was all in his head, but he knew in his heart that Danielle's spirit could not rest until justice . . . Josh looked at the invitation again. It looked so warm and inviting. Brenda Lysik sure had class. She didn't judge people like his skittish boss, who thought business would be adversely affected for employing a murder suspect.

Joshua Deveraux wondered if he could muster enough courage to go to the party. After everything that had happened, he wondered if he would be welcome, if they'd still think him guilty. If only he'd been more outgoing, but he had never been able to overcome his shyness. Rachel had only made matters worse. She'd fed his insecurities and prevented him from enjoying life. His grandmother was right. He now realized that now, and he was glad Rachel was dead.

Bryant Logan peered out his bedroom window. He craned his head to see up the street, but saw no sign of anyone. He plopped down on his bed and picked at his fingernails.

Where was he?

He had phoned Tim Dewitt just after his father had left for work. His brother had been flying high again last night. Again their father hadn't noticed.

Bryant couldn't understand why his dad seemed so preoccupied these days. Yeah, he had dated that dead girl, but that hadn't been serious. So why? Could Dad know about D.J.'s problem? Or was it something else? Dad did seem rattled by the murders. Bryant had seen him reading today's newspaper. They'd been eating breakfast at the kitchen table, and his dad had been muttering to himself. Bryant had only caught a few words, but they hadn't made any sense until he saw the headline, "Murders on Stoneridge Still Under Investigation."

He'd heard his dad swear and junk the paper in the trash before leaving for work. He'd remembered how his dad had called the hospital last night to check on that lady who'd been hit by the car. She'd been in critical condition then.

Bryant shook his head. He didn't want to think about this morning. He went over to the window again. Still nothing. He stalked out of his room, but came to a stop outside his brother's bedroom door.

D.J. lounged on his bed as he read the latest *Sports Illustrated*. His head bobbed up and down to the beat of the music blaring from the headphones he wore. He didn't notice his brother watching him. But then, D.J. didn't notice much of anything these days. Ever since he had broken up with that girl, he had taken to building a cocoon around himself. More and more, he spent time alone in his room. It was so unlike him.

Bryant hurried past his brother's bedroom. Reaching the living room, he looked at his watch and then at the front door. Tim promised he would stop by before his father came home around one o'clock. It was just past eleven. What if Tim didn't show up? What if he did? Would D.J. hate him the rest of their lives because he had ratted on his big brother?

When the doorbell finally rang, Bryant raced to the door.

Tim was on the front steps.

Before he could say anything, he heard muffled music. He saw D.J. enter the room. Amazingly, his brother must have heard the doorbell over the Stones!

"I was just going . . . biking . . . yeah," stuttered Bryant, who raced past Tim.

As Tim entered the Logans' house, D.J. unhooked the headphones from his ears and draped them around his neck. He hadn't bothered to turn the music off.

D.J. looked up and asked, "What do you want?"

"To talk to you," Tim said, descending into the living room, which in the Logan house was down a step.

"Are you still looking for the murderer?"

"Not exactly."

Somewhat interested in what Tim might have to say, D.J. switched off his player.

"So what could I possibly know that would help you?"

Tim began officially, "Sgt. Griffin and I, in investigating the deaths of Rachel Stuart and Lisa Collins, found enormous sums of money in their bank accounts which did not readily make sense. Neither woman was in a position to amass such funds. Upon further investigation it was determined that Rachel may have been blackmailing Lisa over a certain enterprise Lisa was running. Apparently, Miss Collins was dealing drugs and turning quite a profit. Upon further investigation, a notebook in Lisa's handbag contained a partial list of some of her clients. D.L. wouldn't happen to be you, would it?"

The information Tim related had been discovered last night as he and Sgt. Griffin had poured over evidence that had been recovered at Lisa Collins' house and in her car. This same information now caused D.J. to shift uncomfortably under Tim's gaze.

"You know, it would help matters a lot if you helped us out, D.J. If you're not D.L., just say so. That way we can move on and track down the real D.L."

"But I don't know what you're talking about."

"Ah, come on, of course you do, D.J. It's not that hard to figure out. Either you're D.L. or you're not. It's that simple."

"I would never . . ."

D.J.'s face reddened. His eyes darted around the room as if looking for escape.

Tim suspected the boy had never been confronted like this and didn't know how to handle it. He wasn't one of his friends. He wasn't a member of his family. He was a cop.

Standing up, D.J. replied, "I—I can't help you, Mr. Dewitt. It doesn't surprise me that Lisa was dealing. I mean, well, she wasn't rich, and she had that car."

D.J.'s father walked through the door at that moment.

Craig Logan saw Tim and demanded, "What are you doing here? I thought I told you to leave my sons alone."

"I needed to ask D.J. a couple questions. I wanted to make sure he didn't see or hear anything while he was playing basketball with Justin Griffin. You know, something that might not have registered at the time."

"I'm sure my son doesn't know any more about the murders than I do, Officer," Craig said brusquely.

"Of course." Tim turned to D.J. and said, "If you should think of anything you want to tell me, just stop by."

D.J. just slapped his headphones on and jacked up the music drowning him out.

Marie's persistent knocking finally paid off as the front door opened. Smiling innocently, Marie said, "Hi, can I come in?"

Shane Lysik led her inside his house as he said, "I hope you don't mind if things are a bit messy around here. I've been assigned clean up, preparation, and errand duty for tonight's party. How can I help you?"

"Are you sure you don't need any help?"

"No, not really," Shane said. "Brenda and I planned this whole thing last night. We gathered most of the stuff we need, and I said I would take today off to whip everything together. Her thought is that if I like parties so much, then I ought to love everything that goes into the preparation of one."

"So will everyone be here tonight?"

"I should think so. I know Brenda called up a lot of her bridge friends to tell them, and she dropped off invitations to everyone this morning before she went to work."

"Oh, yeah," Marie said, "Tim found the invitation when Bryant Logan rang the bell. That poor boy. I really think he's been terribly affected by all this. After all, he found Lisa's body and apparently he was mowing the lawn when Rachel was killed. His backyard is right next door!"

"It can be a traumatic event for an impressionable boy to witness. The impact of death and its relative finality is rough on anyone really."

"If that's true," Marie began, deliberately pausing. Though his back was to her while he was setting out silverware on the dining room table, she knew she had his attention. "Why did you try to kill my husband?"

Marie saw his back stiffen. Then his body froze. From where she stood, Marie couldn't read his facial expression, but she was sure her question had hit its mark.

Slowly, Shane turned around, a few knives still in his hands. His deep brown eyes locked on Marie for a moment, and then he turned away. With a heavy sigh, he set the knives on the table. Gripping the table's edge with his hands, he murmured, "How did you know?"

"Tim's allergic reaction isn't known to many people outside the family. Your wife is a secretary at Dewitt Enterprises and she's worked with the family. I assumed she likely knew and must have mentioned it to you. Yesterday, you were the only person, aside from Dr. Logan, who could have gotten hold of the bee toxin. And after talking with Mrs.

Icarios last night, I knew. She saw you outside that night. Why did you do it?"

"I hadn't wanted to," Shane began, turning to face Marie. His sepia brown eyes were like those of a lost puppy dog. "I was blackmailed into it. You've got to believe me. I never wanted to hurt anyone. When I was sitting and talking to your husband, I just couldn't . . ."

Trying not to let her fury get the better of her, Marie asked, "Why didn't you go to the police, if you knew?"

"You know then?"

"Since last night. I finally pieced it together .."

"Then you know it was all her fault. She blackmailed me. She was frantic that night. She called me and begged me to help her. Said it had been an accident. She said if I didn't help, she'd tell my wife."

He bowed his head.

"I told Brenda it was a patient calling. I was making her some tea, and I slipped in one of my sleeping pills. We staged that whole murder scene for the neighbors. It was stupid, I know, but I guess I panicked. I love my wife. I didn't want her to know I'd been unfaithful."

"You could have gone to the police!"

Marie always tried not to chastise other people for their faults or shortcomings, for God knew she had enough of her own. But Shane's sob story was too much. "You ought to know better. You are a psychiatrist! People are always placing the blame or trying to find an excuse for their actions. What you did was far worse than blindly helping a murderer. You could have spoken up, told the police, and everything would have been fine. Rachel Stuart wouldn't have died."

"You don't understand. It would have crushed Bren to know. I couldn't, I couldn't let my wife . . . I love her. I do."

"Well, apparently you loved someone else just a little bit more."

Shane averted his eyes from Marie's gaze. He was beginning to feel sick to his stomach. His repressed guilt surfaced in full force, and his whole body shook.

"I don't know what to say. I really don't. Sorry won't cut it. So what do you want from me? What do you want me to say?"

Before Marie could say anything, Brenda Lysik walked through the door. Her face was all smiles, but they quickly vanished when she saw the glum looks.

"What's going on? Hello, Marie. What brings you here?"

"Do you want to tell her? She'll find out anyway. It's all over."

"Tell me what?" Brenda asked, struggling to understand. "Marie? Shane? What is it?"

"I'll let you two talk," Marie said. "I need to phone my husband."

Marie stepped into the kitchen to use the Lysiks' phone as Brenda approached her husband.

"Shane?"

Sonya Schwartz straightened the throw pillows on the couches in her living room. With the television in the den beyond the kitchen, the living room in the Schwartz household was elegantly kept. The bedrooms and den might be a little worn or messy, but the dining and living rooms were always immaculate. Of course, Mama had always taught her girls how to keep house properly. Mama had also advised her girls on raising children.

Sonya recalled how adorable and sweet Rachel had been as a girl. Granted she had been spoiled because she was the only grandchild for a good twelve years. But where could her parents have gone wrong? They had always taken such care to raise a morally upstanding young woman.

"I guess Mama was right in the end when she said no matter how much loving, caring, or discipline, children will grow into whatever they were meant to be. Parenting is merely guidance."

Sonya turned to see her twelve-year-old son, Aaron, enter the room. Her husband and the children had arrived home last night. Though she'd told her husband everything that had happened the last few days, she'd shielded the children, except for Aaron. She'd told her eldest son an abbreviated truth. Now he was getting ready to go biking with his friend down the street, that Logan boy. Sonya had given her full approval, of course; she liked Aaron's friend. Bryant was not the bad influence that some of Rachel's friends had been.

When the phone rang, Aaron volunteered to answer it. Picking up the receiver he said, "Hello, ah, just a moment." Covering the phone, he said to his mother, "It's Mrs. Esterhazy. Do you want to talk with her?"

Sonya rolled her eyes.

Knowing it probably wasn't, but considering that it might possibly be something of interest, she said, "All right."

After Aaron handed his mother the phone and left the room, Sonya said, "Hello, Anne . . . oh, just straightening around the house . . . Yes, I got an invitation . . . oh, I think it's a wonderful idea. So few people welcome new neighbors nowadays . . . No, of course not . . . Well, no, I don't think it's surprising your husband isn't going, Anne."

Anne Esterhazy babbled on for a few minutes before Sonya was able to say anything other than "uh- huh."

"I wish they would solve those murders, too . . . Yes, Rachel was my niece, but I can't feel all that sorry for what happened . . . Anne, she wasn't all that nice a person . . . I really don't like to speak ill of the dead . . . Who knows what Tim Dewitt is up to . . . No, I didn't go to him . . . Look, Anne, I need to go out for a moment. I called Brenda last night, and she said it was all right if I brought something . . . I'm making a special treat . . . you'll see. I just need a few ingredients. I'll see you there . . . Okay, Anne, yes . . . All right . . . Okay, good- bye, Anne."

As quick as she could, Sonya replaced the phone on its hook. Then she sighed. For a moment, she relaxed but then a thought occurred to her. Whirling about her house to snatch what she needed, she escaped to the supermarket before Anne decided to drop by.

Evelyn Martino knocked on the Dewitts' front door until Tim opened it.

"Hi," Evelyn said, catching her breath. "I just remembered I can't make Brenda's party tonight."

"Do you want to come in?" Tim asked.

"No, I don't have that much time. Where's Marie?"

"Out."

"Well, I just wanted to wish you both well and hope you have a good welcoming. Tell Brenda I had a previous engagement and that I'm sorry I couldn't come."

"I will."

Evelyn was about to go, but on second thought, she asked, "Do the police have any idea who committed those murders?"

"It's only a matter of time. I believe the police are just checking up on some last minute details. Everything should be over with by tonight or tomorrow."

"Splendid," Evelyn said with a smile. "I always like to see justice served."

David Yates groaned. He ached all over, but felt much better, considering he'd nearly had a fatal accident. Miraculously, he had escaped the wreckage with only a few bruises and minor cuts. He had had a mild concussion, for which the hospital had kept him overnight for observation. Now, he was trying to recuperate and to forget. He lay on the couch with the shades drawn, casting the room in near darkness though it was the middle of the day. He shut his eyes. Try as he might, he could not shut out the image of an elderly woman's horror-stricken face staring at him moments before his car hit her. If his grandfather hadn't pulled some strings, he'd probably be resting in jail right now. His life was spiraling out of control, and he couldn't fathom a way out. He desperately wanted to fall asleep, slip into oblivion if possible, but then he heard footsteps on the stairs. He opened his eyes to see her enter the living room.

Linda took a look at David and sighed. Walking over to him, she said, "David?" He looked up at her, groggy-eyed. "I just want you to know it's over. I'm leaving you tomorrow."

David struggled to sit up.

"No, you can't. You just can't. What would I do?"

"I can't stay here."

"But—"

"No, buts, David! We are going to the party tonight. Act like everything's fine for the old cats. Tomorrow I'll be gone. Tell them whatever you want."

"How could you?" David asked, struggling to stand up. His tone was getting more hurt, angrier. "After everything. After you . . . How could you leave? Why should I let you?"

Linda glared at him. "Oh, you'll let me. You don't have any choice." Then she turned her back on him and left the room.

Mildred Hawthorne hurried over to Claudia Icarios' house. To an outsider, seeing the stout Mildred nearly running across Stoneridge would have been quite comical. It was certainly out of character for the normally prim matron, but Mildred had never been so distressed before. She had left early that morning to visit with her daughter Margaret and her granddaughter Sharon. As a result she hadn't seen Brenda Lysik's invitation until her husband handed it to her when she got home.

Preoccupied with recent events on Stoneridge, as well as the Dewitt Enterprises board meeting she had attended on Tuesday, Mildred had completely forgotten about the Lysiks' welcoming party for the Dewitts. Apprehensive about the party, especially after last night's talk with Claudia and Marie, Mildred felt compelled to speak with Claudia at once.

Mildred knocked frantically. Words were swirling in her head, and she didn't quite know what she should say first.

Calm yourself, Millie, she thought, trying to catch her breath.

The door had barely been opened partway when Mildred burst in, nearly bowling Claudia over.

"I simply had to speak with you about tonight," Mildred said. "Are you going? I don't know how the Lysiks could go through with this party of theirs. Not with these murders still unsolved. Why it's simply unthinkable!"

Mildred sat herself down in the nearest chair and held her hand to her throat to steady herself.

"Are you all right?" Claudia asked, as she shut her front door.

"I'm fine," Mildred said. "What do you think, Claudia? Should we go to that party?"

"I don't think it could hurt anything," Claudia said calmly.

"I suppose not, but you know what they say."

Claudia shook her head to show she did not understand her friend's meaning.

"One should always be careful where one trends after death," Mildred explained. "You have to be careful what you do, what you say, how you act. That's what my mother always told us, children. Death is nothing to laugh at. And murder is something to fear."

Angela Sparrow tottered to her front door. Though she still used her cane, her ankle was healing much faster than her doctor had anticipated. She'd visited her doctor that morning, and his latest prognosis was very good. Apparently the strain had appeared far worse than it actually was, because of the swelling at the time. Now, it appeared Angela would be cane-free in just a few days.

Presently, Angela opened her door to find Tim Dewitt on her doorstep.

"Hello, Miss Sparrow. I just wanted to know if you were coming to the party tonight. I wasn't sure with your ankle and all."

"What is it, Tim?" Angela asked suspiciously. When he didn't respond, she added, "You know, don't you?"

"Yes, Marie told me. It's quite fantastic, but she's right. I'm sure of it."

"I've had my suspicions, too. Todd Stuart's near suicide did confuse me, but on reflection, I think I know who it is. If I'm right, well, I just hope you both know what you're doing."

"Don't worry, Miss Sparrow. One way or another, it'll all be over by tonight."

"Well, for all our sakes, I hope you're right."

Later that evening at the party . . .

"Thank God, you arrived," Mildred Hawthorne said to Claudia Icarios. "I was beginning to go batty from listening to Anne Esterhazy gab on and on. She's incessant!"

"I'm glad I don't live next door to her," Claudia said.

Mildred rolled her eyes.

"I can't even begin to tell you, but that's not why I wanted to talk. What do you suppose has become of Brenda Lysik."

"Isn't she here?"

"No," Mildred said. "I haven't seen her, and Mr. Lysik will say nothing about it. Of course, he and my husband hit the bar right after we arrived, leaving me alone with Anne. At least until Angela and Sonya showed up." Mildred paused as she looked at Sonya and Anne in the opposite corner of the living room. Then she added, "Poor Sonya. She's been cornered by Anne since she arrived."

"What do you suppose has become of Brenda?" Claudia asked, alarmed.

"I can't imagine. It's not like her at all."

Presently, the doorbell rang, and Mildred and Claudia watched the newcomer's arrival. Both were surprised to see Tim arrive without his wife.

"You don't think anything's happened to Marie?"

"Oh, Mildred, don't even think that," Claudia said, as she eyed Tim. "Besides, he doesn't look too concerned."

"He's certainly captured Angela's attention," Mildred observed.

"Yes, but Tim is a police officer. I'm sure he's involved in investigating these murders."

"Why talk to Angela then? I'm sure she has nothing to do with this. If anyone is involved, it's that Yates character. He was obsessed with Joshua's wife, you know. And he has been suspiciously quiet tonight. And what about Todd Stuart? He's been awfully cheerful tonight, considering his wife's recent demise."

"Well, I'm concerned about Dr. Logan. He has been sullen of late, and I might add that he seems a little jumpy about the murders."

"He did date Lisa Collins a few times," Mildred said, eying the doctor suspiciously.

While Mildred Hawthorne and Claudia Icarios were watching the movements of their neighbors in the living room, Shane Lysik slipped down the basement stairs. A few moments later, Linda Yates followed.

"I still don't understand why you wanted to talk to me in private," Linda said. "Aren't you supposed to be hosting a party for the Dewitts upstairs?"

"Yes, but I need to talk to you."

"I don't understand." Linda laughed nervously.

"Marie Dewitt knows everything. She came and confronted me this afternoon."

"What did you do?" Linda whispered, her eyes wide.

"Come downstairs. I don't want to be overheard."

"Where are you going, Linda?" David asked from the top of the stairs.

Linda turned to look up at him, and she said sharply, "Go mingle. I'll be right back."

David started to follow Linda and Shane, but her withering glance made him stop in his tracks and he withdrew. She then followed Shane down into the gloom of the basement, which was broken only by the light piercing it from the top of the stairs.

Once at the bottom, Linda glanced around. She felt surrounded by darkness and found herself unable to leave the comforting rectangle of light that formed itself like a door on the floor. She looked toward the fireplace opposite the stairs and then back at Shane.

"Couldn't we have discussed this upstairs in the kitchen?"

Shane shook his head. "Too many people around."

"Outside then! The weather isn't half as damp as it is down here. Why don't you turn on some lights?"

"Are you nervous?" Shane mocked.

"Look if you're going to act like that, I'll just go back upstairs."

Shane grasped her arm.

"What are you doing? Let go of me."

"No," Shane said. "It's time."

"Time for what?" asked the woman, her hazel eyes reflecting fear in the light.

"A reckoning," said a voice in the dark.

The woman turned as Marie Dewitt stepped into the light.

"You?" The woman looked at Shane, and sputtered, "You. What have you done?"

"It's over, Lisa," Marie said.

The woman stared long and hard at Marie. "What? Are you mad? What have the two of you concocted? Are you planning to do away with me like the others?"

Shane reached for her, but she slapped him. Then Marie sprang forward and tore the wig from the woman's head, revealing blond tresses that loosened from the pins that had held them for so long.

"It was Linda Yates who was murdered Thursday night," Marie said as she threw the wig down to the ground. "Isn't that right, Lisa?"

No response.

Marie continued, "I wonder when things started going wrong? You've been making money dealing drugs for years. How long has David Yates been one of your clients? Too bad Rachel Stuart found out. Power monger Rachel Stuart got more than she bargained for, didn't she? One would almost think it was a competition. Unfortunately, Syracuse wasn't big enough for both of you."

"For a while you two were stalemated. Rachel Stuart knew about your drug dealing, but you knew she had arranged to have her parents killed. Then Danielle Deveraux stumbled onto the truth. With a little help from Rachel Stuart no doubt, she discovered David was taking drugs he got from you. So you decided to get rid of her by faking her suicide. You used your brief relationship with Dr. Logan to acquire his scalpel and then used to kill Danielle.

"Again another stalemate. Then more trouble. David Yates was hooked on drugs you supplied, but that costs money. So David started breaking into other people's homes to afford his habit. I suspect Linda knew about her husband's crimes. Most likely she questioned him and learned that her own sister was responsible, so she confronted you Thursday night.

"Perhaps you didn't mean to kill your sister, Lisa. The autopsy report indicates Linda died from a blow to the head. Ms. Llewellyn heard you both arguing." Marie tilted her head. "You pushed her, didn't you? You pushed her and she fell, hitting her head against the corner of your front steps. Specks of brick were found in the wound at the back of her head. They discovered that during the autopsy. The gunshot came later."

Marie stared sharply at Lisa Collins. "You staged all that. The gunshots, the cries for help, all of it. But why?"

Shane confessed, "She conned me into staging a fake murder. She told me it was for Rachel's benefit. She feared that Rachel would find out and then it would be over for her. She broke into Joshua's house to get hold of his gun and a spare uniform."

"Shut up, you liar," Lisa screeched.

"I told you to go to the police. It was an accident." Shane shook his head. "You wouldn't listen to me. You probably already planned to kill Rachel."

"That's why you took your sister's place," Marie said. "After blackmailing Shane and dumping your car off down by the creek, you walked up the street. That's when I saw you. You were on your way to your sister's house to take her place. You knew David wouldn't talk. After all, he was dependent on you for drugs. But the burglaries stopped."

Marie continued. "I don't know whether or not you had already planned to kill Rachel, but on Saturday I saw Rachel go to David's house. She saw you that day. She must not have seen through your disguise. Not then. But you feared she would sooner or later. She was asking too many questions. You used an extra uniform of Joshua Deveraux's, and wore it to use Mrs. Icarios' shovel. You crept up to Rachel and killed her! It was simple enough. She probably didn't hear you creep up on her since Bryant Logan was mowing the lawn next door.

"You probably thought you were home free then. You'd taken up Linda's role with the ease of a gifted actress, but I suspect David began having second thoughts. And he started slipping up. He called you Lisa in front of me, and I'll bet he had done it before. You gave him an overdose of insulin because he was becoming a danger. Unfortunately, David came to me that day, and I recognized the symptoms and saved his life."

Marie smiled. She could see Lisa losing control. The wannabe actress tried to maintain her composure, to keep her visage's neutral facade, but her eyes betrayed her anger.

"That's when you got cocky. You knew my husband was on your trail, so you went to Shane. You threatened to tell his wife about your affair. Foolishly, he thought he had no choice but to try and kill my husband. Thankfully, that plot failed. But I have to wonder why you wanted Shane to try and induce my brother to commit suicide. I suspect you were extremely wary of anyone who had known you when you had lived on Euclid Avenue. And that included Joshua Deveraux, who you tried your best to frame for your crimes. When all of that failed, you tried to implicate David, didn't you? That chat you had with me Wednesday wasn't that of a devoted wife trying to protect her husband. It seemed like you were purposely trying to suggest that David was guilty!

"I think you purposely drove David to flip out like he did, nearly killing himself in a car crash. You may not have intended for Ms. Llewellyn to get hurt, but considering what she knew, I'm sure it was only a matter of time before you would have decided to do away with her." Marie paused a moment as she thought of poor Ms. Llewellyn in the hospital; then she said, "It must have been annoying for David to have pushed you into that stone wall. You were probably afraid that someone would realize you were wearing a wig because of the wound to your head. Unfortunately for you, I did see blond hairs, which weren't covered up by your wig!"

"Enough!" yelled Lisa. Then she laughed. "I don't have to listen to this! It's a complete farce. None of it's true."

"Yes, it is. All of it. Just like Marie said," David said.

Tim Dewitt had cajoled David Yates into listening at the top of the stairs. They'd heard everything, and now David bounded down the stairs followed by Tim.

"Shut up," Lisa snapped.

"Screw you," David snapped back. "You almost killed me, and I was a fool to believe you. If I hadn't been addicted to . . ."

Turning to Shane, he added, "And you bastard."

David lunged at Shane and tried to land one solid punch, but Tim grabbed him and held him back. Taking advantage of the distraction, Lisa grabbed the fireplace poker. She turned to advance on Marie, who stood between her and the nearest exit.

"Drop it!"

A light switch flicked on, and standing next to it, Sgt. Jack Griffin trained his gun on Lisa. The poker clanged to the floor as the sergeant stepped forward to arrest Lisa Collins.

Marie moved closer to her husband, as he put an arm around her and said, "It's all over. Finally."

Mr. Lysik, Mr. Yates," Sgt. Griffin said. "You both need to come with me."

Jack Griffin ushered the group upstairs and led them past the gaggle of neighbors, who watched the proceedings in stunned silence. Two police cars idled outside the Lysiks' home, and the sergeant led David, Shane, and Lisa to them. Three Town of DeWitt officers assisted in the arrest. The neighbors watched the police cars disappear out of sight up the street before dispersing and returning to their respective homes.

As Tim closed the Lysiks' door behind them, Marie asked him, "What do you think'll become of David and Shane?"

"It all depends. If Shane testifies against Lisa, he'll probably get an immunity deal. As for David, even if the neighbors he robbed don't press charges, the district attorney may."

"Isn't there anything we could do for him? I just can't help thinking that what he did isn't really his fault."

"Let's just see what happens," Tim said stoically. "Let's go home."

EPILOGUE

The following Tuesday night, the Dewitts hosted their first bridge party, attended by Angela Sparrow, Evelyn Martino, the Col. and Mrs. Hawthorne, and Dr. and Mrs. Icarios. As often occurs at such social gatherings, the conversation turned to recent events.

Evelyn—partnered with Claudia against Tim and Marie—opened with the eight of clubs as she said, "I think it was quite responsible of David Yates to make reparations for what he stole."

Tim glanced across the table at Marie, but she merely shrugged. Her Aunt Evie often switched topics midstream. They'd previously been discussing the Syracuse Botanical Gardens opening set for next month.

"It is a nice gesture," Tim said begrudgingly, as he played his nine of clubs. "But it's no excuse for what he did. I know Todd doesn't care one way or the other, and Brenda Lysik has told David not to bother repaying her for her home's burglary. She feels guilty because of her husband's actions." He lowered his voice for a moment as he added, "Only the Hawthornes have expected any repayment, in return for not pressing charges."

"Do you think the district attorney will file charges?" Evelyn asked.

"I'm surprised he hasn't already."

"Oh, Tim, I hope it doesn't come to that," Marie said.

Tim just shrugged.

"I still have a few questions?" Evelyn said.

"Just a few?" Claudia commented sarcastically.

"Marie, how did you know it was Lisa and not Linda?"

"Well, Aunt Evie, I saw Lisa that Thursday night. I'm not sure what woke me up exactly. I suppose it was the car driving up the street, but I remember feeling thirsty so I went and got some water. I'm not sure why, but I drifted over to the window there to look out." She indicated the bay window in the living room with a gesture. "I saw a woman walking up the street. I got a good look at her when she passed under the streetlight at the end of the Lysiks' driveway. I didn't know it at the time, but it was Lisa. It wasn't until a week later, when I was thinking about the whole mess, that I happened to catch sight of the streetlight."

"And that's when you remembered what you saw," Evelyn finished.

"Yes," Marie admitted. "And I remembered three things. Tim had told me that the body found in the creek was wearing blond wig. I had seen blond hairs on the back of the fake Linda's neck after David knocked her against the retaining wall. And I recalled how much the two sisters looked alike."

"How did you know the gunshots were a ruse?" Evelyn.

Marie answered, "Well, I thought about what Ms. Llewellyn told Tim before she lost consciousness that horrible day. You remember what she said, Mrs. Icarios? You were the only other person besides my husband to hear her."

"Vaguely. She said something about having seen the whole thing and that the gunshots came later."

"Exactly. Don't you see? The murder actually happened at twenty past ten. The events that occurred later were played out to mask the time of the real murder. What some of you may not have known is that Ms. Llewellyn told my husband that at ten-twenty, she heard Lisa arguing with a supposed boyfriend. She mistook Linda Yates' voice for a man."

"And the gun? Who took that gun Todd Stuart dropped?"

"Yes," Claudia said, joining with Evelyn in asking, "I don't understand how it disappeared."

"Shane Lysik moved it. He was attempting to cover his implication in the matter," answered Marie. "I can't explain when or how he took it, but in all the confusion, I suppose it wasn't too hard. I suspect he took it just before he joined the rest of us."

Evelyn nodded in appreciation.

"But what about David and his children?" she asked.

"According to David," Tim said, "Lisa sent the children to stay with their grandmother. And he was so dependent on her for his fix, that it was easy for her to keep him silent. As for David and his kids now, I hear his mother is going to look after the kids while he's in rehab."

Evelyn began the next trick by playing her five of clubs. "What about Joshua?"

"Oh," said Angela, who had been listening from her seat at the other table. "He's very enthusiastic about the future. Kelly Repair Co. offered him his old job back, but he turned them down. He plans to go to college—"

"Which I have agreed to pay for," Mildred interjected. She was partnered with Angela against her husband and Dr. Icarios.

"Then I take it, he's over his wife's death?"

Mildred frowned. "Not entirely, Evelyn. But his mind is more at ease. I think the not knowing caused him to withdraw from polite society. Since Lisa's arrest, he's felt . . . shall we say, relieved."

"Oh, good. I do so like happy endings."

"Well, Aunt Evie," Marie said with a smile, "then you'll be happy to hear that Tim and Jack have received commendations for their efforts."

"Yeah, we may even be closer to being promoted than we thought," Tim said wryly.

"Does this mean you'll be getting a raise?" Mildred asked from the next table.

"No, Mrs. Hawthorne," Tim said. "But don't worry. We'll have a chance to play, and I will beat you."

"We shall see," Mildred said self-assuredly.

The game continued as did the conversation, veering onto other topics. Sadly, the neighborhood bridge nights would become more sporadic, despite intentions to the contrary.

The next morning, Marie emptied their mailbox. As she sorted through the mail, she came across an elegant envelope addressed to Edith Baxter. An R.S.V.P. appeared in script on the outside.

Looks like Ms. Baxter's been invited to a party, Marie mused.

She made a mental note to have Tim call his grandmother and tell her about the invitation. She looked at the return address. C. Robin Lyons. Wasn't he that mystery author?

DID YOU KNOW…?

Gustav Stickley (1857 – 1942) is considered a leader of the Arts & Crafts Movement and credited with creating the Craftsman style. The simplicity of the Stickley furniture appealed to many Americans in the early part of the 1900s, including renowned architect Frank Lloyd Wright. Stickley inspired an open floor plan and groupings of window to allow ample light, and he encouraged the use of built-in benches, bookcases, and sideboards which created practical, uncluttered houses.

The eldest of eleven children, Gustav Stickley first came to Syracuse, New York, in 1893. He stayed at the newly opened Yates Hotel in Downtown Syracuse and within a year moved his family to the city.

He got his start working in his uncle's furniture factory part of the Brandt Chair Company in Pennsylvania. In 1884, with his brothers, Albert and Charles, he established the first Stickley Brothers & Company in Binghamton, New York. By 1898, he had opened a factory in Eastwood, a suburb of Syracuse, and two of his brothers, Leopold and J. George, had branched out on their own, opening a shop in Fayetteville, New York, by 1902.

The shop in Fayetteville made furniture that resembled Gustav's work as well as pieces designed by Frank Lloyd Wright. The brothers continued to operate the L. & J.G. Stickley Company in Manlius, NY, until the 1960s as interest waned in the Craftsman style.

Distributors of the furniture, the Audi family purchased the company and holdings in 1974 and helped revitalize the brand.

Today, the company the Stickley brothers started is known as the Stickley Audi & Co. with a store in Fayetteville, NY (as well as stores in six states), and a warehouse in Syracuse, NY. The Audi family also run a museum near the factory and several pieces can also be viewed at the Everson Museum in Downtown Syracuse.

In 2003, The Fayetteville Free Library moved from its original East Genesee Street location to the former Stickley Factory on Orchard Street in Fayetteville, NY.

Gustav Stickley is buried in Syracuse's Oakwood Cemetery.

Reference:

Bavaro, Joseph J. & Mossman, Thomas L. The Furniture of Gustav Stickley: History, Techniques, Projects.
Linden Publishing Inc. Fresno, California. 1996.
Previously published by Simon &Schuster. © 1982.

CPSIA information can be obtained
at www.ICGtesting.com
Printed in the USA
FFOW01n1657151015
17736FF

9 781619 359284